OUR

DARKEST

SCAR

OUR DARKEST SERIES
BOOK THREE

SARAH BAILEY

Cover Art by Sarah Bailey
Photo from Adobe Stock

Published by Twisted Tree Publications
www.twistedtreepublications.com
info@twistedtreepublications.com

Paperback ISBN: 978-1-913217-20-4

To Ash and Eric,
Your son put me through the wringer. He challenged me in ways I
never expected. I'm grateful to you for bringing him into my world and
giving him life.

PROLOGUE

Raphael

Nothing about the way I felt could be quantified in words. It was like some deep-seated self-hatred had taken up residence inside my soul and infected everything, but there was more to it than that. I didn't know the right way to express what went on inside my head other than it being messy as fuck.

Life couldn't be called simple or easy for me. When you grow up with five parents, the world doesn't want to understand it. Instead, subjecting me and my siblings to ridicule. It wasn't our fault. We hadn't asked for this. Nor had we asked to find out what kind of darkness had forged our family either.

Things weren't supposed to happen this way. I wasn't meant to find someone who made me open up and divulge secrets long buried. Who understood me on a level I wasn't prepared for. Who became my friend and gave me their ear as I needed someone to listen. I wasn't supposed to give this person an insight into my complicated soul, nor allow them to care for me the way they did.

I was the one in the wrong here. I did something I couldn't take back. And all I could do was spend the rest of my life paying the price for ruining everything.

You're not meant to let your friend's older sibling comfort you.

You're not meant to tell them your parents did things they should've been locked up for in the not too distant past.

You're not meant to kiss them.

You're not meant to fall in love.

And you're certainly not meant to lie about it.

What I did to Meredith's brother was unforgivable. I can't undo a single thing I said to him that day. The day I destroyed the only good thing I had in my life.

I had a few choice words to say to the teenage version of myself. I would have told him never to run into the arms of someone older than him. Especially not when he was already confused over his own sexuality and beating himself up over things he couldn't control.

The past cannot be erased. All I want is to ask him to forgive me.

But I can't.

Jonah Ethan Pope hates me for what I did to him.

And I don't blame him for it.

PART I

mitigate

verb, mit·i·gat·ed, mit·i·gat·ing.

to make (a person, one's state of mind, disposition, etc.)

milder or more gentle; mollify; appease.

CHAPTER ONE

Jonah

Thank fuck it was Friday. I could curl up in a ball and not deal with the world. No doubt my sister would be spending all her time with her best friend, Celia. Meredith and I were close as siblings could be, but I wanted to be alone without the world's emotions crowding my head. The first week of school after the summer holidays had been unnecessarily long. I needed to fall into bed and sleep for a year.

Trudging into the toilets at the end of my last lesson, I stopped at one of the urinals and went about my business. Whoever decided to schedule maths as the last lesson on a Friday clearly wanted us sixth formers to suffer. I swear our teacher, Mr Kirk, got a kick out of it. He'd been smirking the whole time.

Dick.

As I washed my hands after I stepped up to the sinks, a weird choking sound came from the stalls. I shut off the tap and listened, wondering if I'd been hearing things.

It came again, except this time I recognised it as a sob.

A part of me knew I should ignore it, considering it was none of my business. Logical and rational Jonah didn't give a shit about other people's drama. He often got drowned out by compassionate Jonah. I couldn't pretend I hadn't heard someone crying. Human suffering always got to me. Perhaps I was overly sensitive, but I had a need to soothe those I cared about. To make their pain go away. It was a burden. A part of me I hated because of how exhausted I got being around other people. But I'd learnt to live with it and its many pitfalls.

The muffled sobbing came again.

Fuck. I can't leave whoever it is crying by themselves.

It didn't sit right with me. I had to do something, but at the same time, I didn't want to intrude. They'd think I was trying to interfere.

Why did I always face this dilemma?

Why did I care so much?

I should walk out of here and forget about it.

"Um, hello?"

The sobbing abruptly stopped.

Shit. I shouldn't have said anything. No going back now.

"Okay, look, I'm sorry. You don't know me and I don't know you. I just couldn't help overhearing and well… I wanted to know if you're okay."

I waited for a long minute, but no other sounds came. Rubbing my face, I decided I'd tried and now I had to leave even if it made me sick to my stomach.

Trust me to be the idiot who asks a complete stranger if he's okay and it ends up backfiring.

I took a step towards the door.

"No… I'm not."

His voice was soft and full of emotion. My chest ached intolerably within moments. I felt their agony in those few words. It made me want to shelter whoever it was from everything they were experiencing.

What the fuck?

I'd never felt this way for anyone except Meredith, my little sister. Why would I feel this way about someone I'd not even seen?

You must've temporarily lost the plot. No other explanation for it.

"Do you want to talk about it?"

The question fell out of my mouth without me thinking about it.

"No."

"Do you want me to go?"

I took another step towards the door.

"No!"

It sounded like the word was torn from his lips.

Who is this boy and what the hell is going on with him?

I knew I should've left this well alone. It wasn't any of my business. Except now I'd made it so. Why the fuck did I do this to myself again and again? I needed to quit being nice to people. It only got me in trouble.

The sound of the door unlocking behind me had me turning around. Out walked the last person I expected to see. He stood staring at me with wide bloodshot verdant eyes, his chestnut hair ruffled and his glasses slightly askew. I couldn't help noticing how tall he'd become over the summer holidays. And how those wide-framed glasses suited him a little too much.

Raphael Nelson was my little sister's friend and two-and-a-half years younger than me. There were two years between me and Meredith. We'd both turn sixteen and eighteen respectively at the end of this year. Raphael's older sister, Aurora Knox, and I were in our last year of school together, but she and I didn't hang out or anything. To be honest, she was probably the most intimidating girl I'd ever met in my life. I tended to avoid her if I could help it.

"Oh," he said, his voice still soft. "It's you."

I'd only ever shared brief conversations with Raphael. Whilst he and Meredith were friends, they rarely spent time together outside of school. I got the feeling it had a lot to do with his family being a little unorthodox. Raphael and his siblings caught a lot of shit off people for having five parents. It'd never mattered to me. What other people got up to was none of my business. Besides, why would I want to cause harm to anyone else? I got enough stick for being who I was. I wouldn't wish it on anyone else.

"This is embarrassing," he muttered when I said nothing.

"You needn't be embarrassed. I won't tell anyone, but maybe I should…"

The way he looked so defeated made me want to stay and find out exactly why he was crying in the toilets. It's not like it should matter to me… but it did.

"Yeah… um…" He rubbed the back of his neck. "I'm sorry, you're probably busy."

"I'm not really. I mean, like, if you wanted some company or something."

What the fuck are you saying?

He adjusted his glasses before levelling his gaze on me. Something in those green depths made me very aware of how miserable he felt right then.

"You don't have to, not like you owe me anything."

"I wouldn't have offered if I didn't mean it."

He didn't say anything straight away, only stared at me with confusion. Like he couldn't understand why I was offering him help. I couldn't quite understand it myself.

"Well, okay."

Turning away, he went over to the sinks and set his glasses down. I couldn't help watching him clean up his face even though I shouldn't.

What are you doing right now, Jonah?

Nothing I should be. I always did as I should, so what was it about Raphael which made me want to help him?

When he put his glasses back on and walked over to me, my spine stiffened. For a moment, I didn't know what to do or where we should go. Probably not a good idea to spend any more time at school.

"Um, come on then."

I didn't wait to see if he was following as I left the toilets. We walked out of the building together a few minutes later. There were still kids milling around, but no one looked our way. Raphael said nothing when I guided him out of the school gates. It made me wonder why he was so trusting of me right now. I was Meredith's brother. He probably thought I was safe. I only wanted to make sure he was okay. Perhaps he needed someone to be there for him.

A few streets over was a small, independent café I liked to take Meredith on the weekends when she wasn't hanging out with her best friend, Celia. I walked up to the counter with Raphael trailing along behind me.

"Afternoon, what can I get you?" said the girl who looked to be in her early twenties behind the till.

"Could I get an Americano and…"

I looked over at Raphael.

"Tea, please."

"A pot of tea." My eyes flicked to the selection of cakes. "And two slices of the Victoria sponge, please."

She gave me a smile and a nod. I didn't know what type of cake he liked but figured he needed something sugary.

There you go again, Jonah, doing everything in your power to take care of someone. You don't even really know Raphael. Why are you doing this?

I told my brain to do one. He needed help. I couldn't walk away.

"I'll bring it over to you."

I paid and led Raphael over to a table in the corner, away from all the other customers. He put his school bag on one of the spare chairs and sat down, eyeing the place warily. I sat across from him, folding my hands on the table.

"You didn't have to get me anything," he mumbled, pushing his glasses up his nose. "But thank you."

"You're welcome."

He tapped his fingers on the wooden table, eyes darting around like he wanted to look at anyone else but me.

"Look, I realise this must be weird for you with me being your friend's older brother, but if you need to talk about anything, I don't mind lending an ear."

Raphael set his gaze on me. I noticed his eyes were a slightly darker shade of green to mine, reminding me of pine trees. It's not a detail I'd ever picked up on before. Then again, I hadn't taken the time to really look at him nor take in his finer features.

"I don't know if I can talk about this."

Waves of unhappiness radiated off him, battering me with their intensity like knives against my skin. I dropped one of my hands under the table and closed it over my thigh, fingers digging into my flesh to stop myself from reacting to his emotions. He didn't need to know how much other people's feelings affected me, even when I didn't want them to.

"We could talk about something else… as a distraction."

"I guess so."

The waitress interrupted us, placing a tray down before emptying it of its contents onto the table. Raphael tugged the pot of tea towards him as I thanked her. He opened the lid and stirred the water with a spoon before closing it again. I watched him eye the plates of cake.

"How's school?" I asked before sipping my coffee.

"Fine, mostly."

"So that's not why you were upset?"

He shook his head as he picked up a fork and dug into one of the cakes.

"Some stuff at home," he told me before he stuck the cake in his mouth.

I watched him chew and swallow. His eyes fell on his hands.

"You're not like weirded out by my family or anything? Everyone else seems to be."

"No. Meredith has told me a little, but to be honest, even if she hadn't, I wouldn't have thought anything of it anyway."

My motto in life was each to their own. People should be allowed to go about their daily lives and live the way they wanted. It's not like they were harming anyone. So what if it wasn't the norm? Nothing in life really ever was.

"Oh."

He looked stumped. Who knew why, since Meredith had never hassled him over it as far as I knew. She never judged people for those types of things. The things you have no control over. When I'd come out to her a few years ago, she barely batted an eyelid and asked me if I had the same taste in boys as she did. I didn't, but it was nice to have someone to talk about it to. That's if I ever actually found someone I liked. No one I knew had piqued my interest, but I guess I might be a little picky. I'd always been careful who I gave my time to.

"I'm the last person to judge anyone for their relationships or whatever else."

He looked at me, his eyes narrowing.

"No?"

I shrugged.

"Why would I? I get enough shit for who I am. I'd rather not put that out in the world myself."

A furrow appeared between his brows.

"Why would you get shit for who you are?"

I wondered why Meredith hadn't told him, but then again, she didn't view the world by people's sexual preferences.

"People are pretty open-minded and tolerant these days but it doesn't stop idiots giving me shit for being openly gay. The world can be black and white when it comes to being different. Not that I really care what anyone else thinks."

Raphael's eyes widened a fraction as if he hadn't been expecting my answer. Then he looked away, picking up the teapot and pouring some out into a cup. He set it down and poured some milk in before stirring the hot liquid.

I wondered what he thought about my admission. Not like I hid it. I doubted it would be an issue for him considering the environment he'd grown up in. Those who were different tended to be more understanding in my experience. They weren't quick to judge.

"I like to think the world is varying shades of grey and instead of trying to understand things, people lash out with anger when their view of the world is threatened. That's the reason they give you shit for it. Just like they give me shit about my parents… but you're right. Doesn't matter what anyone else thinks. It only matters how we feel inside."

CHAPTER TWO

Raphael

I 'm not sure why I'd not wanted Meredith's brother to leave the moment I realised he'd found me crying in the toilets at school. It's not like I knew very much about Jonah. Only a few things Meredith had told me like his age and how he was planning to study psychology at university next year.

Jonah raised his eyebrow at my statement as he sat back in his chair. He and Meredith looked alike except his hair was blonde and hers more coppery. He had a strong jawline and was slightly taller than me. I'd always avoided looking at him too much since I didn't like the way he gave me an odd feeling in my chest. Considering I already felt like an outcast, it didn't help matters. I didn't want alien feelings for random people I didn't know very well. Jonah wasn't completely random, but he wasn't someone I ever thought I'd have a conversation with. A real conversation, that is. Not the bullshit small talk we made whenever we crossed paths before.

I gripped my cup in both hands and stared down at the tea in it, feeling distinctly out of place and like I'd said something I shouldn't to him.

Why did you even open your mouth?

"I guess you're right. Sometimes I wonder if the world is really as progressive as people like to think it is."

I scoffed.

"Hardly. People call my mother a slut to my face for her relationship with my dads. I can only imagine what they say to you."

Looking up, I found Jonah raising his mug to his lips, watching me with a spark of interest in his eyes. I hadn't put my foot in it.

Thank fuck. Don't want him thinking I'm weird. Enough people think that already. Hell, I think I'm weird.

"Probably not worth repeating."

Neither was what set me off earlier. You'd think hearing people talk shit about your family your whole life would have given me a thick skin. No such luck. Sometimes what they said hit far too close to home. Especially after what my parents had told me before the summer holidays started. I shivered, not wanting to think about that shit again. It'd plagued me for months already and nothing made it better.

"Can… can I ask why you offered to keep me company?"

Most days one of my parents picked us up after school, but I'd wanted to get a head start on homework. I told my dad I'd make my own way home. Kind of lucky I guess because Miles

16

Anders and his idiot friends gave me shit. I'd snapped and ran away like a coward which had only made them laugh at me.

Usually, I'd find Duke if Miles and his gang started on me, but he'd already left for the day. It had me hiding in the toilets in floods of tears like a baby instead. Having Jonah find me crying was possibly the most embarrassed I'd been in a long time. I didn't want to look weak and pathetic in front of him. Only Jonah hadn't looked at me with anything other than compassion and friendliness since we'd left school. Maybe he didn't think I was one gigantic baby.

I hope not.

Jonah's green eyes darted away. They were light in colour. And kind of beautiful. When he blinked, his blonde lashes fluttered across his cheeks, drawing my attention to the light dusting of freckles across his nose. The weird sensation I got in my chest when I looked at him for too long started up again.

This is so disconcerting. I don't understand it.

"I don't like seeing people suffering," Jonah said in response to my question after a moment, his voice just above a whisper.

"I'm not—"

"You are."

I frowned.

How does he know that?

No one knew how I felt inside. I'd become adept at hiding it, especially from my parents. Well, most of them anyway. You couldn't get anything past Rory, but he never pried. He waited for you to come to him. Dad hadn't noticed the way I'd withdrawn into myself since they told me about their past.

17

How every taunt I got from kids about them became magnified because of the knowledge of what they'd done in the past. The tidal wave of misery overwhelmed me at times. Like today.

So how did Jonah, who knew next to nothing about me, know I was suffering? He'd said it with such conviction as if he could see inside my mind.

I didn't ask. Instead, I sipped my tea and tried to work out why I felt uncomfortable around him. Perhaps it was the way my skin itched with urges I couldn't understand nor wanted to acknowledge.

Jonah dragged the other plate of cake towards himself and took a bite. My eyes fixed on his hand, admiring his long fingers and noting the way they trembled. Was he as nervous as me about this? Or uncomfortable with hanging out with his little sister's friend?

"Meredith told me you want to study psychology," I blurted out, wanting to fill the silence.

His eyes fell on me, curiosity in them.

"Yes, hopefully far away from here."

I cocked my head to the side, fiddling with my glasses.

"Oh, you don't want to study in London?"

His eyes turned haunted for the briefest of moments.

"No."

I didn't think he'd want me prying any further. I decided not to ask the question burning on my lips. However, I had little else to say. What did I even talk to him about? Why had I agreed to this?

I snagged some more cake, stuffing it in my mouth. As I chewed, I stared at his hands again. He had one curled around his coffee mug and the other resting on the table, tapping the wood. The noise mesmerised me, keeping my gaze pinned to the drumming of his fingers. I'd never understood why I felt this way about Jonah. From the few times I'd spoken to him before, he seemed nice enough and was always polite to me.

"I don't think my mum would be happy if I moved away from London to study or anything," I mumbled, looking up at his face again.

Mum would hate it. She didn't want any of her babies moving out of our house. Personally, I couldn't wait to get away. It would mean I didn't have to face the horrifying nature of their past every single day when I looked at them.

"No? Have you decided what you want to do?"

The curiosity in his eyes had me answering honestly.

"Environmental sciences. People think that's a bit geeky, but I like nature, you know. The city is so... oppressive."

"Yeah, I know the feeling. It's like you can't escape from anyone here no matter where you go."

"Is that why you want to leave?"

Idiot. You just told yourself not to ask that question. What is wrong with you?

My curiosity about Jonah had got the better of me.

His eyes turned sad and his expression caved in. I felt like shit for causing him any distress.

"One of many reasons. I mean, you must know our dad died last year. Things haven't really been easy for me and Mer since."

I hadn't forgotten about his dad having a heart attack a year ago. Meredith had been withdrawn for months after it happened. She seemed to be coming out of herself a little more these days, but she was still guarded around everyone. It's like she had this wall up and no one could get past the barrier except Celia and clearly, Jonah.

Is he going to try to break through my walls too? I can't show anyone what's inside me. Those demons need to stay where they are.

"I'm sorry, I shouldn't have asked."

He canted his head as his hands gripped his coffee mug.

"It's okay, guess it's still a little… raw."

I nodded. No one close to me had died. I didn't know how it must feel. Thinking about death only reminded me of shit I fought hard to forget about. Why did everything always come back to that? I needed to quit thinking about it.

I took a sip of my tea to distract myself from the way Jonah was looking at me. It felt like he could see right through me. I didn't like it.

"Do you have anyone to talk to about what's going on with you?"

I jumped, my eyes flicking up to his again.

"Not really. I guess I could talk to Duke, but he's got his own shit going on with… you know."

Duke's troubles were way worse than mine. What he'd gone through six months ago was fucked up and he'd changed because of it. Sometimes events in people's lives could derail everything and make you think about who you really are. It had shaken all of us on some level. But not like Duke. It was as if he had a personality transplant, at least, outwardly. He was the same Duke with me, even if he didn't like to talk about it. We'd always been close, what with our dads being together.

"Yeah, that shit was…"

"Tragic and fucked up?"

Jonah gave me a sad smile.

"I was going to say it must have been devastating for him."

"Yeah, well, he's not okay. He doesn't talk about it, but I know he's not."

"It's not like anyone can relate, you know, if they've not gone through it themselves."

I sighed and dug into my cake. Honestly, I didn't know how to get through to my brother. I'd tried, but I was only met with a wall of anger over the whole thing. If he didn't want to talk to me, then I wouldn't force him. I suppose it's why I was reluctant to talk about my own shit with him. He didn't need me piling my insignificant worries on top of his own.

"Guess you have to let him work through it himself."

I wished I didn't, but Jonah was right. Duke needed space. Besides, he wasn't completely alone. He had Kira. If anyone could reason with Duke, it was her.

"Yeah, he tells me to stay out of it, so I do."

Jonah's eyes softened. My hands trembled at the sight of it. I hid them under the table, hoping he wouldn't notice how his presence affected me. It's not like he would talk to me after this, but I didn't want to make a shit impression on him.

"Well, it's like I said, if you need someone, I'm willing to listen."

I didn't know what to say to that this time. Imposing on my friend's older brother didn't feel right, but if Jonah was offering then should I really turn it down?

"Um, thanks," I muttered, looking away because I couldn't take his staring. It's like the longer Jonah looked at me, the more my skin prickled and my heart started to race.

The two of us fell silent, both finishing our slices of cake. I looked around the café, wanting to find a way to make this less awkward, but failing miserably. My eyes fell on my watch, checking the time. My parents would probably be wondering why I wasn't back yet. It's not like they kept tabs on me, but I had told Dad I was only staying a little later to catch up on homework.

"I probably need to get home," I said, finally meeting Jonah's eyes again.

I picked up my cup and swallowed a mouthful of tea.

"Okay… should we go then?"

I nodded. We finished our drinks and got up, walking out of the café together. I glanced around, knowing I'd have to catch the bus because there was no way I was walking. Mum would hate it. She'd tell me I should have called one of them to pick me up. I rubbed the back of my neck, unsure of how I should say goodbye.

"I need to go catch the bus."

"I'll come with you."

I stared at him. Jonah stuck his hands in his pockets giving me a half-smile.

"You don't need to do that."

"I want to. Let me at least make sure you get home okay."

I shuffled my foot on the pavement.

"I mean okay, if that's what you want."

I didn't know how to say no to him, to be honest. I let Jonah walk me to the bus stop and get on the bus with me when it arrived. We sat together near the back. I tried not to flinch when his thigh brushed up against mine. The odd sensation in my chest was back, but this time it was joined by my heart racing out of control. I didn't understand what it was about this boy that made me all kinds of nervous.

Jonah rested his hand on the seat in front of us, tapping his fingers on the fabric. His green eyes were fixed outside whilst mine were on him. Why I couldn't look away was a mystery to me.

"You must have a big house if all nine of you live there," he said, startling me.

"Um, yeah, we do. Thankfully our bedrooms are downstairs so we don't have to hear my parents."

I watched him smile.

"I can imagine there being five of them makes that a bigger issue for you all."

I snorted. My parents had no shame when it came to their relationships. The number of times us kids had to put up with them being all loved up was not okay. No one wants to see their parents all over each other, especially not when there's five of them.

"Just a bit."

We lapsed into silence again until we reached my stop and the both of us jumped off. He walked along beside me. It took a concerted effort on my part to not look at him too much.

Not the way his blonde hair glinted in the sunlight, nor at his beautiful hands.

What is wrong with you? Since when did you start finding hands attractive? Jesus, get a grip!

By the time we got to my house, my need to be away from him was making me anxious. My palms had got all sweaty and my clothes itched against my skin.

"Um, this is me," I told him, waving at the house. "Thanks for… everything."

"You're welcome." He put his hand out to me. "Give me your phone a sec."

I dug it out of my pocket, unlocked it and handed it to him without considering why he wanted it. Jonah fiddled with it for a moment before handing it back to me.

"If you need to talk, you let me know, or if you just need company, I'm here."

I looked down at the screen, finding he'd added his number to my contacts.

"Um, okay."

Jonah gave me a smile, which made my heart rate spike. I hurried up the steps to my house, digging my keys out of my bag. I unlocked the door and turned back to him before I opened it.

"See you at school, Raphael," he said, giving me a wave.

"Yeah, see you."

No one called me by my full name these days. It was always Raphi. I wasn't sure how I felt about him saying it. I opened the front door and hurried in. Shutting it behind me, I leant against it, taking a few deep breaths.

"Oh good, you're home, Mum was about to send out the cavalry," came Duke's voice.

I looked up, finding my brother leaning against the doorframe of the living room, eyeing me with a raised eyebrow. I shoved off the front door and rolled my eyes.

"Shut up, no she wasn't. She would have called if she was worried about me."

"You okay? You look kind of pale."

I walked along the hallway and past him to go to my room.

"I'm fine, long day."

"You sure about that?"

"Yeah, Duke, I'm sure."

I didn't want to talk to him right now. Not after the weird reaction I'd had to Meredith's brother. Duke thankfully didn't follow me to my bedroom. I shut the door behind me after I walked in. I dumped my bag on the floor and collapsed on my bed. My phone was still in my hand. I looked at it.

Jonah Pope.

Why had he been nice to me? It seemed odd for him to offer to keep me company. I was two-and-a-half years younger than him. It didn't make any sense why he'd want to hang out or anything. Guess it didn't matter. I wasn't going to take him up on the offer. I shouldn't have let him take me out today.

I threw my phone down and dug my hands into my eyes, pushing my glasses up on my forehead. No point dwelling on it. Besides, I needed to change and make sure Mum didn't start hassling my dads to go searching for me. Duke might have been making a joke, but I wouldn't put it past her to do something like that. She constantly worried about us, especially after what happened with Duke. I couldn't blame her, but her overbearing nature drove me insane. It was bad enough having Quinn on our cases and now Mum was at it too.

I just wished my parents would leave me alone. Maybe I'd be able to deal with all the shit going on my head if they gave me some space. Especially since I had yet to really deal with my feelings towards them regarding their past. I'd have to do it eventually because I couldn't keep running away from it. Or I could and hope to fucking god I could bury it deep and never address it again. That would be easier than accepting reality… wouldn't it?

CHAPTER THREE

Jonah

The fact I'd spent the entire weekend staring at my phone, willing a notification to appear to let me know he'd texted me went to show I was an idiot. I don't know what had got into me. It's not as if I wanted anything from Raphael. Not really. He seemed so sad and it tugged at my heartstrings.

Why am I doing this to myself? He clearly doesn't need me.

I didn't know why I wanted to help him. It's not like he was my friend. He meant nothing to me. He was just a boy who hung out with my little sister. That's it. Anything else wasn't my business.

Why are you wanting to make it your business, huh, Jonah?

I sat out on the benches outside the sixth form block since it was break time, staring down at my phone and wondering why I couldn't get a grip. He'd probably forgotten all about me and my offer to be there if he needed someone. I couldn't imagine why he'd want me as a friend. It's not like we had a ton in common.

Yeah, you keep telling yourself that.

"You look like someone just kicked a puppy," came a voice from next to me.

I looked up to find Olive and Teddy taking a seat next to me.

"Do I?" I muttered, shoving my phone back in my pocket, irritated with myself and my inability to stop thinking about why he wasn't taking me up on my offer of help.

"Good weekend?"

I shrugged, sitting back and watching the kids milling around, wondering if he would be outside right now.

"Just slept and did homework." *And worried yourself sick about a boy you shouldn't be thinking about.* "You?"

The two of them looked at each other with a secret smile. Olive and Teddy had been together since forever or at least it felt like it. I didn't think anything could split them up at this point.

"Yeah, it was good," Olive said.

I snorted.

"Yeah, I bet it was."

She shoved me in the arm.

"Some of us are allowed to be loved up, J, even if you aren't."

I rolled my eyes.

"I have no interest in being 'loved up', got more important shit to do."

Olive gave me a look.

28

"Yeah, because you're a right nerd who only cares about school and making sure your sister stays out of trouble."

"Mer doesn't get into trouble," Teddy put in. "You don't need to worry about her so much."

That wasn't the reason I worried about Meredith. Our mother had fallen into a pit of depression since Dad died and had neglected us. Grandma wasn't any help either. She kept telling my mum it had only been a matter of time before our father worked himself into the grave. I ignored the two of them arguing all the time. At least it meant my grandmother wasn't on my case. She might say she didn't have an issue with my sexuality, but she did. The snide remarks pissed me off. I did nothing about it. Wasn't much point since she was stuck in her ways and wouldn't change.

Meredith hadn't taken our father's death very well. That's why I worried. I wanted her to smile again. It took a lot for her to smile at anything these days.

"Yeah, I guess so."

I didn't talk about it with Olive and Teddy even though they were my friends. To be honest, I'd never had what I'd call close friends. The person I was closest with was my sister. We didn't fight or argue in the way siblings usually did. We relied on each other, especially since Dad died. Our mother had never been the maternal type, which meant we had to fend for ourselves a lot of the time.

Being close to people meant I got sucked into their drama and emotions. I couldn't afford that. It hurt too much when it all went to shit.

This is why you should not be worrying about Raphael. Resist the urge to check your phone again. It's not worth it.

I wanted to drop my head in my hands but Teddy and Olive would ask me what was up with me. A conversation I didn't want to deal with.

What the fuck was it about Raphael which had me feeling this way? I'd felt comfortable in his presence. Like we could sit in silence together, watching the world go by and it wouldn't be a big deal. Most people liked to fill the void with noise, but I liked the peacefulness of being next to someone without the need to talk.

It's how I'd felt when the two of us sat on the bus together on the way to his house. I imagined he didn't get much quiet time with his family. Not that I'd actually met his parents, but I'd seen his brothers around school and was in the same year as Aurora.

"You want to come bowling on Friday after school?" Olive asked.

"And get my arse kicked by Teddy? Hard pass."

She grinned and Teddy flexed his hands.

"I'll take it easy on you, J," he said. "You can always have the barriers up."

I stuck a finger up at him and turned away, glancing towards the main school building. I noticed my sister and Celia huddled together with some other kids. My heart rate spiked when I spied some very familiar chestnut hair. He nudged his glasses up his nose as he dragged his foot across the tarmac. I wondered if he was okay after Friday and what was bothering him.

Stop it. You shouldn't care about that. It's none of your business.

So why the fuck couldn't I look away?

"You sure, J? You never come out anymore," I could hear Olive saying, but my attention wasn't on them any longer. It was fixed firmly on Raphael, who'd looked up and caught me staring. Even from this distance, I could see his cheeks flush. He rubbed his hands against his sides. I should look away. I should stop this in its tracks, but apparently, my rational side had gone to sleep.

"Yeah, okay, I'll come. It could be fun," I replied to Olive on autopilot because it was probably a good idea for me to get out. I needed the distraction.

"Oh great, we'll make sure he has a good time, won't we, Teddy?"

Their words faded into the background as they discussed plans. All I could think about was this boy across the fucking playground whose verdant eyes had drawn me in. Raphael hadn't looked away either. I didn't know what to make of it. Nor when I watched him take out his phone. His eyes flicked down as he fiddled with it. When they rose again, he cocked his head to the side. My phone buzzed in my pocket. I tugged it out, knowing it must be him.

Unknown: Thank you for Friday. I appreciated it.

Jonah: You're welcome.

I watched him check his phone again. His lip twitched.

Raphael: You didn't tell Mer about it, did you?

Jonah: No. I won't if you don't want me to.

Raphael: She doesn't need to know.

It's not like I had planned on saying anything to her. It wasn't my place. I wasn't the type to betray someone's trust. Didn't matter if I hardly knew Raphael, his secrets would be safe with me.

Jonah: My lips are sealed.

I watched a slow smile spread across his face as he read the message. He looked up at me again, biting his lip before he stuffed his phone in his pocket and turned back to his group.

"So, we'll meet you at the school gates, yeah?" Olive said.

I turned to her and Teddy, having no idea what they'd said before.

"Yeah, school gates on Friday," I said, my eyes flicking back to Raphael one last time.

Perhaps that would be the end of it. Perhaps not. I just had to wait and see if Raphael reached out again. Maybe he needed someone outside of his circle to talk about the shit going on in his head. And I knew if he asked it of me, I'd be that person for him. Because, apparently, I cared about what happened to him and whether he was really happy... or not.

CHAPTER FOUR

Raphael

A ll week I'd thought about why I'd texted Jonah the day I caught him staring at me. The way his eyes bored into me like he was seeing right through me. Beckoning me with them and telling me I could trust him with all my secrets if I dared. It made me throw caution to the wind.

It sounded crazy.

Hell, it felt fucking crazy.

My mind ran rampant, considering all the reasons how it could be okay to unburden myself to my friend's older brother.

Would it be cathartic? Would it help me? Would I feel a sense of relief afterwards?

Stupid thoughts I should not be entertaining.

The whirlwind of emotion inside me wasn't something anyone should have to deal with. I'd been raised to be open and honest about my feelings by my parents, but that had been shattered the moment they told me the truth about themselves.

A part of me wanted to unburden myself to someone I could trust with the truth. Jonah had offered to listen. No one had given me the option. Then again, no one knew anything was wrong. My parents were worried about Duke's wellbeing. I didn't want to give them more shit to fret over. And every part of me was ashamed over the whole thing.

It wouldn't be right to go to Jonah, would it? He owed me nothing. He was Meredith's brother. Why the hell would he even want to help me?

Fed up with feeling all this shit, I left my bedroom to go in search of one of my dads. I needed to get my mind off everything. They could distract me for a while. Not like I had anything better to do. I had friends, sure, but I never invited them back to mine. My family could be a lot and we got so much shit over it. I didn't feel like giving anyone further ammunition to use against me and my siblings. No one would get it. How could they unless they lived it? Unless they saw the way my parents worked. How they'd walk through fire for each other. They were my heroes because of how they loved and cared little for anyone else's opinions.

At least… they used to be.

I passed by Duke's bedroom. The door was wide open and the light was on. My eyes were drawn inside, finding my brother sitting on the end of his bed, his hands resting at his sides as he stared down at the floor. My feet came to a standstill.

"Duke?"

He didn't raise his head. If anything, he looked defeated.

"You okay?"

His lack of response was telling. I walked into his room, shutting the door in case someone else came by. Duke didn't like anyone seeing him show emotion. He liked to make jokes the same way his dad did, but he was also incredibly aloof. Kept his walls built so high, I didn't know how anyone could scale them. The only person other than me Duke ever opened up to was his best friend.

I sat down next to him, noting the way his shoulders sagged. Seeing him like this made my heart ache. My brother wasn't as strong as he liked to make out, but given what had occurred six months ago, I couldn't exactly blame him. I'd defy anyone to go through it and come out unscathed.

"Do you want to talk about it?"

His fists enclosed around the covers.

"No," he murmured.

"Do you want me to go?"

He shook his head. Then one of his hands uncurled from the duvet and he rubbed his face.

"Why is everything so fucked up, Raphi? I feel like I grew up too fast when…" he faltered.

Neither of us wanted to voice aloud what he was referring to.

"I don't know why. The world is cruel for no reason. Chews us up and spits us out when it's done torturing us."

Duke's ice-blue eyes met mine. He frowned as if he wondered where the hell I came up with that idea. If only he knew what kind of fucked up shit went on in my head.

"Since when did you get so smart about the world?"

I shrugged.

"I've felt that way for a while… people giving us shit about our family is draining."

Duke was the only one I'd admitted what being bullied felt like for me. No matter how many times he came to my defence, it didn't stop the idiots. I didn't even tell my friends about it. I wasn't ashamed of my family or anything, just my inability to keep people's barbs from getting to me.

"Are those fuckers still on your case?"

"What do you think? Doesn't matter what you say, they just start up again. Like it's our fault we have five parents. Didn't ask to be born. I'm just tired, Duke."

He looked away, nodding slowly.

"Me too. Tired of it all. It's times like this I understand why she did it."

His words prompted me to wrap an arm around his shoulder as his body shook.

"Hey, it's okay… it's not anyone's fault that happened. Especially not yours."

He turned his face into my shoulder.

"Why does it feel like it is?"

I didn't know how to answer his question. It's not like I could relate to his pain. At least not this type, anyway. I put my other arm around him and stroked his back. Duke didn't hold back, wetting my t-shirt within minutes as he silently cried out his agony.

"I've got you," I whispered. "Always."

It didn't matter what shit my brother was going through. I'd always be here for him even when he pushed me away. He'd withdrawn into himself for the first couple of months, refusing to talk about it. Then the personality transplant happened. He went from being this kind, upstanding guy to someone who didn't give a shit any longer. And it had resulted in him using a lot of girls. No to mention the increasingly reckless shit he and Kira got up to with their so-called dares. I didn't judge him by any means even if I didn't strictly agree with it. Everyone dealt with their pain in different ways.

When Duke pulled away, he rubbed his eyes with his sleeve and looked at the floor.

"Thanks," he mumbled.

"You know you can come to me if you need to."

He nodded. I felt the change in him, the way the shutters came down, sealing away his emotions. It's not like I could push him into opening up to me further. It would only make things worse.

"You want to be alone?"

He nodded again. I got up to give him some space, patting his shoulder.

"Okay."

He didn't acknowledge me as I walked away, opening his bedroom door and closing it behind me. I leant against the wall outside, rubbing my hand across my mouth. It reminded me of why I couldn't talk to Duke about my own feelings. Not the ones I held deep inside. The bullying, sure, but everything else? Not so much. He was too lost in his own misery. I didn't want to pile mine on top of his.

I walked away to my bedroom, not wanting to be around anyone else right then. Not after having my brother cry on me. My heart felt heavy and my mind was in disarray.

I lay on my bed staring up at the ceiling and wondering when life had got crazy difficult. When did everything get this fucked up? I was only fifteen, but I felt a lot older. The weight of the world was on my shoulders.

Maybe it's why I reached out and grabbed my phone from my bedside table. And maybe it's why I stopped caring about the reasons I shouldn't lean on someone I had no business being friends with.

Everyone needed someone in their corner. Someone who had an outsider's perspective.

Raphi: Do you ever feel so lost you don't know what's up or down any longer?

CHAPTER FIVE

Jonah

I regretted agreeing to go bowling the minute Teddy, Olive and I met up with what felt like half our year at the school gates. The number of people made me anxious. My hands were all sweaty. My pulse had spiked. I couldn't deal with the onslaught of overwhelming emotions hitting me from every side.

This was my idea of hell.

Olive and Teddy knew I was an introvert, but I'd never told anyone other than Meredith about the way crowds affected me. How it made me uneasy. I'd end up withdrawing into myself rather than being social. I couldn't exactly blame them for inviting other people even though it made me want to run far, far away.

We took up four lanes next to each other at the bowling alley. Thankfully, I was on a lane with my two friends and could sit in the corner without garnering too much attention. I pulled out my phone and sent a text to my sister.

Jonah: Half of sixth form is here.

She'd understand what I meant. I glanced around, checking to see if I was up next or not.

Meredith: You okay with that?

Jonah: Not really.

Meredith: Didn't O and T tell you loads of people were coming?

Jonah: They might have, but I wasn't exactly listening.

I suppose it might have been my fault for getting distracted by Raphael.

What are you doing thinking about him?

I hadn't stopped. I'd attempted to stop looking around for him at school and wondering how he was all week. Attempted to but failed miserably. I didn't understand why I felt compelled to help him. Perhaps a part of me recognised the pain in him. The suffering. And my idiot-self wanted to soothe him. To make him smile again because his smile was kind of beautiful.

You need to stop thinking like this.

Meredith: You? Distracted? Who are you and what did you do with my brother? Did someone steal your phone?

Jonah: You really aren't funny, you know that right?

Meredith: I made you smile though.

I realised the corners of my lips had turned up. Meredith hadn't been in the mood to make jokes for a while. I was happy to see her doing so now.

Jonah: You did. Thank you.

Meredith: Just try be social, yeah? I know you hate it, but you have to put yourself out there or you'll end up alone with twenty cats.

Jonah: At least cats are antisocial so wouldn't be harassing me every five minutes. The perfect pets.

Meredith: Jonah…

Jonah: I know. I know. Putting the phone away.

Meredith didn't respond. I tucked my phone back in my pocket, noticing it was my turn to bowl. I needed to stop being such a recluse, but my dad dying only made me want to retreat further into myself. It was the suddenness of it which got to me the most. Even a year later, I still missed him.

Our home life pretty much sucked as Mum didn't seem to give a shit. I'd felt like it was down to me to keep it together. To make sure my sister got what she needed. Meredith hadn't noticed our mother's attitude quite yet, but it would only be a matter of time. She'd need me more than ever when it happened.

I got up from my seat and picked up a bowling ball.

"You sure you don't want the bumpers up?" Teddy quipped.

"I'm sure."

Having never been any good at sports or anything involving hitting targets, my aim when it came to bowling sucked. I didn't want to look like a complete wuss though. People already gave me enough side-eyes as it was. The poor gay kid whose dad died of a heart attack.

Got to love those labels people brand you with.

I took aim, walked forward, swinging my arm back before throwing the ball down the lane. For once in my life, it actually stayed in a straight line and hit some of the pins.

"Have you been practising without us, J?" Olive asked as I picked up another ball.

I threw her a smile and a wink.

"Nope, an absolute fluke. Watch, bet this goes straight in the gutter."

True to my word, it was a gutter ball. Olive gave me a pat on the shoulder and said better luck with the next one. I was proud of myself for getting any pins down in the first place.

The rest of the game was much of the same with me hitting very few pins, Teddy getting several strikes and Olive not far behind him on the scoreboard. A couple of the other kids who were with us did well too.

"Just going to get a drink," I told Olive before the next game started.

She gave me a nod. I ambled off in the direction of the bar area and ordered myself a soft drink. As I stood there drumming my fingers on the bar, my phone buzzed. I slid it out of my pocket and stared down at the message. My heart thumped hard against my chest.

Raphael: Do you ever feel so lost you don't know what's up or down any longer?

It seemed like a rather odd thing for him to text me out of the blue, but he'd actually reached out to me. The bartender set my drink down. I paid, wondering how to respond to Raphael. I picked up my drink but didn't walk back over to the bowling lane. Instead, I stood at the bar staring at the message like it would give me an answer. My palm felt sweaty as I held my phone tighter in it.

What is an appropriate response? Jesus, why am I overthinking this?

Jonah: Yes.

It seemed stupid to only give him a one-word reply, however, it was the truth. Some days I didn't know what to do with myself. Life had got a lot more difficult for me when my dad passed. It forced me to confront a lot of things. I couldn't hide who I was any longer. Life was too short. I'd come out at school and it made things way more complicated than they should be.

Raphael: Duke just cried all over my shoulder. It made me feel so...

Jonah: So what?

Raphael: Alone. Like I have no one to talk to. Then I felt shit. It's selfish of me to whine about my lot when he has it worse.

Jonah: It's not a competition.

Raphael: I don't want to burden him or my parents.

I sipped my drink. Every part of me wanted to reach out through the phone and give him what he needed. An outlet. He suffered as I did. I locked away my own pain to allow me to take care of my sister. Raphael was, in essence, doing the same thing for his brother.

Jonah: Would you believe me if I told you I know how that feels?

Raphael: Yes.

Jonah: The offer still stands if you need someone.

"Jonah, are you coming back to the game?" Olive's voice registered with me.

Raphael: Are you busy right now?

I looked up at Olive. Technically I was but being here wasn't exactly fun for me.

Jonah: I have time for you.

You… are… so fucking stupid.

Raphael: Come to mine? Can go for a walk.

Was I really doing this? Ditching my friends for someone I barely knew but who I inexplicably wanted to help.

Jonah: Be there in twenty.

Yes, yes I was.

I downed my drink, popping it back on the bar. Olive was still waiting for my response with a raised eyebrow.

"I have to go… it's Meredith, she needs me."

Lying to Olive made my stomach roil in protest. I only felt worse when her eyes softened.

"Oh no, is she okay?"

I shook my head.

"She's upset and wants me to come home. I'm really sorry, Olive. We can do something on Sunday maybe… you, me and Teddy?"

She reached out and squeezed my arm.

"Of course, go be with your sister. I'll text you and we can have brunch, maybe."

Did you really just use your sister as an excuse to flake out on your friends to go see Raphael?

I gave Olive a tight smile.

"Sure, brunch sounds good."

"Let me know how she is later, yeah? I'll tell the others."

Olive gave me one last squeeze and walked back towards the lanes. I went to exchange my shoes back and then left, feeling like a shit friend. Why couldn't I have been honest and told her the real reason I wanted to leave? Raphael was an excuse for me to get away from the crowds of people who'd turned up to this.

And you want to know what's going on with him.

Clearly, I had more issues with trusting people with who I was inside than I realised. And I was beginning to think maybe I needed someone to talk to as well.

CHAPTER SIX

Jonah

I sent Raphael a text to let him know I was outside considering I didn't know how he'd feel about me ringing the doorbell. Who knew if he would answer it, or one of his parents. I wasn't sure if he wanted them or anyone else knowing he was going to see me. It didn't bother me either way because this wasn't about me. It was about giving him an outlet which he didn't feel like he could get anywhere else.

It took two minutes for him to open the front door and walk down the steps, meeting me on the pavement. His green eyes were wide and his cheeks flushed. I tried not to smile. Raphael was cute in this boyish, slightly nerdy way.

Did you really just think that about your sister's friend? Cute? You never think anyone is cute.

"Hey," he said with a sheepish smile on his face.

"Hi."

I dug my hands into my pockets.

"Um, so, should we?"

I gave him a slight nod. I didn't know what to say now I was next to him. Raphael didn't seem to know either. He stared at me for a long moment before he shook himself and made to walk off toward a nearby park. I followed along next to him, watching as his chin dropped to his chest. He reached up, his fingers tugging on one of the arms of his glasses.

"Is Duke okay?" I asked when the silence seemed to go on for too long.

"Not really, but he doesn't want to talk about it. I guess he doesn't see the point in rehashing the whole thing, you know, since it won't change anything."

That I could completely understand.

"And are you okay?"

He gave me a shrug, raising his chin and turning his head to look at me.

"Trying to be there for someone who won't let you help them is hard, especially when you feel like you're half drowning yourself."

The waves of self-doubt coming off him hit me like a ton of bricks. I refrained from reaching up to rub my chest, not wanting to bring attention to the way his emotions affected me.

"You… you said people give you shit for being who you are."

"I did."

"How do you deal with it? I know you said you don't care and it doesn't matter what others think… and I agree, but it doesn't make it any easier."

How did I deal with other people's judgement? That was a question and a half. Mostly I ignored it, shutting out the world because it was the way I'd learnt how to protect myself. It wasn't what he was asking me. He wanted to know what to do when it got too much.

"There's no easy answer to that."

Raphael tugged at his glasses again.

"Nothing is ever easy. I don't want easy, just real."

His eyes fell down between us and I wondered what he was looking at. They seemed to drift over my arm, landing on my hand. I don't know why his gaze made my skin start to itch, but it wasn't in an uncomfortable way. More like he drew something out of me. Made me crave some kind of contact? Connection? I didn't know how to explain it. Only I'd never wanted a connection like this from anyone else before.

"How about I promise this here is a no bullshit zone between us, if you do the same."

I waved between us, watching his eyes track my hand.

"I can do that."

He met my eyes again. Those verdant depths held so much pain in them, I didn't know what to do with myself. I got lost in his gaze behind those wide-framed glasses. We almost matched each other in height. He was slightly shorter, but he might continue growing since he hadn't yet turned sixteen.

We reached the park which made him look away as we passed through the gates. It broke the weird spell I was under.

I shoved it away, not wanting to consider what the fuck it even meant.

"I don't deal with it, that's the truth," I blurted out in a rush, knowing I should probably answer his question.

"You don't?"

He glanced at me, eyes full of curiosity this time.

"No, I can't afford to. I bottle it up instead so I can be there for Meredith. She needs me."

"She seems okay."

"She hides it well, but Dad's death affected her way worse than she lets on."

"Does that mean you need someone to talk to as well?"

I nodded. Considering I'd just declared this a no bullshit zone, I didn't think keeping it from him would start us off on the right track.

"Okay, that makes me feel slightly better about talking to you. I didn't want it being one-sided."

"I wouldn't have minded if it was."

He raised an eyebrow.

"No?"

"I like helping people. Meredith calls it my superpower."

He smiled at me. The way the corners of his lips turned up had me focusing on them. It did funny things to my insides. Making them warm because I'd caused that expression on his face. Me. It shouldn't make me as happy as it did.

"Why would you want to help me when you don't really know me?"

A question I'd like answering myself. Something about Raphael made me want to offer my support. It wasn't something quantifiable. I was just drawn to him.

"Everyone needs someone and Mer keeps telling me to stop being so…"

"Antisocial?"

I shook my head.

"Did she tell you she says that to me?"

"Lucky guess."

The two of us stopped by a bench. Raphael sat down, gripping the wood below him with both hands as he stared out across the grass. I took a seat next to him, probably a little too close as our hands brushed together. He didn't move his away. Neither did I.

"When you found me last week, I was upset because some kids called my family disgusting since my mum sleeps with four different men. They said she's a slag and a whore, saying I was going to turn out as fucked up as them. In a lot of ways, I'm used to them saying those things, but it hurts, you know, to get judged like that because of something I have no control over. I guess I'd had enough. No matter how many times Duke tells them to leave me alone, they won't. I'm tired of being called names simply because I have five parents."

His voice shook as he told me why he'd been crying in the toilets. Without thinking, I shifted my hand from where it was resting next to me and settled it over his. His mouth parted on an exhale before he looked down at our hands. Now I'd done it, I didn't know what the hell had possessed me. If I pulled away now, it might make things awkward.

"Not going to say I know how that feels, but I know what it's like to be judged for something you have no control over. It's hard to ignore when it's constant."

He nodded slowly, still staring at our hands.

"That's not the only reason it gets to me."

I cocked my head to the side, watching the way his hair fell in his eyes as he shifted. He pushed it off his face with his free hand, readjusting his glasses.

"I'm not supposed to talk about it outside of my family… for good reason."

"You don't have to tell me."

He folded his top lip over his bottom one. Then his eyes flicked up to mine.

"You make me feel safe."

I hadn't been expecting him to admit such a thing. Nor the way he released the bench, allowing my fingers to slide between his. My heart thundered in my ears at the strangeness of being this close to someone I was beginning to like a whole lot more than I should.

You're my little sister's friend and yet I can't help myself. I want to know you.

"Sorry, that was probably too much. I swear I didn't mean anything weird by it. I don't have many people in my life I feel like I can be myself with."

"No, it's okay. I understand what you mean."

His eyebrow quirked upwards.

"You do?"

"I'm glad you feel that way. Means we can be friends… I hope."

He smiled then.

"You want to be my friend?"

Why would he think otherwise? I had offered to lend an ear on several occasions. It's not like I did it for just anyone. I wasn't great at making friends on the whole, but talking to him felt normal, natural even. Maybe because I understood him in a lot of ways.

"Yeah, Raphael, I do."

"Even though I'm your sister's age?"

I shook my head, grinning at him.

"I don't care how old you are."

"Okay, but you have to admit it's kind of weird. We don't know each other that well."

My eyes fell to our hands. Neither of us had moved them. It didn't feel uncomfortable. If anything, it made my pulse race having his skin against mine.

"Then we change that. Though I'm going to warn you now, I'm not easy to get to know. Meredith calls me antisocial for a reason."

"I don't think you're antisocial, Jonah. More like picky about who you spend your time with and you should be. Most people aren't worth it."

"You are."

He looked away, but his smile remained.

"If you say so." He stared out over the grass again. "Okay, I told you what really upset me last week. Tell me something about you."

I thought about it for a moment.

No bullshit zone, remember?

"I ditched my friends to come see you by telling them Meredith was upset."

His head whipped around to me, his green eyes wide.

"What? I thought you said you weren't busy."

"I think you'll find I said I had time for you, not that I wasn't busy."

His cheeks went red.

Cute. So fucking cute.

"You didn't have to do that."

"I didn't, but I wasn't enjoying myself. They invited way too many people to bowling. I don't like crowds, it makes me feel anxious… like I'll say something stupid. I end up not talking instead. The thing is, I haven't told Olive and Teddy how I feel. It wasn't their fault. I didn't want to disappoint her since she keeps telling me I don't come out with them enough, but lying made me feel worse."

It took a second for his expression to change. It morphed into understanding and it made me feel at ease.

"Well, I appreciate it and you should tell them. It's nothing to be ashamed of. Some of us just prefer one-on-one conversation."

"Us… meaning you?"

He nodded.

Raphael said he felt safe with me. I sort of felt safe with him too. I mean, shit, I'd admitted something I'd only ever told Meredith.

"I'll keep that in mind when we hang out."

"We're going to hang out again?"

I bit my lip.

"Yeah… I told you I'd be here if you needed to talk."

He gave me a smile.

"I'm teasing. You did say you wanted to be my friend."

I had. My mind hadn't changed either. It didn't matter to me if he was Meredith's friend first or that this might not be the best idea. I just wanted to know more about him. It was clear we had stuff in common and I didn't feel awkward.

I pulled my hand away since I shouldn't still be holding his. Instead, I knocked his shoulder with my fingers.

"Yeah, did you not want to be or something?"

It took him a second to respond. I'd only been teasing back, but his expression turned serious.

"You're like the complete opposite of your sister, you know."

"Is that a bad thing?"

"No, not at all." He nudged my shoulder back. "In answer to your question… I do want to be your friend, Jonah. To be honest, I'd like that a lot."

CHAPTER SEVEN

Raphael

I didn't know what I'd been expecting when Jonah agreed to meet me but it wasn't this. He'd been open, honest and seemed very at ease. Not only in his words but his expression. He had this soothing presence, making all my worries feel easier to admit to. He wasn't judging me or my family. He simply listened and understood.

It's why I'd reciprocated in his offer of friendship. Every part of me wanted him to stay right next to me. I wanted to talk to him. See his light green eyes brighten with amusement. Watch the wind breezing through his blonde hair, giving him a ruffled sort of look.

What I did not want or expect was my reaction when he'd rested his hand on mine. It caused my heart to slam against my ribcage. My skin prickled and heat spread up my hand, along my wrist and further up my arm. I didn't understand it. It's not as if I'd experienced this with anyone, let alone a boy.

And I wasn't about to admit it to him even though we'd agreed no bullshit between us.

I'd known I was straight my whole life. I liked girls, but I was too nervous and shy to ask anyone out. Especially considering what most people thought about me and my family.

Why do I keep looking at Jonah like this? Feeling things I don't understand when I'm near him.

"Do we need to shake on it or something?" he said with a quirked eyebrow.

His smile made my palms clammy.

"On being friends? No, not necessary."

Jonah reached out and grabbed my hand, giving it a firm shake despite my words. My mouth went dry and the twinkle in his green eyes only made my pulse pick up all over again. When he released my hand, I didn't know what to do with myself or where to look any longer.

Jonah turned back to the park, leaning his arm across the back of the bench. If he moved his hand lower, it would brush over my shoulder.

I'm in two minds as to whether or not I want him to.

"Do your parents know you're out here with me?"

I shook myself at his words.

"Not exactly. I told my dad I was going for a walk. Had to or my mum would start worrying about where I am."

"Are they protective?"

"Mum is, but my dads? They're all different."

It was hard to explain to someone who had never seen us together before how our family worked.

"How do you handle that stuff?"

I stared at Jonah's profile. The way his blonde eyelashes fluttered over his cheek when he blinked. He had a beautiful bone structure. His jawline was neither too strong nor too soft.

"Having four dads? Um, we call our biological fathers dad, and the others by their names. It's easier that way because we all know who we're referring to."

"What are their names?"

"Quinn, Xavier, Eric and Rory. Eric is my dad. Mum says I'm like a carbon copy of him, except I wear glasses and he doesn't. Her name is Ash."

I watched Jonah smile.

"You all have the same nose."

"Huh?"

"You and your siblings. You have the same nose."

I touched mine the moment he said it before adjusting my glasses.

"It's from Mum, well, technically, I guess, from our grandpa."

Talking about my parents to Jonah didn't exactly feel weird, it's only I never did this with anyone. Not even Meredith, Celia and our other friends. I avoided talking about them at all costs because of the judgement we got over it.

"So is your dad protective?"

I shook my head.

"No, he's more nurturing. Mum keeps saying I get my sensitive side from him. He takes care of us in a way the others don't, like he loves cooking and is always willing to listen. I look up to him… or at least, I did."

Jonah glanced at me then, his brow furrowing.

"Did something change?"

"Yeah, but that's the thing I can't talk about."

A huge part of me wanted to tell Jonah everything, but you didn't go around informing other people your parents were killers who had covered up their crimes. It's not as if I didn't understand why they'd done it or thought they were terrible human beings. It had, however, reshaped my view of them. They weren't these infallible people who could do no wrong. They were just as flawed as the rest of us. No matter how kind, caring and compassionate they were now. It didn't change the fact that once upon a time, they had done things which made me feel queasy thinking about it.

"That's okay. You never have to tell me anything you don't want to or can't. I'm not going to push you into anything."

I might not know much about Jonah, but it seemed as though he had infinite patience. He would probably need it with me. I was beginning to see why Meredith said her brother was her saviour.

"I do love my parents, they're still some of the most amazing people I know, but this stuff made it… weird for me."

"Have you told them that?"

I shook my head.

"I don't know what to say. Duke and Aurora took it well, but me, I'm here seeing them without rose-tinted glasses and it's confusing for me. As if I'm not confused enough already about my entire life."

"Cole doesn't know?"

I shook my head. He was only thirteen and going through puberty. My parents didn't want to put that shit on him right now. I couldn't blame them. I wish they hadn't put it on me quite yet either, but people don't always get what they want in life. More often than not, I got lumbered with a crap hand.

"He's too young to understand."

"And you're not also?"

I shrugged.

"Didn't exactly have a choice in the matter."

"Did they not say you could talk to them about it?"

"They did, but I don't know what to say, to express how I feel."

It would be easier if I could. If everything hadn't happened with Duke not long afterwards, then maybe I would have said something. Whenever I had the urge to talk to my dad about it, it would only take one look at his eyes and I'd freeze up. My dad had this compassion unlike anyone else I knew. It broke me inside knowing I felt this way about him and the rest of my parents. I didn't want them to think I loved them any less because of what they'd done.

"I get that. It's hard to tell them something they might not want to hear."

I nodded. For some strange reason, I wished Jonah would reach out and touch me again. Just to reassure me he was there for me.

Or maybe you just like the feel of his skin against yours.

The thought terrified me. Along with the way he stared at me as if he was ripping every thought I had about him out of my head. The ones I shouldn't be having. Like how I found his hands beautiful, his face, his jawline, the way he smiled and the vibrant green of his eyes.

What the hell is wrong with you? You… you can't feel this way about him.

I reminded myself we were becoming friends and not to read into these alien feelings. Not to examine them too closely. They were just feelings. I could deal with them. Fleeting feelings which didn't mean a single thing.

Liar. You're a liar.

"I wish they hadn't told me. People say ignorance is bliss for a reason."

His lips parted, but he didn't say a word. Instead, he breathed in and his fingers, which were resting on the bench, brushed over my shoulder. I internally shivered.

Nope. Don't think. Don't read into anything. Be calm.

"Sometimes it is." His lip twitched. "I can't say if it's better for you to know or not since I don't know what it is."

I knew why they'd told me about it. To protect me in case their past came back to haunt them. Given what they'd been involved in, it was a very real possibility despite all the years which had passed by. As Quinn said, no one escaped the life completely even if they were on the straight and narrow now.

"Do… do you mind if we head back now?"

I felt very comfortable with Jonah, but if I didn't leave now, I might end up blurting out the whole story to him. I couldn't do that. It needed to remain a secret to keep my family safe.

"If that's what you want."

He lifted his arm off the bench and went to get up. My hand reached out of its own accord and landed on his shoulder, stopping him. Jonah frowned, staring down at my hand.

"I like talking to you. You're not like anyone else I know… in a good way. Thank you for listening."

"You're welcome."

My eyes focused on his lips. On their fullness. I almost unconsciously licked my bottom one.

"Can we do this again?"

His lips curved upwards.

"Of course."

"Okay."

I didn't want to pull my hand back. I might not be touching his skin, but he was warm and real. Those thoughts made me release him and stand up, pacing away because I wasn't sure what the hell was going on with me. I felt his presence behind me a moment later. My skin prickled with awareness. And that was a bad sign. A really fucking bad sign.

Jonah said nothing about the strange way I was acting as we walked out of the park and back to my house. I stopped myself from staring at him the whole way, not trusting my thoughts and feelings. When we stopped outside my house, I gave him a slight shrug.

"I'll see you then."

"You have my number, Raphael. Use it if you need to."

He lifted his hand for a moment, then seemed to think better of it and dropped it. We stared at each other for several seconds. My chest got all tight. I fought the urge to rub it.

"Well, see you at school," he said before he turned and walked off towards where the bus stop was on the next street over.

I watched him until he disappeared, unable to help myself. How had I found someone who didn't judge a single thing I said? Who listened and understood. Who didn't make me feel stupid or ridiculous.

I rushed inside, scared by my thoughts. Scared by the whole thing. I didn't encounter anyone on the way to my bedroom, shutting the door and leaning back against it. I stared down at my shaking fingers and asked myself why this was making me feel so anxious.

You're just going to be friends. There's no need to freak out.

It wasn't the friend part making me feel this way. It was the knowledge I might actually see Jonah in a different light. I might think of him in a way I shouldn't.

No. Don't say it. Don't do it. Just keep cool. Friends. Nothing more. Nothing less.

I held onto that mantra, forcing myself to calm down and stop getting worked up over a… boy. I'd never been worked up over anyone in my entire life. I couldn't understand it.

Why on earth did it have to be the completely wrong person for me to be feeling this way about?

CHAPTER EIGHT

Jonah

I sat up on my bed with my homework scattered around me on Sunday morning. A cup of coffee rested on my bedside table. It was kind of early, but I hadn't wanted to do it yesterday. Plus, I was seeing Teddy and Olive in a couple of hours. Yesterday, I'd had to go deal with getting food in for the family and cleaning the house. My mother wasn't in any state of mind to even get out of bed, and my grandmother was out visiting her not so secret boyfriend, Leonard. She kept telling us he was just her friend, but I didn't believe a word coming out of her mouth.

"You're such a nerd."

I looked up, finding Meredith leaning against the doorframe with a grin.

"You're a fine one to talk."

"I don't start homework right after I get up."

I shrugged. She knew I'd had to get a lot of shit done yesterday. Meredith walked into my room and sat on the edge of my bed, running her fingers along the covers.

"So, did you actually have fun on Friday?"

I hadn't told her about the ditching part. Meredith had been at Celia's when I got in and we didn't have time to talk yesterday. And I did have fun, it was just not with my friends but with hers. A part of me felt incredibly guilty over it and the other didn't care. Spending time with Raphael had made me smile.

"Sort of."

"Jonah."

"I didn't stay very long."

She rolled her eyes and crossed her arms over her chest.

"Why not?"

I'd promised Raphael I wouldn't tell my sister about us hanging out. Having to lie to both her and my friends was not my idea of fun, but I kept my promises.

"I felt awkward, Mer. You know I can't deal with that many people at once. I'm making up for it today, going for brunch with Teddy and Olive."

The way her eyes lit up made my stomach twist.

"Can I come?"

"Um…"

"Come on, J, I don't want to get stuck with Grandma."

I was going to have to come clean to Meredith about my little white lie. My sister was my weakness. I couldn't deny her anything. It's not like I hated it. She needed me. I always gave her what she asked for. It's what you did for the people you loved. Especially when they had suffered the loss of a parent. Of course, I had too, but Meredith and Dad had this special bond because of their love of the theatre.

"You can, but… you're going to have to do something for me."

Her eyebrow quirked up.

"What?"

"I need you to act like you were upset on Friday and needed me because that's the excuse I used to leave early."

Meredith stared at me for a long moment. Then she threw back her head and laughed.

"Oh, for god's sake, J, you are something else."

I gave her a smile. My sister always came through for me just as I did for her. After Dad died, we'd stuck together like glue. It was me and her against the world.

"It's that or you stay here with Grandma. Your choice."

"You drive a hard bargain, but I'll do my best." She put a hand to her forehead. "Oh, my dear brother, I cannot possibly cope at home without you. Not like I was at Celia's or anything."

I stuck my tongue out at her before staring back down at my homework. After a minute, I realised she hadn't got up and left.

"Did you need something else? We're leaving at quarter to eleven."

"No, I'm just bored."

"Go be bored elsewhere." I waved at my books. "Some people have to get their work done."

"Nerd."

I rolled my eyes.

"You giving me shit for wanting to get into a good uni?"

"No."

"Then shush."

I watched her smile out of the corner of my eye before she slumped back against my covers and stared up at my ceiling. My eyes went back to the text I was reading. For a long while, neither of us said anything.

"Do you want a boyfriend, J?"

I looked over at my sister with a frown.

"I don't have time for a relationship."

The truth was I didn't like anyone I'd met so far. Not like there weren't other openly gay kids at school, but a few of them were too overt. It wasn't my thing. I didn't know if I had a type, only I wanted someone like me. Someone who wasn't too out there with their personality. Who liked the quiet times more than going out and partying. I wasn't looking for someone to push me out of my comfort zone or challenge me in that way. Not when I already had Meredith on my case about being more social and less in my own head.

"That sounds like an excuse to me."

"It isn't when I've not met anyone I want to date, Mer. Maybe I'd feel differently if I had."

She turned her head to look at me.

"You sure there's no one?"

A niggling thought in the back of my head told me there was, but I shoved it away.

"You'd be the first to know."

"Celia thinks we should try to set you up with Jeremy."

I stared at her. Jeremy was a boy in sixth form who, quite frankly, I couldn't stand because he was just about the most irritating person I'd ever met in my life. Constantly talking about everything and nothing. Always up in people's faces for no reason. Not to mention vapid as fuck. I couldn't think of anyone worse.

"Celia should mind her own fucking business."

"I told her you wouldn't go for that."

"I don't need a couple of fifteen-year-old girls setting me up on dates."

Meredith grinned.

"We could be amazing matchmakers for all you know."

I gave her a look.

"But no, don't go out with Jeremy. He would piss you off within seconds."

Too bloody right he would.

"Celia doesn't understand that just because you both like boys, doesn't mean you'd be interested in each other."

I didn't like to say it to Meredith, but her best friend could be a right pain. She wasn't exactly the nicest girl to other people and whilst she never gave my sister any shit, I didn't trust her.

"And you still hang out with her despite her, quite frankly, backwards and insulting view of gay men?"

"I did tell her, you know, that it's not okay to make assumptions since you're no different to anyone else."

"Hmm."

"I know you don't like Celia."

I looked back at my books, not wanting to have this discussion again. Meredith could hang out with whoever she wanted, but it didn't mean I approved. Whilst Celia might have been a good friend to my sister over the years, she'd become spiteful and mean when she hit puberty. It was only a matter of time before she turned on Meredith. It was a fucking given at this point.

"I've got nothing to say about Celia. She's your friend."

"You know I don't think the way she does."

"Because that makes it so much better. You know it's hard enough for me and everyone else who isn't straight when people continue to have attitudes like that."

Meredith looked away for a moment.

"I know. I'm sorry people still think that way. It's shitty and you don't deserve it. You're like the most amazing person I know and if idiots can't see that, well they can all go get drowned in the Thames."

I snorted, eyeing her with no small amount of amusement.

"That's a bit extreme, the water in the Thames is gross."

"They deserve it."

The determined look in her eyes when she turned back to me made me smile wider.

"You are savage."

She shrugged and sat up.

"And?"

"It's why I love you."

She grinned and jumped off my bed.

"I'll leave you in peace since you're in full nerd mode. And I love you too."

I sat back as Meredith ambled out of my room. She might be okay today, but she had bad days as well. It's why I didn't want to say no when she'd asked to come out with me, Teddy and Olive. She wouldn't enjoy staying at home with our grandmother who would no doubt give her a hard time.

My phone buzzed on my bedside table. I reached over thinking it might be my friends. My pulse skittered when I saw who it was.

Raphael: Sorry if I was acting weird on Friday.

I hadn't noticed him acting strangely. If anything, he seemed nervous, which I understood. He had been telling a near-stranger about how he felt. He didn't feel like a stranger to me though. Somehow, Raphael just felt real to me. Like he wasn't putting on some kind of act to fit in or impress me.

Jonah: I didn't think you were.

Raphael: Oh. I felt like I was.

Jonah: You okay?

Raphael: A lot on my mind.

Jonah: You need to talk about it?

I no longer wanted to question why I needed to help him so badly. Why my heart kept beating faster whenever I saw him or thought about him. And, admittedly, I'd thought about him far more than I should.

Raphael: No, you've helped me enough already.

Jonah: I really don't mind. Like I keep saying, I'm here if you need me.

I understood it might be difficult for him to accept I wanted to be there for him even though we didn't know each other well. I wasn't asking for anything in return. Well, maybe other than being my friend.

You keep telling yourself that.

I couldn't afford any other thoughts. He didn't need me getting ideas in my head which were inappropriate. Fuck, Raphael was only fifteen and my little sister's friend. Not at all who I'd expected to feel anything for. The way he'd been open and vulnerable did something to me. Not to mention the way he looked at me.

Stop. Just stop. Don't go there.

Raphael: My grandparents are coming over for Sunday lunch. It's always crazy. Grandma hates Grandpa's wife, Lily. Mum always ends up in an argument with her over my dads or one of us. It's just exhausting.

I couldn't begin to imagine what it was like to have such a big family.

Jonah: I bet it is.

Raphael: I really hope Grandma doesn't bring up Andie.

Jonah: Would she?

Raphael: You have no idea. She has no tact.

She can't have if she would bring up that topic at the dinner table.

Jonah: Your family sounds like a lot.

Raphael: Tell me about it. I wish I didn't have to deal with them today.

I would have offered to give him an excuse to get out of the house, but I could not ditch my friends again. Besides, not sure his parents would allow him to get out of a family Sunday lunch.

Jonah: Feel free to text me if it gets too much.

Raphael: Mum would literally kill me if I used my phone at the table, but thanks. You're sweet.

My face grew hot at his compliment. I knew I shouldn't read into it, but I couldn't help it. My heart hammered against my ribcage in this completely disconcerting way.

What is wrong with you?

Jonah: Me? Sweet? Are you mistaking me for someone else?

Raphael: Are you incapable of taking a compliment?

Jonah: Not exactly.

Raphael: If I was to shower you with them, would that make you feel awkward?

Jonah: Very much so.

I couldn't help my smile. This was very bad. I didn't know how the conversation had got turned around onto me.

Raphael: *Calculates the sheer amount of ammunition he now has.* You shouldn't have told me that.

Jonah: You going to use it against me?

Raphael: Perhaps… you'll just have to wait and see.

This funny side of him had my stomach twisting in knots. I had no idea what to make of it. Raphael couldn't be flirting with me, could he? To be honest, I didn't even know how to recognise when someone was.

Jonah: Are you going to be as much trouble as my sister is?

Raphael: Didn't you know that's why we hang out?

Jonah: Oh wonderful. I'll get it from all sides now.

Raphael: Aw, don't worry, I'll go easy on you.

I should be getting back to my homework. Instead, I was clutching my phone, holding onto every fucking word he typed out to me like I couldn't get enough.

You are messed up, you know that. Completely messed up.

Jonah: I'll just have to give it back if it's going to be like that.

Raphael: Them's fighting words.

Jonah: You're a little bit funny, you know that?

Raphael: I do try. Am I making you smile?

I put my free hand to my lips.

Jonah: Maybe.

Raphael: Mission accomplished.

Raphael: I have to go... Dad just stuck his head around my bedroom door. Apparently, I'm on kitchen helper duty today.

It was probably a good thing because if this conversation continued, I might end up embarrassing the hell out of myself by saying something stupid.

Jonah: Good luck!

Raphael: I'll need it!

I put my phone down on the bed and stared at my books. The thing I hadn't wanted to acknowledge reared its ugly head. There was denying it now. Not after that exchange. Not after the way I'd reacted to his words. My body felt hot all over and I was sure my face must be bright red.

I think I have a crush on my little sister's friend.
Well… fuck.

CHAPTER NINE

Raphael

After the complete and utter shitshow that was Sunday lunch with my grandparents, I'd felt like crawling under my covers and never reappearing. It didn't get any better over the next few days either. Honestly, I don't know why Grandma insisted on bringing up the most inappropriate topics at the dinner table. Mum had lost her shit completely. My dads had been no better.

I shuddered at the memory of Duke storming out of the room, then everyone except me, Aurora and Cole were shouting at each other. Mum sent us into the living room. The three of us sat on the sofa silently listening to the mayhem going on next door until Lily, our step-grandmother, came out and tried to distract us. It hadn't worked. Nothing could prevent us from hearing what was going.

I didn't want to think about it, but it had brought up all sorts of shit for me. Like how Grandma accused them of raising us all wrong. Mum telling her she couldn't talk given how she'd allowed my mother to be raised by a monster. It went on and on in the same vein until Quinn basically kicked Grandma out of our house telling her she wasn't welcome here if she was going to give my mum shit.

The rest of lunch had been a subdued affair. Likely it would all blow over before the next Sunday lunch gathering, but it had soured the atmosphere in our house completely. Probably why I'd ended up texting Jonah earlier today whilst I was in lesson asking if I could see him after school. I needed an outlet. Some way of dealing with how I felt.

Here we were, sat across from each other in the same café he'd brought me to the first time we'd hung out. This time we only had drinks. I'd cupped my mug in my hand and was staring down into my tea.

"Did something happen?" he asked when we'd been sitting there in silence for at least five minutes.

Everything had happened. It wasn't just my family. It was the boy in front of me too. Before everything went to complete shit on Sunday, I'd enjoyed our back and forth banter a little too much. I'd tried not to text him since my feelings towards Jonah were all kinds of messed up, but I couldn't help it. My mind was too full and he told me to let him know if I needed to talk.

"Just a full-blown shouting match between my grandma and my parents on Sunday."

I looked up, finding Jonah frowning heavily at me. A part of me wondered if it was because I hadn't told him about it until now, a full three days after it happened. He had told me to tell him if it got too much. It had. And I'd not reached out.

You were too messed up over it all and dealing with the aftermath.

I told myself that, but it didn't stop the pit of guilt forming in my stomach. Why the hell did I even care so much anyway? We were still getting to know each other. It was unlikely he was that invested already.

You know that's bullshit. Jonah's the type of person who doesn't offer friendship lightly.

I was seriously a mess over him and we'd barely even started down the road to being friends. What was happening to me?

"About what?"

"Oh well, Grandma was being her usual interfering-self, questioning how we were being raised, giving Mum shit and, as predicted, brought up the Andie thing."

"She sounds a bit like my grandma."

I raised an eyebrow.

"Oh yeah? She bad too?"

Jonah nodded, circling a finger around the rim of his mug. I don't think he was doing it consciously, but it was distracting. I had to stop looking at his hands. I just had to plain stop looking at Jonah in all the ways I shouldn't.

"She's very judgemental about everyone and everything."

"So is mine. Don't think she was very happy when Quinn forcibly ejected her from our house. He full-on told her she wasn't welcome any longer."

My eyes flicked up to Jonah again. He cocked his head to the side and appraised me with an expression I couldn't read.

"He actually kicked her out the house?"

"Yeah, it'll blow over and she'll be back next month. Not like it hasn't happened before."

"I didn't realise your family was so…"

"Fucked up and crazy?"

I saw him hide a smile as he bit his lip.

"Not quite what I was thinking, but it'll do."

I leant back in my chair and glanced around. The café wasn't very busy. I liked it. It was quiet and unpretentious. No one was looking at us, which made me feel safe.

"Does your grandma accept you?"

I don't know why I asked that. Perhaps it was something in his voice when he mentioned her.

"She says she does, then proceeds to make snide remarks like referring to anyone who's not straight as 'those people' as if we're some kind of lesser human beings."

"Well, that's shit."

"I ignore it. No point arguing. She was born in the wrong era. She blatantly thinks we should be back in the days where being gay was a crime."

I had no idea that's what Jonah had to put up with from his own family. I was lucky mine would accept us any way we came.

"That's rough. I didn't think people still had those sorts of attitudes. Don't think mine would bat an eyelid about one of us coming out. My dad is pan and Xav is bi. It's no big deal in our household."

Jonah's eyes widened slightly.

"Oh really? I had no idea."

I almost smiled. No one did because people were too busy talking about my mum's polyamorous relationship with my dads.

"Xav and Dad have been best friends since they were kids and well, they're also together, but it didn't happen until after they met Mum."

I don't think Jonah knew what to say. He stared at me as if I'd told him I'd jumped over the moon or something.

"Your family is complicated."

"You're telling me."

He waved a hand and looked a little contrite.

"I'm not judging, you know. It's cool that they're so open."

"I know."

It got me thinking. Mostly about myself and my feelings towards Jonah because, by now, I had to admit they weren't exactly on the spectrum of just being friendly. It made me feel all kinds of crazy. I'd never felt this way about someone who wasn't of the opposite sex. My rather fleeting crushes on girls had made me sure I was straight. Jonah made that surety fly right out the window. And it terrified me. Not because there was anything wrong with me finding another boy attractive. That wasn't even a thing since I'd grown up with two parents who weren't straight. No, it was the impact it would have on my life.

I hadn't told Jonah the true extent of the bullying I received at school. Aurora, Duke and even Cole were able to defend themselves against the taunting. I wasn't. At all. It upset me far more than I ever let on. Even to Duke. To be honest, it made me hate myself even though none of it was my fault.

When you get people constantly putting you down for being the product of some sick, twisted relationship which was unnatural, it begins to sink into your bones. The feeling of worthlessness eats away at your self-identity. You begin to think they're right. That you should never have been born.

I couldn't imagine how much worse it would get if they knew I was something other than straight. These feelings I had towards Jonah? Well, they couldn't happen. I couldn't be anything that would give the bullies like Miles more ammunition to use against me. I was already drowning under the intense waves of self-loathing and despair.

My parents weren't exactly innocent people. They were killers. All five of them had blood on their hands. The knowledge fed into my twisted view of myself. Made me crave normality so people couldn't say shit about me any longer. But I wasn't normal. My family wasn't fucking well normal. And I hated myself for even thinking those things. For resenting the fact I wasn't born into a household with two parents who weren't murderers.

I loved my parents. So damn much. I respected the hell out of them for their relationship. They were loving, kind and caring, but they were all dark too. So fucking dark. A part of me was scared of them after they told me the truth. Scared of what they were capable of. Scared of what they would have to do if their past ever came back to haunt them. I was just plain fucking terrified of everything rushing through my mind because it was screwed up.

"Raphael, are you okay?"

I jolted in my seat. My eyes flicked to Jonah who was looking at me with concern. How long had I been sitting here saying nothing?

Crap.

"I am… sort of." I let out a sigh and rubbed my face. "No, I'm not okay. I'm… I'm really… fucked up."

"What makes you say that?"

Why did he have to look at me like that? As if he just wanted to help me. Jonah had become part of the bloody problem and yet I didn't want to stop talking to him. Didn't want to stop being around him. He had this calming presence, especially when he touched me. I'd never met anyone who just exuded peace and serenity. It made me want to be closer. To hold on to him.

Jesus, you know that can't happen.

"I don't really like myself," I all but whispered.

Jonah leant forward and reached out, placing his hand over mine. My whole body went tense at the warmth of his skin against mine. The understanding in his eyes almost broke me clean in two.

"Do you want to tell me why you feel that way?"

He made me want to tell him just by being himself. By the way he'd been there for me.

"I'm not normal."

"No?"

I shook my head.

"I told you about the bullying. It's every single day. Sometimes small things like people muttering 'your mum's a whore' under their breath, shoving me in the corridors, calling me a freak, four-eyes, nerd. One person said they bet my sister would follow in my mum's footsteps. It's constant and it's exhausting. Duke knows about it, but he doesn't know how bad it is. No one does."

I stared down at our hands, my heart sinking with every word I spoke. The back of my neck was clammy. I felt completely uncomfortable in my own skin.

"All I can do is ignore it, but it gets to me. Their words get inside my head and I can't stop these messed up thoughts about myself. Some days I feel so alone, I cry myself to sleep, which is embarrassing to admit."

Jonah's hand left mine. I looked up, finding him getting up. He walked around the table and took a seat next to me. I stared at him as he reached forward and took both of my hands, holding them in his. They shook from my frayed nerves and his closeness.

"What thoughts?" he murmured, leaning ever closer.

My breath got caught in my throat. I had to swallow before I spoke.

"That I'm worthless and I should never have been born."

"You know neither of those things are true."

I nodded. The logical and rational part of my brain knew that, but it didn't stop those thoughts from taking over. Didn't stop me feeling like I was nothing and nobody.

"My parents told me some really fucked up stuff about themselves," I blurted out the next moment. "It's made it worse. So much… worse. I can't look at them the same way.

I can't… I can't talk to them about it either. I just feel… alone… so… alone."

Those light green eyes held all this compassion in them. I almost got whiplash from staring into them. Jonah understood. He saw me. I don't think I'd ever really been seen before. Not like that. Not in the way he did.

"You're not alone anymore. I'm here."

The pounding of my heart hammered in my ears, making them ring. He was so close. I couldn't stop the onslaught of emotion driving through every inch of me. It's like he was everywhere, flooding all of my senses and forcing me into admitting everything to myself.

I like you, Jonah. I like you too much. And I hate it. I can't afford to like you in that way. I can't.

He was my friend's older brother. And a boy.

It didn't stop me from wanting him to stay. From needing his presence. Because somehow through admitting to my problems to Jonah, he'd become important to me. I couldn't let go now.

"You promise?"

"Yeah, Raphael, I promise. I'm not going anywhere."

CHAPTER TEN

Jonah

I had to hold myself back from pulling Raphael into my arms and soothing him. His green eyes were wide with a mixture of fear and misery. The sight of his brokenness made my heart ache. The way he talked about himself with such venom and horror in his voice had my stomach in knots. He'd been made to feel like crap by kids who probably saw him as an easy target to pick on. He didn't deserve any of the shit being thrown his way. Especially not because idiots refused to try to understand his parents and their relationship.

I made the promise I wouldn't leave him because I couldn't not. Even though we'd only spent a little time together, I was attached. Probably a little too much, but it's not like we'd been complete strangers the day I'd found him crying in the toilets. There was just something about him. Perhaps it's the stuff I recognised in myself. Like internalising your suffering because the people you care about need you to be strong for them. I could see how everything with Duke, his grandmother and his parents had worn him down. Made him feel like he couldn't open up to them. And how the bullying had all but ruined his own self-image. I felt for Raphael. For all of his pain. I wanted to help him. I wanted to make it go away, so he didn't have such a sad look in his eyes and the waves of misery didn't roll off him, slamming into my chest instead.

I wanted to take his pain away even if it meant I got hurt in the process.

"I feel stupid admitting all of this to you," he said in a quiet voice.

"Why?"

I didn't think any less of him. If anything, his vulnerability with me only made me like him more. I wasn't going to kid myself into thinking he would ever like me back. Especially when he tugged his hands out of mine, his eyes darting away. I couldn't help but feel the loss of contact keenly. It made my chest ache. I pulled my hands back, settling them in my own lap and trying not to take it personally. He was clearly feeling embarrassed for having admitted some of his darkest thoughts to me.

"I don't want you to think badly of me."

"I would never… you haven't done anything wrong."

"I can't even stand up for myself. My parents would be disappointed in me if they knew."

What parent would ever feel that way about their child being harassed and tormented?

"Didn't you say your mum is super protective?"

"Yeah."

"Then I'm pretty sure the last thing she would be is disappointed. More like appalled you're going through this."

Raphael met my eyes again.

"Can I be brutally honest?"

"You weren't doing so before?"

He smiled in a hollow sort of way.

"Well, yeah I was, but this is…" He adjusted his glasses. "Jonah, I'm scared of what my parents would do if they found out. Not to me… but to the bullies."

What on earth would make him scared? Why would they do anything other than report it to the school and get them to deal with it?

"Why?"

"I can't tell you."

He kept bringing this stuff up about his parents and then skirting around the truth.

"Is this to do with them telling you something which changed your view of them?"

I wondered what he'd meant by that. Raphael didn't need me pushing him though. If he wanted to say it, he would.

"Yes. They… they did stuff in their past and it's… god, I can't say anything else. They wouldn't be happy if I did."

I wanted to reach out to him again.

"You can trust me. I won't breathe a word of what you tell me to anyone. Meredith doesn't know we've been talking and I tell her everything."

Almost everything. She was still only fifteen. There were things I held back to keep her safe. Like how our mother no longer cared about us and I'd picked up all her slack. I did it for my sister. To protect her from the reality of what our father's death had caused within our family dynamic.

"I just can't. If you knew, you'd understand. It isn't stuff you tell people about. It's a secret for a reason. I'd be putting my parents and you at risk. Like at huge risk. Even me, Aurora and Duke knowing is dangerous, but they know we'd never get them in trouble."

The seriousness of his tone made it very clear it wasn't some small thing Raphael was keeping quiet about. It had huge ramifications.

"Did they do something illegal?"

"Jonah…"

"Did they?"

He gave me a nod.

"Please don't make me talk about it. I can't do that to them. I can't betray their trust. I love them. They aren't bad people. They had terrible childhoods in different ways. My dads grew up together, their entire lives were marred by poverty, drugs and violence. All you need to know is, they did what they did to survive."

I wasn't sure how to feel about what he was saying to me. It's not like I'd ever met his parents. I certainly didn't want to judge them when I didn't know them nor what they'd actually done. Whatever it was, it clearly had a negative effect on Raphael's state of mind.

"I'm sorry. I didn't mean to push you."

His eyes turned sad behind his glasses.

"No, it's okay. You're just trying to help me and I'm—"

"You're loyal to your family."

He closed his mouth, his hand curling into a fist on the table.

"Raphael, I'm not trying to make things harder for you. I just… care."

Admitting it was probably stupid. Everything about this was. Being around him when I felt these things. This attraction to the boy next to me. The sweet, funny, beautiful boy who I couldn't stop staring at. Even when Raphael went on radio silence, it didn't stop me seeking him out with my eyes at break time when we were in school. The moment I admitted to myself I *liked* him, I couldn't help but want to be closer to him.

"I still wonder why you care so much."

His hair had fallen in his eyes. Without thinking, I reached up and pushed it off his forehead.

"I understand what it's like to go through shit with your family that hurts beyond belief but you have to bottle it up. You have to hide it because your sister needs you and your mum doesn't care about anything any longer since the only person she gave a shit about died."

I heard him suck in air.

What are you doing?

I snatched my hand back, feeling stupider than ever. Especially since I hadn't meant to tell him that about my mum.

"Your mum doesn't care about you and Mer?"

"She… she only had us because our dad wanted kids."

"Why do you think that?"

I looked away, feeling the pain of it tear into my soul.

"She told me."

"Seriously?"

I raised my shoulders and dropped them again before reaching over and dragging my coffee towards me. I took a sip, needing a moment.

"When Dad had his heart attack, all of us waited in the hospital for news. It was… difficult. The doctors told us he didn't make it and Mum just sat there staring into space like she'd just checked out. It went on like that for months."

I swallowed, staring down at the table.

"Grandma took care of Mum whilst I looked after Meredith. One night, I had to check on Mum as Grandma was at her boyfriend's. For the first time in fuck knows how long, she was lucid. She started talking to me and the first thing she said was, 'Jonah, I never wanted kids. I never wanted you and your sister. That was Phil's thing. Your father wanted you. I had you for him, not me. Never me,' and I stood there wondering why the hell she was saying these things. What mother tells her child she never wanted them?"

I felt his hand close over my shoulder. My heart tightened at the contact.

"I couldn't move as she kept talking, telling me all this shit I didn't want to know about how she felt. It's like somehow she was trying to absolve herself of her guilt but instead, she just made me feel…"

"Feel what?"

"Like I wasn't wanted."

For a moment, he didn't say anything. It's not like I thought he would judge me. I had a feeling he understood.

"Jonah?"

"Yeah?"

"Would it be okay if I hugged you?"

I exhaled on his words, not being prepared for them.

"Yes," I all but whispered.

He moved slowly, shifting towards me and wrapping his arms around my body. He leant his forehead against the side of mine. I felt a sense of relief and belonging. As if this boy accepted me. I didn't realise I needed it until that exact moment when Raphael hugged me for the first time.

"You are wanted. Mer calls you her superhero. She wants you."

She did. Having her in my life was everything. The only reason I didn't fall apart was knowing Meredith needed me. I'd crawled into her bed the night of my mum's revelation and cried into my sister's hair. She kept asking me what was wrong but I couldn't tell her. I kept everything bottled up inside. And now, I felt relief having finally told someone about it.

"And I want you in my life."

My hand shook at his words. I tried not to read into what he was saying.

"You do?"

"You're such a good person, Jonah. I don't know why anyone wouldn't want you as a friend."

Even though it should make me happy, it didn't. My stomach sank. Raphael wouldn't see me as anything but a friend. I knew that. It didn't stop it hurting. I'd never felt this way about anyone before. Raphael was the first person I really… wanted. The first person I felt an actual connection with.

You should never have allowed it to get this far.

My heart hurt when he pulled away. I internally scolded myself for my ridiculous emotions. I had to shut it down and be his friend.

"Thank you… for listening," I said as I didn't trust myself to say anything else.

"You've done it enough for me, about time I got to do so for you. Thank you for opening up to me."

I watched him sipping his tea out of the corner of my eye. He had a sad smile on his face like the knowledge I suffered as much as he did was painful for him.

"You told me you didn't want this to be one-sided."

"I guess I did. Maybe we need each other or something."

I nodded.

"Yeah, I guess we do… or something."

He chuckled and nudged my shoulder with his which in turn made me smile. The tension between us dissipated.

I tried to be okay with the fact he and I were only ever destined to be just friends. Tried being the operative word. It was the only thing I could do. Try. And hope I didn't fail. I couldn't fail the boy next to me.

He needed me.

CHAPTER ELEVEN

Raphael

The day I almost told Jonah the truth about my parents only confused me further. I had severe word vomit around this boy. I only had to look at him and all I wanted to do was spill all my secrets. Every thought I had rattling around in my head. I wanted him to know everything about me, which was crazy since I'd never wanted that with anyone.

Jonah wasn't like anyone else I'd met. He was kind, caring, and a little broken on the inside. Just like me. Every time I saw him, my feelings got more and more tangled, like I was trapped in a web with no way out.

We hadn't had any further deep conversations like the day at the café. A couple of weeks had flown by in the blink of an eye. I'd seen him a few times and we texted a lot. To be honest, it was daily. Our budding friendship had grown into something more. Something magical in a lot of ways. And it was driving me absolutely crazy. I couldn't afford to feel this way about him.

It's not like Jonah was exactly forbidden to me. I wasn't crushing on someone straight, which would have been worse. I'd just forbidden myself from feeling these things. Held myself back because of everything going on in my life. And I didn't think he liked me in that way either. It was kind of a moot point.

It, however, didn't stop me from wanting to understand myself better when it came to my sexuality. I'd thought about broaching the subject with my dad but decided against it. I knew he'd understand, but I guess I didn't feel comfortable asking questions since he'd never struggled with his identity. He'd known who he was since he was young.

There was someone else I could talk to. Someone who I knew might give me shit over it, but he could be relied on to be serious when needed. Hence why I was standing outside his bedroom door and had raised my hand to knock.

"Come in," came the muffled noise from beyond.

I opened the door and stepped in, finding Xav sitting at his desk with his laptop open. He turned his head to look at me.

"Hello, cheeky monkey."

My parents always called me that. It had been a thing since I was a kid running circles around them. And because I used to climb all over the furniture in my effort to explore my environment. I was more interested in the outside world than my siblings had ever been.

"Hey," I replied, shutting the door behind me.

Xav frowned a little.

"What can I do for you?"

I walked over and sat on the edge of his bed, staring down at the covers.

"Can I ask you some questions? They're kind of… serious."

I raised my eyes in time to see him spin around in his chair and splay out his hands.

"Serious, eh? You sure I'm the right person for that? Your dad is better at serious conversations."

"I'm sure."

I wasn't, but I was still all kinds of messed up. I wanted to find some kind of clarity. Or at least to understand how I could go about working my feelings in a less chaotic manner.

"Well, I suppose I can try. What's this about, Raphi?"

I fiddled with the blanket on the end of his bed.

"How and when did you know you were… bisexual?"

Xav's eyebrows shot up. After a moment, he leant forward in his chair, resting his arms on his knees. There was concern written all over his features.

"Is there a reason you're asking me this?"

"Sort of. I'm curious. Dad told me he always knew he didn't have a gender preference, but I know that's not the case for everyone."

He didn't respond to me straight away. Instead, he stood up from his chair and came to sit next to me.

"Have you spoken to E about this?"

"Not exactly, no. He brought it up in conversation a while ago. I didn't ask him."

"Are you confused in some way?"

I didn't know how to tell him I was. How being around Jonah had made me question everything about myself. How I wanted to act on these feelings, but I held myself back. Jonah didn't see me in that way. And I didn't want the backlash I would get at school. I couldn't deal with any more bullying about things I had no control over.

"I don't know. Will you answer my question?"

He let out a sigh and looked over at his bookshelves.

"I always had this niggling feeling in the back of my mind I wasn't just into the ladies. I didn't meet anyone I seriously considered getting involved with until I was in my teens. I guess I was the same age as you are now when I met Marcin. It was like a switch flipped, you know. Not that it was right, but I'd already lost my virginity to a girl by then. Don't get any ideas in your head about doing it before you're sixteen or your dad would kill me, yeah?"

"Don't worry, I'm not planning on it. Besides, I'm not with anyone."

I hadn't even considered the possibility of sex until I was over the age of consent. It wasn't like I was in a rush. It could wait until I met someone I really liked.

You really like Jonah.

Shut up, brain. Not helping!

"Good, you just wait until you're ready and it's with the right person."

I smiled. Xav was a good dad to us even though he drove my other dads and my mum crazy half the time with his jokes. He gave solid advice and never made me feel stupid. It's why

I felt comfortable asking him this stuff. He was always the most open and out there with himself. Never backing down from a challenge. I admired that about Xav. I didn't think I would ever have his courage, too much like my dad with being in my own head all the time.

"Dad said the same thing to me."

"Of course, he did. E is a little sensitive sap who believes in only fucking people he actually cares about. Anyway, sorry, I'm sure you don't want to think about that."

I grimaced.

"Yeah, not something any kid wants to think about their parents."

Xav smiled and nudged me with his shoulder.

"As I was saying, I met Marcin and things just kind of clicked for me. He was the first guy I slept with. I haven't been with many men compared to women, but your mum might kill me if I talk about that part of my life."

"Why would she?"

His smile turned devious.

"I was quite free with my… affections."

"So what, you were a manwhore?"

"Now where did you learn a word like that?"

I rolled my eyes.

"I'm fifteen, Xav, not exactly an innocent, uncorrupted child any longer. How can I be with you, Dad, Rory and Quinn as parents?"

He chuckled. My parents couldn't be called nice, polite people. They all swore like sailors, told it like it was, and had never hidden who they were from us.

"You have a point. And to answer your question, yes, I was. Your mother changed that. She was like an angel sent to save us all. She taught me how to love. And it's how I was able to accept your dad's love."

I'd heard this before… too many times. My parents' love story wasn't exactly what you'd call orthodox or romantic. More like fucked up and often made me wonder how they even navigated such a thing. The fact they'd stayed together for the past twenty-one years and were still so in love was no mean feat.

"Yeah, okay, I know, you, Mum and Dad are all grossly in love with each other and will always be."

"Nothing gross about being in love, Raphi. Love makes the world go around. You'll work that out one day and then I can say I told you so."

I knocked his arm with my hand.

"Shut up, Dad would tell you off for gloating."

"E and Ash tell me off for everything. I'm used to it."

Xav got in trouble with Mum way more than my other dads. He was notorious in our family for it.

We lapsed into silence for a long moment.

"I am wondering why you would come to me about this rather than your dad," Xav said. "Do you think you might be bi? Is that what this is about?"

I folded my hands in my lap and stared down at them.

"If I answer that question you have to promise me you won't tell anyone else."

"Can I ask why you don't want E to know?"

"I just don't. I came to you, Xav. I know it's weird, but I feel safer talking to you about this stuff."

I glanced over as his eyes softened and he wrapped an arm around my shoulder.

"Well, okay. You have my word, I won't tell a soul."

I didn't know why exactly I felt confiding in Xav was the better option. Somehow, I couldn't bring myself to speak to Dad. He would understand more than anyone else how I felt about Jonah, but I couldn't tell him about my feelings. I didn't like knowing they even existed.

"I honestly don't know. I like girls, but…"

"You can like boys too, Raphi."

"I know I can. I don't know if I do or if it's just one… boy."

"So, there's a boy?"

I nodded, feeling miserable about it. Jonah made my heart ache with longing. He was such a beautiful person on the inside and out. The person who ended up with him would be one lucky guy. He'd take care of them, give them everything they needed in life. I had a feeling Jonah loved hard and would do anything to make his partner happy.

I wish that boy could be me, even though I can't ever see it happening.

"Is he straight?"

"No."

"Then what's the problem?"

Everything. My whole life was the problem.

"I don't want to ruin my friendship with him."

It was the only safe answer. It's not like I could tell Xav I was being bullied and I was terrified of what would happen if people at school found out I wasn't straight.

All I wanted was to be normal.

I wasn't normal and I certainly didn't fit in anywhere. Sometimes I didn't feel like I fit into my own family. Aurora wanted to follow in our parents' footsteps and work at their casino, the Syndicate. Duke didn't know what he wanted out of life, but I couldn't blame him with everything he'd been through. They didn't have the same problems I did about my parents' past. They fit into this life just fine. Then there was me, who wanted to go to university to learn more about the environment and how I could make things better for the world. I didn't stand up to people. I didn't like confrontation. And I didn't feel like I was who my parents expected me to be. I had too much of Dad in me, but not in the ways that mattered in this family. He had a much tougher skin than I did. He was more logical and didn't let his emotions run his life.

Dad loved me, but sometimes I wasn't sure if he was proud of who I was becoming.

"Well, that I understand all too well with me and your dad's situation. He didn't want to ruin things between us. And honestly, I don't blame him. Not sure I wouldn't have done the same in his position."

"I need him as a friend more than anything else. And I don't know about my… sexuality. It's confusing for me. I've always seen myself as straight."

"If that's how you feel, then it's okay. You don't have to have it all worked out right now. If you're not ready to explore these things, you don't have to. It's you who decides who you are, no one else. If you want to keep identifying as straight, it's your choice, okay? But know I'm here for you if and when you decide it's not the case any longer."

This was exactly why I'd come to Xav. He didn't push or judge.

"But I do think you should have a conversation about your dad about this."

I sighed.

"I know."

He wrapped his other arm around me and I hugged him back. Xav gave the best hugs in the world. Maybe it was because he was huge and bear-like. It meant I felt safe and secure with him. Mum once said he was her protector, keeping her from falling apart completely.

"You're my dad as much as he is," I whispered into his shoulder.

"Don't make me start getting emotional, monkey."

"It's true though."

He patted my back but said no more. He didn't have to. It was my way of telling him how much he meant to me. How much I loved him.

When we pulled apart, he smiled and ruffled my hair.

"Any more serious questions?"

"No. I should really go get on with my homework."

He nodded. I stood up and walked over to the door, opening it wide. Standing outside was my dad with his hand raised to knock. He looked a little startled when he saw me.

"Raphi."

"Dad."

He peered around me at Xav, his eyebrow quirking up.

"Everything okay?"

"Yeah, just having a chat is all."

Dad looked at me with a strange expression on his face. Instead of allowing him to question me, I stepped forward and hugged him. A second later, he wrapped his arms around me.

"I love you, Dad."

I don't know why I needed to say it. I just did. We were incredibly close, even if recently it hadn't been the case. The distance between me and my parents felt vast. I hated it. I wanted to close the gap so I could confide in them and tell them how they'd made me feel.

"I love you too, monkey."

I tried not to get choked up. My emotions were all over the place. It hurt so fucking much. I pulled myself together before I stepped back from him. Dad gave me a smile. It only made things worse for me.

"You sure you're okay?"

"Yeah, Dad, I'm fine."

He stepped out of the way and I left Xav's room, walking away towards the stairs. Before I reached them, I heard Dad's voice filter along the hallway.

"What were you and monkey talking about?"

"Nothing much."

"Xavi, if there's something I should know…"

"There's nothing, E. Now, did you want to see me for a particular reason?"

I hurried downstairs before I overheard any more. As much as I was grateful to Xav for keeping my secrets, it also made me feel shit. Forcing any of my parents to keep secrets from each other for my sake wasn't something I ever wanted to do.

I promised myself I'd tell my dad how I was feeling when I was ready. When I worked how to deal with what was going on with me.

When I got to my room, I pulled out my phone and typed out a message. I shouldn't have, but my heart was hurting too much.

I wanted him. To talk to him. I just wanted Jonah.

CHAPTER TWELVE

Jonah

Mum walked into the kitchen just as I was pulling dinner out of the oven. Everyone was home this evening for once. I didn't mind taking on the responsibility for making sure Meredith got fed, but I resented the fact my mum hadn't started giving a shit a year after our dad had passed. With me being seventeen going on eighteen, she assumed I was old enough to take care of everyone. Even though Grandma didn't approve of my sexuality, she took more of an interest in mine and Meredith's wellbeing than Mum did.

"That smells nice."

I looked over at her.

"Thanks."

She cocked her head to the side as she appraised me with an icy stare.

"Are you okay, Jonah?"

"Yeah, I'm fine. Would you set the table or is that too much for you to manage?"

It's not like I wanted to resent my own mother, but I did. Things had been strained between us since the night she'd confessed her true feelings. I hadn't done what she wanted and forgiven her. In the intervening months, I'd only grown colder towards her. Now, it was hard to keep myself from being outwardly hostile.

She frowned and crossed her arms over her chest.

"Is that any way to speak to me?"

"Let's see, Mum, do you think it's okay to make your seventeen-year-old son take care of his younger sister all the time because you don't give a shit about us?"

I wasn't usually confrontational, but she'd been rubbing me up the wrong way for months. After I'd told Raphael the truth, Mum's presence only irritated me further. I'd had enough.

"I see you're in a mood."

She huffed and walked over to the cupboards, pulling out plates, cutlery and glasses. I wasn't going to apologise even though I probably should. Being around her was fucking exhausting. As if I didn't have enough on my plate to deal with.

My phone buzzed on the counter. I snatched it up before she had a chance to glance over at it. I ignored her pointed stare as she carried the plates over to the kitchen table. My heart skipped a beat when I saw who it was.

Raphael: I feel like shit.

Jonah: Why?

Raphael: I lied to my dad about being okay. I'm not. It's like every time I see him, my heart starts hurting. I wish I could talk to him like I used to.

As much as hearing from Raphael made me smile when he told me things like this, it made my heart hurt too. I hated how much he suffered.

Raphael: Sometimes I feel like you're the only person I can talk to.

Jonah: I wish I could do more for you.

Raphael: In what way?

Jonah: I want to take your pain away.

The moment I said it, I knew I shouldn't have. The words exposed too much about me. Showed my feelings towards him. At least, I felt like they did.

"Are you going to bring that over then?"

I glanced up at Mum to find her staring at me expectantly.

"Need to get Grandma and Meredith."

She walked away to the door and called for them. I tucked my phone in my pocket and took the dish over to the table, setting it on a mat so it wouldn't burn the wood. Mum had, thankfully, set the table. I grabbed the bowl of salad I'd made next and brought it over as my sister and grandmother came in.

We all sat down and served ourselves. Meredith started talking to both Mum and Grandma, but I wasn't paying attention. My mind was on Raphael. On what he thought about what I'd said since he'd not replied yet.

"Jonah?"

I looked up, finding Meredith staring at me expectantly.

"Sorry, what?"

"Grandma asked how school is."

I looked over at our grandmother, who had a disapproving look on her face.

"Oh, um, it's fine. Just busy since it's my last year."

I was looking forward to finishing and getting into university. It meant I could get as far away from here as possible. Even though now my plans had been thrown into question because if I got into a university outside of London, I'd be away from Raphael. The thought of it made my heart feel tight.

"Good. Are your teachers happy with your progress?" Grandma asked.

"Yeah, very happy. They think I'll get my predicted grades."

"I'm pleased to hear it."

I dug into my food when she didn't say anything further. This was how it went in our household. Grandma asked how school was. Mum pretty much ignored everything. Then the conversation between us petered out.

"Meredith, don't stuff your face like that," Grandma said, scowling at my sister. "It's not polite."

"I'm not," Meredith retorted. "I'm eating normally."

"You're going to start putting on weight if you don't slow down."

"Hey, Grandma, don't say stuff like that to her. She's not overweight," I said, hating how they'd started picking on her for no apparent reason.

It was another thing which drove me insane. Their insistence on giving Meredith a hard time.

"Maybe not now, but if she ever wants to find a good man, she needs to stay slim."

I looked at my mum, trying to get her to say something, but she was staring down at her food.

"You're going to give her a complex. She's fine. I'm taking care of her."

Grandma gave me a look. I looked after my sister the best I could. It's all I ever did. Not like she was doing a good job of it. Meredith needed someone. So I took on the role of her parent in a lot of ways.

Meredith gave me a nudge as if to say thank you. I would always defend her. It also worried me I'd be leaving her alone here with them when I went away. Meredith understood. She wanted me to do well and fulfil my dream of becoming a psychologist. Raphael was right about one thing. Meredith did call me her superhero. She wanted me to save other people too. To rescue them when things got dark.

The only person I wanted to rescue right now was Raphael. Rescue him from himself.

My phone vibrated. No one gave a shit if I looked at it when I was at the table. I pulled it out.

Raphael: I wish you could too.

I stared at his words for a long time, my food forgotten. How did I answer that? It's not like I could reveal my hand further or let on that I *liked* him. It would make things complicated.

Jonah: You sure you can't talk to your dad about all of this?

It seemed safer to direct things back on him than start bringing my feelings into it.

Raphael: I don't know. Maybe. It would mean I have to be honest about everything. I don't think I'm ready for that.

"J, who are you texting?" Meredith whispered.
"No one," I responded on automatic.

Jonah: Whatever they did, it must be bad for you to feel this way.

"It's not no one. You're concentrating pretty hard there." I glanced at my sister, who was giving me raised eyebrows. "I told you, it's no one and it's also none of your business."

Raphael: It is. Like properly messed up.

Jonah: I think you should talk to your dad if you can't tell me.

"None of my business? You never keep anything from me."

"Not everything is to do with you, Mer."

She reached over and tried to snatch my phone out of my hand. I held it out of her reach.

"Come on, J, stop being so secretive."

"Eat your dinner."

She scowled at me but turned back to her food. I lowered my phone, keeping an eye on her in case she tried to grab it again. Mum and Grandma weren't paying attention to either of us, which could only be a good thing considering Grandma would only give my sister shit for being 'unladylike'.

Raphael: I know you're right.

Raphael: Can I see you tomorrow?

Jonah: What did you want to do?

It was Saturday and I hadn't made any plans. Seeing him would make my entire weekend, even if it would torture me at the same time.

Raphael: Don't know yet. Just keep the afternoon free.

Jonah: I have the house to myself… if you want to hang out.

Meredith was going to Celia's for a sleepover, Mum was going to see her friends and Grandma would be at Leonard's place.

Raphael: Sounds good. Text me the address. Is 2pm okay?

Jonah: Yeah. I'll pick a film or something.

Raphael: Just no horror!

Jonah: Don't worry, I hate them too.

Raphael: I knew there was a reason why I liked you.

My heart raced out of control in my chest. I was not going to take this the wrong way, but him saying it did things to me.

"What's with the smile on your face?" Meredith asked.

"Shut up, I'm not smiling."

"Yes, you are. I haven't seen you smile like that in forever."

I put my hand to my lips, finding she was right.

Jonah: I've only been showing you my best side so you won't run.

Raphael: Not going anywhere. Seeing you is like the highlight of my week.

Did he have any idea what he was doing to me? I didn't think so or he wouldn't say stuff like that.

Jonah: I feel the same way.

Raphael: Ugh, Mum is calling me for dinner. Text you later!

"Seriously, J, you're like beaming right now. Oh my god! You're texting a boy, aren't you?"

I looked at Meredith. Her green eyes were wide with excitement.

"No. I'm not."

"I don't believe you. You're totally crushing on whoever you're talking to."

I rolled my eyes and went back to my food, stuffing my phone in my pocket. She could try to pry the information out of me, but I wouldn't break. For starters, I'd made a promise to Raphael and I was going to keep it.

"I'm going to find out exactly who it is," she continued. "You've never liked anyone before. This is huge."

"I don't have a crush on anyone, don't start getting ridiculous ideas in your head."

She waved her fork at me.

"Okay, I get it, you're feeling shy about it. That's okay."

"I am not."

"You're protesting too much, means you've got a massive crush."

I ignored her. Meredith knew me too well. I wasn't going to give her any further ammunition. It didn't matter if she was right about me having a crush on Raphael. She couldn't find out about it. No one could. Raphael and I were secret friends, and it would stay that way if I was going to keep him in my life. And I wanted him in it… desperately.

CHAPTER THIRTEEN

Jonah

I wiped my sweaty palms on my jeans when the doorbell rang. Even though I'd told myself I had nothing to be nervous about, it didn't stop my anxiety. Having the boy I was beginning to have serious feelings for in my house and soon, in my room was terrifying, nerve-racking and exciting all rolled into one.

Raphael was fiddling with his glasses when I opened the door. My mouth went dry at the sight of him out of his school uniform. Not that I hadn't seen him like this before, but it felt different. His other hand was stuck in his jean's pocket and he had a navy pea coat on.

"Hey," he said with a smile when he saw me.

His chestnut hair was a tad windswept which gave him this rakish appearance. I felt tongue-tied, but I had to say something.

"Hi, please come in."

I stepped back, allowing him to walk in before I shut the door behind us.

"No family today?" he asked as he shrugged out of his coat.

I took it from him and hung it up on the rack.

"No, Mer is at Celia's. Mum and Grandma are out."

We stood in the hallway awkwardly for a moment before I started towards the stairs. When I reached the bottom step, I looked back, finding he was still in the same place.

"You coming?"

"To… to your room?"

"Um, yeah."

He looked nervous and unsure of himself as if being alone with me in my room wasn't something he'd been expecting. I had a very good reason for not wanting to hang out in the living room to watch a film. Perhaps if I showed him, he'd understand. Instead of going upstairs, I changed tack and walked towards the living room. After a minute, Raphael followed me. When we both got in the room, I dug my hands into my pockets.

"We can sit in here if you want, but you might want to try out the sofa before you make a decision."

I almost shuddered at the sight of the pink monstrosity. Mum bought it not long after Dad died. I don't know why Grandma allowed it since it was the vilest thing I'd ever laid eyes on.

Raphael looked between the sofa and me for a moment. His nose scrunched up. I bit my lip, trying not to smile. He gingerly moved towards it and sat down.

"This is…"

"The worst sofa in the history of sofas and should be burnt in the fiery pits of hell?"

He jumped up and turned around, frowning down at it.

"More like a torture device. Who buys something like this?"

"My mum, after one of her weird shopping sprees she went on when my dad died."

He gave me a sympathetic look.

"Wow, okay, I definitely think your room is a better option if this is the alternative."

I grinned.

"Glad you agree. Come on, I promise it's far more comfortable than that… thing." I waved at the sofa. "I do really wish I could burn it."

He followed me out of the room and upstairs to my room. I opened the door and directed him inside. He turned his head from side to side as he went in, looking around with interest. I had pale blue walls with a few pictures up on them. My bed was in the middle of the room with my desk against one wall and on the other, I had a TV mounted, which I'd turned on before he'd got here.

I fidgeted by the door, watching him take in my space as if he could learn things about me from it.

"Is what you expected?"

He jolted and looked back at me with a sheepish expression on his face.

"Yeah actually, it's exactly what I thought your room might look like."

I wondered what he meant by that when he gave me this amused sort of smile. I walked into the room, rubbing my chin with my hand.

"Oh? Am I that transparent?"

"No, you're not. I just knew it would be neat as a pin."

He was right. My room was organised down to the last detail. Not a single thing out of place. Meredith told me it would make any potential love interest think I was a control freak. I wasn't, just liked things to be in order.

"Do you want to sit?" I waved at the bed. "I picked out a couple of potential films."

I watched him look at my bed and then visibly swallow. Not wanting to read into it, I moved closer and sat down with my back up against the headboard. Raphael kicked off his trainers and sat next to me but left a gap between us.

"What are our options?"

"Okay." I picked up the remote. "We can go action, sci-fi or maybe… a romcom."

His eyebrow quirked up.

"Are you a secret romance lover, Jonah?"

I spluttered.

"What? Um… I mean I watch them with Meredith."

He grinned and shifted, nudging my arm with his.

"It's okay, Mum makes us watch them all the time. Also, Rory is an avid romance reader. It's not like it's some weird taboo or unmanly thing in our household."

I was not expecting him to reveal that bit of information.

"Wait, seriously?"

"Oh yeah, Cole thinks it's embarrassing, but I think it's cool. Rory said it helped him learn about relationships and how to treat my mum right. He had the hardest time out of my parents growing up. Not sure why you're so surprised, we are a rather *progressive* family, don't you know."

I almost laughed. His family was a little bit more than progressive. They were unique. And I was insanely curious about them, but I would never pry into Raphael's life. He could tell me things when he was ready to open up.

"I take it Rory is Cole's dad."

"Yeah, sorry, I didn't explain that part. Duke's dad is Xav and Aurora's is Quinn. If you saw all of us at the same time, you could tell straight away. We look way more like our dads than we do our mum."

"Maybe one day I can meet them."

Raphi's body seemed to go tense at my words.

Does he not want me to meet his parents? It's not like I don't already know his siblings.

"Maybe… why don't we watch an action flick, hey?"

The abrupt change of subject made my stomach sink. I'd hit a nerve and I wasn't sure why. I knew his parents were a sore point for him. Maybe I shouldn't have said anything. The last thing I wanted was for him to shut down on me. I was here to help him not make it worse.

"Um, sure."

I fiddled with the remote and selected the film. The title credits filled the screen. I got more comfortable, shifting the pillows behind me. Raphael didn't look my way, merely fixed

121

his gaze on the TV. I'd made things awkward between us and I hated it.

I tried not to look at him, but I couldn't help myself, especially when he bit his lip. I watched the indents his teeth made and the way his eyes tracked the movement on the screen. Those green eyes behind his wide-framed glasses which I could drown in.

You have it really bad for him, you do realise that, right?

It was far worse than I realised. My feelings kept growing and deepening. I wanted to know what the heat of his palm felt like against me. To experience my first kiss with the boy next to me. And it was really fucked up since this was my little sister's friend. He was also straight, so me having this crush was ridiculous. I needed to quit it and fast before I did something worse. Like fall for him.

You're in serious danger of that, anyway.

"Jonah."

I jumped, finding his eyes on me whilst I'd been staring at his mouth.

Oh fuck, he's caught me staring. Shit, I hope I haven't freaked him out.

"Yeah?"

"I'm sorry about before."

I met his eyes, not understanding what he meant.

"Before?"

"I got weird about my parents."

"Oh, it's fine. I know that's a weird subject for you."

His eyes flicked down to my mouth, which made my skin prickle. We were less than a foot apart from each other.

"It is."

"Don't worry about it. I know you find it hard to—"

My words died in my throat because he'd leant closer.

"I want to tell you. I keep going back and forth with myself over it all. I trust you, but I don't want to betray my parents."

I got stuck in place. He was so close to me, I could hardly breathe. Could hardly think straight.

"I feel like there's no one else in the world except you and me when we're alone. I don't know what it is about you, but sometimes I just want to blurt out all of my inner thoughts and feelings because I know somehow you'd understand."

My hands curled around the covers to stop myself from doing something reckless. Like reaching out and touching him or pulling him closer and kissing him. What did two-and-a-half years between us matter when he looked at me as if I was the very thing he needed to survive his pain?

Shit, I want to kiss him. This is wrong. This is so bad. I can't be feeling this way.

"Jonah, my parents... they... they're killers."

His words broke through the strange spell he had on me.

"What?"

He pulled back abruptly and tugged his hand through his hair.

"Fuck, that came out the wrong way."

"Wait, hold on, did you just say your parents are killers? As in they've killed people?"

"Yes, but it's not that simple. Nothing about their lives is simple." He dropped his face into his hands. "Shit, I should not have told you that."

"I don't understand. What do you mean, Raphael? You can't say that and not explain."

My mind whirled with all sorts of insane scenarios. Insane reasons to explain why he'd said it and whether it was actually true. It's not like I thought he'd lied. He wouldn't say those things to get attention. If anything, he didn't want to bring down any further heat on himself. He was already being bullied at school.

"It means exactly what you think it does."

"You're going to have to give me a bit more than just, my parents are killers."

He let out a long sigh, then he dropped his hands from his face and raised his head. When he met my eyes, I saw something in them I hadn't before. There was a strange intensity as if he was about to do something that scared him.

"I know. I know I do, but… first, first I need to…"

He moved so fast. One moment he was staring at me, the next his face was right up in mine as his hand curled around my jaw.

"I need to know," he whispered.

And before I could begin to work out what he meant, Raphael kissed me.

CHAPTER FOURTEEN

Raphael

The questions and emotions whirling around my brain stopped the moment I kissed Jonah. It was as if everything stopped. Time its-fucking-self went still, leaving just me and him. Just us and nothing else. His mouth was warm. His skin under my palm where I was holding his face felt soft. I was surrounded by his scent. It was earthy, like rosewood or something. Who knew. All I knew was his lips were soft and he'd frozen in place when I pressed my mouth on his.

Seconds ticked by and I thought about pulling away until Jonah made this whimpering sound. Then he kissed me back. He released the covers he'd been holding and grabbed me, one of his hands threading in my hair whilst the other curled around my shoulder. As he pressed his mouth more firmly against mine, my glasses got all squished up against my face. I reached up, prying them off and tossing them away from us. I didn't need those to kiss him.

What am I doing? This is madness. Oh shit, he's kissing me back.

I shouldn't be kissing him, but I couldn't stop myself. After my conversation with Xav yesterday, all I'd thought about was how I felt about Jonah. How I had no idea if I was bisexual or not. How I'd never experienced these emotions for another person before. The need to be as close to them as possible. The want and, if I was honest with myself, desire. Not that I could act on the latter or anything, but it didn't stop me wanting to feel him against me.

I'd never kissed anyone before. It was everything and nothing like I imagined. My heart hammered in my chest. I thought it might explode with the way it was pounding. All I wanted to do was press closer. To feel more.

It was me who pushed him back against the headboard, momentarily breaking our kiss. Me who climbed into his lap. Me who gripped his face and kissed him again, this time pressing my tongue against his lips. I had no idea what I was doing, acting purely on instinct. Acting on whatever insanity had overtaken me. But it was Jonah who responded to me. He gripped my waist, tugging me against him. Our bodies became flush with one another. He opened his mouth and let my tongue meld with his.

My body felt so hot being this close to him. Having his chest against me. Feeling his heart hammering in tandem with mine. Our kiss was uncoordinated, but it didn't seem to matter to either of us. Nothing mattered. Not him being Meredith's brother nor me being utterly confused about my sexuality.

And it definitely didn't matter I'd told him my parents were killers without giving him a real explanation.

"Raphael," he whimpered against my mouth, his hands tightening around my waist.

My name on his lips spurred me on. No one else said it the way he did. I kissed him harder, wanting to bury myself inside Jonah, then I'd never have to come up for air. He made me feel secure. Safe. He just made me fucking well feel something other than emptiness and self-loathing. Jonah considered me worthwhile. He gave me his time and attention. Being with him made me feel… seen.

I didn't want reality to intrude on us, but it hit me like a freight train. The realisation I was messed up as fuck for doing this. For needing to know how deep my attraction to him ran. For needing to work out if I liked boys as well as girls.

I'd got one thing straight. Kissing Jonah, feeling his body against mine had provoked a reaction. One which was quite obviously pressing against him. My reaction to him made me pull back abruptly, putting space between him and my state of arousal.

Jonah blinked rapidly as if coming out of a daze. His green eyes were wide and his pupils dilated as if he'd taken a hit of something. Being this close to him meant I could still see without my glasses since I was only short-sighted.

"I… I'm sorry," I blurted out, my voice all breathy, "I don't know why I did that."

He hadn't let go of me, his hands firmly circled around my waist. I looked around, finding my glasses hadn't gone far. I reached out, grabbing them and shoving them back on my face. Jonah was still staring at me with his mouth closed as if he wasn't sure how to respond.

"Jonah, you can let go of me."

He looked down at his hands then back up at me.

"What if I don't want to?"

I sucked in a breath at his words. Did he like me in that way? And if so, how the hell hadn't I noticed before?

He kissed you back. I think you can assume he was into it.

"What's that supposed to mean?"

He swallowed.

"I don't know, Raphael. You kissed me out of the blue and I'm completely thrown by it. I… I haven't done that with anyone else."

Well, that's great. I just stole his first kiss… but I did give him mine in return.

"Neither have I."

His cheeks pinked up. I would have said it was adorable if this entire situation was different. He removed one of his hands from me, reaching up to rub the back of his neck. His teeth sunk down into his bottom lip. It only made me want to bite it myself. Our kiss hadn't been enough. The urge to do it again drove through me.

"Was… was it okay?" I asked before I had a chance to think about it.

"What? The kiss?"

"Yeah."

His blush deepened, spreading down his neck. I took it as a yes since it was clear he was having trouble forming a sentence. He dropped his hand from his neck onto my thigh.

I was beginning to believe him when he said he didn't want to let me go.

"It was more than okay," he murmured the next moment. "I didn't want to stop."

I swear to god my heart went batshit crazy at his words.

"You didn't?"

He shook his head, staring at me with nothing short of an open invitation to kiss him again. I swallowed, unsure if I should or not. Unsure of everything now I'd come to the realisation being with Jonah turned me on as much as the thought of being with a girl did.

I'm not… straight.

I didn't know how I felt about it. It shouldn't make me feel nervous and insecure. Sexuality was a spectrum. This I knew. Yet the fact still remained, I was already being terrorised for who I was. If they knew about this, it would be worse.

So. Much. Worse.

"Raphael?"

My eyes dropped to his mouth.

"Why did you kiss me?"

I remembered I'd told him I needed to know before I kissed him. But knowing for sure my feelings towards Jonah weren't platonic only confused me further.

"I wanted to… because… because I like you."

You idiot! Why the fuck did you tell him that?

"You like me. Oh. I thought you were straight."

I closed my eyes for a second, wondering how to explain it. Being this close to him wasn't helping matters. His presence scrambled my brain. When I opened my eyes, I moved, forcing him to drop his hands from my body. I sat next to him, pulling my knees up against my chest and wrapping my arms around them. I stared down at them rather than looking at him.

"I am… at least, I think I am. I don't really know."

"So it was just an experiment to you?"

"No, that makes it sound like you were my guinea pig or something." I looked over at him. "I swear it's not like that. I'm just confused. You make me… confused."

He eyed me with a cautious expression as if he didn't know what to make of what I was saying.

"Look, I'm really sorry I did it. I don't want you to think I'm like trying to mess you around or anything."

"You don't need to apologise."

I lifted my hand from my leg and rubbed my face.

"Yes, I do. Your first kiss shouldn't have been with me. I don't even know what I want or who I am, Jonah. I'm totally fucked up and you deserve better than that. So I am sorry."

He stared at me for a long moment. I couldn't read his expression and it bothered me. I didn't intend to make things weird between us. To make things awkward. I'd just wanted to kiss him and the consequences hadn't really registered. Now I was seriously regretting doing it.

He licked his lip, making me even more nervous about what he was going to say.

"I'm not."

Wait, what does he mean? Does he not regret it?

"What?"

"I'm not sorry you kissed me because, if I'm honest, I've wanted to kiss you for weeks."

CHAPTER FIFTEEN

Jonah

I 'd gone and done it now. There was no taking it back. There was no taking back our kiss either. Not when it had been the most alive I'd felt since my dad died. It was like all those films describe when fireworks go off inside your head and your entire world shifts underneath you. He felt… right. It's not as if I wasn't sure I was into boys or anything but kissing him had solidified it.

"You have?" he whispered, his eyes wide with shock.

"Yes. I like you too."

He blinked then looked down at his knees.

Him kissing me hadn't completely distracted me from what he'd said before it happened. Before he flipped my world upside down. I still needed to understand why he'd told me his parents were killers.

"Why? I'm not anything special."

I reached out, taking his chin in my hand and tipping his face back towards me.

"You are special to me, Raphael."

The day I'd found him crying in the toilets had been the beginning. Raphael might be confused and had buried himself under all that self-loathing, but to me, he was beautiful inside and out. Everything about him made my heart sing. All I wanted to do was help him be the best version of himself. To protect him from all the shit he had to deal with. To save him.

He bit his lip, his eyes full of conflicting emotions.

"I owe you an explanation about my parents."

It was clear he couldn't deal with what I'd said to him. Maybe it had been too much. He had just told me I confused him. I dropped my hand from his chin and nodded slowly. Despite wanting to press him on the subject of what the hell it meant now we'd kissed, I knew it was a bad idea.

"I don't want you to think they're bad people. What they did was to protect themselves."

He shifted, dropping his arms from his legs and digging his phone out of his pocket. I reached over and grabbed the remote, pausing the film since we weren't watching it. Raphael fiddled with his phone and then held it out for me. I took it and looked down at the webpage and article he'd brought up.

Frank Russo.

"Who is this?"

"My mum's… well, I guess you could call him her stepfather. She was raised by him and thought he was her real father until she was twenty-one. That's when she met my dads and my real grandfather, Viktor."

My eyes scanned over the page, seeing things like *crime family* and *most powerful man in the criminal underworld*.

"He sounds like a monster," I said after reading further details about his penchant for beating people to death with brass knuckles.

The more I read, the more I thought the whole thing was like something out of a true crime documentary. Frank Russo had met his demise twenty-one years ago, which I couldn't exactly be sorry over if half of what was said about him was true.

"It says his killers were never found. His death and everyone else's at his building was a massacre. Wait, is this what your parents are responsible for?"

I glanced up at Raphael who looked resigned.

"Yes."

"But why?"

This was way more fucked up than I'd ever imagined. I didn't think when Raphael told me his parents had done something illegal it would involve corruption, crime and murder.

"Well, the way my parents tell it, their whole lives had been affected by his empire. My dads parents' were involved with the Russo family in one way or another. Their childhoods were violent and unforgiving. My dads wanted to destroy Frank and his legacy so he couldn't spread his corruption any longer. They made their own fortune to combat Frank. Not all of it was legal and they had to do things they weren't proud of. They didn't tell me all the details, only that they took my mum from Frank to use as leverage. It's how they met and somehow fell in love. Things got complicated, she switched sides and together, they took down Frank and his empire."

He fiddled with my covers, not meeting my eyes.

"I understand if this is too much for you to handle and you don't want to talk to me again, but I'm going to ask you to keep it a secret. No one else can know. I don't want the past dragged up and for them to get in trouble. I love my parents. They're good people. They're kind and would do anything for me. Please… please promise me you won't tell anyone."

His voice shook on the last words as if he thought I might actually betray him. Yes, the whole thing shocked me and I didn't know what to think, but it didn't mean I was planning on going to the police and turning his parents in. I couldn't prove it and I wouldn't want to do that anyway. Why on earth would I dig up something that happened so long ago?

"I promise."

He looked up at me then.

"You do?"

"Yes. You can trust me, Raphael. I would never betray you."

A sad smile appeared on his face.

"You can call me Raphi like everyone else unless you want to be like my parents and call me monkey."

"Monkey?"

He shrugged.

"When I was a toddler, Xav called me a cheeky little monkey because I ran circles around him and the rest of my parents. The name kind of stuck. Sometimes it's cheeky monkey, but usually, just monkey."

Holy shit, that's so fucking cute.

I could picture him when he was small and it did things to my heart. He had to have been the most adorable kid imaginable with those green eyes and chestnut hair.

"Are you freaked out by what I told you about my parents?"

My hand reached out, finding his fingers and holding them.

"A little or maybe a lot. I don't know what to say about it in all honesty, but it doesn't change how I feel about you."

"How you feel about me?"

Had he not been listening to anything I'd said to him?

"Nothing you say or do would make me like you any less."

He shook his head, his eyes darting away.

"You can't say things like that."

"Why not? It's the truth."

He pulled his hand away from mine. It felt like rejection and it hurt way worse than it should have.

"It just confuses me even more, Jonah. I'm already fucked up from all this shit with my parents, the bullying at school and now this…" He waved a hand at me. "This with you. I don't know how to feel. How to even begin to work out what it is I actually want when everything is all just so messed up."

He shifted further away from me and the distance made my chest burn. I wanted him right next to me where I could touch him. Where I could feel him against me. I just plain wanted him. He kissed me. He made me feel alive. I didn't want to shove it back in a box. And I couldn't let him do it either.

"You said you like me… you kissed me."

137

"I do and shit, I want to kiss you again, but I won't when I can't make you any promises about what this is."

I want to kiss you too. Fuck. I really want to.

"I'm not asking for that."

He stared at me.

"Then what are you asking for?"

"Nothing. I'm not asking you for a single thing other than to be honest with me."

I couldn't exactly force him into doing anything with me. It wasn't fair. Not when he looked at me with distress written all over his features. As if this whole thing made him agitated.

"Honest? You want me to be honest?"

"Yes, that's it. Nothing's changed. We're still friends, Raphi."

He blinked and I realised I'd finally called him by his nickname. It fell out of my mouth like it was natural.

"I can do honesty. I've been nothing but honest with you, but are you going to be honest with me? I don't think you're saying everything you want to say right now."

There was a level of challenge in his eyes as if he was daring me to tell him what I really wanted. If I was expecting him to be honest, then I had to do it too. And when I said nothing had changed… it was a huge fucking lie.

"Fine. You want the truth? I want to kiss you."

His eyes darkened at my words like it was exactly what he wanted me to do.

"Then why don't you?"

"You said you won't kiss me. I'm not going to force myself on you."

"How would it be forcing when I also literally just said I want to kiss you again?"

We stared at each other for a long moment. This conversation wasn't getting us anywhere. I don't know how we even reached this point either.

"I'm going to kiss you."

"Then kiss me."

So I did. I leant towards him and I planted my mouth on his. His hands went to my hair, digging into my scalp as he pulled me closer. It wasn't gentle. It wasn't sweet. It was like a fucking bomb going off between us. The messy, uncoordinated dance only made me crave more. I couldn't help the way I reacted to it. The way it flooded me with want and need.

You're not going to let it go further than this. It's just a kiss.

It didn't feel that way. I attributed it to teenage hormones. Or something like that anyway. I reminded myself how old he was and whatever was going on between us, there were lines we couldn't cross. I pulled back, panting. He opened his eyes, gave me this sort of half-smile before reaching up and smoothing my hair back down where he'd tugged at it. I adjusted his glasses for him as they'd become a little askew in our desperation to be closer.

"You say nothing's changed, but I think everything's changed," he murmured.

He was right. Things had changed. You couldn't fake this kind of intensity between two people. At least, I didn't think you could.

"Where does that leave us?"

139

He sat back, putting some distance between us.

"I don't know. Depends on what you want."

I swallowed. He said honesty. I couldn't be anything but at this point. Might as well lay my cards out on the table.

"I want you."

A pained look flashed across his face.

"I can't give you that."

I knew he was going to say it, but it didn't make it hurt any less. My heart squeezed in my chest at the rejection. I'd felt his want and need in his kiss. He wanted me back even if he couldn't admit it.

"I'm too messed up, Jonah. It wouldn't be fair on you."

"I don't care about fair. I care about you. I just want… you."

I sounded desperate, but the truth was I'd never felt this way about anyone. I could help him. I could save him. Nothing else mattered but that. He'd become important to me even though it hadn't been very long. Perhaps it was all the deep conversations we'd had which accelerated this. I knew what I wanted. And it was Raphael Nelson.

"No, you don't. You don't want this." He waved at himself. "Not when I don't know who I am. Not when things are so fucked up. I can't even look at my own parents without seeing them as murderers even though I love them. All I want is to be normal. A normal kid who doesn't have five parents who have this really fucked up past. Who I'm actually shit scared of now I know the truth. When I said to you I'm scared of what they'd do to the bullies, this is why. They do whatever it takes to protect their family even… even kill people, Jonah. How the hell do you think that makes me feel?"

He dragged his hands through his hair. All I wanted to do was wrap my arms around him. Take away all of his pain.

"I feel like shit and I hate the fact I can't tell them about the bullying. If I did, it would hurt them as much as it hurts me. They never wanted that for us. Never. But I'm fucking lost and alone. I hate that I can't go to school without getting people saying shit about me. It's made me hate myself because I'm not normal. And now there's this… confusion I have over who I am. What if they find out? What will I do then? They would give me so much more shit if they knew I was dating a…"

The words hung in the air. I knew he didn't have a problem with anyone's sexuality. It wasn't about that. Raphael wanted to be normal so badly he wasn't willing to entertain the idea of me and him.

Despite all of that, I couldn't help reaching out and cupping his face in both my hands. He didn't stop me. His eyes were full of caution and sadness.

"I don't care," I whispered. "I don't care if it has to be a secret. I still want you anyway. Whatever way I can have you."

"Jonah…"

I couldn't hold back. All my thoughts and feelings bubbled up to the surface. The ones I'd been repressing when I thought he wasn't into me. They couldn't be restrained any longer now I knew for a fact he was.

"You wanted honesty, Raphi. This last year has been miserable for me since my dad died. I closed myself off to the world, but you… you came along and I told you things I've never told anyone. You made me feel like I wasn't drowning any longer. You make me smile every day. I look forward to seeing your name pop up on my phone. I'm happy because of you. I think you are beautiful inside and out even if you don't see yourself that way. So no, I don't care about other people. I don't care about any of that shit. I just care about you."

He searched my face as if he was trying to work out whether or not I was being serious. If I truly felt that way about him. Then he put his hands on mine, pulling them away from his face.

"I care about you too."

"I'm not asking you to decide right now… just think about it. I'm not going anywhere."

I hoped he would. It wasn't asking too much.

After a long moment, he let out a sigh.

"Okay. I'll think about it."

"Thank you."

"I think I kind of ruined movie afternoon."

I smiled.

"We can still watch one if you want, but I understand if you want to go."

He shook his head. It made my heart fucking hurt in a good way.

"No, I don't want to go yet."

I sat back against the headboard again, grabbing the remote and deciding we should watch something different. Raphael sat next to me, rubbing his arm with one hand. I picked a new film out and put it on. It was a romcom this time. I figured we needed a laugh. He didn't object. No, he reached out and took my hand, entwining our fingers together. I tried not to smile, but I couldn't help it. His little gesture gave me hope. Maybe this would work out the way I wanted it to.

I wasn't lying when I said I didn't care about it being a secret. I'd keep Raphael's secrets until my dying day if I had to.

The truth was… I was falling in love with him with every moment, every conversation, every touch. And I'd do anything for him.

CHAPTER SIXTEEN

Raphael

I hadn't spent much time alone with Jonah since the whole kissing and revealing the truth about my parents' incident. Partly because I didn't trust it wouldn't happen again, but mostly because of him being busy with schoolwork and taking care of his sister. I'd been thinking a lot about what he'd said. Probably too much. Going over and over it in my head about what I should do. And even weeks later, I was still no closer to a resolution.

The bullying hadn't stopped. My feelings about my parents hadn't disappeared. My confusion about my sexuality still remained. But somehow I felt lighter because I had him. He was still there for me just as he promised he'd be. He responded to my texts straight away. Kept me sane whilst I tried to sift through my thoughts, feelings and fears.

I thought about the kisses I'd shared with him all the time. They proved to me I wasn't completely straight, but a part of me still couldn't accept it. I was getting in my own way with my need to be normal. To not suffer with all these self-doubts. To not hate myself any longer. No matter what Jonah said, it wouldn't be fair of me to pull him into this mess. To force him into keeping a relationship with me a secret. We were already secret friends. It would only get worse if we were involved further.

I was walking down one of the hallways in school when I almost ran into someone. When I looked up, I found it was Jonah himself. He steadied me with his hands on my shoulders. The warmth of his palms seeped into me, making me want things I couldn't have. Like him.

"Hey," he said with a smile.

"Hey… you okay?"

"Yeah, you?"

I nodded, wondering why he'd not dropped his hands yet.

"We still meeting up after school?" he asked.

I bit my lip. It would be the first time we'd be properly alone together in weeks and I'd been looking forward to it.

"Definitely."

His smile widened and I couldn't help smiling back.

"Good. I'll see you later then."

We stared at each other for a moment longer. I would never get over the way his light green eyes glinted. Jonah was so handsome. He would make anyone who was with him the happiest person alive. And for a moment, I wished it could be me. I imagined what it'd be like to hold his hand in public. To kiss him. To be honest and open about how I felt about the boy in front of me. The kindest and most caring person I'd ever known with the exception of my dad.

I don't know when it started. It crept up on me and slapped me in the face with its intensity. He'd found a way past my barriers without even trying. He saw me as something more than I was. Jonah made me feel like I was worthy. My heart went wild whenever I was near him. I longed to be closer, to hold him tight and never let go.

It didn't matter if he was a boy. That doesn't matter to your heart when it wants the person it wants.

I'm in love with you, Jonah Ethan Pope.

And even though I felt that way, all of my conflicting emotions held me back. They prevented me from telling him the truth. From being open to the possibility of us.

Jonah dropped his hands from my arms and stepped back, letting me go on my way. I walked a few steps along the hallway before turning my head back. He was watching me with affection in his expression. My heart lurched.

Maybe I could be open to it. Maybe… just maybe I can be brave and admit to the truth.

When he looked at me like that, I didn't feel so alone. He was here for me if I needed him. I gave Jonah a smile and turned away again, making my way towards my next lesson. And for the rest of the day, I was feeling on top of the world. I hoped I could get through this shit I was feeling. I had him. Jonah. He'd make sure I was okay. If I let him, he'd take care of me in all ways I knew he could.

I was happy up until I stepped out of the building at the end of the day only to be confronted by Miles Anders and his gang of idiots. I found myself hustled away to a quieter part of the playground behind the school by his friends. I swallowed hard when I looked up at Miles, not wanting any trouble.

Why are they doing this now? I'm going to be late to meet Jonah.

"Well, well, here I thought you were just a freak because of your parents but clearly I was wrong," Miles spat, pressing a finger into my chest.

I tried to back away but Clive was behind me, keeping me from running.

This is bad. Really fucking bad.

"What are you talking about?" I asked, unsure if I even wanted to know.

"I saw you with that gay kid with the dead dad."

I swear my heart just about stopped in my chest. He'd seen me with Jonah. And where did he get off calling him the gay kid with the dead dad? That wasn't Jonah's whole identity. He was kind, sweet and caring. Wasn't his fault his dad had died. And him being gay wasn't something to be sneered at in the way Miles had done.

"You two were getting a little cosy. Something going on there, freak? Something you want to tell us?"

I shook my head, knowing it was better to keep my mouth shut. Miles laughed and pointed at me again as he looked around at his friends.

"Pity, I don't believe you. So, not only do you come from a sick, fucked up family, you're also into dick, huh?"

"I'm not," I mumbled. The fact Jonah was a boy had nothing to do with why I liked him.

"Look at this freak, trying to deny he's a little pussy boy who wants to get fucked raw. Aww, isn't it so sweet? Are you all loved up? Why didn't you tell us, freak? We'd have been happy for you."

I didn't believe a word coming out of his mouth. The disgusted look he was giving me told a different story. The same look they were all giving me. I wanted to curl up into a ball and make them go away.

"He's just my friend."

Miles laughed and the others joined in.

"Oh no, no, I don't think so. The looks you were sending each other's way tells a different story. You're just a sick, little pussy boy desperate for dick."

My worst fears were confirmed. They weren't going to let this go. His taunt made tears well in my eyes. He made the fact I liked Jonah sound like it was wrong. Like I was some kind of abomination for feeling this way about someone of the same sex. It wasn't wrong. It didn't make me a freak nor did it Jonah. Miles was a bigoted piece of shit who didn't want to understand anyone who differed from him.

"Shut up," I whispered. "That's not true."

Why couldn't my voice sound stronger? Why was I this weak pathetic excuse for a human being cowering from my bullies? I felt useless staring up at the people who'd tormented me for so long, I couldn't remember when it started.

"Aw, look, he's trying to say no."

I felt sick to my stomach. The tears behind my eyes burnt. I couldn't take this. I needed to be away from them. My hands curled into fists, trying to keep my emotions from overflowing.

"Shut up," I all but growled at Miles. "Just shut the fuck up. You're wrong. All of you are wrong. I'm not like that. You know nothing about me."

Miles's eyebrows shot up into his hairline.

"What's that you say? Telling me to shut up." He gave me a cruel smile. "Look at the freak, he's grown a backbone." He waved a dismissive hand at me. "Pity really. Too fucking little, too late."

It was then I realised this time I wouldn't be able to talk my way out of things like I had done before. This time things were going to be worse. Much, much worse.

As Miles raised his fist, I tried to take a step back, but Clive held onto my shoulder, forcing me to stay where I was. The crunching sound of his fist connecting with my glasses made me flinch. The pain radiated outwards from the impact the next second. I tried to raise my hands to stop another blow, but he was too fast. He socked me in the jaw, making my head snap back. Next thing I knew, another kid had punched me in the stomach. I almost doubled over, but Clive threw me on the ground. There were some kicks for good measure as I curled into a ball, trying to protect myself.

Everything hurt from the blows and I knew my glasses had shattered under the impact of Miles's fist. Everything went still for a long moment. I peered out from behind my hands, finding them all standing over me with evil smiles on their faces.

"Let that be a fucking lesson, freak."

Miles laughed then indicated with his head they should go. He and his friends slopped off, leaving me on the ground like I was nothing to them. Nothing and nobody.

I didn't move for a long moment, trying to assess what hurt. Trying to work out how things had escalated to the point where they'd actually physically hurt me.

I tugged off my glasses. One of the lenses was broken. I had a few spare pairs, but they were at home. I touched a hand to my eye, wincing. My jaw hurt. My stomach did too from where they'd punched and kicked me.

I sat up, holding my ruined glasses in one hand. I wanted to burst into tears, but I didn't. No, I had to pick myself up. All I wanted to do was to go home and curl up in a ball under my covers. And I knew then I couldn't hide what was happening to me from my parents any longer. It was all very well having Miles and his friends verbally abuse me, but to cause me physical harm was a different matter altogether. They'd done it on school grounds and it meant they could get in trouble. Real fucking trouble.

I pulled my phone out of my pocket and dialled a number, still trying to hold myself together.

"Hello, monkey," came my dad's voice.

My heart burnt at the sound of it. Everything just fucking well hurt.

"Dad, who's picking up Cole, Duke and Rora today?"

"Me, why?"

"Are you still here?"

"No, I left five minutes ago."

I realised he must still be in the car since we lived twenty minutes away.

"Can… can you come back and get me, please?"

I tried to keep my emotion out of my voice but it was almost impossible.

"I thought you were making your own way home later as you had things to do."

I'd told him that because I was seeing Jonah. Now, I wanted my mum and dad. All I wanted was my parents to hold me and tell me everything would be okay. I didn't care what they'd done any longer. I didn't care about anything but having them right here with me.

"Dad… I… I need you."

My voice broke then. I sniffled as a tear fell down my cheek.

"Are you okay, Raphi? Did something happen?"

"No, I'm not," I choked out. "Please, Dad."

"I'm turning around now. I'll be there soon, okay?"

I could hear the worry in his voice. It made me feel worse, but in all honesty, I really needed my dad more than anyone else right then.

"Okay."

Knowing he was coming made it possible for me to put the phone down and haul myself up off the ground. I'd have to go wait by the school gates and hope no one saw me because fuck knows people would question why I looked like a mess right now. I smoothed my hair down and straightened my uniform as best I could. Not being able to see that far ahead of me properly would have made things difficult, but I knew my way around the school well enough.

As I rounded the corner of the building, I found the playground mostly empty which I was thankful for. I walked across it and scraped a hand across my face, wiping away the tear that had leaked out of my eye.

A hand landed on my shoulder and I almost jumped out of my skin.

"Raphi?" came Jonah's voice.

I turned around, finding him behind me with concern on his features. My heart lurched. The dam almost broke when he looked me over, his features falling further.

"Are you okay? What happened to you?"

I shoved his hand off me, not wanting to be touched right then.

"No, I'm not fucking okay," I ground out. "I just got hit in the face and kicked, so I'm not okay."

I felt like absolute crap for snapping at him, but my emotions were all over the place. I was done with everything. The world could just go away as far as I was concerned.

"What?"

"Miles Anders hit me in the face because I tried to talk back to him. He was giving me shit because he saw us in the hallway earlier. He saw us! He thinks we're a thing and we're not. Fuck. He called me a fucking pussy boy desperate for dick. I told him to shut up. He didn't like that. He hit me and then they shoved me on the ground and started kicking me. And now… now I fucking hurt everywhere all because of… of this shit between you and me."

Jonah looked horrified. I knew it wasn't his fault, but I'd lost all sense of a filter and rational thought. I was angry, upset and overwrought. And the person I didn't want to see because it hurt too much was standing right in front of me.

"They hurt you for that? Oh shit, I'm so sorry, Raphi."

He tried to reach out to me. I didn't want his comfort. I wanted nothing from him. My heart was heavy. Nothing felt good. Everything just felt wrong.

I backed away, staring into the eyes of the boy I'd fallen in love with. The one who was kind, caring and deserved someone who could give him everything. Who wouldn't make him hide in the shadows. Who would be there no matter what. He didn't need someone like me. A messed up boy who didn't know who the fuck he was. I should never have allowed this to happen in the first place. Him comforting me. Him making me feel okay. Him being there for me. It was wrong of me. So. Fucking. Wrong.

I couldn't have Jonah Ethan Pope. I didn't deserve him. I deserved nothing. And I was going to make sure he knew that. Then he wouldn't try to make me change my mind.

"Don't. Just don't, Jonah. I can't… I can't do this with you any longer."

CHAPTER SEVENTEEN

Jonah

I had been wondering where Raphi had got to when he didn't appear straight away after school finished. I waited, thinking he was probably running late. It's only when I saw him striding across the playground with his glasses gripped tight in his hand, I knew something was wrong.

Discovering he'd been hit in the face was like a punch to the gut. I could see the redness around his eye and his jaw was colouring up too. I hated how cruel kids could be. Hated that he'd been attacked for being himself. That wasn't the worst part though. Not by a long shot.

It was him telling he couldn't do this with me any longer. It was as if he'd reached into my chest, grabbed hold of my heart and tore it out. He held it in his hand as it fought to keep beating, the bloody mess coating his fingers, leaving me hollow and empty.

"Can't do what?" I asked almost dumbly because I already knew what he meant.

"Whatever the fuck we are."

My heart wheezed in his hand, trying to pump blood but failing miserably.

"We're just friends, Raphi."

He shook his head. Each movement brought a fresh round of pain. Each denial made my chest burn.

"No, no we're not, and you know it. You know this is more than that but we've been refusing to admit it, walking on eggshells around each other, skirting around the fucking truth." He waved a hand around, wincing at the action. "I'm not the person you want, Jonah. I'm not that boy. I'm not like you."

I took another step towards him, unable to let him go because I wanted him too much. The fucked up, crazy part of me had believed for a second he would let me in. Let me be there for him as more than just a friend. I wanted him to be mine because I was already his.

"You are that boy. You're everything to me."

He blinked. It was strange to see him without glasses. They were still clutched in his hand.

"No. Don't say that. Don't make this harder. You barely even know a thing about me and if you did see me, truly see me, you wouldn't like me. You'd hate everything about me. So don't say that. Don't."

I took another step, closing the distance. I didn't care about us being school grounds any longer. No one else was around. He sucked in a breath when I cupped his face, stroking my thumb down the bruise forming on his jaw.

"I could never hate you, Raphi. I do see you. I see every part of you. And I want all of it."

I could see in his eyes he hated that I could. He hated it because it was breaking him on the inside. All of his pain was destroying him. I wasn't helping. I was pushing and I knew it. Somehow, I couldn't stop. My future was rapidly disintegrating before my eyes with every ragged breath he took.

I knew what he was going to say before he said it. I didn't stop him. And it killed me.

"I don't want you."

He said it like he meant it even though I could see in his eyes he didn't. He didn't mean a single fucking word of it.

"Don't lie to me."

He knew how to hit me the hardest. Raphi was aware of what my mum had told me. Him saying it now wasn't lost on me. It fucking well stung.

"I'm not. I don't want any of this. None. You make me too fucked up. I can't be who you want me to be."

"I'm not trying to change you."

I wanted him the way he was. He was beautiful, kind, funny, and he made me happy.

He wrenched away from me. His green eyes were full of torment and it cut me deeply. Raphi held my heart in his fist and squeezed. My chest lit up with agony all over again, his words and his denial ripping me to shreds.

"You are trying to make me into someone I'm not so you can have me. I'm not that person! I'm not… I'm not like you. So just stop. Stop pushing. Stop trying to fix me. I'm not fucking well yours to rescue."

I took a step back as if his words had physically hit me this time. My hand went to my chest. It hurt. It just fucking hurt. I had been trying to save him and he threw it back at me like all of my help had meant nothing to him.

"You don't mean that."

His expression shut down. Raphi shut down on me.

"I mean every single word."

The conviction in his voice decimated me.

"Believe me when I tell you this is the last time I'm ever going to let you come near me. I'm not what you need so just leave me alone. Let me fucking drown because that's where I belong, in the fucking gutter with the rest of the dregs of the world. I'm not worth saving. I'm not fucking well worth rescuing."

He sucked in a breath and I knew this was the final blow. I wasn't ready for it. Not at all.

"Everyone is better off in this world without me, especially you. I don't want you, Jonah. I can't afford to. I just… can't."

Then he turned and walked away. The blood trail he left behind him as he carried my bleeding heart away soaked into the tarmac of the playground, staining it crimson red. I stared at his back. Stared at the boy who I'd stupidly fallen for. Who I thought I could rescue. Turns out I couldn't rescue him at all. He was too far gone. And what happened today had only pushed him over the edge. Forced him into saying all that shit to me to make sure I couldn't go after him. He'd hurt me to force me into leaving him alone.

I hated knowing exactly what he was doing. Hated it so fucking much. He didn't mean any of those words. He didn't mean a single damn thing. And yet it killed me because he'd said them. We'd come to the point where he felt like he had to lie to me to make me stop. He used my mother's words against me knowing how much it would destroy me. He'd done it so I wouldn't go after him.

The horrific truth was we'd brought this on ourselves. I'd tried to save someone I had no business saving. He leant on me when he felt like he had no one else. We had no reason to be near each other. Yet we'd been drawn together. Drawn into a fucking web of our own making. Now Raphi had ripped himself out of it.

I let him go. What was the use of fighting the inevitable? Knowing what I did hadn't made it any easier. My heart was still broken. The hollow cavern of my chest echoed with its emptiness. I raised my hand and rubbed it, hoping the ache would lessen. It didn't. Nothing would stem the flood of my agony. I bit the inside of my cheek to stop tears from spilling down my face. No way in hell I could cry at school even if no one was around.

I took a few steps towards the school gates when I couldn't see him any longer, but I froze a second later when I spied him again. This time he was with someone. Someone who looked exactly like him. I watched Raphi and his dad stride across the playground and into the school building, then I walked out of the school gates and went home. I didn't have to question what was happening. Raphi had told his dad about the bullying. There was no way he could hide it any longer when the evidence of it was on his face. In that regard, I was happy because he needed to deal with it. He needed it to stop.

The whole way home I was fighting with myself. Fighting to keep my emotions in check. Fighting against everything. The dam was breaking. Nothing I did could stop the flood. I knew it was going to drown me. Drag me under and keep me there whilst the waves of pain washed over me again and again.

When I got in the door, I tugged off my coat, kicked off my shoes and chucked my bag on the floor. Then I trudged up the stairs. Instead of going to my bedroom, I went to my sister's. Meredith was laid out on her bed flipping through the TV channels. She eyed me as I walked in and crawled onto her bed.

"Jonah?" she said when I wrapped myself around her, burying my face in her chest. When I finally let my tears fall.

I felt her drop the remote and then stroke my hair, wrapping her other arm around me.

"Jonah, what's wrong?"

I let out a pitiful sob. How could I explain it to her? Just because he'd broken my heart, didn't mean I was about to reveal everything. Tell her all his secrets. I couldn't do that to him. I wasn't vindictive. I wasn't the type to want revenge.

I want him. I just want him and I can't have him.

"Hey, hey, J, what happened?"

"You were right," I whispered into her clothes.

"About what?"

"About me liking someone… and… and he rejected me."

It was the most I could say. It wasn't far off the truth. Raphi had rejected me.

"Oh, J, I'm so sorry. That's awful."

She kept stroking my hair and I kept crying. It was like I couldn't stop now I'd started.

"Will you tell me who it is?"

I shook my head.

"It might make you feel better."

I only cried harder. Telling her it was her friend made me feel like absolute shit considering we'd kept our meetings a secret from her. As if I didn't feel bad enough already. The whole thing was absolutely fucked up.

"Raphael," I sobbed, unable to stop the name spilling from my mouth.

"What? Raphael… you… you mean my Raphi?"

I nodded, clutching her tighter.

"Oh, J. I could have told you he was straight if you'd asked me."

She had no idea he was struggling with his sexuality. I wasn't going to tell her.

"I'm so stupid."

"No, no, you're not. You're the best person in the world, Jonah, and if he can't see that, it's his loss, okay?"

I didn't believe her. No, I blamed myself for ruining everything by pushing. By wanting someone I couldn't have.

"I didn't know you two even talked or anything."

A part of me regretted ever talking to him that first time. For ever giving a shit about someone else's pain. Now I was suffering worse than ever. Not only was my pain razing through me, but his pain also consumed me. His agony. This was my problem. I took on the hurt the people I cared about felt. I experienced it right alongside them.

I hated it. I hated it so fucking much.

"We were kind of," I sniffled. "I was just stupid enough to think it meant something more when it didn't."

"What exactly happened?"

I shook my head. I wasn't going to tell her. No one could find out. I wouldn't out him to his friend. It wouldn't be right.

"I can't tell you. Don't ask me to. Please just be here for me and don't ask questions, Mer."

She was silent for a long moment, her fingers still tangled in my hair.

"I'm right here, okay? I'm not going anywhere."

I would have breathed a sigh of relief if I wasn't in so much pain.

I want to hate you, Raphi. I want to hate you for this… but I can't. I just fucking can't.

I didn't think I could hate the boy I'd fallen in love with. I didn't even hate my mum and she'd done worse to me. Hate wasn't something I felt capable of feeling.

Instead of hating Raphi, I cried. I cried into my sister's chest and wondered if I would be okay. I wondered if I would be able to fall out of love with him in time. If this would stop hurting the way it did.

Too many questions. Too many what ifs.

None of it mattered to my heart. It was shattered. And I was in purgatory over the loss of the person I wanted to take care of and love the way he deserved.

CHAPTER EIGHTEEN

Raphael

Every step I took away from Jonah decimated me. It fucking stung. I could feel myself falling deeper and deeper into the abyss of torrid torment I'd sentenced myself to. There was no one else to blame but me. I'd given him the horrified and broken look in his eyes. I'd subjected him to the agony he must be feeling alongside me right now. I knew Jonah. He was sensitive. He felt my pain just as he did his.

It was what killed me the most. Knowing I'd forced this misery on him. I'd used what I knew about him against him, which was completely unfair of me. I should never have told him I didn't want him. It would only have reminded Jonah of what his mum said. Of the fact she didn't want her own children.

None of this was Jonah's fault. He hadn't really done anything wrong other than try to save me and want to care for me. It was me who couldn't let him. Me who couldn't see beyond his need for normality. Need to not feel this way about another boy. I knew all of this and yet I could do nothing to stop it. Nothing at all.

Fucking Miles Anders had pushed me over the edge. His bullshit had been the last straw. I'd never been hit before and it hurt like a bitch. I didn't want that for myself again. I didn't want any of this.

I walked through the school gates. My dad was leaning up against the car right outside. The moment he saw me, he shoved off it and his green eyes, which matched mine, grew concerned.

"Monkey, what on earth happened to you?"

I didn't want to cry. Seeing him made my heart hurt worse. Everything hurt too much.

He reached out and gently took my chin between his fingers, looking over my face with so much concern, it almost broke me clean in two.

"Did someone hit you? Where are your glasses?"

I raised my hand and showed him them. Dad looked down at them, his expression turning grim.

"Raphael, what happened?"

There was nothing for it but to tell him the truth.

"Some kids beat me up, they've been harassing me for a long time but today… today they got physical."

"How long?"

I flinched.

"A while… like maybe a year or two or three," I mumbled.

166

He sucked in a breath, then put his fingers to his nose as if this was not what he wanted to hear at all. I could hardly blame him. I'd kept the truth of it from all five of my parents.

"Right, we're going to speak to your headteacher. I sincerely hope he's still here or I will be coming in with you tomorrow and we'll talk to him then."

"What? No, Dad—"

"Do not say another word, Raphael. We are going and that's it."

I could hear the anger in his voice. I shut my mouth because it was useless arguing. He walked away to the car and pulled the door open.

"Rora, Duke, stay in the car and watch Cole. Raphi and I will be back in a bit, okay?"

I didn't hear the response from my siblings. Dad shut the door and took me by the arm, forcing me to go with him back into the playground. I stared up at him, wondering if he was angry with me or the situation.

"I'm sorry, Dad."

"You should have said something long before now."

"I know."

"Do your brothers and sister know about this?"

We'd reached the entrance by then. Dad ripped the door open and tugged me inside. He wasn't being rough with me or anything, but I could feel the tension and frustration radiating off him.

"Duke does. He's told them to stop so many times, but they haven't. They never do."

"Jesus Christ, and neither of you thought to tell us what was going on?"

"I'm sorry."

"Well, it's neither here nor there now. I'm going to make sure this doesn't happen again."

I was silent then, letting him lead me through the school building. A teacher came out of a classroom and looked a little startled when she spied us. It was my biology teacher.

"Raphi?"

Dad stopped, looking her over.

"Um, hello, Miss Dennis," I mumbled.

"Are you okay?" She looked at my dad. "Is your son okay, Mr Nelson?"

Dad had met her at parents' evening a few times as he was usually the one who attended with Mum.

"Hello, Miss Dennis. No, he's not. Do you think Mr Hanover is still here? I need to speak to him. Urgently."

"He normally stays late on a Thursday, so yes, he should be. Here, I'll take you to his office."

Miss Dennis gave me a concerned look as she led us down the corridor, but I stayed quiet. I was already in enough trouble as it was for not saying anything about the bullying earlier. I had no idea what Mum would say when she found out.

I barely registered when we got to the headteacher's offices and when Miss Dennis went in to let him know we were there. Too busy worrying about what would happen when I got home and trying to shove down the pain in my chest. It was agonising. I couldn't think about Jonah any longer even though my heart was fucking shattered.

Dad hustled me into Mr Hanover's office and they were talking whilst I sat down in a chair in front of his desk. I stared down at my broken glasses, not knowing what to do or say.

"Raphael?"

I looked up finding Mr Hanover looking at me expectantly.

"Sorry, I wasn't listening."

"That's okay. Would you like to tell me what's been happening? Your father said you were hit on school grounds."

I set my glasses on the desk for him to see. He frowned when he noticed the shattered lens.

"I was… they hit me in the face twice, punched me in the stomach, threw me on the floor and kicked me repeatedly."

I saw Dad's hand curl around the arm of the chair he'd sat in like he was holding back his emotions over hearing what happened to me.

"Well, this is very serious. I'd like you to start at the beginning, if that's okay? I need to know when this started and the names of all the pupils involved."

I told him the whole sorry tale. Everything I remembered. How they'd call me names in the hallway, shove me and make me feel small. How Duke had told them to stop it but they wouldn't. I told him all the horrible things they'd said about my parents knowing my dad was growing ever more agitated next to me. Then I told him in detail what they'd said to me today. What they'd done. And by the time I'd finished, I felt numb.

It didn't matter that in the aftermath of this, most of the kids involved were suspended and Miles was expelled. Nor that Duke had found Miles outside of school days later and given him a black eye for hurting me, telling him if he dared uttered a word about this, Duke would fuck him up worse. None of it really mattered because I felt like shit for it coming to this and my world had fallen apart around me.

When we left Mr Hanover's office, Dad said nothing. He merely led me back to the car, turfed Aurora out the front seat and made me sit there instead. No one spoke during the ride back to our house. The atmosphere was heavy like a black cloud had fallen over us.

Dad unlocked the front door and the five of us walked into the house. He helped me out of my coat and put my bag by the door.

"Kids, go find your mother for me and I want you to make Raphi some tea, okay?"

"Okay, E," Aurora said, looking over at me with sadness in her eyes like she understood I'd been hurting and didn't want to give me shit over it.

"I'm taking him to his room."

Aurora, Duke and Cole ambled off whilst Dad led me down the hallway and into my room. I sat down on my bed, letting him take my ruined glasses from me. He set them on my desk and dug through the drawers, finding one of my spare pairs. He brought them over and set the case on the bed next to us as he sat down.

A moment later, Mum rushed in with her face a picture of concern.

"My baby boy."

That was all it took. I burst into tears, feeling utterly desolate. She hustled over, sat down and took me in her arms.

"Shh, shh, it's okay, I'm here."

"Mum," I sobbed, clutching her like my life depended on it. "I'm sorry. I'm so sorry."

"Oh, monkey, you have nothing to be sorry for, nothing at all."

I could feel her and Dad looking at each other over my head.

"What happened, E?"

"He's been getting bullied at school and today, they hit him. I've spoken to Mr Hanover and they're going to be dealt with. I'll explain the whole story later as I'm sure Raphi doesn't want to go over it again."

Mum stroked my hair and held me tighter. She leant her face against my head.

"It's okay, my baby, I'm here. I'm right here," she murmured.

I wasn't even crying over what happened with Miles and his gang at school. I was still in pain from it, yes, but it was my heart which had me sobbing into my mum's chest. My damaged and bruised heart. I had done this myself by utterly destroying any last shred of hope between Jonah and me.

"It's… it's not school, not the bullies," I cried. "It's not."

"What is it then, monkey?"

"My heart… my heart."

Mum and Dad were silent for a long moment. Then I felt Dad hug me from behind. Having both of them holding me only made it worse. The pain ripped through me, tearing my insides to shreds.

"What do you mean, Raphi?" he asked.

"My heart… it's broken."

"Your heart is broken?"

"Yes," I practically wailed into Mum's chest.

I heard footsteps then.

"I think I might be able to shed some light on that," came Xav's voice.

I peered out from where my face was buried in Mum's chest. Xav had come in and was holding a steaming mug of tea in his hands. Behind him appeared my two other dads, Rory and Quinn. Everyone was here. I didn't even know they were home. I thought they might have been at the casino.

Xav walked over and squatted down in front of me. I pulled away from Mum, both my parents releasing me at the same time. He had a compassionate look in his eyes as he pressed the mug into my shaking hands.

"Do you want me to tell them?" he asked, his voice quiet.

Quinn and Rory came closer, the latter having closed the door over. I nodded since I wasn't able to voice out loud that I'd gone and fallen in love with a boy.

"Raphi came to me a few weeks ago. He's been a little confused about himself, haven't you, monkey?"

I nodded again, staring down into the mug of tea.

"It seems our boy has developed feelings for his friend."

"Which friend?" Mum asked.

"Well, that he didn't tell me, but what I can say is, it's another boy."

A fresh set of tears made their way down my cheeks. The thought of Jonah tore my fucking soul to pieces. I'd said terrible things to him. I had no other choice. He wouldn't stop pushing so I had to do something drastic.

I regretted it.

Every. Single. Word.

Mum wrapped her arm around me, giving my shoulders a squeeze. Xav sat down on the floor properly. Then Rory squatted next to him and reached out, taking one of my hands from around the mug and holding it.

"You know it's okay if you like boys, right?" he said without any sort of judgement in his voice.

That was the thing about Rory. He never made any of us feel like we were in the wrong or stupid for our choices.

"I don't know if I do," I mumbled. "I don't want to feel that way about him."

"That's okay too."

It didn't make me feel any better. Somehow their acceptance of my feelings made it worse.

"It doesn't matter anyway, I ruined it. I made it clear to him I didn't want that. I hurt him and myself in the process."

Mum squeezed me again. None of them looked disappointed or upset with me. All of them had these understanding expressions on their faces. I sipped my tea, feeling it warm me from the inside out. It made me smile a little as it was so typical being given tea to calm myself down. It was the universal solution to anything.

"I'm sorry I didn't tell you about the bullying. I didn't know how because it made me feel like crap, especially since it was about you guys. I guess… I guess after you told me about… about your past, it made it worse." I looked down at my mug again. "Like their taunts were kind of valid which I know they aren't… I know that, but it messed with my head, messed with everything."

"Raphi, we're sorry we had to tell you about that," Dad said, rubbing my arm.

I shook my head.

"It's okay. I understand why you did. I'm sorry too."

Quinn squatted down on the other side of Xav. I met his eyes a moment later. They were full of understanding.

"You have nothing to be sorry for. We all knew this wouldn't be easy for any of you. We're the ones who are sorry for making you feel like you couldn't come to us about it. None of us wanted you kids to ever feel like that, Raphi. You are our son and we love you so much."

My heart hurt at his words. The sincerity and love radiating off him and the others was almost too much. Why had I been stupid enough to think my parents wouldn't understand? Having them all be here for me in my hour of need was everything to me. Absolutely everything. It didn't stop my heart bleeding over what I'd said to Jonah, but it kept me from sinking completely.

"I was scared," I whispered.

"We know and it's okay, monkey," Xav said. "We're not upset or angry with you. We're worried and we care, that's all."

I looked over at my dad because he was who I'd always been the closest to. His eyes were sad as if he hated how much I was suffering.

"Dad…"

He reached up and stroked my face.

"You're okay, monkey. I love you, remember that."

Xav took my mug from me to enable me to hug my dad. He held me close and murmured everything was going to be okay whilst rubbing my back.

I wasn't sure it would be when I'd really hurt someone I cared about, but having my parents give me exactly what I needed right then. It helped me work through my pain. They stopped me from falling into a pit of despair I couldn't get out of. If they hadn't helped me, I'm not sure I would have been able to make it.

I'd gone and done something stupid. I'd hurt the one person who I knew would have been there for me through thick and thin. Who would have cared for me if only I'd let him. I didn't think I could ever forgive myself for what I'd said to Jonah. He deserved better. And I hoped he'd find someone who would give him everything I couldn't.

PART II

entice

verb, en·ticed, en·tic·ing.

to lead on by exciting hope or desire; allure; inveigle.

CHAPTER NINETEEN

Raphael

Three years later

I t's over.

Those two little words have the power to change everything. They'd run through my head on repeat for the past two days. It's not that I felt bad about it being over or it was some kind of profound moment in my life which would stick with me forever. They signified the end, not just of my relationship, but the end of an era. She'd said them to me on the last day of school. The day I truly felt like I'd stopped being a kid and started being an adult. I had turned eighteen before then, but it didn't hit me until that day.

I thought perhaps Lana and I would remain together throughout the summer until we both went to university. Wishful thinking on my part. Stupid thinking really, since she and I had nothing real in common except we'd been lonely.

Sometimes loneliness draws two people together and keeps them next to each other for a time. After all, Lana and I had started talking because Duke had dragged me out to a party his friend had thrown and we were the two quiet ones in the corner. She was sweet, kind and funny. We ended up in bed together. It was the first time I'd been with a girl, but she didn't seem to notice as we were both drunk.

We saw each other regularly after that and sort of fell into a relationship. And then, just like that, we fell out of one. There was no crying or raised voices. No hard feelings. It was just over. She didn't plan on staying in London for university. I did, since I'd already got an unconditional offer. Long distance wasn't something Lana wanted. I respected it. Even so, the words remained.

It's over.

They reminded me of words I'd uttered to someone three years ago. Words which had ruined everything. They weren't the same ones, but they had the same intent. They brought things to an end.

"I don't want you."

Those words were the real words which haunted me. They weren't true. None of what I'd said that day was true. And I'd paid for them every single day since.

My door was thrown open and in walked my younger brother. I eyed him from beneath the covers. Even without my glasses, I knew it was Cole. Only he and Duke barged in here without knocking, but my older brother had heavier footsteps.

"Why the fuck are you still in bed?"

"Why do you care?" I retorted as he came closer. It was only ten in the morning and it wasn't like I had anywhere to be.

Cole had become more irritable than ever recently, but I blamed it on his breakup.

"I don't."

I hauled myself up into sitting position and grabbed my glasses off the bedside table, shoving them on.

"What do you want, Cole?"

He looked away for a moment.

"I need you to give something back to Meredith."

I gave him a look. If he was going to fuck with her feelings some more, he could count me out. No way in hell I was enabling that shit. To say I was pissed with my brother for hurting my friend was an understatement. I'd wholeheartedly supported their relationship. Him breaking Meredith's heart? Yeah, I wasn't happy about it.

"What exactly?"

He held out his hand.

"I found this under my bed. She lost it here and she deserves to have it back. Her dad got them for her."

There was a small earring nestled in his palm. Cole had this pained look on his face. I knew how important Meredith's dad had been to her, and so did he.

"Hand it over then, I'll make sure she gets it."

I didn't want to upset her with a reminder of Cole, but she would want the earring back. She'd told me why they broke up since Cole had kept silent on the subject. No matter how pissed I was at him over the whole thing, I was still relatively sure he was broken up inside about it. The catalyst had been someone I had desperately tried to forget. Except you can't ever forget the person you said the worst things imaginable to when you still had feelings for said person, which you've tried to bury deep inside you in an attempt to make sure they didn't resurface. Only it was impossible to do that. To cut the person out of your heart.

"Is she okay?"

"She's fine, no thanks to you."

He gave me a dirty look.

"Don't start on me."

"I'm not. Give me the earring."

He closed the distance and dropped it into my outstretched hand.

"I just want her to be okay. I… I miss her."

"You do realise she told me why you broke up with her, right?"

He shifted on his feet.

"I wouldn't have had to if you hadn't told her brother about our parents."

I flinched at the mention of her brother. I wasn't sure why he'd felt the need to tell Meredith when he'd kept it a secret for years.

"Oh no, you do not get to blame me for your mess with her. I'm not responsible for his actions and it was three years ago, Cole. How the fuck was I supposed to know you liked her back then?"

He rubbed the back of his neck and let out a sigh.

"Why did you even tell him in the first place?"

"I was struggling, you know this. It's not some big fucking secret in this family how fucked up I was back then."

I was still fucked up now if I was honest. Still so fucked up about my sexuality and how I couldn't reconcile myself with it. Especially since it was all wrapped up in my feelings for… him.

"What happened between you, Raphi?"

"None of your business."

He raised an eyebrow.

"It is my business when it almost single-handedly ruined my relationship."

I understood why he was mad at me over it, but the demise of his relationship was between him and Meredith. It had fuck all to do with me. I was not responsible for other people's actions. Only my own fucked up ones.

"You didn't have to walk away. That's on you. And it was a fucked up thing to do after she told you she loves you."

He scowled.

"Don't remind me."

"Then don't ask me about… him."

Cole threw his hands up.

"You can't even bring yourself to say his name, can you?"

"Shut up."

He gave me one last look before walking away to the door. He paused on the threshold, and I really wished he hadn't.

"Just give her the earring, okay?" He shifted on his feet. "And whatever happened between you and Jonah, deal with it, Raphi, because no one here is ever going to judge you for wanting to be with another man."

And with that statement stabbing me in the chest, he left.

It had nothing to do with my family. I knew they wouldn't judge me. They'd be happy. It wasn't about that. It was me and my fucked up need to be normal. To be away from this suffocating environment. Ever since my parents had found out about the bullying, Mum had become insufferably protective over me. It was non-stop and I couldn't take it any longer. I wanted some freedom. It's why I was moving out into halls for university. Something I knew Mum hated since I'd be in London, but not with them. My dads had accepted it without comment. They'd always encouraged us to make our own choices in life.

I loved my family, but I needed to find myself outside of them. My entire life had been marred with the fact I was the kid with five parents. I wanted a new start, so I didn't have to be that person any longer. All I wanted was to be my own man. Be Raphi and not freak or four-eyes. Just me without the labels and baggage.

I popped the earring down on my bedside table before grabbing my phone and taking a photo of it. I attached it to a message.

Raphi: Is this yours?

Meredith: Oh my god! You found it?

Raphi: Well, I didn't, but he thought you'd want it back.

Meredith: I do. Can you drop it around mine?

I figured she'd want to skirt around the fact it was Cole who'd given it to me. And I didn't blame her for it.

Raphi: Sure. Today okay?

Meredith: Yup, just let me know when.

Raphi: Could be there in an hour.

Meredith: Sounds good.

She'd never taken sides when it came to me and her brother, but Meredith didn't know what really happened between us. I'm not sure she'd like me much if she knew what I'd said to him that day. I didn't like me much for it.

Don't sugar-coat it, you hate yourself for it.

I hauled myself out of bed and took a shower before dressing and grabbing breakfast. My parents had left for the day. Well, Rory was still here, but he didn't go out much. Cole was nowhere to be seen, and quite frankly after what he'd said to me, I didn't want to talk to him.

I walked out into the sunshine, breathing in the fresh air. Well, as fresh as the air can be in London, anyway. It was a nice day. I was only in a t-shirt and jeans as I walked up to the bus stop. It was only a few stops over, so didn't take too long for me to get to Meredith's.

I walked up the street and stopped outside her house, reaching up to ring the doorbell. Running my fingers through my hair, I waited. A minute later, the door was pulled open and the breath was stolen from my lungs. It's not as if I didn't think there was any possibility he would be here or I would never run into him again because I was friends with his sister. I wasn't prepared for the sight of him right then.

Jonah was wearing a t-shirt and shorts. He had a hand stuck in his pocket. His blonde hair was messy as if he hadn't bothered to sort it out this morning. His light green eyes went wide the moment he set them on me.

He looks so good. Fuck.

I didn't think my heart could slam any harder against my ribcage, nor my mouth could get any drier. Of course, he looked older. He was twenty now and had been away at university for two years. I hadn't seen him since he'd left school. There'd been no reason for us to run into each other… until now.

Why does he still look so handsome?

It was a stupid question. A stupid fucking question since I had no business thinking that about him. I'd hurt Jonah. I should not still have feelings for him. And yet… I did.

"Hello," he said, his tone clipped.

"Um, hi… is Mer here? I'm dropping something off for her."

How I even got the sentence out without tripping over all my words was beyond me. It's like my entire fucking soul was on fire and I didn't know what to do about it. He was right there in front of me. The first person I'd ever loved. He didn't know about my hidden feelings. And those feelings had only come flooding back with his presence.

God, I want his presence. I'm such a fucking idiot. Those things I said were such bullshit. I want him. I want every part of him. He's the only person who truly sees me.

He didn't look very happy to see me right then. I didn't blame him. I owed him an apology. A huge fucking apology. And he owed me a fucking explanation as to why he told Meredith about my parents. After Cole's reminder of it today, I couldn't get it out of my head. He shouldn't have said anything. Meredith didn't need to know about what they did. She didn't need that shit in her life. Neither had Jonah in all honesty, but he'd wanted to know the truth. He'd been there for me. And I'd thrown it all in his face.

"Yeah, she is. Hold on…" he turned his head back, "Meredith, Raphael is here for you."

When he met my eyes again, I could feel all of his pent up resentment towards me slamming into my chest. I wanted to hang my head in shame. I wanted to fall to my knees and beg him to forgive me. Tell him I didn't mean a single word.

I heard the thundering of footsteps down the stairs before Meredith appeared next to Jonah. She gave him a look and he stared at the two of us.

"Sorry, I meant to answer the door myself," she said with a nervous laugh.

I dug the earring out of my pocket.

"It's okay… here you go."

I reached out a hand to her. Meredith opened her palm and I dropped the earring in it. She stared down at it for a moment.

"Thank you. I'm so glad you found it."

"Like I said, wasn't me."

The tension in the air cranked up a notch. We were all thinking about what Cole had done to Meredith and how our actions had led to the demise of their relationship.

"Uh, I should get going," I said when the silence had gone on for too long.

"Yeah, uh, I'd invite you in, but… yeah."

She looked at Jonah, who was still staring right at me with that fucking damning look in his eyes. Like he didn't know if he wanted to shout at me or not. I wouldn't blame him if he did. I deserved it.

"It's cool. I'll text you, yeah?"

She nodded.

"Yeah, we'll do something soon."

I shrugged, gave her a tight smile and then turned, leaving them in the doorway. I heard the door shut a second later as I walked away. I only got a few steps before the crippling pain started. I gripped the railing outside their house, putting a hand to my chest.

What the fuck was that?

Seeing him had brought back all of my fucking torment. All of it slammed into me. It made me want to cry and rage all at the same time. At myself. And at him.

I couldn't leave it at that. I couldn't. Every part of me was screaming. Screaming so loud it fucking hurt my ears. Without me even thinking about it, I dug my hand into my pocket and brought out my phone. And I was almost frantically typing out a message to a number I hadn't used in three years.

Raphi: We need to talk. Now.

CHAPTER TWENTY

Jonah

I stared down at my phone, reading the words over and over like they would tell me something else. Like they wouldn't fuck with me in the way they were. Because seeing Raphi again had fucked with me to the point where I thought my knees would give out.

Meredith had gone back upstairs. I'd lingered in the hallway. I don't know why, but I couldn't walk away. Every part of me wanted to rip the door open again and go after him. There were so many things I hadn't said all those years ago when he'd walked away from me. I wanted to hate the very sight of him, but I didn't. Fuck, I didn't.

Time had done nothing to heal the gaping hole in my chest he'd left me with. Time hadn't altered my feelings. Time hadn't fucking well changed a damn thing.

He'd only become more attractive in the intervening three years, having filled out more and grown a few extra inches, meaning we now matched each other in height. I hated myself for the fact my mouth had watered when he'd been standing there on my doorstep in jeans and a t-shirt. Hated that I'd wanted him to shove me up against the wall and kiss the shit out of me. Wanting the passion and fire between us since I'd never found it with anyone else.

You shouldn't want him. He hurt you.

I couldn't help it. Raphi still meant far too much to me.

The moment my phone had buzzed in my pocket, I'd known it was him. There had been so many emotions in his eyes when he'd looked at me. So many unspoken words between us.

Even though I knew it was a fucking stupid thing to do, I shoved it back in my pocket and walked back over to the front door, pulling it open. He was still there, standing with his hand on the railing and looking like he was about to keel over.

"Raphael."

The boy who held my fucking heart in his hand turned around, his green eyes full of things I didn't want to see. Why did it hurt this much? Shouldn't three years have settled this shit? And why the fuck did I still want to save him after all this time?

He let go of the railing and walked over to me. My heart was wild in my chest. My hands clenched at my sides to ensure I wouldn't do something stupid. His closeness affected me. I couldn't do a single fucking thing about it.

"Why did you tell Meredith about my parents?"

Those were not the words I'd been expecting to come out of his mouth.

"We shouldn't talk about this out on the street."

I stepped back and he walked in without hesitation. We were going to have a conversation whether or not I was ready for it. I shut the door and walked towards the stairs, feeling him at my back following me as I took the stairs two by two. When we got into my room, I closed the door firmly behind us.

I walked away a few paces before turning to him. We stared at each other for several long moments. My whole body called for his in this desperate manner which took my breath. I couldn't act on it. It would be fucking insane given how much he hurt me when he said that shit to me three years ago.

"That's what you want to talk about? Meredith and Cole?" I asked before he had a chance to say a word. "You sure you don't have anything else to say to me?"

He swallowed. I didn't like getting confrontational, but my emotions were all over the place. Not to mention how I was fighting against my urge to go to him and hold him.

Stupid. Fucking. Idiot.

"I have a lot of things to say to you."

"Then say them."

He shook his head.

"I asked you a question, Jonah."

The moment I knew Cole was interested in Meredith, I couldn't fucking deal with it. It had brought all those horrifying feelings about Raphi back to the forefront. All the heartache and pain. And reality had hit. The reality that their family had a dark past. His parents had killed. The thought of my sister getting wrapped up in their bullshit brought all my protective instincts to the forefront. I had to keep her safe at all costs since Meredith had already been through too much. Our father had died. Our mother didn't give a shit about us. She and Grandma constantly picked on Meredith. They'd got worse since I'd gone to university. I'd seen red when it came to matters of the person I'd give my fucking life for if I could.

"Can you blame me? That's my sister and your brother is two years younger than her. He's not even an adult."

"That's bullshit. You don't even know Cole. He treated her with so much respect and care. He loves your sister with every ounce of his being. Cole might not be perfect, but he gave Meredith everything he has and you… you fucking well ruined that for them."

I was a little taken aback by the vehemence in his voice. And I hated the fact he had a point. I didn't know his brother. All I'd thought about was my sister. Protecting my sister from a family whose past, quite frankly, scared the shit out of me just like it did Raphi all those years ago.

"I did what I had to. Meredith doesn't need to be wrapped up with your family."

The moment I said the words, I regretted them. I fucking regretted them because they weren't true.

"My family? Hold on… hold fucking well on. You didn't seem to have a problem with them when I told you about what they'd done. You didn't seem to care when you wanted to be with me. Why is it any different for her, huh? She's not in danger. Cole would never have let anything happen to her, and they aren't even involved in that life any longer. I told you that. I fucking well told you that."

I didn't want to tell Raphi I'd gone looking for more information about his family. I'd found every article and detail I could about who they were and what they'd done. It hadn't made me feel good about myself. Not when I'd find out about his dad, Xavier's father being in prison for murdering his wife and sister. Nor finding out that his other dad, Quinn had some sinister as fuck name which people feared. All of it had made me ill.

It hadn't really been about Meredith and Cole, it had been wanting more of the story than Raphi had told me. Needing to know everything because I was too fucked up about the boy in front of me. So fucked up about him I couldn't stop wanting him even though he hurt me.

"It doesn't matter. She's my sister!"

"Oh I see how it is, one rule for you and another for her, is it?"

"No!"

"Then what the fuck is it?"

"You, it's fucking well you." He kept pushing. Fucking pushing me just as I'd pushed him all those years ago. I couldn't help the words spilling out any longer. "You fucking well broke me, Raphi. You. All I have done for the past three years is suffer because of you and what you said to me. You hurt me so fucking much, I saw red when she told me about her and Cole. I had to protect her. I just fucking had to."

He took a step towards me, his eyes flashing with anger and I was pretty sure mine were too. Why did he look hot when he was pissed off?

"Me? You did this because of me?" He pointed at his chest. "Do you know how fucked up that sounds, Jonah?"

"Yes, I fucking well do. I know it's fucked up and I'm sorry."

"Well, I'm fucking well sorry too. I'm fucking sorry I hurt you so much you had to ruin my brother's relationship with your sister."

The words I'd wanted to hear all this time hit me like a ton of bricks, tearing me up inside even worse than anything else he'd said.

He'd apologised.

He'd actually said sorry to me.

We stared at each other from across the small expanse between us. His chest was heaving and his eyes were like molten fire. I don't know who moved first. I didn't care. It wouldn't have mattered either way. What did matter was what happened next.

We practically slammed into each other then it was lips, tongues and hands everywhere. His mouth was so hard against mine, our teeth almost smacked together. I felt like he was trying to crawl inside me just as I was him. His hands were in my hair, pulling at the strands whilst mine were gripping him just as tight.

The kiss was brutal and unforgiving. It fucking hurt when he bit down hard on my bottom lip like he was trying to punish me for fucking up Cole and Meredith's relationship. I only bit him back in retaliation. It was like a taunt, daring him to do things to me. Daring him to take what he wanted.

Raphi shoved me backwards until my legs hit the bed, still kissing me all the while like he couldn't stop. I didn't want him to. I found myself flat on my back with him on top of me a minute later. He pulled back for only a second to rip his glasses from his face and throw them on my bedside table. Then his hands were pinning mine against the covers and his lips were back on mine.

I had no idea how to feel about him being dominant with me. There was no doubt who was in control, even if we were both running off anger and desire, especially when he ground himself into me. I whimpered into his mouth, desperate for more. I'd grown hard the moment he planted his mouth and hands on me. I ached for his touch. For all of him.

"Raphi," I moaned when he nibbled his way down my jaw, his teeth grazing against my skin. "Please."

He didn't say a word, merely let go of one of my hands and dug his between us. I gasped when he wrapped it around my cock. It made me wonder if he'd actually done something with another boy, but then I threw the thought away. Raphi had struggled with his sexuality so much, I didn't think he would have gone there.

"You make me fucking crazy," he hissed in my ear. "I hate that you do."

I didn't know what to say to him since he was rubbing his hand up and down my cock like he owned it. I could feel him hard against my hip. It wasn't just me who was insanely turned on right then. He captured my mouth again. Now he'd let go of one of my hands, I wound it into his hair, holding him close because I never wanted this to end. I didn't want him to stop what he was doing. How he was making me feel.

Please, fuck, please just touch me. I want you so fucking much, Raphi.

His body left mine as he sat up. I almost whimpered in protest, but his hands were at my t-shirt, pushing it up my chest. I let him take it off me. His eyes were dark and intense when they roamed over me. And his hands, his fucking hands ran down my skin, lighting it up and sending sparks down my spine.

I let out a pant, wrapping my hands around his thighs as I needed something to hold on to. His touch utterly intoxicated me. I needed all of it. All of him naked against me. His fucking skin on mine. And most of all… most of fucking all, I wanted him in me, taking everything from me.

He leant down and planted his lips on my chest, trailing his tongue down my skin. My hips arched up into his by instinct. Fuck, it felt so good.

"Fuck," I gasped when his tongue swirled around my nipple.

"You like that, do you?" he murmured.

"Yes… yes, yes."

"Good."

He sat up and tugged his t-shirt off, throwing it away from us. The way his body flexed with the movement made my mouth water. Shit, he wasn't overly muscly, but he wasn't skinny either. Just perfect. I couldn't help myself when I reached up and ran my fingers down his stomach. He sucked in air, watching me with hooded eyes filled with… desire.

"Tell me what you want, Jonah," he said, his voice all low and gravelly.

What do I want?

You.

I want all of you.

What would he say if I was honest? What the fuck would he think? I didn't know what he wanted out of this. I didn't even know what the hell we were doing with each other, but I wasn't about to stop. No, I needed it. I needed him. And I didn't give a flying fuck about consequences.

"I want you to fuck me, Raphael… I really want you to fuck me."

CHAPTER TWENTY ONE

Raphael

As I stared down at Jonah, bare-chested and panting and his words registered with my brain, I found myself aching with the need to do exactly what he'd said. I had no fucking clue what I was doing when it came to being with a man intimately. I'd only ever been with Lana, and her body was nothing like Jonah's. He was hard in places she had been soft, but it didn't matter to me. He made me lose my mind because I was so insanely attracted to him.

I wanted him.

I wanted all of him.

I bit my lip as he waited for me to say or do something. It never occurred to me he'd want me to fuck him. I hadn't honestly thought about what it would be like to be intimate with Jonah, or any other man.

"If you want that, you're going to have to tell me what to do."

He swallowed as if he hadn't expected me to concede to his desires. What the fuck did I know about sleeping with a guy? Not like I'd come here with the expressed intention of having sex with him. Hell, I'd never even expected to see Jonah today.

"You want to?"

I leant over him and ran my nose up his face.

"I want whatever you want right now."

His hands around my thighs tightened and he let out a pant.

"Going to assume you have experience since I don't. I've only been with a girl."

"Yes," he hissed when I licked his jaw. "Only one guy, but yes."

It bothered me a little, even though I'd hoped he'd found someone else. Someone who deserved him unlike me. I didn't deserve him and yet this was going to happen. We were going to have sex.

My hand ran down his chest, making him gasp and pant more. When I reached his cock, I stroked it again. Feeling him only made mine throb harder.

"Raphi, please."

"Tell me, Jonah, fucking tell me what you want me to do."

"I want to see you… all of you."

I smiled against his skin.

"Do I get to see you in return?"

"Yes."

Every part of me ached and longed for it. For all of him. The boy I'd never fucking well been able to forget, no matter how hard I tried. This beautiful man below me who was practically begging me to give it to him. He sounded so needy and desperate, his voice shaking on all of his words.

I got up off the bed, kicking my shoes off and tugging at my jeans. He lay there, staring at me as if he couldn't believe I was going to get naked for him. Honestly, I couldn't believe it either, but here we were and I couldn't stop. I was still pissed as hell at him, but I was turned on as fuck. My socks came off with my jeans and then my fingers were tugging at my boxers, freeing my cock from their tight confines. It slapped against my stomach. I could feel his eyes on me. Feel him staring.

"Fuck," he whispered.

I knelt over him again, watching Jonah take in every inch of me. Watching his normally light green eyes turn dark with unrepressed need. He didn't stop me when I peeled back his shorts and boxers, tugging them down his legs. And he certainly didn't stop me staring at him too. All of him. My mouth watered at the sight of Jonah's solid body. I had to swallow it back when I looked at his cock. His beautiful, hard cock. I couldn't help touching it, wrapping my hand around his girth and stroking slowly. He whimpered but didn't move, allowing me to explore him. I raised my head and looked into his eyes.

"Is this what you want from me, Jonah? Do you want me to give it to you? Is this what you fucking well imagined when you thought about us together? Or did you think it would be the other way around, huh? Me on my back with you towering over me."

His mouth opened but no sound came out. It made my lips curve upwards. Perhaps it was my anger coming out. My anger with myself and him. I'd never spoken to Lana like that, but there was history between me and him. Fucking history we couldn't erase. It wouldn't disappear and leave us alone because we'd forged a connection which went far deeper than I ever realised.

"Answer me."

"This, exactly this," he panted out as I continued to stroke him. "I don't… I don't like to top. Fuck, don't stop."

It wasn't what I expected from him. For him to want me like this, but fuck, I wasn't going to complain about it.

"I won't, but you did tell me you want me to fuck you."

"I do."

"Then what's next?"

He reached out towards his bedside drawers, tugging it open. He gave me a look. I shifted up and peered inside. Then I pulled out the lube and a condom, dumping them on the bed next to us.

"Can… can I touch you?" he all but whispered.

"You think I wasn't going to let you?"

He shrugged a little like he'd given over all the control to me even though he was telling me what to do. This was fucked up, but I didn't care.

"Touch me if that's what you want, I'm not going to stop you."

His hand met my chest and ran down it. The softness of his touch surprised and thrilled me at the same time. When his fingers curled around my cock, I grunted, loving the way he gripped it firmly and stroked me back. His eyes flicked up to mine.

"I've pictured you so many times, but in reality… you're perfect."

I leant down and caught his mouth. It was a wild battle again, each of us wanting more and more. His hand left my cock and wrapped around me, pulling me closer to him like he wanted my body flush with his.

"Please," he moaned in my mouth. "I need you."

I fumbled next to us, finding the lube and flicking the cap open. I had some idea of how this would go even if I'd not done it before. Pulling away slightly, I squirted some on my fingers and reached down. Jonah's eyes travelled the length of us and he let out a groan as I touched him. When I ran my finger around his hole, he swallowed hard. I couldn't stop staring at him. The way his pupils looked like they'd blown and his chest rapidly rising and falling.

"Put it in me," he panted out. "Please."

I did what he asked, I pressed against him with my finger. The moment it slid in, he groaned and I almost fucking died. He was hot and tight in a way I wasn't expecting. Having only experienced touching pussy, this was different, but in a good way. In a really fucking good way.

"Stretch me out, Raphi, then fuck me," he whispered as if the words scared him because once we did this, there was no going back.

My mouth was on his again, swallowing his words whilst I did as he asked. I fucked him with my finger before adding a second and not long after, a third. He was arching into me and writhing as if this was exactly what he needed. His cock rubbed against mine and it only made me want him more. Want all of this.

"How do you want me to fuck you?" I murmured against his mouth.

"Like this, just like this. I want to see you."

"Now?"

I pressed my fingers deeper and he moaned in response. His acquiescence to me was intoxicating. I thrived off it. It made me all the more eager to have him. To be inside him.

"Jonah, now, do you want me now?"

"Yes," he whimpered. "Now, please."

I pulled my fingers from him and sat up on my knees, grabbing the condom. He watched me roll it on and when I coated myself in lube. He pulled his legs up, bending them at the knee. I looked down, placing a hand on the back of his thigh for leverage as I shifted forward. Seeing him waiting for me to impale him on my length like this only turned me on further.

I glanced up at his face, finding him staring at me with nothing but desire and need. He bit his lip as I pushed against him with the tip of my cock. There was some resistance, but I applied more pressure. He gave way a moment later, letting me slide the first couple of inches of my cock inside him. I choked out a breath.

Fuck me, he's so tight.

"Oh fuck," he moaned. "Fuck… don't stop, don't… don't stop."

I pushed deeper, trying to breathe through it since I was so fucking turned on right then. He panted with each inch, making me wonder if I was hurting him in any way, but he looked like he was in ecstasy. I pulled back and drove back in, keeping a slow, but steady pace.

"Yes, Raphi, please, fuck… please fuck me."

"You sure?"

"Please."

I pulled out and thrust in a few times, not really putting too much weight behind it as I was trying to loosen him up a little more. He reached out and grabbed my arm, tugging me over him and forcing me into giving more. Then his mouth was on mine, kissing me for all he was worth as my hands landed next to his head. He bit down on my bottom lip as if ordering me to give it to him properly. Give it to him in the way he and I both wanted.

I pulled back and thrust harder this time, making him moan in my mouth. I could feel his cock against my stomach with each thrust, throbbing restlessly. It only spurred me on further.

"Oh fuck, there, fuck, right there," he groaned, turning his mouth from mine.

I shifted my hips and kept hitting the spot he'd asked, realising I was rubbing right up against his prostate. He gripped me so tightly, making it hard for me to stop from coming. This experience was nothing like being with a girl, but it was just as good. It felt just as fucking wonderful. In a lot of ways, doing this with Jonah felt right.

I kissed him again as he reached between us, gripping his cock and stroking it. My thrusts became harder and more erratic, right on the edge of orgasm, but keeping a lid on it so this didn't end too quickly.

"Harder," he grunted. "Fuck me harder."

"If I do that, I'm going to come."

"Then come, fuck, please, just give it to me."

The need in his voice made it impossible to say no. I gave it to him harder, listening to his erratic breathing and moans of pleasure. His fist around his cock moved faster between us, driving him towards the edge.

Everything inside me tightened and I could no longer stop the onslaught of need. I pounded into him harder. Then I erupted, groaning and shuddering into his neck as I came. A moment later, I felt his hot cum splattering against my stomach and his hand.

"Fuck," he gasped, his body twitching against mine.

We were both panting as we came down. I didn't think I could move. The whole experience had been overwhelming and completely unexpected. I kissed his neck, running my tongue over his pulse point as his free hand curled around my waist.

"Raphi," he whispered.

"Yeah?"

"Was it okay for you?"

I raised my head and stared down at him. His eyes were wide and full of caution.

"What do you mean, was it okay for me?"

"You're not freaked out, right?"

I frowned.

"Why on earth would I be freaked out?"

"Because… because you said you didn't want this before. That you didn't want me."

His words hit me square in the chest, making it ache. The worry in his eyes had me swallowing.

"I didn't mean what I said three years ago. I didn't mean a single fucking word of it. I'm sorry I said any of it. I'm sorry I hurt you and used her words. I'm so sorry." I reached up and brushed his blonde hair out of his eyes before cupping his cheek. "I want you, Jonah, so fucking much it hurts. So no, I'm not freaked out." I dragged my thumb over his bottom lip. "Admittedly, I wasn't exactly expecting you to want me to fuck you, but the moment you said it, I wanted it too."

And I had. I wanted all of him like this, but I also knew we had a lot to talk about. There were many things we needed to say to each other. I didn't want to yet. I needed a few more minutes of me and him together like this. I wanted to savour it. Those precious moments where anger had given away to desire and desire had given way to hot, explosive sex.

It hadn't been like that with Lana. Not at all. No, with Jonah it had been pure passion, want and need. I didn't want reality to intrude and force me into facing up to the fact I'd confirmed to myself I was way too into Jonah to be anything other than not completely straight.

CHAPTER TWENTY TWO

Jonah

The words I'd been desperate to hear from his mouth for so long made my bottom lip tremble.

"I want you, Jonah."

I'd been scared after we'd come down from whatever madness had overtaken us when our lips met he would run from me. Or he'd be completely uncomfortable with what we'd just done. I didn't want that. It would have ruined the very best sexual experience of my life. The pleasure he'd given me was intense and unyielding. Feeling the boy who I'd loved for three years fuck me like he meant every thrust had driven me higher than I'd ever been before. I hadn't wanted it to end but we were both so turned on and pent up, it wasn't surprising it hadn't lasted long. It didn't matter. It was everything to me.

I hadn't told my sister I'd lost my virginity a few months ago. She would probably give me a hard time over it. Mostly because it had been with my housemate, Robin, who considered himself 'try-sexual' in the sense he'd try anything once. I hadn't been drunk and neither had he. It was simply a conversation we'd had one evening which led to more. I wanted to get it over with since I was tired of wanting Raphi so much, I couldn't be with anyone else. It hadn't been romantic between me and Robin. He'd taught me about sex as he'd been with other men before. When it came to me and Raphi, I'd already been sure of what I wanted.

Being with him had been everything and more. Nothing fucking well compared to what we'd just done. I would do it again and again to feel the sheer joy he brought on. I desired this boy more than life itself. He was the sun to me. No matter how much he'd hurt me, I still saw him as the person I wanted to spend eternity with.

The way Raphi was looking at me right then had my heart aching. There was such tenderness in his eyes like I was something precious he had to take care of. I didn't know if it was the aftermath of sex. If this sense of euphoria was because we'd been high off each other and later on, reality would hit him square in the chest. Knowing Raphi, it would likely fuck with him. I wasn't going to get my hopes up about there being a positive outcome to us sleeping together.

He leant down and kissed me again. I let myself get carried away in it. His kisses felt like fucking magic to me. They warmed me from the inside out.

When he let me go, I had to keep myself from uttering a protest. He pulled out of me and cleaned up a little after he'd grabbed the tissues off my bedside table. He stood up to throw everything in the bin before tugging on his boxers and slumping down next to me. I watched him roll on his back, placing his hand on his chest. I sat up to clean myself up before pulling my boxers on too.

My need to touch him overrode my common sense. I curled myself around him, my arm slung across his stomach as I laid my head on his shoulder. He wrapped his arm around me, stroking his fingers down my bare side. The contentment I felt at being this close to him almost overwhelmed me.

"You okay?" I asked, my voice sounding loud in the silent atmosphere of my room.

"Yeah… you?"

"I guess so."

He looked down at me, his eyes full of questions.

"You guess so?"

"I don't know what this means… for you and me."

He tapped his chest with his free hand.

"What do you want it to mean?"

I could feel him deflecting this all back to me and I was going to assume it meant he didn't know what he wanted. It's not as if I thought we would end up in bed together. Hell, I wasn't even sure how we'd got this far. We'd been fighting over Cole and Meredith, although really, it had been about us. How our past with each other had affected the people around us.

"You asked me that three years ago and it didn't go well. I'm not sure I want to answer now."

He grimaced and shook his head.

"I'm sorry. I said some pretty awful things to you. Hurting you is my single biggest regret. You didn't deserve that."

"I appreciate you saying that."

I stroked my fingers along his side, revelling in the way his skin felt against mine. Then I kissed his shoulder, wanting him to know I accepted his apology.

"I'm not sure what I want," he said with a sigh. "I don't want to hurt you again, I hope you know that."

I nodded. He'd been terrible to me, yes, but I understood why. He'd been through a traumatic event and everything had been too much for him to handle. I hadn't helped by trying to push him.

"I… I just got out of a relationship like two days ago."

My heart ached at the thought of him being with someone else. I had no claim to Raphi, but it didn't stop me feeling… jealous. He'd met another person he shared a connection with. Someone he wanted to be with intimately. And it was a girl. I didn't give a shit if he liked women, but he had no issues being with a girl openly. I didn't know if he would ever reach a point where it was an option with me.

"You did?"

"Yeah, Lana and I got together not long after Cole and Meredith split up."

I dragged my fingers along his chest, hating myself for the stabbing pain in my chest.

"Was it serious?"

I must be a masochist for asking questions about his relationship. Thinking about him with anyone else made my stomach roil in protest. I was a masochist for even having sex with Raphi in the first place. My fucked up need for him had overridden common sense, but I no longer cared whether or not it was right. The honest truth was I wanted him and the mess it would create didn't matter.

"Yes and no."

"What does that mean?"

"She's the first girl I've been with, but we always knew it was finite as I'm staying here for uni and she wants to go up north."

"Did you not want to do long distance?"

He stilled my hand on his chest and laced our fingers together.

"She didn't. We didn't have much in common, to be honest. Not… not like you and me."

I stared up at him. He had this softness to his eyes which made my whole body ache for him.

"You and me…"

"You don't think so?"

We had a ton of things in common. Shit with our parents. Feelings of being lost and lonely. I understood him and he got me. It's why we'd become close in such a short period of time.

"Not what I was questioning."

He raised an eyebrow.

"Then what?"

"Is there a you and me?"

He didn't answer, merely stared into my eyes with an almost blank expression on his face. I didn't know what to make of it. I knew I shouldn't have asked the question since I was well aware Raphi didn't know what he wanted.

"You don't have to answer that," I told him when I couldn't stand the silence.

"You need to give me time to think about it. I meant what I said about not being freaked out by us having sex, okay? It's not the thing I'm struggling with."

He didn't have to tell me. I already knew. It was his sexuality. It's what he'd always struggled with since we'd started talking and why he'd even said all that shit to me before. Even if it killed me to be stuck in some kind of limbo with him, I still cared about Raphi more than anything else. My feelings hadn't disappeared. I knew my answer.

"I can do that."

"Yeah?"

I nodded, squeezing his hand in mine. He gave me a smile. He was so fucking beautiful when he smiled like that. As if he was happy. As if I made him happy.

"Come closer."

"Why?"

"I want to kiss you."

I felt my face growing hot. He'd told me he wanted to think about things and yet still wanted to kiss me.

What do I even do with that? Fuck, I don't care right now.

"You do?"

"You going to make me come to you?"

Instead of responding, I shifted, raising my head to bring my lips closer to his. The moment he caught them with his own, I was lost. His touch was everything I craved and desired. I wanted him so fucking badly. Wanted this intimacy I'd missed out on. It was more than just the mechanics of sex, which is all I'd experienced before. This connection was real and alive.

I let go of his hand and traced my fingers down his jaw as we kissed. Raphi's arm around me tightened, his hand curling around my waist in a possessive manner. I attempted to remind myself not to get carried away. Attempted and failed miserably. My whole soul called out for him. Needed this boy who held my heart.

I shifted over him, straddling his waist whilst not breaking our kiss. My fingers dug into his hair and his did the same to mine.

"Do you have to go?" I murmured against his lips.

"No."

"Stay then."

He pressed his mouth against mine, his tongue delving between my lips seeking mine. The kiss became heated and passion flared between us.

Stay forever, Raphi. I need you. I've needed you for three years and now here you are. I can't let you go. You are the only person I've ever felt this way about. The only person I want. Don't leave me again.

All those words were on the tip of my tongue, but I didn't utter them. No, I continued to kiss Raphi, showing him without words just how much I wanted him. How much I needed him. I couldn't say those things for fear he would run from me. For fear he wouldn't want this with me. I didn't want to rock the boat. I'd said I'd give him time. I had to stick to that even if it killed me in the process.

CHAPTER TWENTY THREE

Raphael

I 'd promised Duke I'd do lunch with him today. It wasn't much of a chore if I was honest since I hadn't made plans for the summer. He was working at the Syndicate, our parent's casino whilst he was off from uni. Duke was studying accountancy like my dad had done. It's the part of the business he'd eventually take over from our parents, whilst Aurora was working directly with Quinn and Mum. Cole and I had no interest in working at the casino, but our parents didn't mind. They wanted us to be happy.

Aurora had pestered Quinn to upgrade the restaurant and hire some high-flying chef whose name I kept forgetting. He'd finally relented a year ago and it had been thriving ever since. The members certainly appreciated it. It's where I'd met Duke whilst he was on his break.

I stared out the window, tapping my fingers on the table whilst my mind ran rampant with thoughts of Jonah. It's as if my whole being had been consumed by him and what happened between us a couple of days ago. The memories assaulted me, taunting me with the need to do it again. To shove him up against a wall, pin his hands to it and fuck him whilst he begged me for more.

I didn't know where this side of me came from. When Jonah and I kissed, a part of me I didn't know existed had unlocked. The part that got off on those pants and moans he made. The neediness in his voice. The way he'd begged me to give it to him. It fuelled a fire under me which kept burning hotter. And I'd had to outright restrain myself yesterday from texting him to see if he was busy.

It wasn't the way I acted normally. I was relatively quiet and unassuming, at least it's what my brother kept telling me. Me being dominant as fuck in the bedroom? Well, it shocked me just as much as it probably surprised Jonah.

"Earth to Raphi."

I shook myself, turning to Duke who had a raised eyebrow and a sceptical look in his eyes.

"Sorry, what?"

"You were away with the fairies. What's up with you?"

"Nothing."

"Yeah, okay, totally nothing when you've got some weird as fuck smile on your face like you did something bad and liked it."

I felt my face blaze. I looked down, fiddling with my cutlery instead.

"Do I?"

"Yeah, Raphi. Did you suddenly forget I'm like the only person in this world who knows you better than you know yourself?"

I sighed. Duke did as well. He was the only person I'd actually told the full truth of what happened between me and Jonah. I didn't feel comfortable revealing it to anyone else given it painted me in a bad light.

"No," I muttered, looking up at him again.

"Then spill."

Getting out of telling Duke would be impossible. He was a dog with a bone. The two of us had always been as thick as thieves. We didn't keep secrets from each other.

"I slept with Jonah."

He blinked before his ice-blue eyes widened in shock. I gave him a shrug. I hadn't been sure how he'd react to the news.

"When?"

"Two days ago."

He put a hand on the table and leant closer. I did not like the look in his eyes.

"Let me get this straight… you and Lana broke up then you jumped into bed with the guy who you're so fucked up about you can't even decide whether you're straight or bi?"

For fuck's sake!

"I didn't jump into bed with him like 'oh hi, Jonah, let's have sex because my girlfriend broke up with me'. It was an accident."

"An accident? So your dick accidentally slipped into him or was it the other way around? Because, you know, without adequate lube that's going to hurt."

I scowled. Trust him to say something crude.

"No! Not an accident like that. Jesus, Duke."

He shrugged and leant back in his chair.

"Well, you're not exactly giving me much to go on here."

I rubbed my face and adjusted my glasses.

"Cole asked me to return something to Meredith. I went around hers and Jonah answered the door, then we got into a fight over the whole him sabotaging their relationship and… and then we were kissing and then we were…"

"You were fucking, right?"

I rolled my eyes. Duke was just as crude as Xav. I didn't know why I was even surprised.

"Yes."

"And? Was it good?"

"That's what you want to know?"

"Yeah, Raphi, you just fucked a guy. Of course, I'm going to want to know if you enjoyed it. And you didn't tell me if it was you doing the giving."

Again, why I was surprised by this was beyond me. I should have told him in graphic detail what happened because clearly, it's the kind of shit my brother wanted to know. I wouldn't do that. The details of what I'd done with Jonah should be kept between us.

"I did enjoy it. And who did who is none of your fucking business."

He grinned and gave me a wink.

"Oh, a little shy, are you? It's okay, I can guess."

"No, you can't."

I was annoyed by his idiotic grin widening and the twinkle in his blue eyes.

"I'm willing to put money on it being you giving him a good, hard pounding."

"Fuck off."

"See, the protesting confirms it."

How the fuck he guessed was beyond me. I didn't even know I was into that until Jonah had asked me to fuck him. And there I went again having images of him naked assaulting me at every fucking turn. I gripped my knife handle, trying to calm down. It was difficult since all I wanted to do was get Jonah naked again. I wanted to do bad things to him. I wouldn't go there when I didn't know what the fuck I wanted from him outside of sex. A lot of hot, explosive and passionate sex.

Stop it. You can't. He's not someone you can just have some kind of fuck buddy relationship with. It's not fair on him or you.

It wouldn't be a fuck buddy situation since he meant more to me. I cared about him deeply.

"Look, it doesn't matter which one of us is the fucking top, Duke. It's not about that. I don't know what to do about me and him."

"So it's still the same thing, eh? You don't want to like guys."

"It's not that I don't want to like guys. You know why."

He waved a hand and rolled his eyes.

"Yeah, yeah, you're just confused, fucked up and everything in between. You're going to have to make up your mind at some point, Raphi."

My insecurities about myself were something I'd battled with for years. Finding this new side of me made it worse. My skin itched. I didn't feel comfortable in it. I never had.

We were interrupted then as the waiter came over with our meals. He gave us a bright smile and a nod. All the staff knew who we were. Not like you could hide being the owner's kids, especially not when Duke worked here.

I dug into mine whilst Duke continued to stare at me, waiting for an answer no doubt. What did I even say? I didn't have an answer. I wished it was as easy as just clicking my fingers to make all of my doubts about myself go away. Didn't work like that though. Accepting myself was nigh on impossible. I wished it wasn't.

"How did you leave things with Jonah?" Duke asked after a minute of me remaining silent.

With a major make-out session that had almost escalated into sex again, before I'd left with a promise I'd be in touch. No doubt he'd be wondering when I was going to text or call him.

"He said he'd give me time to think about it."

"And have you been thinking about it?"

I sighed, placing my fork down.

"Only every second of every fucking minute of every damn hour since it happened."

Duke picked up his knife and fork, giving me a look.

"That says a lot."

"What's that supposed to mean?"

He pointed his fork at me.

"It means you want him, but you're too chicken shit to admit it."

"Fuck off."

"The truth hurts, little bro."

I gave him a dirty look before picking my fork up again, watching him dig into his food. I did want Jonah. It's not like it had changed in the past three years even though I'd buried my feelings for him deep inside me.

"You know, if you just gave it a chance, I think you'd be happy," Duke commented after he'd swallowed a mouthful of food. "Lana was okay and all, but she wasn't Jonah now, was she?"

"I hate you right now," I muttered, staring down at my plate.

"You always hate me, but what did I do this time?"

He knew I didn't hate him. My brother might be a royal pain in the arse, but he was also the only person I could talk to about this. Well, I could talk to my dad. In all honesty, I probably should. Keeping stuff from him last time hadn't gone very well.

"Just being right about me all the fucking time."

His smile pissed me right off.

"So, that means you definitely want to be with Jonah and you're definitely the one who gave him a good hard dicking."

I cannot with my brother. He literally is the fucking worst.

"Really, Duke? We're back to that again?"

"We're going to be back to that until you admit it."

"For fuck's sake, fine, I fucked him. Now, can you please stop going on about dicking and pounding?"

We stared at each other for a long moment before both of us started chuckling at the utter ridiculousness of the situation.

"Way to fucking go," he told me through his laughter. "You've grown a pair finally."

"Shut up, I have not grown a pair just because I slept with Jonah."

He waved a hand at me before going back to his meal.

"Yeah, you fucking have. You were a repressed little shit who blushed at the mere mention of sex before today. You refused to even tell me what Lana's pussy was like."

"I'm still not telling you."

He winked. It was none of Duke's business. My dad had always taught me to treat everyone with respect, especially someone I was in a relationship with. I'd never divulged those types of details. I didn't think Lana would have appreciated it.

"Well, she was kind of fucking boring, Raphi. She better have had a good pussy or there would have been no point going out with her."

"You are such a…"

"Cunt?"

"Yes."

"I know."

I shook my head. I didn't like to say it, but Duke had a point. My family had been polite to Lana, but they'd never taken to her the way they'd done with Meredith when she was dating Cole. Lana never really tried with them and I didn't press the subject. Loneliness and the need to be normal had

224

driven me to stay with her. It was wrong of me, but I had a feeling she was using me for the same reason.

"Look, I'm not going to tell you what to do, Raphi, but you should just give it a chance, okay? You don't have to work out what it is you are right now. Go with the fucking flow and be with the person you care about. Doesn't fucking matter if he's male, yeah? Do what makes you happy."

"Don't you think that's the pot calling the kettle black?"

He gave me a dark look.

"Shut up, it's not the same thing."

I shouldn't push him on the subject, but he had screwed up with the person who made him happy.

"Is it not? When are you going to man the fuck up and sort your shit out with her then?"

"She doesn't want to see me, Raphi. What do you want me to do? Force her? I can't do that. It's already fucked up enough as it is. Don't need to make it worse."

I rolled my eyes.

"Oh yeah, it's fucked up all right. When are you going to tell our parents, hmm? Because I'm pretty sure they'd like to know."

I might have been awfully cruel to Jonah three years ago, but the shit Duke had got himself into? Well, it was a hundred times worse.

"How about never?"

"No? You don't want me to show them the bit of paper you keep in your drawer proving just how much you royally fucked up then?"

His knife and fork clattered on the plate before he pointed a finger at me.

"Don't you fucking dare, Raphi. I mean it. You promised me you'd keep your mouth shut."

"I'm not breaking my promise, Duke. I just think you need to take your own advice."

He looked down at his plate.

"I'll think about it. So should you. He's not going to wait around forever for you to get your shit together."

I knew he wouldn't. It would be unfair of me to expect him to. It didn't stop me wanting to see Jonah. From wanting to touch him. I was screwed up.

"I know. I'll think about it too."

Duke and I were like two fucking peas in a pod. All we did was think. Perhaps we needed to act. Act on what we wanted instead of being chicken shit. I could do that. I might not have made up my mind, but one thing was for sure. I didn't want to deny myself now I'd experienced mind-blowing sex.

You should not text him to see if he's free when you haven't made up your mind. How fucked up are you!

I stared down at my hands. It made me feel like shit, but I was *that* fucked up about Jonah. So fucked up that when I left the Syndicate, I had a hard time not pulling my phone out and seeing if he was around.

Fuck.

CHAPTER TWENTY FOUR

Jonah

I couldn't stop myself glancing at my phone every five minutes like some fucking lovesick fool waiting for the boy he's obsessed with to contact him. The ball was in Raphi's court. He had a decision to make. I wasn't going to pressure him even if I wanted an answer. Needed one with every fucking passing second.

Here I was, stuck at my part-time job in the care home Grandma volunteered at, moping around the place. Even one of the residents when they passed by reception asked me why the long face. I didn't mind the work. It wasn't difficult. I didn't technically need the extra money with my student loan covering my expenses but I hated being idle and the girl who worked at reception had gone on long-term sick.

Robin had attempted to persuade me to stay in Durham for the summer but I needed to come back to London for Meredith. I wanted to help her prepare for university since

Mum and Grandma were useless. Besides, I felt awkward being around Robin since we'd spent the night together. He'd gone back to his old ways of fucking anything which moved. His fucking spree didn't bother me. It was more every time I looked at him, I wished I'd waited. The person who should have been my first was Raphi.

You are a fool.

I didn't think losing my virginity was a big deal. Only now I knew what true passion felt like, I had second thoughts about my decision to give it to Robin.

My phone buzzed in my pocket. As there was no one around, I pulled it out and stared down at the message.

Raphael: Are you free?

I swallowed.

Jonah: I'm at work. Will be done at like 6.

Raphael: Can I see you this evening then?

Had he made up his mind already? It didn't seem like it would be the case. He would have said.

Why did he want to see me?

Jonah: When and where?

Raphael: Mine... whenever you want to come over.

His words made me swallow again.

Jonah: I have to do dinner. Is eight or nine, okay?

Raphael: Yes. Just text me when you're here.

My mind raced with possible outcomes to me going to see him.

Would he tell me he wanted us to be together?

Would he tell me he didn't?

Would it be about something else?

Did he just want to spend time with me?

I shook myself and stuffed my phone back in my pocket. Now was not the time to be worrying about this shit. I had to get on with work.

The rest of the day dragged. The resident who'd commented about my dreary face earlier said I looked happier before I left for the day. He was a nice man who said hello to everyone who came through the doors, loitering around the entrance to the care home much to the care workers' annoyance. They wished Mr Kavanagh would stay in the lounge with the other residents.

During dinner, Meredith kept talking to me but I was too busy fretting over what would happen later to respond with more than one-word answers. By the time I left my house and got on the bus, I was a fucking mess inside.

Get a grip!

I couldn't. My nerve endings burnt and my heart was racing out of control. The thought of being near him made my mouth water. I shouldn't be having dirty thoughts about him. Shoving them away, I tried to focus on something else. Anything.

How can I when he is all I can think about?

Pretending was futile. I wanted to see him. Wanted to touch him. Have him touch me. I just fucking well plain wanted everything that came with Raphi and me.

By the time I stood outside his house, I was breathing heavily and I had no idea how to stop. The thought of him being next to me had driven me crazy.

Jonah: I'm outside.

It took a minute before the front door was pulled open. There he stood in a t-shirt and shorts without his glasses on.

"Come in."

I walked up the steps and into the house I'd always been super curious about. He shut the door quickly, took my hand and dragged me down the hallway. We turned into another corridor. I didn't know what the rush was, but I tried to keep pace with him.

Raphi shoved me through a doorway and all but slammed the door closed behind us. I heard the distinct sound of a lock turning. I barely had a chance to turn around when he was on me. His hands were in my hair and his mouth on my lips. My back hit the wall next to his door. His body pressed into mine as he kissed me, hunting my tongue down.

"Jonah," he groaned.

I had no idea what the fuck to do other than to surrender. My body did it of its own accord whilst I battled with my response to his boldness. He pressed his lips to my jaw, kissing his way down to my ear. His fingers ran down my chest, diving beneath my t-shirt.

"I can't stop thinking about you," he murmured in my ear. "About this." He ground into me. "I want to touch you so fucking much."

My breath whooshed out of me with his words. His fingers were at my jeans, tugging at the buttons. I barely had time to form a sentence as his hand stroked across my cock. My body trembled as I grew hard. How could I not? Raphi was touching me. His exploring fingers made me feel alive. His teeth grazed along my earlobe. A strangled cry of pleasure left my mouth.

"I think you like this. Do I make you as fucking hot and bothered as you do me?"

"Yes," I panted without thinking too hard about it.

"Good… there's so much I want to do to you."

His hand delved beneath my boxers, wrapping around my half-hard cock as he kissed down my neck. The rational part of me should tell him to stop. He got buried under all the desire and need Raphi brought out in me. Especially when he stroked my cock.

"Raphael," I whimpered.

"Shh, I'm going to take care of you, J."

His hand left my cock, then both of them grabbed a hold of my clothes, tugging them halfway down my thighs. I sucked in air when Raphi dropped to his knees. His hands ran up my bare legs. I looked down in time to see him lean closer and run his tongue up my shaft.

"Oh. What—"

My words died in my throat. His mouth had closed around the head of my cock. The very last thing I expected was for him to go down on me. I stared at his chestnut head, wondering what the fuck I had done to deserve this heaven. My body didn't care about us talking. My body wanted Raphi. And I gave in, burying my hand in his hair as he swirled his tongue around me.

He pulled back for a moment and stared up at me with those verdant green eyes full of possessiveness. They made me want to give him every part of me.

He already has you, idiot. You've given in.

"Do you want me to make you come?"

I nodded, biting my lip.

"I want you to tell me if I'm doing it right. Tell me what you need."

"Okay," I whispered, not trusting my voice.

His mouth was on me again as his fingers wrapped around the base, stroking up and down. For someone who'd never done this before, he didn't hesitate for a second. I might have underestimated how much Raphi liked me… and desired me.

He was careful as he took more of my cock. His tongue curled around my shaft. I had no words. His mouth was wet and warm. It felt so fucking good.

"Yes, fuck."

My fingers dug into his scalp, encouraging him to keep going. His other hand stroked up my thigh before he cupped my balls, playing with them as he worked my dick in his mouth.

"Raphi," I groaned. "Fuck, don't stop."

Never in my life had I been this turned on by another person. His hands on me scrambled my brain, making it hard to think straight. There was nothing rational about letting him suck my dick like this. Nor would there be when I'd no doubt beg him to fuck me after this.

I want it, fuck how I want it.

"Please, fuck, Raphi… I want you in me."

My mouth had run away with me. I let out a cry of protest when he pulled off my cock.

"The way you sound so needy turns me on."

"You make me needy."

I couldn't believe what I'd said. Raphi's eyes turned dark. Like me admitting these things pleased him no end.

"Do I now? Does that mean you're going to beg?"

"Do you want me to?"

The sly smile he gave me made my pulse quicken.

"You already know the answer."

I swallowed. Oh, I did. I fucking well did.

"If I beg, will you fuck me?"

"Make me believe you want it."

His taunting tone made my dick throb. Raphi had never struck me as the confident or dominant type in an intimate setting. And I'd have never thought I would find it this arousing. But… fuck did I.

"Please make me come first."

Oh god, his smile.

It was wicked and deviant.

"With pleasure."

233

He pulled something out of his pocket and flipped the cap on the bottle. It made it clear he'd planned on us having sex when he asked me over. I wasn't sure how to feel about it, but right then, I was on board for every part of it.

He coated his fingers in lube, dumping the bottle down and gripping my dick in his hand. His lube coated fingers delved underneath me. On instinct, I widened my stance to allow him better access. I let out a pant when he touched my hole and his mouth enclosed over my cock. The extra sensation almost sent me over the edge. My hand in his hair tightened since I hadn't let go.

This didn't feel like it had done when I'd lost my virginity to Robin. Being at Raphi's mercy was like a drug, intoxicating me and making me want to fall deeper into whatever fucked up madness had overtaken us.

I cried out when he slid his finger inside me, not quite expecting it but loving it all the same. He worked me with both his mouth and his finger. I struggled to hold on to the last shred of sanity I had left.

"Raphi," I groaned. "Fuck, I'm going to… fuck."

He didn't stop. If anything, he sucked harder. And when he slid a second finger inside me, I was done. I let out this ridiculously high pitched whimper as my cock erupted in his mouth. He looked up at me, his eyes full of heat and I could do nothing but watch myself come apart for him. My knees threatened to buckle when I was spent. He pulled his mouth from me and swallowed. Then he smiled as I let go of his hair and planted my hands on the wall to keep myself upright.

"You done, J?" he taunted as he continued to thrust his fingers inside me.

"No," I panted even though I didn't know if I could take any more.

He slid his fingers from me, picked up the bottle and rose to his full height.

"Turn around."

The way he said it was like a command. I could do nothing but obey. I turned around and faced away from him. He leant into me, his hand between us as he slid his fingers back inside me. His lips brushed against my ear, making me shiver.

"Hands against the wall."

I did as he said, planting them palms down against it.

"You're so good for me," he murmured, teeth running along my earlobe. "But I'm still going to fuck you until you can't take any more."

I don't know why the thought of it made my already-spent cock twitch. He kissed my cheek and down my jaw.

"You're so fucking hot like this, do you know that?" He pressed his front to my back, grinding his hard cock through his shorts against my bare behind. "All I've been able to think about is this. You like this up against my wall. It's driven me insane."

He slid a third finger inside me, stretching me out further which had me panting more. Knowing he'd had filthy thoughts about me was a surprise given how adamant Raphi had been three years ago about not wanting to be in a relationship with a man. Not wanting me. Those had been lies. It had never been about me. It had always been about him.

235

His view of himself. It was my biggest hurdle when it came to the man behind me. I needed him to accept himself, then he could be open about being with me.

"You want to fuck me like this?" I whispered.

"So much."

"Then fuck me, I want your cock inside me."

"I'm going to."

"Do it."

"Patience, J. I don't want to hurt you."

I had none. My cock was already springing back into life at the thought of him taking me like this.

"You won't… please, I need you in me."

He licked my neck as his fingers continued to thrust inside me. It wasn't enough. I wanted to feel him. All of him.

"Raphi, please. Fuck me."

My voice was all breathy with my desperation.

"How can I say no when you're begging?"

He tugged his fingers from me. I could feel and hear him fumbling behind me. My head turned further. He had his shorts tugged down, his cock in his hand whilst he rolled on a condom. Then he squirted lube into his hand and covered himself in it before pushing the rest inside me. I rocked back against him, which only made him smile.

"So fucking needy."

"Please!"

He gripped my hip with one hand whilst he pressed himself against me with the other. My body relaxed into his, knowing he'd take care of me. He'd give it to me just the way I wanted. We both groaned when he pressed his way inside me, filling me up with his beautiful cock. He kissed his way down my jaw as he thrust deeper. When his lips met mine, I kissed him, pouring out all of my need into this moment whilst keeping my hands firmly on the wall.

He rewarded me for being good by giving me his cock. The moment he pulled back and thrust inside me again, making me feel alive, I couldn't fucking take it.

"Raphi," I cried into his mouth. "Please."

He pressed one of his hands over mine whilst he continued to use the other as an anchor, holding my hip in a vice.

"You want it hard, *cuore mio*?"

"What does that mean?"

"Answer the question."

It sounded Italian. In my research, I'd discovered his mother's stepfather had Italian roots. It might be why Raphi had said it. I made a mental note to look it up.

"I want it hard, please."

Raphi pulled back and thrust in again, this time with more force. I whimpered. It felt fucking good. I wanted to fall into oblivion with him forever. I revelled in each stroke, listening to the way he grunted in my ear each time I clenched around his cock. Driving him crazy was such a fucking high. Knowing I brought this out in him. This passion and fire. The possessiveness in his voice which made me feel needed and wanted. I felt safe with him. So fucking safe to let go.

"Jonah, fuck, you feel good," he groaned, his pace increasing as if he was getting closer to the edge.

"I want you to come in me."

"Oh yeah? You want to feel that, do you?"

"Yes… so much."

I'd felt it last time. Each pulse and twitch. It had triggered my own orgasm. The way he had me pinned prevented me from touching myself. Raphi shifted his angle. I moaned when he thrust against my prostate.

"Mmm, I think you like it when I hit you there."

"Yes, don't stop, fuck, don't stop."

He chuckled like the idea of stopping amused him since it wasn't going to happen. Not with the way he was pounding into me with such force, it almost knocked the breath from my lungs. And I loved it. Every fucking second of it. The way he felt inside me. The hardness of his body pressed to mine. All of it.

"Fuck," he grunted. "Going to come, J. Come all the way up inside you. Fuck."

Next thing I knew, he'd bitten down on the side of my neck, making me cry out as I felt him thrust as deep as he could go. His body shuddered as he climaxed. A moment later, he let go of my neck and my hip, his hand curling around my body and gripping my cock. He jacked me hard and fast, making me moan and buck into him. He continued to give me these shallow thrusts even though he'd come until I couldn't take it any longer.

"Fuck, Raphi," I cried into the wall as it hit. The waves of my orgasm washed over me, my cock spurting over his hand.

Both of us were panting messes as we came down. Him still pressed against my back, with his face digging into my shoulder and me just there trying to hold myself up.

A few minutes later, he pulled away from me. He tugged me from the wall and the two of us somehow stumbled towards his bed and collapsed on it. He rid himself of the condom and cleaned up his hand then lay back, staring up at the ceiling. I couldn't move any longer. The way he'd fucked me had been intense and I needed a moment. Being with Raphi like this was something else. I never expected any of it. But I adored it. Every single second. And I wanted more. I wanted it again. I wanted it forever.

CHAPTER TWENTY FIVE

Raphael

I didn't know what to do with myself as I stared up at the ceiling above us. The intensity of my feelings when it came to Jonah overwhelmed me. Especially since I'd called him *cuore mio* during sex. I almost wanted to smack my hand against my head. Smart idea to voice my feelings aloud in such a way. I didn't doubt Jonah's curiosity would get the better of him and then he'd discover I'd referred to him as my heart. Didn't matter if it was the truth. I wasn't ready for him to know. Fuck, I didn't even know what I wanted with him.

It should be simple. All of it should be easy, but for me, it wasn't. It just fucking well wasn't. I was too fucked up to be in a relationship with him even if it was the right thing to do here. The thought of us just sleeping together didn't sit well with me. Not when I had feelings for Jonah.

I sat up and grabbed my glasses off the bedside table, along with a few wet wipes. I shoved my glasses on and glanced to my side. Jonah was laying there, his breathing heavy as if he'd run a marathon. He watched me wipe him clean and tug his boxers back up. I chucked the wipes away before lying on my side next to him and stroking a hand down his arm. I wanted to take care of him after the way I'd fucked him. This man was precious to me. He deserved more than I could give him. Reaching up, I stroked his hair back from his face, watching him let out a long breath at my touch.

"Okay?" I asked, my voice quiet in the silent room.

"Yes."

"I wasn't too rough with you or anything, was I?"

He shook his head and gave me a slight smile.

"No… I… liked it."

I leant closer and brushed my nose against his.

"I liked it too."

He captured my mouth and his hand came up, cupping the back of my neck to keep me there. I melted. His touch just did something to me. He did something to me. There was a certain vulnerability between us because we'd shown each other our darkest parts three years ago. Our scars. Except mine ran deeper now. My self-hatred and loathing hadn't disappeared even though the bullies had been dealt with. It's as if they were cemented in my psyche and I couldn't do a thing about it.

"Will you stay?" I whispered when I pulled back.

"What… the night?"

"Yes."

"I don't know."

I didn't blame him for being cautious. It's not something I should have asked of him. Hell, getting him to come over so I could fuck him the way I had was a bad idea in the first place. I didn't want him to go. His presence calmed me. Gave me a small pocket of peace from the internal war being waged inside me.

"I would like it if you did, but I understand if you can't."

"You really want me to?"

"I wouldn't say it if I didn't mean it."

Please stay, Jonah. Please don't leave me alone right now.

His lips curved up.

"I don't have work tomorrow. I'll stay as long as you want me here."

My heart thumped hard in my chest. My hand curled around his face, my thumb stroking down his jaw. I kissed him again for a brief moment before I pulled away. Jonah watched me sit up and drop to my knees off the end of the bed. He raised up on his elbows in time to see me unlacing his trainers and tugging them off. I could see him biting his lip as I helped him out of his socks and jeans. He probably wasn't used to anyone taking care of him. He was always taking care of others, especially Meredith.

It wasn't particularly late, but I got up off the floor and pulled back the covers. I encouraged Jonah to get beneath them and kissed his forehead.

"Just going to get some water, do you want some?"

He nodded and I smiled. Then I straightened, adjusted my clothes, walked over to the door before unlocking it and slipping out. The house was quiet. My parents were upstairs and who knew what my siblings were up to. I padded out to the kitchen, washing my hands in the sink before I grabbed the Brita filter from the fridge. I poured two glasses of water after getting them out of the cupboard.

I felt someone behind me. I looked around finding Rory leaning up against the doorway.

"Sometimes I think you deliberately sneak up on people," I muttered.

He smiled wide at my words.

"Sometimes."

"You're admitting you do it on purpose now?"

He shrugged, so I rolled my eyes.

"You have a guest?"

He nodded at the glasses on the counter. I fidgeted, not wanting to admit it but out of all my dads, Rory was the one you couldn't get anything by.

"Yes."

"A friend or…?"

I felt my face heat up. Jonah was not exactly my friend but he wasn't my boyfriend either.

Boyfriend? That word doesn't feel… right.

"Just… someone."

Rory raised an eyebrow. I picked up the glasses, not wanting to talk about this any further. I wasn't ashamed to have Jonah here, but I didn't know how to explain what we were to each other.

"You don't want to talk about it."

"No… just don't tell Mum, okay? She'll get all weird because Lana and I only just broke up."

Mum had been more than a little angry when I came home from my last day of school and told them I'd been dumped. She tended to get overprotective of us kids, but with me, it was worse. Any time she thought I was in trouble or danger, her hackles would rise and she'd be out there defending me to her last breath. I found it frustrating since I wanted to live my life without her worrying about me every five minutes.

Rory nodded slowly as I walked towards him on my way out of the kitchen.

"She's with Xav and E, but I won't tell her."

"Thank you."

I stopped next to him in the doorway.

"It's not someone you're ashamed of, is it?"

"What? No." *How does he always bloody know what we're thinking?* "It's… complicated."

"Everything always is with this family."

Didn't I know it. My family had so many secrets they were hiding from the world, not to mention we were about as unorthodox as they come.

"I'm just not ready to tell anyone yet."

He reached out and squeezed my arm.

"It's okay, monkey. Just be safe, yeah?"

It took me a second to understand what he meant. I scrunched up my face.

"God, you're as bad as Xav and Dad with their sex talk."

He grinned.

"I heard about that."

I shuddered. Even though it had happened years ago, I still remembered the horror I felt at the two of them sitting me down and talking to me about sex. Xav went into far too much graphic detail. Dad had to tell him to cut it out.

"I'd rather not be reminded of it ever again."

"My lips are sealed."

I gave him a nod as he dropped his hand and I walked away back down the hallway. When I got in my room, Jonah was sitting up in my bed on his phone. I took a second to watch him from my doorway. His hair was mussed and he had this little line of concentration between his blonde brows. My chest tightened. He was absolutely beautiful. And if I could be brave enough… Jonah would be mine. The thought of anyone else touching him sent a hot wave of jealousy rushing down my spine.

I don't want anyone else to touch you but me.

This possessiveness had come out of nowhere. I wasn't like this normally, or at least, I hadn't been until a few days ago when this man had awakened it in me.

"Are you watching me?"

I jolted, almost spilling the water in my hands.

"Um… yes."

Jonah's eyes flicked up and he smiled.

"Should I be flattered?"

I left the doorway, pushing the door shut with my hip.

"Absolutely. I mean, I don't know if anyone has told you how hot you are."

His cheeks heated, but he smiled wider.

"No, only you."

I walked further into the room and popped the glasses of water down on the bedside table, flipping on the lamp whilst I was there. Retreating to the door, I locked it and turned out the main light.

"Well, you are in my eyes."

"Did you get waylaid?"

"Huh?"

I walked back over to the bed and slid in next to him, popping my glasses down on the table.

"You took longer than I expected."

"Oh." I rubbed my face. "Rory came into the kitchen and made some enquiries as to what I was doing."

Jonah's eyebrow raised.

"Enquiries?"

"Here's the thing about Rory… nothing, and I mean nothing, gets by him. He has eyes like a hawk and ears like a bat. He sees and hears everything."

"You told him I was here?"

I looked away.

"I didn't tell him it's you, just that I had a guest." I didn't know how he'd react to it so I couldn't meet his eyes. "Lana and I just broke up and I don't know what we are… yet."

His fingers curled under my chin and he turned my face to his. Those light green eyes were full of compassion, it almost broke me clean in two.

"It's okay, Raphi, you don't have to explain. I'm here and I'm not going to push you. I want you to decide on your own terms and in your own time."

"Why are you so nice to me? Like you're the kindest, most understanding person I've ever met. I don't know how you can forgive me for being such a dick to you."

The words fell out of my mouth without me thinking about them. They made his eyes soften further.

"It's simple. To me, you're worth the pain."

I swallowed hard.

Cuore mio, I don't deserve you.

There was that fucking phrase again. I knew why it resonated with me. Mum called Xav her treasure in Italian. *Tesoro mio.* When I was small, I kept trying to pronounce it but couldn't do it quite right. She taught me it and several other Italian phrases she learnt when she was a kid. Mum might not be a Russo any longer but she hadn't forgotten the culture she was raised in. She kept the parts important to her. Italian was something only the two of us shared as Aurora, Duke and Cole had never been interested.

"Jonah…"

His fingers slid around my jaw, pulling me closer as he dumped his phone on the bed.

"I never stopped caring about you even after you said all those things. You have always meant something to me. I don't want to hold grudges or live with hate. I only ever wanted to help set you free."

He kissed me then, perhaps knowing I couldn't speak. My emotions clogged my throat. He saw me. Jonah was so fucking good, he wouldn't hurt a fly.

"Just don't push me away again," he whispered against my lips. "Even if you don't want to be with me, don't leave. I'll take whatever you're willing to give."

I didn't want to leave him.

I wanted him to be mine.

No one else could have him because he was the person I needed. And I had to let myself feel what I did towards him or things would fall apart. Whether or not I was capable of it was a question I had no answer to.

"I'm right here," I murmured against his mouth before I pulled him down under the covers. He lay back and I curled myself around him, my head resting on his chest. "I just don't know how to accept myself the way you do."

He stroked my hair, wrapping his other arm around me.

"Let me help you."

If anyone could, it was him. Jonah wanted to be a psychologist. He would make an amazing one. His kindness and compassion were some of his biggest assets.

"I'll try."

He kissed the top of my head.

"That's all I ask."

Except it wasn't and we both knew it. The unspoken words still hung in the air.

Let me be with you because I want you to be mine.

I didn't say them and neither did he. Instead, I lay there feeling content for the first time in a long time. No matter the problems between us, being with him made me feel safe.

I couldn't let him go. Because… I loved him.

CHAPTER TWENTY SIX

Raphael

A loud banging dragged me from the depths of a deep, peaceful sleep. I cracked my eyes open, finding myself wrapped around a solid body. He was warm and I didn't want to leave.

"Raphi, why is your door locked?" came a muffled voice which sounded like my mother.

Oh, Jesus Christ, really? I can have my door locked. The rest of them do.

The banging came again. I knew why she was worried. Mum was overprotective of me.

"Raphael!"

I carefully extracted myself from around Jonah's back, not wanting to wake him. He was still dead to the world. I smiled and kissed his shoulder. Dragging myself out of bed, I pulled a t-shirt and shorts on, which I'd discarded before we fell asleep and shoved my glasses on my face.

I walked over to the door, unlocked it and stepped out, pulling it closed behind me. There stood my mother with her arms crossed over her chest. She did not look happy at all.

"What do you want, Mum? I was asleep."

"It's breakfast time."

I rubbed my face and yawned.

"And?"

Her frown deepened.

"And you promised your dad you would go shopping with him for Xav's birthday. Or did you forget?"

I hadn't, but clearly, Mum was stressing since she wanted to make sure Xav's birthday celebrations next week went off without a hitch. She was like this every time one of us had a birthday.

"I remember, but we're not leaving until twelve."

I planned to spend the morning with the man in my bed. Wrapped up in his warmth and calming presence before reality intruded on me again.

"Well, come and have breakfast anyway."

I gave her a look. Being babied by her was a regular occurrence even if Cole got it way worse than I did.

"I'm eighteen, Mum. I can do it myself. Besides, I'm kind of busy."

"Busy? You just told me you were asleep."

"Yeah, but I'm not alone."

Her blonde eyebrows shot up. I knew right then in my sleep-addled state, I'd fucked up. I hadn't meant to tell her I had a guest.

"You have someone here. Who?"

She looked past me as if she could see through the closed door of my bedroom.

"A friend."

"A friend who slept in your bed with you. Spare me the run-around, Raphael. What is going on? You only just broke up with Lana."

I was well aware of the fact. Far too aware.

"You didn't even like Lana. Why does it matter how much time it's been?"

I wanted this conversation to be over. Just another reason I needed to move out. I loved my mum, but she was exhausting.

"You're dating someone new already?"

"No! I just told you we're friends. Can I please go back to bed?"

It was better she thought that than whatever was going on between me and Jonah.

"Raphael—"

"Mum, please stop. I'm fine. I know what I'm doing. When I am ready to tell you about them, I will, until then, please, please, please leave it alone."

She closed her mouth and stared at me for a long moment. I hated upsetting my mum but she was being overbearing.

"Okay, monkey. I'm doing it again. Being too much."

I reached out and tugged her into my arms. Mum had always been tiny compared to the rest of us. Aurora favoured Quinn so even she was taller than Mum.

"I love you, Mum, but I'm an adult now. Let me decide when and how I tell you things."

"I just worry because you kept some very big things from us and I don't want that to happen again."

I held her tighter. It's not like I didn't understand where her fears stemmed from. The whole bullying incident had been a wakeup call for my parents about what was going at school. How all four of us had been given shit for their relationship, but I'd got the brunt of it. Didn't matter anymore since those days were behind me, but Mum never forgot. She would probably remember the bruises on my face and my stomach for the rest of her life.

"This is not one of those things."

She rubbed my back.

"I trust you."

"Thank you."

She pulled away and reached up, stroking my cheek.

"I'm going to make you both breakfast. I'll leave it outside the door, okay?"

I knew arguing with her over it would be futile. She would only tell me not to be stupid. She was my mother and wanted to take care of me.

"Okay."

She smiled and turned, walking down the hallway towards the kitchen. I watched her until she disappeared from sight before going into the bathroom. I went about my business and brushed my teeth since I didn't want morning breath. Then I went back into my room, shutting the door, setting my glasses on the bedside table and slipping into bed again.

Jonah was still fast asleep. I curled myself around him, kissing his bare shoulder. As if on instinct, he shifted further back into my embrace and murmured something unintelligible. It made me smile. He and I fit together. I couldn't deny it.

Would it really be so hard for me to be with him?

I hated myself for making it this complicated. Hated I couldn't accept I was in love with a boy. My feelings for him had nothing to do with his gender. I loved the person he was. The way he understood without judgement or reservations. It was all about my own fucked up self-image. How I couldn't accept the way I was. Labels made my skin itch even though I knew I was bisexual. Dad had always told me he hated being labelled. Maybe I'd got it from him. He only ever said he was pansexual for other people's benefit so they could understand who he was. For him, he was just Eric Nelson and it's all the label he needed.

Maybe I needed to be more like my father. Just be who I was without labels. It wasn't that simple. Nothing with me was ever *that* simple.

I nuzzled my face in Jonah's neck, kissing his skin because I couldn't stop myself. My body craved his. It ached for his touch. His fingers on me since I hadn't allowed it last night. I would now. I'd let him do whatever he wanted to me.

"Raphi?" came a mumbled, groggy voice.

"I'm here, J."

"What time is it?"

I peered over at the clock on the bedside table.

"Eight-thirty."

"Mmm."

I couldn't help smiling at how adorable he was being all sleepy and shit. This man made my heart do backflips in my chest.

"Um so, Mum's making us breakfast in bed."

He looked around at me, his green eyes wide.

"What… why?"

Jonah had no idea what my mum was really like.

"She turned into the inquisition and demanded to know why I wasn't alone. Arguing with her is futile, she wins every time. I only told her I have a friend over."

It's not like I didn't want to tell them about Jonah, I just wasn't ready yet.

"I think we're a little more than friends." He rubbed against me. "You wouldn't be hard if that was the case."

I bit my lip at the dirty look in his eyes. No, I wouldn't be rock hard against him if I didn't desire him more than anything else.

"Are you teasing me?"

"Maybe."

"Rather bold if you're not intending to follow through."

He smiled. That smile of his could light up the whole room.

"I will after you direct me to the bathroom."

My mouth watered wondering what he had in mind.

"It's just across the hall, like almost directly opposite my room to the left."

"I'll be back to follow through."

I let him go. He got up and stretched. My dick twitched watching the muscles on his back flex with the movement. He tugged on his t-shirt after snagging it off the floor. I watched him leave the room, half worried he'd run into someone in my family. Wouldn't go down well if I went so far as to keep watch.

I lay there, trying not to let my anxiety about it get the better of me until he returned, closing the door behind him. Jonah approached the bed with a sly smile on his face. He knelt at the end and tugged the covers off me, exposing my body to him inch by inch. I swallowed as he crawled over me when the covers were bunched up by my feet.

"Will you let me make you feel good?" he asked, leaning down to press his lips to my jaw.

"Yes."

His hands went to my t-shirt. I allowed him to tug it off me. His eyes darkened as he stared down at my bare chest.

"Since you were complimenting me last night," he murmured. "I want you to know just how much I desire you. Every part of you is beautiful to me." He ran his fingers down my chest, making me stifle a groan. "Even your flaws." He shifted lower, kissing along my collarbone. "You're perfect to me, Raphi. I've never looked at anyone the way I do you. I can't. You're all I want."

I trembled at his words. His eyes were still on my face, watching my reaction, gauging my feelings about what he was saying to me. What he was admitting. He had no idea I'd already admitted to mine last night when I called him my heart in Italian. It was only a matter of time before he did.

He trailed his mouth lower, his hot breath following the path of his tongue. I gripped the bed below me, trying not to direct proceedings even though my instincts cried out to grab him by the hair. Jonah had admitted to me last night he liked me being rough with him. I didn't think he'd get upset if I did. He'd told me he wanted to make me feel good. This was me letting him.

His fingers curled into my shorts and boxers, tugging them down as he went. I panted when he ran his tongue along my stomach, dipping between the subtle grooves. Dad and I went running three times a week with each other, something Cole had started joining in with since he and Meredith broke up.

"Jonah," I breathed when his fingers circled my cock, stroking slowly as he continued to trace his tongue along my stomach.

I tried not to make comparisons between him and Lana. The way he made me feel was a hundred times more intense and overwhelming. His touch electrified me, bringing me back to life after years of fucked up misery and resentment towards myself.

I groaned when his mouth finally met my cock, his tongue circling the head. My mind ran riot with the thought of him doing this to someone else. It made me agitated because he was mine.

What the fuck? He's not yours.

But he was. This man was mine. Even if we weren't yet in a relationship. Even if I refused to admit how I felt about him. He was still… mine. And I was his.

I forgot in those moments my mum was making us breakfast. I forgot I still had so much to think about and decide. All I could see, feel and hear was him. The way his mouth closed over me. How hot and wet it was as he sucked me deeper. How I didn't think I could get enough of this. I wanted more with him. I fucking well wanted everything.

My hand curled into his hair of its own accord, pushing him further down on my cock, making him take it. His green eyes glittered with need and I knew he wanted this. He liked me taking control. Why was it such an exciting prospect? Why did it make me feel this fucking alive?

"I want you to take it all," I all but grunted at him.

His eyes burnt with the need to obey me. And he did. My cock sunk into his mouth, hitting the back of his throat. Jonah swallowed and took me deeper. I all but fucking died at the tightness and the sheer bliss of being in him like this.

"That's it," I moaned. "Fuck, don't stop."

To my utmost surprise, he did take it all. I didn't know what the fuck to do with myself, but I didn't want to choke him. I loosened my grip on his hair. He pulled off me, leaving strings of saliva coating my length as he took several deep breaths.

"You okay?" I murmured, wanting to make sure I hadn't hurt him.

He gave me a smile and nodded. Then his mouth was on my cock again and he went to fucking town on me. I was so far gone, I didn't even stop him or direct proceedings. All I could feel was ecstasy. My hand fisted the covers, my knuckles whitening under the strain. His hand planted firmly on my stomach to keep me in place as I struggled to stop bucking.

"Fuck, shit, Jesus, fuck, Jonah."

My body tensed up. I felt it hit me before I could even utter a sound. I fought against closing my eyes because I wanted to see him. I needed to. The way he stared up at me, eyes dark with satisfaction as if pleasing me made it all worthwhile for him. The words I wanted to say burnt in my throat.

I want us to be together… as a couple.

I didn't know how to admit it to him. It felt wrong to ask him to be mine considering I wasn't even okay with telling my parents about him. Duke was the only person I could talk to about this.

I closed my eyes, unable to fight against it any longer. Allowing the waves of pleasure to wash over me, I stopped my wandering thoughts in their tracks.

When I finally came down and opened my eyes, Jonah had moved to lay next to me. I heard a sharp rap at the door.

"Monkey, just leaving it outside the door," came my mum's muffled voice.

"Okay," I called back, my voice sounding a little hoarse.

I turned to Jonah who was smiling at me, his fingers stroking down my chest.

"Hungry?"

His eyes glittered with amusement.

"Yeah, though you did just feed me."

I felt my face growing hot.

"You're bad."

He leant down and brushed his lips against mine.

"I think you like it."

I reached up and cupped the back of his head, kissing him. I could taste myself on him, but I didn't care much about that. When he pulled back, I smiled.

"I'll warn you now, Mum's probably gone all out. She likes to take care of us."

"Good thing we worked up an appetite."

I shook my head as he sat up. Pulling myself up, I dragged my clothes back on and walked over to the door. True to my word, Mum had gone all out and made us a crazy amount of food. There was fruit, toast, yoghurt, granola, orange juice and tea. I picked up the tray and took it in. Jonah's eyebrows raised when I placed it on the bed.

"I could get used to this."

I smiled. Maybe he would if I was brave enough to be with him. I watched him pick up one of the bowls and dig in.

"My parents are throwing Xav a birthday party next week. Do… do you want to come?"

Jonah looked up at me, his eyes widening.

"Um, where is it?"

"At the restaurant in the casino, but like it's not some sit-down thing. There'll be food, dancing and games and stuff. It was Dad's idea to do a children's birthday party but an adult version. I'd… I'd like it if you came. And you can meet my parents finally."

He was silent for a long moment. I thought he was going to say no because he looked conflicted.

"I'd love to."

I leant closer to him and kissed his cheek.

"I'm glad."

The thought of introducing Jonah to my parents was terrifying, but it wasn't like I had to tell them we were anything other than friends. I was going to have to decide where he and I stood. And it needed to be soon because it wasn't fair of me to have us remain in limbo. I just hoped by the time next week came around, I would know what exactly I was going to do.

CHAPTER TWENTY SEVEN

Raphael

I trudged after my dad, wondering whether I should talk to him about me and Jonah or not. We'd been walking around for an hour now, having gone to a few shops in the shopping centre already. Dad stopped in front of a display and glanced over the items. Then his eyes flicked over to me as I came to a standstill next to him.

"Don't tell me you're tired already, monkey."

I shook my head.

"No, just thinking is all."

"About anything in particular? You've been rather quiet today."

I wasn't the most talkative person in general, but I usually made an effort with my dad. Everything with Jonah was making my head spin. When he'd left earlier, I'd felt bereft of his presence immediately. He said he'd come to Xav's party, but it was a week away and the thought of not seeing him until then almost sent me into a blind panic. It's as if when I'd finally given myself permission to want him, I couldn't deal with being away from him.

What do I even do with that? It's not like I can monopolise his time.

"A lot of stuff really."

Dad eyed me with a curious expression on his face. He knew I went to Duke if anything was bothering me. This didn't feel like something I could talk to my brother about since he was just as fucked up as me about the person he cared about.

"That's a little vague, monkey."

I shrugged. If I started asking him questions, he might get suspicious as to why.

"What do you want me to say?"

"I'd like it if you told me what's wrong."

I fiddled with the bags in my hand. We'd already got all Xav's birthday presents, now we were just looking for party supplies. The staff at the casino were mostly handling the preparations, but Dad wanted to get some specific things to match the adult theme we were going with. I was pretty sure when Quinn saw we'd bought a whole bunch of penis straws, dick-shaped confetti and ordered a birthday cake shaped like a pair of breasts, he might have something to say about it. Xav would find it funny, which is why we'd even gone out of our way to get them in the first place. My dads were nothing if not unique. I didn't tend to get embarrassed by them any longer except when they started going on about their sex life. It was a subject I never wanted to think about let alone listen to them go on about.

264

"Everything and nothing."

He rolled his eyes and moved along the aisle. I followed, wondering how long he was going to tolerate my reluctance to communicate. Dad was one of the most patient people I'd ever met, but even he had his limits. I didn't know how to broach the subject of Jonah with him. Mum would have told him about my guest. Dad hadn't brought it up. He was probably waiting for me to.

"Do you want to get some lunch, monkey?" he asked me a few minutes later.

"Sure."

I followed him out of the shop once he'd paid and we found a chain restaurant to eat in. When we'd sat down with our bags under the table and had duly ordered at the counter, Dad shifted in his seat and stared at me. I felt mildly exposed as if all my thoughts were on display.

"If I ask you something, can you promise me not to read into it?" I blurted out, wanting to rip the bandage off because this was driving me crazy.

"Yes."

I fiddled with the sauces on the table, my nerves getting the better of me.

"How did you know when it was the right time to… confess your feelings to Xav?"

It's not as if I wanted to make some big declaration to Jonah about how I felt. Just to make it known I wanted him to be mine. I couldn't deal with the thought of him having a relationship with another guy. It made me jealous and possessive. Perhaps a product of growing up with four very different fathers. I knew who I might have got that kind of attitude from.

Might? You know you get it from Quinn, don't kid yourself into thinking anything else.

Dad folded his hands on the table.

"I didn't."

"No?"

"There's never a right time, monkey. Life doesn't come with perfect moments and opportunities."

"That's not helpful."

He smiled and chuckled as if I was being unreasonable.

"I don't think I would have told Xav if it wasn't for your mother, but that, in turn, made it complicated. There was a lot of jealousy, miscommunication and assumptions made between the five of us when we were working things out. It's why we've always tried to instil the importance of honesty and communication in you kids."

Of course, I was well aware of how my parents had come together, but there were certain parts of their story they'd never talked about.

"So what you're saying is I should always be honest if even the timing isn't right?"

He shook his head.

"Only you can decide whether it's the right time or not. Yes, it could be a mistake, but that's the risk you take. Don't let fear of a bad outcome stop you if you really want something."

I looked down at my hands. The only thing which scared me was fucking up royally with Jonah. I was worried about how possessive over him I'd become. Worried about how my own inability to fix myself could get in the way. Every part of this scared me. But did it scare me enough not to try?

"Sometimes I struggle with who I am," I said, my voice rather quiet in the busy restaurant. "And it makes me scared of taking risks."

"Struggle in what way?"

I took a sip of my drink, trying to work out what else to say. How to even explain it. It's not a subject I'd broached with any of my parents before. Only with Duke and Jonah. Even they didn't know the full extent of it. Mostly because I was ashamed of how much I hated myself for the way I was. It's like no matter what I did, I couldn't see myself in a positive light.

"My own self-identity."

"You know you don't have to label yourself, right?"

"It's not that, Dad. It's…" *Everything. Absolutely everything. All the horrific thoughts I have about myself. The way I can't seem to do anything right. How I've hurt people I care about. How I know I'm going to keep doing it because I'm too fucked up to be good for anyone.* "It's not the way other people see me. It's how I see me."

He frowned.

"How do you see yourself?"

"Not in a good way."

I didn't feel great admitting it to him, but I didn't want to lie either. It's not as if I wanted him to do something about it. It had always been my burden to carry. My fucking burden which was beginning to drive me insane. Coping with all these negative emotions had worn on me. It only reinforced my feelings towards myself. The feeling of worthlessness since I couldn't even deal with my own fucked up bullshit.

"How long have you been feeling like this?"

"Long enough."

"Raphi…"

"Years, I've felt this way for years. I'm only telling you because I feel like I need to start being honest… and I really don't want you to tell Mum. She already worries about me enough."

His green eyes were full of his own worry, but there was understanding there too.

"I won't talk to her about this."

"I don't know how to change how I feel."

The waitress came over, interrupting us so he couldn't respond. Dad thanked her as she set our plates down. I immediately started putting sauce on my plate because I was starving. Trudging around a shopping centre could be tiring.

"Have you ever thought about getting some help?" Dad asked after I'd started tucking in.

"What kind of help?"

"Like therapy or counselling."

I looked down at my plate. It had never crossed my mind.

"No. I don't want to do that."

Not when I had Jonah. He said he'd help me. I trusted him. I didn't trust some random stranger.

"It helped Rory."

"Are you really comparing what he went through to me being unable to see myself in a positive light?"

"No, that's not what I meant. Counselling isn't just for people who've been through trauma, Raphi."

"I know, but it's not something I'm comfortable with… I don't want to talk to a stranger."

He cocked his head to the side.

"Okay, it was just a suggestion."

I shook my head and continued to eat. If he was expecting me to just jump at the opportunity, he was mistaken.

"I want to help you, monkey, you know that, right?"

I nodded, swallowing my mouthful.

"I'll be okay."

"You don't have to go through this alone. You've always been so independent and closed off. I let it be because that's what I thought was best, but I'm your dad and I can't help worrying. I care deeply about your wellbeing."

His words only made me feel like shit for keeping this from him. For not having the courage to be open and honest. That was my problem. I had something to prove which meant I tried to deal with everything myself. Things always seemed to come easier for my siblings than for me. They were confident and had no problem going after what they wanted. That trait had skipped over me. I wanted to make my parents proud and instead, I ended up feeling as though I was always disappointing them.

"I know, Dad."

He reached across the table and took my hand.

"You're never on your own. I'm right here if you need me. Just remember that."

I nodded, not knowing what else to say. Not as if I could promise I'd get better. All I could do was try. Try to be a better person even though deep down, I didn't know how.

One thing our conversation had made clear to me was the need to stop being so afraid, to be honest.

"Dad…"

"Yes, monkey?"

"You remember I once told you my heart was broken over… over a boy?"

"I do."

I looked away as he retracted his hand.

"We've been talking again. I invited him to Xav's birthday."

"I take it he was your visitor last night and this morning."

"Yes, we're just friends though. I want to introduce him to all of you, but I don't want anyone getting the wrong idea about us."

I might want Jonah to be mine, but I wasn't ready to admit it to anyone else except Duke yet. I had to take things one step at a time.

"Okay, if you say you're friends then I believe you. Does this boy have a name?"

"That's the thing, Dad, I don't know how Cole is going to feel about this."

"Why would it have anything to do with Cole?"

I sighed and set my cutlery down.

"It's Meredith's older brother, Jonah, and he had something to do with their break-up. I promise he's a good person, he's just protective of his sister is all. I'm sure you can understand."

"I see. Well, I don't think your brother is going to be particularly happy, but it's not about him."

Dad was right. Cole had accepted what Jonah had said about him and Meredith. He was the one who'd broken up with Meredith. I could keep Jonah away from Cole for the night somehow.

"I just don't want anyone to give him a hard time."

"Hey, hey, no one is going to do that, monkey. I'll talk to the others, okay?"

I nodded.

"Make sure you tell them we're just friends, yeah? Nothing else is going on."

The lie made my throat tight, but I wasn't ready to cross that bridge yet.

"I will. I'm looking forward to meeting him since he must be important for you to be so concerned over what we're going to think."

I felt my face grow hot. I wasn't worried as Dad would really like Jonah.

"He is. I'm lucky to have him as a friend."

"If he's anything like his sister, I'm sure we'll all love him."

I almost snorted. Jonah was the opposite of Meredith. Whilst she was loud and out there, Jonah was quiet and introspective. It's what I liked the most about him. He didn't feel the need to fill the silence.

"You'll just have to wait and see."

Dad smiled at me and I hoped everything would be okay. After all, I felt like I'd finally made up my mind about the boy I'd invited to Xav's birthday. Even if I wasn't ready to tell everyone else, I could tell Jonah. I could make him mine if he was okay with it being kept quiet. He'd told me he'd take me any way he could have me. It wouldn't be forever.

I'll tell him next week. I'll make him mine then.

Just a little longer, cuore mio. I'm only going to keep you waiting a little longer, then I promise, I'll be with you even if I don't deserve you.

Somehow I'd have to silence those doubts and try. Because all I could do was try. He was worth trying for. He was worth… everything.

CHAPTER TWENTY EIGHT

Jonah

I took a deep breath as I walked up to the Syndicate. Meeting Raphi's parents made me more nervous than I thought it would. The worst thing was knowing I would have to see Cole and the last time that had happened, it hadn't gone very well. I felt responsible for pushing him into breaking up with Meredith. Seeing how much pain it had caused her only made me regret my choices. The whole thing hadn't made me feel good about myself considering a lot of my complaints about her boyfriend were all mixed up with his brother.

I walked into the non-descript looking building with the sign 'The Syndicate' in red lettering above the door. There was a reception area. I walked up to the desk. The lady behind it gave me a smile.

"Hello, welcome to the Syndicate. How can I help?"

"Hi, I'm here for, um, Xavier's birthday party."

"Oh yes, could I take your name please?"

I shifted on my feet.

"Jonah Pope."

She scanned something on her computer screen for a moment then gave me a nod. I imagined Raphi had put me on the guest list.

"If you go through the doors and take the lift up to the second floor, the restaurant is on the left."

"Thank you."

I went through the doors she'd indicated and found there was a lift already waiting. Hopping in, I pressed the button for the second floor and the door closed. My fingers tapped on the mirrored walls as I leant back. I resisted the urge to text Raphi and ask him to meet me outside. It was being cowardly. I just didn't like crowds and I wasn't sure how many people would be at this party.

The doors slid open when the lift stopped on the right floor. I walked out, hearing music. I followed it, walking to the left and glancing up at the name of the restaurant.

The Underworld.

It made me smile a little considering it reminded me of Raphi's parents' past.

The room was rather busy as I walked in. It made my pulse spike. Taking a deep breath, I looked around, seeing if I could spot Raphi. All the tables had been pushed back to make a clear space in the middle of the room. Near the bar area, several people stood in a group next to a table with what looked like presents and a cake on it. One of them, a tall man with greyeing dark hair kept looking over at the cake with disapproval. Next to him was a short blonde woman who had her arm wrapped around his waist. She was talking to two other men, one with auburn hair and the other, a carbon copy of Raphi but his chestnut hair was greyeing. The last man stood next to Cole and they looked almost exactly alike. Aurora, Duke and Raphi stood off away from them, seemingly deep in conversation.

Raphi's family. I took a second to take them in before I made a beeline for them. I wiped my sweaty palms against my dark jeans. No one else looked like they were too dressed up. I breathed a sigh of relief about my attire.

Duke spied me first and smirked before nudging his brother. It made my face grow hot since it was quite obvious Raphi had told him what was going on between us. The moment Raphi saw me, his smile made my heart squeeze in my chest. He looked so fucking happy to see me, I almost didn't know what to do with myself. He then eyed his brother and said something to him I couldn't hear which prompted Duke to laugh and Raphi to give him a dark look.

Raphi moved away from his family and met me a few feet away.

"You made it."

"I said I'd come," I replied, giving him a smile.

"I'm glad you're here. I'll introduce you to my parents."

He started to reach his hand out to mine, but then thought better of it and snatched it back. I didn't know what to make of it. I followed him over to his parents, who all looked over at us.

"This is my friend, Jonah." He waved at me. "J, these are my parents, Quinn, Ash, Xav, Eric and Rory." He indicated each of them in turn. "And you know my siblings already."

The first person to step forward was Raphi's dad, Eric who gave me a smile and shook my hand.

"It's nice to meet you. Monkey tells me you're studying psychology."

I glanced at Raphi who was still smiling. I found it adorable how his parents had a nickname for him.

"Yes, it's my last year after the summer."

"And do you have plans after that?"

"I want to do a postgraduate doctorate. It takes another three years but then I'll be able to work as a counsellor."

I hadn't exactly told Raphi about it. Neither had I said I planned on returning to London to get my doctorate. It was a conversation for a later date considering I had no idea what we were to each other.

I didn't know what Raphi had said to his parents about me but they were all smiling as if I hadn't fucked up their youngest son's relationship. Cole, on the other hand, had moved away towards Duke and Aurora. I couldn't blame him. Eventually, I would apologise for what happened when he was more open to it.

"Interesting. Aurora's boyfriend's uncle is a psychotherapist."

"Is Logan coming tonight?" Raphi asked.

"I think so."

Raphi leant closer to me.

"If he does turn up, expect some tension between him and Quinn," he murmured.

Xav stepped forward, the auburn-haired man who looked a lot like Duke.

"So, you're Raphi's secret late-night visitor."

"Xavier, behave," Raphi's mum, Ash, hissed.

Raphi's ears went red. I was pretty sure I wasn't much better as the memory of the way he'd fucked me flashed through my mind.

Not now, brain, not now!

"That's me," I said, with a nervous laugh.

"I would say ignore him as he's always like this but it is his birthday," Raphi said, giving Xav a dark look.

"Oh, monkey, I'm just playing," Xav said, ruffling Raphi's hair. He stuck a hand out to me. "It's nice to meet you."

"You too," I replied. "And happy birthday."

Xav gave me a grin and a wink.

"Getting old like this lot. Well, our girl isn't yet fifty but we'll throw her a big do then."

"Still five years away, *tesoro*," Ash said as she stepped forward, placing a hand on Xav's arm.

He leant down and kissed her forehead.

"And you're still as beautiful as the day we met, angel."

"Flattery will get you everywhere with me tonight."

Raphi rolled his eyes and inched closer to me.

"Excuse them and their lovey-dovey shit."

"It's okay," I said, giving him a smile.

His parents clearly loved each other. And it didn't escape my notice Ash had called Xav, *tesoro*. I hadn't yet looked up what Raphi had called me but now I knew for sure where he'd got it from. His mother.

Ash let go of Xav and took my hand, giving it a firm shake.

"My son failed to mention how much you look like your sister. How is Meredith?"

"She's fine, I've been helping her prepare for uni."

"I'm happy to hear it."

It didn't feel awkward to talk about her since Cole was out of earshot. Ash shifted closer to Raphi who leant down to allow her to speak to him.

"He's rather handsome, monkey," she murmured.

"Mum!" Raphi hissed, his blush spreading from his ears to his cheeks.

"I'm just saying."

She patted his arm and moved away towards the cake table. Now I was close enough I could see it was shaped like breasts.

Well, that's... I don't know what to say about it.

It's not like I didn't appreciate female beauty, but this was a little in your face.

"The cake is Dad's idea of a joke. Xav loves it, but he's got the dirtiest mind imaginable. Quinn doesn't approve," Raphi said when he noticed me staring at it.

"No?"

"He accused Dad of indulging Xav's childish behaviour and questioned what their employees would think but loads of people have taken photos and laughed about it."

"Your family is quite something."

Raphi's fingers brushed over mine. The small touch made me swallow and want more. So much more. The thought of us tangled together was never far from my mind. His closeness did a number on me. A week of being apart felt like too long.

You're a mess, you know that? You promised him you'd wait for him to make a decision.

I might have promised that, but it didn't stop impatience from rearing its ugly head. It didn't feel good to be stuck in limbo with him like this.

"They're one of a kind. We should say hello to Rory and Quinn."

Those two had moved closer to each other. Raphi directed me towards them. They both looked over at the same time wearing joint expressions of curiosity.

"You waiting for Xav to cut the cake so you can have a slice?" Raphi asked.

Quinn gave his son a dark look.

"E and Xav have been wearing off on you too much."

"Quinn just hates sipping from a dick straw," Rory said with a smile.

"Oh, shut up. I should never have let E be in charge of decorations."

I stifled a smile and Raphi shared a look with Rory.

"Anyway, enough about dicks, it's nice to meet a friend of monkey's." Quinn extended his hand to me so I shook it. "Raphi is notorious for keeping his life private. This is a rare occurrence."

"If I didn't, then Mum would be on my case even more than she already is," Raphi said. "Roll on September is all I can say."

Rory gave Raphi a sympathetic look whilst Quinn grinned.

"Your mother is a force to be reckoned with. How else do you think she deals with the four of us and four kids?"

"I'd rather not think about how she deals with you four."

Quinn chuckled and Rory looked outright amused.

"I'll spare you the details, unlike Xav."

Raphi shuddered. I couldn't blame him. Talk of parents and what they got up to alone was enough to embarrass any child.

"Do you want a drink?" Raphi asked me.

"Um, sure."

This time, he took me by the arm and pulled me away from his family towards the bar. As we waited for the bartender to make his way down to us, Raphi glanced at me.

"They're a lot… I know."

"It's nice to finally put faces to names and they're fine, Raphi."

"Are you okay? I know you don't like crowds."

The fact he remembered that about me warmed my fucking heart.

"I'm okay because I'm with you."

He smiled and touched his hand to my arm again.

"I'm glad."

The two of us made the rounds with our drinks after we'd got them. Raphi told me more about the restaurant and the casino. How exclusive the membership was and about some of the celebrities who'd attended before. We both filled up plates from the buffet. The food was way fancier than anything I'd ever had before, but Raphi didn't bat an eyelid. He must be used to it. I didn't think his parents lived a lavish lifestyle, but it was clear they didn't want for money. The only reason I even lived in Kensington was because it was my grandma's house. We weren't exactly super rich or anything.

After we'd eaten, the music changed and people were starting to get on the makeshift dancefloor. Raphi and I stood near the doors of the restaurant. It's not like I didn't dance. The thought of doing it with anyone else but the boy next to me was unappealing. I doubted he'd be comfortable dancing with me in front of his family so I didn't suggest it.

Raphi turned to me. There was a twinkle in his green eyes. "Come with me."

He slid his hand into mine. His touch warmed me from the inside out. I glanced around to see if anyone had noticed us, but everyone seemed to be engaged in conversation, eating or dancing.

"Where?"

Raphi smiled wide.

"You'll see."

And the boy I loved led me out of the restaurant, leaving me wondering what he had planned.

CHAPTER TWENTY NINE

Jonah

aphi took me over to the lifts and hit the button for up. His palm was warm in mine and his smile had me in knots. I didn't ask questions as the lift arrived and we got in. Raphi pressed the button for the top floor. He moved closer to me, his arm brushing against mine as he stepped back. My skin tingled all over and my heart raced. We were alone for the first time in a week. My lips craved a taste of his.

I didn't think it was possible to desire a person in the way I do him. It's making me crazy.

Resisting the urge to shove him against the wall and kiss him proved harder than I anticipated. I preferred it when he was in control. When he took what he wanted. Didn't stop me wanting him though. Craving everything with him.

My nerves were shaky as the lift door opened. He pulled me out and along a corridor. At the end were a set of doors with a security panel. Raphi punched in some numbers and then pushed the door open. We walked into a large office. There was a bank of monitors along one wall, a desk in the middle of the room and a couple of other desks along another wall.

Raphi turned to the panel on the wall next to the door and did something to it, but I wasn't paying much attention to him.

"Where are we?" I asked, realising the monitors showed all angles of the casino.

"Oh, this is my parents' office. That's not what I want to show you."

He pulled me away towards the window. I looked out on the London skyline. It wasn't quite dark yet, but it was still a beautiful sight to behold. The city was spread out below us, the lights twinkling.

"That's some view."

"Right? I like to sit here and look out whenever I'm at the casino, which isn't often to be honest. Not like I could go out on the floor until I turned eighteen. I'm not into gambling though. Quinn holds VIP poker tournaments, but otherwise, my parents don't gamble either."

"You didn't want to go into the family business."

He shook his head.

"No. My parents are proud of me for wanting to follow my passion. Besides, Duke and Aurora will take over from them when they retire."

Raphi turned to me, dropping my hand. I angled my body towards him as his hands came up and landed on my chest.

My breath stuttered at his touch and the way he was looking at me.

"There are no cameras in here." He pushed me up against the window, my back pressed to the glass. "Have you been wanting to kiss me as much as I want to kiss you?"

I nodded, not trusting my voice. He leant closer. My mouth went dry and I tried not to think too hard about the fact we were in his parents' office.

"Don't worry, J, no one is coming up here." His hand ran down my chest. "We won't be interrupted."

I let out a pant as his hand brushed over my crotch. He kissed me then, stealing all of my words and the breath from my lungs. His other hand curled into my hair. Mine wrapped around his waist, tugging him against me. Any objections I had to us doing it here flew out of my head. All I could see and feel was him.

"I can't stop thinking about you," he told me as he kissed down my jaw. "I want you so fucking much."

"I want you too."

He smiled against my skin.

"You have me," he whispered. "I'm already yours, *cuore mio*."

My heart couldn't take it. It pumped wildly in my chest, making my body tremble.

"I do?"

"Yes… as long as you're mine."

I nodded, panting as he kissed my neck and rubbed my cock which had hardened under his touch. If I wasn't sure I wanted him to take me in this room with the London skyline behind us before, I was sure now. So fucking sure of everything.

"Use your words."

"Yes, yes, I'm yours, Raphi. I'm all yours. I've always been yours."

"I'm not ready to tell anyone yet. Are you okay with keeping it between us?"

I didn't care about having to be a secret right then. Not when he was touching me, making it clear he was going to have his wicked way with me. Not when it meant I'd have him. He'd be mine. All I'd wanted for the past three years was Raphi. He was the boy I loved so much, it hurt. If this was the way I could have him, I'd take it. I'd take it all to be close to him like this.

"I won't breathe a word to anyone."

"Then consider me yours, Jonah." He pulled back and stared at me with those stunning verdant eyes. "I'm yours and you're mine."

He didn't need to say anything more. The implication was there. We were a couple even if it was only between the two of us.

"Okay," I whispered. "I'm yours and you're mine."

His smile was wicked. He stepped back completely and snagged both my wrists, tugging me with him towards the desk in the middle of the room. When we reached it, he leant against it, pressed a hand on my shoulder and shoved me down on my knees.

"I want you to get my dick nice and wet."

My hands went to his dark jeans immediately, tugging open the fly and pulling them down slightly along with his boxers. His cock was already hard. When I wrapped my hand around it, I felt it throb under my touch.

Raphi reached over to the top drawer of the desk and pulled it open. He took a few things out and set them on the desk before shutting the drawer. Either he'd planned this or his parents kept supplies in their desk because there was lube, condoms and tissues. My money was on the latter judging by the way his parents looked at each other earlier.

Raphi picked up the bottle of lube.

"Whilst you suck my cock, I want you to prepare yourself for me."

I swallowed hard.

"I'm ready for you to be a needy panting mess, J, begging me for it. Tell me now if you're not on board with this."

I stared up at the boy I adored with every inch of me. The one I wanted to worship just like he'd asked me to.

"You sure no one will come up here?"

His eyes softened.

"I'm sure and besides, I may have set the security panel so it won't open from the outside right now."

I raised an eyebrow.

"Won't that piss your parents off?"

He shrugged.

"Like I said, they're not coming up here right now, so you better get to work."

I let go of his cock and unbuttoned my jeans, tugging them and my boxers down my thighs. Raphi's eyes darkened when he looked at me. He held out the bottle of lube and I took it, squirting some on my fingers. As I reached behind me, I curled the fingers of my other hand around his cock, stroking him. I leant forward and licked his shaft, making him grunt. Then I wrapped my lips around the head of his cock, sucking him as I stroked. I groaned against his cock when I slid a finger inside me.

Raphi's fingers curled around my neck, but they were gentle. He wasn't directing me, just keeping me there. I had no intention of going anywhere. I wanted all of this. All of him.

"I'm wondering whether you'd prefer it if I shoved you up against the desk and fucked you, or if you want me to sit in the desk chair then you can ride me."

The thought of both made my skin itch with need. It wouldn't matter to me what he chose. I knew I'd adore it either way.

"Mmm, I think you like the idea of those, don't you? I suppose I'll have to decide what I'm in the mood for."

His voice was taunting. It only served to make my cock throb. I wanted his hand wrapped around me, bringing me to the edge with his dick buried firmly inside me. If I wanted that, I needed to make sure I was ready. I slid another finger inside me, stretching myself out for him. The pleasure was already making me feel wild and needy. I moaned around his dick again, taking more because he told me to get him nice and wet.

A few minutes later, I had three fingers in me and Raphi was panting, his fingers around the back of my neck tightening. I pulled away, staring up at him as his eyes glittered with desire.

"I need you to fuck me."

"Do you?"

"Yes, please. I'll do anything, just please fuck me."

"Get up."

I slid my fingers from myself and rose to my feet. He pulled me closer and kissed me, biting down my bottom lip and making me whimper. He let me go and smiled.

"Bend over the desk and make sure you're ready for me."

I did as he asked, squirting more lube on my fingers and sliding it inside me. I took a tissue and wiped my hand before I leant over the desk. My palms lay flat on the cold surface. Raphi moved behind me. I imagined he was rolling on a condom and coating himself. His hand landed on my lower back a moment later. I shivered as his cock nudged my hole.

"I'm not in the mood to hold back," he told me as he pressed against me. "Seeing you on your knees for me turns me on so fucking much, J."

I panted as he slid inside me. The intensity had me reaching forward and gripping the edge of the desk because he wasn't letting me adjust.

"Going to fuck you so good, you won't even know your own name when I'm done."

"Raphi," I gasped, feeling him stretch me open inch by inch.

"The need in your voice is the most fucking intoxicating thing in the world."

Knowing how much I got him going only made me want to do more to please him. To keep him with me. I'd give him anything he asked for.

"Fuck me," I whimpered. "Fuck me… please."

And he did. Oh, he fucking well did. Raphi pulled back and pushed inside me with a few relatively gentle thrusts. Then he stopped holding back. I cried out when he slammed inside me the first time. The harder he fucked me, the more my thighs dug into the desk, but I didn't care. It felt so good. Being taken by him. Being given everything he had to give.

"Fuck, Raphi, more, please."

I didn't care how crazed with need I sounded. My knuckles were going white with the grip I had on the desk. Raphi's hands were wrapped around my hips for leverage as he continued to fuck me with deep, hard strokes. I could hear him breathing heavily above me and his grunts.

He let go of my hip and leant forward, gripping me by the chin. He forced my head back and stared into my eyes.

"You're mine. All of you. Your pleasure, your pain, everything."

"Yours."

He leant closer and ran his lips over my forehead.

"That's right."

His other hand left my hip and he pulled me almost upright, his hands curling around my body to keep me steady as he continued to pump his cock inside me. I felt his lips meet my throat, kissing and sucking at the skin. His hand reached down and wrapped around my cock, stroking up and down the length. I closed my eyes, the delirious pleasure washing over me.

The only sounds now were our skin slapping together and our mutual breathing. Every so often, one of us would moan or grunt. There were no words. This was us. We were together finally just like I wanted. Raphi's free hand curled around my jaw, holding me still as his head dropped to my shoulder. I could feel him getting close and I was too. His fist around me tightened and his strokes became faster, in time with the way he was fucking me.

"Fuck, Jonah," he groaned.

His cock swelled, then he came, which only made me moan. The sensation of him pulsing inside me drove me over the edge. I gasped as the waves hit, pulling me under and drowning me in him. As my mouth opened, Raphi stuck his fingers inside it, pulling my jaw open as he continued to pound into me with his climax. I could do nothing but let the pleasure take control.

The two of us panted and struggled to catch our breath when we fell back to earth together. It felt like every time we had sex, it grew in intensity and pleasure. We were learning exactly what made each other tick.

Raphi's fingers slid out of my mouth and his hand landed on the desk.

"That was something," he murmured, kissing my neck.

"More than something."

He chuckled.

"My parents would give me a lecture if they found out I'd fucked you in here."

I snorted.

"Maybe we should get back before our absence is noticed."

"Mmm, you're right, but first, we should make sure we don't look like we just got high off each other."

He pulled away but not before kissing my neck one last time. The two of us spent the next few minutes cleaning up the office to make sure it looked like nothing had been disturbed, hiding the evidence of our tryst by taking it into the bathroom off the office and disposing of it. We both sorted out our clothes and hair. The flush of our faces couldn't be helped.

Raphi took my hand and led me back towards the lift.

"Are you sure about all of this?" I asked, unable to help myself.

"What? Us?"

"Yeah."

He turned to me, his smile bright.

"I'm sure I want to try, J."

"Will… will you tell me what that thing you keep calling me means?"

His green eyes were twinkling as he licked his bottom lip.

"*Cuore mio* is Italian for my heart. Take of that what you will. My mum taught me a few phrases when I was younger."

I didn't know what to say. Him calling me his heart. It had all sorts of implications about his feelings, but I didn't want to read into it. Didn't want to think too hard in case everything fell apart before we had a chance to even really begin. Instead of answering, I leant towards him and kissed him. When I pulled back, I smiled too.

"*Cuore mio.*"

He bit his lip.

"That's right. I'll teach you some more words if you'd like. I don't know a huge amount, but enough to get by."

"I'd like that."

He leant his head on my shoulder as we waited for the lift to arrive. And I couldn't help but hope we'd be okay. He'd finally given us a chance and it's all I could ask him for. I was just happy he was here with me. He was open to us.

I love you, Raphael Nelson. I won't tell you that yet. Not until you're ready to tell the world you're mine and I'm yours. Just know I'm going to be here for you whatever you need. You and I can get through this together. I'll protect you, my beautiful, broken boy. I'll protect you forever.

PART III

devastate

verb, dev·as·tat·ed, dev·as·tat·ing.
to lay waste; render desolate.

CHAPTER THIRTY

Raphael

"Okay so, *luce dei miei occhi* is light of my eyes, right?"

I smiled up at Jonah, whose chest my head was resting on. I'd been slowly teaching him Italian terms of endearment like Mum had taught me years ago.

"Mmm, yes, and you are just that."

His cheeks flushed, which was adorable. He got flustered at compliments when I caught him off guard with them. I loved that about him.

The past eight weeks had flown by in almost the blink of an eye. Now I was moving out of my parents' house into student halls and Jonah was going back to Durham where his university was. I'd avoided thinking about it until today since it was our last night together. Being apart wouldn't be easy on either of us.

I was relatively sure my parents had cottoned onto the fact Jonah and I were more than friends given how many nights he'd spent here. And even though I was happy being with Jonah, I still wasn't ready to admit it. To tell them the truth. I still struggled with my own identity and acceptance of myself. So far, only Duke knew. I needed someone to confide in and vent my frustrations to. Opening up to my brother had been the only thing keeping me from losing my shit completely.

Jonah hadn't brought it up. He'd been content to let me take my time since there were no barriers to us seeing each other. I wasn't sure that would be the case going forward. The thought of him not being able to tell anyone he was taken made me anxious. He was mine. He knew that, but it was other people I didn't trust.

This was why the whole thing kept fucking with me. I wanted to be this brave person who was comfortable with who they were, but I wasn't. And I hated it.

"I'm going to miss you," Jonah said after a few minutes of silence, his voice a little shaky. "A lot."

My heart tightened.

"It's your last year, you'll be busy."

He knew I'd miss him too, even if I hadn't said it.

"Doesn't mean I'll stop wishing I could be here with you."

"You're coming back at Christmas."

He nodded, but his eyes were sad. I hated it. All of it. It couldn't be helped. We always knew we'd be apart when the summer ended. I was trying to be the strong one.

You're not strong. You're weak. So. Fucking. Weak.

"J, you know it's not that long, right?"

He tried to smile, but I could see the insecurity in his expression.

"I need to talk to you about something."

My stomach twisted at the seriousness of his tone. I shifted to look at him fully.

"Is something wrong?"

"No, but I've been meaning to tell you this, just hasn't felt like the right time. Now I'm leaving and time has run out."

I didn't like where this was going. What had he been keeping from me? Jonah was very open with me usually.

"Okay… what is it?"

I made sure my voice was calm despite my nerves spiking. He didn't need me going off on one before I even knew what it was he wanted to say.

"I told you I'd only been with one guy intimately before."

My body tensed at his words. Whilst he knew I'd been with Lana, I didn't bring her up in conversation. She was a part of my past, not my present.

"Yeah."

"It wasn't a relationship thing. He taught me about sex and that was it."

"Oh."

If that was it, I didn't know why he was making a thing out of it. Yeah, it did suck since his first experience wasn't with someone he was emotionally involved with, but mine hadn't been either. Not the first time anyway. I'd never developed strong feelings for Lana, but at least we'd had a relationship afterwards.

"And the reason I'm telling you is because I live with him and another guy in Durham."

I didn't speak. The very idea he lived with someone he'd been intimate with had me struggling to not overreact. It wouldn't be fair, considering I'd stipulated our relationship had to be a secret.

This is different. You aren't living with the girl you fucked.

It wasn't quite as bad as him living with an ex, but it was bad enough. Did he think I would be okay with this? Probably not, since he hadn't told me until the very last minute.

"I promise nothing is going on between me and Robin. It wasn't really anything to begin with. He's not interested in relationships. I don't want him like that either. You are all I want. You know that."

His words didn't placate me. They didn't make me feel any less uneasy about it.

Robin? His name is Robin? You know what? Fuck Robin!

Jonah reached up and ran his fingers through my hair, stroking the side of my head.

"Say something. You look kind of pissed."

"I am pissed," I muttered.

Jonah looked contrite at my words. He should have told me about this weeks ago. Springing it on me when we were sharing our last night together for weeks? It was kind of shitty.

"I know I should have said something before."

I sat up, pulling away from him. His expression fell. I wasn't sure what else he expected.

"You think?"

"Raphi…"

Those sad eyes of his gut me. I wasn't overreacting. He knew better than to keep that shit to himself.

"No, don't do that. Don't look at me like that. What the fuck, J? You slept with your housemate?"

He sat up and reached for me, but I backed away, avoiding his hands.

"It wasn't my smartest idea and I wish I hadn't but I can't take it back now."

"Do you really expect me to be okay with you living with a guy you've slept with?"

The words hurt him as much as they hurt me. I didn't have a say in the matter since this was all arranged before I ever came back into his life. Didn't stop me hating everything about it.

"No, but it's not like I can change it."

"I don't care. You knew I would hate it, so you kept it from me."

"Like you're any better when you're keeping me a secret."

He slammed his hand over his mouth right after he said it as if he could put the words back in his mouth. They couldn't be unsaid. I knew he didn't like the fact I wasn't ready to tell the world I was bi and in love with a boy. Jonah didn't know about the love part quite yet. His tone made it sound like he resented me for all of it.

"I didn't mean that, Raphi. I really didn't." His words came out rushed, and he lunged forward, gripping my arms and making it impossible for me to go anywhere. His eyes were frantic, making my chest ache. "I promised you I'd wait. I know you're not ready and it's okay. I understand. You don't need to rush this."

His words did nothing to stop the bitterness towards myself from rearing its ugly head. The self-loathing kicked in. I didn't deserve Jonah, but he was mine anyway.

"I'm sorry. I didn't want to ruin tonight."

We'd had a beautiful day. The two of us had a picnic in Hyde Park in the afternoon, followed by dinner out after we'd done some last-minute shopping together. We'd watched a movie in the games room as my parents were out with Grandpa and Lily. My siblings were doing their own thing.

His hands left my arms, cupping my face instead. My breath hitched.

"Don't run, please. I need you."

"Where do you think I'm going to go? This is my room," I ground out.

He pressed his forehead to mine.

"You pushed me away last time things got too much."

As if my self-loathing wasn't bad enough already, what he said made it intensify. I could only apologise for my actions so many times. If only he knew how much I'd already beaten myself up over it. If only he could see the extent of my brokenness. I hadn't let him. No one was allowed to see how damaged I was inside. How much I hated everything about myself. I didn't see what everyone else saw. This useless boy who couldn't even admit the truth of who he was to himself.

"I'm not doing that."

"Aren't you?"

"I'm trying not to lose my shit with you right now. I'd appreciate it if you stopped pushing me."

Jonah let go of me, pulling back and staring at me with no small amount of pain in his eyes.

"I'm sorry."

"Sorry doesn't change anything you've just said, J."

I didn't want to be angry. This was the worst thing to happen the night before he was due to go back to Durham. All I'd wanted was to hold him tight and forget it was happening. I couldn't do that now.

"Raphi…"

"No, you equated me not being ready to tell anyone about us to you living with a guy you've had sex with. I don't even know what to do with that right now."

Was I being unreasonable? I had no idea. All of this didn't sit well with me.

The horrified look in his eyes affected me. I hated upsetting him. Hated seeing the agony in his expression.

"You're… you're not breaking up with me, right?" he asked in a small voice.

I froze at his words. I'd already told him I wasn't going anywhere. What on earth would give him that idea? I felt worse than ever. All of this shit was my fault. I'd made it hard for him to trust me to stay, even though I'd spent the past eight weeks trying to show him I wanted to be with him. I wanted this to work. I needed it to.

"No, J, that's not what's happening here. I want to be with you. I want this. I'm just… angry with the situation. And angry you didn't tell me sooner."

Why did he have to look so broken? I couldn't take it. It hurt to see him like this. I leant back against the headboard and reached for him, pulling him against me and forcing him to rest his head on my chest. I stroked his blonde hair as Jonah wrapped his arms around my body.

"I need you," he whispered. "I really need you so you can't leave me."

"I'm right here, *cuore mio*, I told you already, you have me. I'm yours, but I need a minute to calm down."

He kissed my chest. I didn't want to hurt Jonah any more than I already had. Whilst I didn't think I could be okay with him living in the same house as the guy he'd been intimate with, I could deal with it. Or at least try to. It would've been worse if they'd had a relationship. It was just sex. It didn't mean anything, did it? What Jonah and I had was more than physical. He and I shared a connection. We could talk to each other about anything and he understood me more than most.

"How did it happen?" I asked.

I didn't want to know, but the need to ease my fears about it overrode that.

"He jokingly suggested he could teach me when he found out I was a virgin… and I'd only ever kissed one boy."

That boy being me. Had he kissed this… Robin? The name made me want to punch a wall but I didn't. I continued to stroke Jonah's hair and hope I could stay calm enough to listen to the rest of this.

"What started as a joke soon became serious. It's not like I'm really attracted to him, to be honest. He's a bit of a manwhore who will fuck anything with a pulse, but… but I wanted to know what it felt like. What I even liked. So we did everything… well, not everything, but you know, the basics."

I hated myself for wanting to know details. Jonah had that experience with some guy who clearly didn't want anything other than sex. He deserved more. The man I was holding should have had someone to care for him. To love him.

It should have been you. All of this should have been you.

Those thoughts only fucked me up more.

"That's how you learnt you don't like to top."

"I'm willing to try with you if you wanted to. It didn't feel right with him."

I hadn't actually considered it to be a possibility. I liked what we had now. Our dynamic was fine the way it was.

"Honestly? I haven't thought about it. You're not unhappy with the way things are now, are you?"

"No, I'm happy… more than happy. I'm just saying if you wanted to, then I would. I'd do anything for you, Raphi."

For some reason, it didn't make me feel good. I didn't want that kind of power over him. The bedroom was different. There I liked having control. Outside of it? I wanted Jonah to make his own choices.

"And I don't want you to do anything you're uncomfortable with."

He turned his head up towards me, his green eyes so full of emotion.

"I want to make you happy."

"You already do. I don't need you to do more."

"Will you do something for me then?"

I cocked my head to the side.

"If you tell me what it is, I'll certainly try."

He smiled then.

"Can you put all of that aside for the rest of the night and give me something to remember you by whilst I'm away?"

CHAPTER THIRTY ONE

Raphael

It took me a long second to work out what he wanted from me. It had been my intention to end our night with sex, but after hearing about Robin, I wasn't entirely in the mood. The whole thing left me with a sour taste in my mouth.

How could I not give him what he wanted though? I already felt like I didn't deserve him. Denying him something made me feel terrible. Especially since neither of us had made any plans to see each other before Christmas. It would be a long time to go without having any physical contact.

"Come here then," I murmured.

He shifted upright and straddled my lap. I let him lean forward and kiss me, his hands moving to tangle in my hair. It wasn't full of our usual passion and fire, more sweet and gentle. Jonah could set the pace tonight. This was for him. To remind him I was his and he didn't need to worry me going anywhere. His insecurities weighed heavily on me since I contributed to them by not being ready to open up to anyone else except Duke about our relationship.

"I don't want to go," he whispered against my lips. "I hate that I have to be away from you."

"I know. It's only a year and then you'll be here in the city again."

He'd told me he'd be applying for a postgradudate place down here after getting some work experience. I could wait a year for him to be back here. I'd be busy with university myself, so I wasn't too worried. We could survive it if we tried hard enough. If things didn't get fucked up. If I could learn to accept who I was and be honest with the people I loved.

I didn't know if I was doing enough to reassure him as I gripped his hips and kissed him a little harder. He didn't need to be scared. Or maybe he did. I had no idea at this point. My fucked up inability to stop this cycle of self-hatred concerned me. It's like the more I tried to be okay with myself, the less I felt capable of it.

Stop thinking about that. Concentrate on Jonah. He needs you right now.

I had to shove aside everything else. His needs were the most important thing tonight.

My hands went to his t-shirt, pushing it up his chest. He pulled back to allow me to discard it and mine too. I don't think I'd ever get over how much I adored this man. His skin against mine. His handsome features. The way he shivered when I touched him.

His hands roamed across my chest as he kissed me again. It felt like he was committing the contours of my body to memory. All the blood was rushing down to my cock, making me painfully hard.

How the fuck could I go weeks without seeing him? I needed him as much as he needed me.

"I want to taste you," I whispered as my hand stroked down his hard cock. "I want you to fuck my mouth, J."

He groaned. I might not be particularly interested in letting him fuck me, but I did love it when his dick was in my mouth. The way he panted and moaned. Giving him pleasure turned me on. I hadn't asked him to take control before. It was always me dictating how things would go. Tonight I wanted something different.

He pulled back and tugged his boxers off. I marvelled at the sight of this man I was captivated by. The man I was in love with. He rose up on his knees, bracing a hand against the wall whilst I leant forward and took his cock in my mouth. I wrapped a hand around his hip, encouraging him to give it to me. The other gripped his thigh as an anchor.

"Fuck," he whimpered as his dick sunk deeper.

I kept my mouth wide enough so I could take him. His little pants gave me the impression he liked this. But it was his hand gripping the back of my head which confirmed it. He pulled back and shoved himself deeper, almost making me gag, but I didn't care. I wanted him to do this.

"Raphi, fuck, yes."

I stared up at him. He leant over me, his hand still planted on the wall and his breathing ragged. His eyes were wild with his desire and pent up need.

That's it, J, fuck my mouth. Take your pleasure from me. Come down my throat.

I couldn't say those words to him, but I hoped my expression and eyes betrayed my thoughts. All I wanted was to give him this night. Then he could survive without me when he was back at university. The desperation in his voice when he told me he needed me almost broke my heart clean in two. Only now did I realise how deeply his feelings for me ran. And it scared me. It shouldn't, but my fears of disappointing him and fucking things up because I couldn't cope with my own crap made it so.

I don't want to hurt him again. I have to get my shit together. For him.

It should be for me, but I'd tried to do that many times. It didn't work. Nothing I did worked. I was too screwed up in the head to ever be fixed. Sometimes I wondered if I even deserved to be. If I was even worth saving. Jonah clearly thought I was, but it didn't matter what other people thought. It mattered what I saw. And it wasn't anything good.

Some days the only reason I even kept going was the knowledge it would hurt those I loved if I wasn't here any longer. I knew what it was like to watch someone go through that kind of loss. I wouldn't wish it on anyone.

My focus should be on Jonah right now, not on my own self-pitying bullshit.

I stared up at my beautiful man, whose movements were growing more erratic by the second. His grip on the back of my head tightened. I could feel him getting closer to the edge. His eyes had glazed over in his pursuit of an orgasm.

Perhaps this would be enough for him tonight. Fuck knows I had too much shit on my mind to lose myself in it. And not being able to only fuelled my self-loathing. I wanted to be with him. To be in this fully. It wasn't fair on him to be lost in my own crap.

"Going to… fuck…"

He shuddered above me as he came violently in my mouth. I let him, trying not to allow any of it to escape.

I hope this makes you happy, J. I hope I've done enough to reassure you. Fuck, do I hope I've given you what you need.

He pulled out of my mouth and slumped down in my lap. I swallowed before tugging him against me and stroking his back. Jonah rested his head on my shoulder, breathing heavily.

"Okay?" I whispered.

"Mmm."

I smiled. He was too high off coming to give me an actual response. I kissed his hair and held him tighter. My guilt over everything between us ate me up inside, but I shoved it away. I tried to keep some semblance of normality, then he wouldn't know what was running through my mind.

After a few minutes, he pulled back and smiled at me. He reached up and stroked my face.

"Do you want me to?"

I shook my head.

"You don't have to."

He ran his other hand down my bare chest.

"I want to."

I was stuck between a rock and a hard place. Whilst I wasn't fully in the mood, I didn't want to upset him. All I could think about was making him happy. Doing what he wanted. Him pissing me off this evening by springing the Robin revelation on me didn't matter. I couldn't do anything but give Jonah what he needed.

"Okay."

His smile widened. I bit my lip as he shifted back and pulled me out. The moment he wrapped his mouth and hand around me, I dug my fingers in his hair. He knew exactly how to make me feel good. I couldn't help but groan. His mouth was heavenly.

"J," I hissed, shoving him down further on my cock. "Don't stop."

My instinct to take control overrode anything else. I directed him with my hand, setting the pace. It's what he liked, me telling him what to do, taking what I wanted.

"You like that, don't you? Taking it all."

He moaned around my cock, the vibrations making me crazy. I let the sensations drown me. I lost myself to him and these last moments we had before we'd be without each other.

"Jonah, fuck… that's it." I could feel him struggling with the whole thing, but I didn't let him up quite yet. "So good for me."

He ran a hand up my stomach as I released my grip on his head. He coughed a little when he pulled off me to catch his breath. Didn't take him long to suck me again, working me with his hand at the same time. I gripped the covers below me, rolling my head back against the headboard. For those moments, the war going on in my head disappeared. It would come back with vengeance later, but I could deal with it. I always did.

When I came, it was with a groan of his name and my body shuddering from the release. Jonah settled next to me after pulling on his boxers and tucking me back away. I slid down the bed and tugged the covers over us. It was getting late. He was leaving in the morning to catch his train. I turned out the lamp, knowing it was time we got some sleep.

Jonah pulled me against his front, curling his arms around me and cradling me against his chest. He kissed my hair. I fought back against telling him I didn't want him to go. I needed him here to get through my bullshit. I said nothing. Merely listened to the sound of his heart thumping in his chest where my face was pressed to it.

"Would you be okay with me telling Robin and Damien we're together?" he whispered.

"Is Damien your other housemate?"

"Yeah, he's… well, Meredith calls him uptight and I suppose that's an accurate description. Keeps to himself mostly and thoroughly disapproves of Robin's exploits."

I'd already decided I didn't like Robin, but I was biased. If I ever met the guy, I would be civil because I wasn't the type of person to get confrontational. Wouldn't stop me wishing he'd never touched my Jonah.

"You can tell them."

I wanted that dickhead to know I'd staked my claim on Jonah. He was mine and no one else was going to have him. My possessiveness when it came to this man holding me knew no bounds.

You really do sound like Quinn.

All of my dads were pretty possessive over my mum, but Quinn was the worst for it. I guess this was a tick in the box for nurture over nature. I might be a lot like my biological father, but I'd been raised by four very different men and one headstrong woman. They'd rubbed off on me in different ways. I hadn't yet realised it until now.

"Thank you. I don't want there to be any misunderstandings. I'm all yours, Raphi. There's never going to be anyone else for me but you."

There he went again, scaring me with his feelings. It didn't matter if I loved him more than life itself. I couldn't safely say we would work out in the long run. Not when I was so fucked in the head. Him saying things like that put pressure on me to fix myself. I wanted to be someone who deserved him.

Are you even capable of that? You're still just as messed up as you were three years ago. You still can't accept who you are.

Whilst Jonah fell asleep, I lay there trying to work out how the hell I was going to make this better. I didn't have the answers. And it fucking killed me.

All I wanted was for us to survive. And yet… the biggest obstacle I had was myself.

CHAPTER THIRTY TWO

Raphael

I stood at the front door with my hand cupping Jonah's cheek. He turned his face into my palm and placed a kiss on it. We'd already shared a rather passionate and heartfelt goodbye kiss in my bedroom. Not to mention before when I'd woken him up with sex. Very hot, passionate and rough sex. I'd had to put my hand over his mouth to stifle his moans and cries. I wasn't about to let him go without one last fuck since last night had become a bit of a mess.

"Let me know when you get there, yeah?" I said, giving him a smile.

"I will."

"I'll see you then."

I dropped my hand, feeling bereft without his touch but knowing I had to let go. He gave me a warm smile before turning and walking down the steps. I watched him make his way up the road, my heart thumping as he turned back and waved. It sunk when he turned the corner and disappeared from sight. I shut the door and leant my head against it.

I hate this. How will I cope without him? He keeps me from drowning.

"You might want to cheer up before our parents see you and start asking questions about why you're so forlorn," Duke's voice came from behind me.

I pulled away from the door and turned to look at him. He'd poked his head out of the living room.

"Shut up."

"I'm just saying."

"Well, don't. I'm not in the mood."

My mind was already at war with itself over Jonah leaving. Over him being away from me. I did not want to deal with my brother poking holes in my fragile state. It wouldn't help matters.

I walked away towards the kitchen, hearing Duke's footsteps as he followed me.

"It would have been the perfect opportunity to tell them about the two of you."

I stiffened as I reached the fridge. The thought of admitting to my parents I was in a relationship with Jonah made my skin itch.

"I don't know why you keep insisting I should tell them."

"They already suspect it, so why don't you come clean?"

I turned around and glared at him.

"You know why."

Duke rolled his eyes, crossing his arms over his chest as he leant up against the kitchen island.

"They're going to accept it if you're with a man."

"That's not what this is about."

It had never been about anyone else's opinion. Never. Maybe it had started that way when I was being bullied. Their words had only fed into the insecurities I already had, amplifying them. I couldn't ignore them any longer.

"Jesus, Raphi. It's not that hard. All you have to do is say… Mum, Dads, Jonah and I are together… that's it."

"Fuck off. I know what to say."

Duke really did like to stick his oar in where it wasn't wanted. I'd told him a thousand times it had more to do with my feelings as opposed to theirs. He could hardly talk anyway with the shit he was keeping from them.

"Then why don't you do it? You're a grown man, just own up to it. What difference does it make if they know or not? It's not going to change how you feel about yourself and would give Mum some fucking peace of mind when it comes to you. You know how she gets."

"Don't use her against me."

He threw his hands up. I turned away and opened the fridge, wishing he'd drop the subject. Grabbing the milk, I set it on the counter. I filled the kettle with water and flipped it on before digging out a couple of mugs from the cupboard.

"I wouldn't have to if you didn't keep getting in your own way all the time. I'm surprised he hasn't said anything to you about it."

I clenched my fist. Jonah had last night, before apologising profusely. Didn't matter. The damage was already done. My inability to be honest was wearing thin on him. And I couldn't blame him. It was on me. All on me.

"He's giving me the time I need because he understands why it's hard for me."

My words sounded hollow to my own ears. The real reason he was doing it was because he didn't want me to leave him. He didn't want to push me for fear I would walk out the door.

"No, he's doing it because he loves you, Raphi. Don't kid yourself into thinking anything else."

"How the fuck would you know that?"

Jonah doesn't love me, does he?

My brain was laughing at my expense. There was no other explanation. He loved me. It was the only reason he'd put up with my shit. The only reason anyone ever put up with being kept a secret. Love.

"You are blind if you don't see the way he looks at you." He waved his hands over his eyes. "It's like he's got fucking stars in his eyes. I don't even have to ask him to know how he feels about you. It's obvious to me so it's going to be obvious to other people. You're in denial since you can't get your fucking shit straight. If you said jump, he'd ask how high, that's how much he loves you. With the way you're going right now, you're going to lose the only person who's ever made you happy. Stop being such a fucking coward and admit you have a boyfriend who you're in love with too."

Since Duke was the only person who knew the truth, the three of us had hung out together more than once. Duke wanted to get to know the man I was with since I was his little brother and he saw it as his duty to protect me. He always had. Duke might like to portray himself as this unfeeling, emotionless manwhore, but it wasn't the real man inside. He was sensitive and caring. He loved with everything he had. It's the way all of us were. Maybe because we'd grown up surrounded by that kind of love.

"I can't."

He gave me a look. I hated how all of his words were true. They cut into me, making my heart bleed. It wasn't Duke's fault. He wanted what was best for me. Tough love was the way he dealt with this kind of shit. I was the one at fault. It was always me.

"It's your funeral… but don't think I won't be here for you when it comes to a head, okay? I'm always here for you."

I looked away, staring at the kettle as his words sunk in. It would come to a point where I'd have to deal with it. All I'd done for the whole summer was put it off to allow me to enjoy the time I had with Jonah. There were no expectations. No need to poke my head out of our bubble. Reality had intruded now. And reality was a bitch.

"Oh, morning."

I looked around finding Aurora's boyfriend standing in the doorway with a dazed look and slightly swollen lips as if he'd been ravaged. I hid a smile. No doubt she'd sent him out here after rocking his world.

"Morning," Duke said, his eyes twinkling. "Surprised you're here, does Quinn know?"

I almost snorted. Quinn might have begrudgingly accepted Logan wasn't going anywhere even after all the shit between him and Aurora, but it didn't mean our super overprotective father approved of the guy. Our sister was determined to be with Logan anyway no matter what Quinn thought. I admired her for it. She wasn't scared to be who she was and choose who she wanted.

You're the one who's a coward.

It wasn't just me. Duke was as bad if not worse.

"He doesn't," Logan said as he walked further into the room. "You two planning on telling him?"

"Do you want me to?"

Logan rolled his eyes. He was used to Duke by now.

"You making tea?" Logan asked me as he came to settle nearby.

"Yeah, do you want me to do some for you and Rora?"

"Please."

I got two more mugs out and dumped tea bags in them. Luckily I'd filled the kettle, so I could do all four mugs. I leant against the counter whilst I waited for them to brew.

"Where are our parents, anyway?" I asked, directing my question at Duke.

"They left early, got to prepare for a big staff meeting today."

Cole trudged in then, giving us all the once over before seating himself at the kitchen island on one of the stools.

"Tea?" I asked, grabbing another mug anyway.

He grunted in response, laying his head on the counter.

"What's wrong with you?" Duke asked.

"Didn't you hear? He's actually having to work hard now with his apprenticeship," I said, grinning.

Cole stuck a finger up at me. He'd been like this for the past few weeks since he started at the garage.

"Aww, is manual labour kicking your arse, little bro?"

"Just a bit," Cole admitted.

I finished all five cups of tea with milk and sugar for those who wanted it. I pushed two mugs towards Logan and took one over to Cole. Aurora chose that moment to walk in, looking perfectly put together as usual. She walked straight over to Logan who gave her a warm smile.

"When you telling Daddy you're moving out?" Duke asked, picking up his mug which I'd left by the kettle.

Aurora huffed and leant against the counter next to her boyfriend.

"Soon."

"Quinn's going to hit the roof," Cole said, picking himself up off the counter. "Not to mention Mum."

"I'm an adult, they'll have to deal with it."

We all knew Logan had asked Aurora to move in with him. Our parents didn't. She was waiting for the right opportunity to tell them.

"Mum's not ready for me to leave. Doubt she's going to be happy about you," I said, sipping my tea.

When I'd told her I wanted to move out into halls for university, she'd cried buckets. Dad had to comfort her for half an hour before she calmed down. He'd been fine about my decision. I think he understood I wanted to find myself since he was the only one other than Duke who knew what plagued me. I'd had a few more conversations with him about it over the summer. His advice about therapy still stood, but I wasn't ready to take those steps. Wasn't ready to admit defeat. I still held on to hope I could fix myself.

You're an idiot for thinking that. You can't fix yourself. You're too broken.

I shoved my wayward thoughts away.

"That's why I'm not telling them yet."

I watched Logan's eyes darken. Whilst Aurora had said he was fine with waiting, I wasn't sure how true it was. He might be the only guy capable of dealing with my sister, but he still had a battle on his hands with her. Aurora liked to get her own way. Probably why they worked. He didn't take shit off her.

My phone buzzed in my pocket. I tugged it out, unable to help the smile on my face when I saw who it was from.

Jonah: Just leaving to catch the train now. Miss you already.

Raphi: Miss you too. Don't forget to send me a train selfie.

I got a winking face back.

"You should tell them, Rora," I said, still staring down at my phone. "Take the heat off me since I'm moving out tomorrow. Reckon Mum's going to be crying for days."

When I looked up, my sister was giving me evils, but my brothers and Logan were smirking, their eyes full of amusement.

"Don't know why you're laughing. You lot are going to have to deal with her whilst I'll be living it up in halls."

I slid my phone back in my pocket, watching my brothers' faces fall. I doubted I'd do too much living it up, but I did plan on having fun during freshers' week. Jonah kept telling me I should have a proper university experience. I was going to try to. I'd be away from home and could do what I wanted without my parents watching my every move for the first time in my life.

"Shit. She's going to be a nightmare," Duke complained, rubbing his face.

"Our dads can deal with her," Cole muttered. "I'm too fucking tired for that."

I smiled. As much as I was looking forward to going to university, I was going to miss my family. They might be a crazy bunch, but they were everything to me all the same. Being away from them was going to take a lot of getting used to, but I was ready for it.

What I wasn't ready for was being without Jonah and how it would break me down piece by piece. And how that would push both of us over the edge.

I wasn't ready for it at all.

CHAPTER THIRTY THREE

Jonah

nlocking the front door, I hauled my suitcases into the house I shared with Robin and Damien. They'd both stayed here over the summer. I'd come back early as I had a lot of shit to catch up on. Most of my time had been spent working at the care home and with Raphi, so I was behind. It didn't bother me since being with him was worth every moment. Every day I was in his presence, I fell deeper in love with the boy who'd stolen my heart three years ago and had kept it with him ever since.

I took my suitcases up to my room and set them down before trudging back downstairs into the living room. Both Damien and Robin were in there, although they were sitting at opposite ends of the room since they weren't particularly big fans of each other.

"Hey, man," Robin said, giving me a lopsided grin.

"How're things?" I asked as I slumped down on the sofa.

"Good. You enjoyed your time down south?"

I shrugged and tried not to smile too hard.

"Yeah, it was good."

"Good? Looks like it was way better than just good."

I glanced at Damien who was eyeing Robin with contempt. The three of us had ended up getting a place together out of ease as opposed to anything else. It was like Raphi said, I only had a year left then I could go back to London. It reminded me I was meant to text him to say I'd got here. I pulled out my phone.

"I had a nice time with Mer is all."

Jonah: Got here okay. You all packed for tomorrow?

Raphi's parents were helping him move into student halls tomorrow. He'd been looking forward to it. As much as he loved his family, he wanted his own space. In a lot of ways, he needed to find himself. This gave him the opportunity to do so.

"Why don't I believe that?"

"You're a nosey bastard that's why," Damien muttered.

Robin gave Damien a dirty look before turning back to me. "Well?"

My phone started ringing in my hand. I bit my lip as I stared down at the screen.

"I have to take this, sorry."

I jumped up and hurried out of the room before either of them could say a word, shoving my phone to my ear.

"Hey."

"I'm not disturbing your reunion with your housemates, am I?"

I shook my head as I took the stairs two by two. I could hear the disdain in his voice but it wasn't directed at me. No, it was for Robin who I was pretty sure my boyfriend hated if his reaction to what I'd told him last night was anything to go by. I'd known I should have told him weeks ago about Robin and me. It wasn't my proudest moment. Raphi had every right to be pissed at me for it.

"Of course not."

Raphi knew I'd always make time for him.

"I haven't finished packing yet. Still trying to decide what to take and what to leave. Not like I'll be far away from home so it's not that important."

I reached my bedroom and shut myself in, taking a seat at my desk.

"You want to be comfortable though."

"I'll be fine. I have your train selfie if I get sad."

I snorted.

"You have way better pictures of me than that."

"There's a certain charm about this one. You look like you want to be anywhere else than in that seat."

The train ride up here had been boring as hell. I'd listened to music and read a book, but my mind kept wandering back to Raphi. How I wanted things to work out. And how I regretted ever mentioning the fact he hadn't told anyone except Duke about us yet. I'd met his parents on several occasions now. Hell, they probably suspected there was more to us than friendship.

The strange thing about meeting them had been the realisation they were just normal people. They might have done a lot of fucked up shit in the past, but it was clear to see they loved their kids and would do anything for them and each other. It made me regret my objections to Cole and Meredith's relationship even more.

"I was bored."

"Poor thing, wish I'd have been there to entertain you."

"Not sure your form of entertainment is allowed on public transport."

He laughed. The rich sound of it made my heart melt. Hell, did I adore everything about him. How on earth would I survive until Christmas without Raphi?

"That wasn't what I had in mind. Didn't I satisfy you enough earlier?"

My face grew hot thinking about the way he'd pinned me down on his bed with his hand over my mouth, stopping me from making too much noise. The absolute brutal pounding he'd given me. How I'd ended up coming not once, but twice because of it.

"You did."

"You don't sound very convinced."

"I'm just remembering it."

One of the many things I'd miss whilst I was up here. We weren't sex-mad for each other or anything, we just had a healthy amount of it. It was the intimacy I'd miss the most.

Being close to him. Sleeping next to him. Talking to him about everything and nothing.

"Oh yeah? You not walking funny or anything?"

I could hear the amusement in his voice.

"Oh my god, no, I'm fine."

It's not like he'd hurt me or been too rough. Raphi knew what I could take and never went too far.

"You're definitely fine."

I put my fingers to my lips, feeling how wide my smile was. He knew I blushed when he complimented me. I hadn't got used to it. I wasn't sure I ever would.

"Flatterer."

"Just a boy waiting patiently until your fine arse comes back home."

There were too many weeks until then. Far too many.

"You'll survive. You've got freshers to look forward to."

"I know. I'm just feeling sad right now. I'm leaving home and you're not here. Feels like so much has changed in the last few months. I'm trying to cope with it all, but it's hard."

If I was with him, I'd hold him tight and tell him it would be okay. He had me. I'd help him cope. What good was I hundreds of miles away?

"Change is hard, so it's normal to feel overwhelmed by it. If it gets too much, I'm only a phone call away, okay? I promise I'll be here whenever you need me."

"I miss you and you've only been gone hours. It doesn't feel real that I won't get to see you for weeks."

My heart was in a vice. What I wouldn't do to be there with him. He revealed a lot about himself in those few words. He wasn't coping very well. Raphi hid a lot of his true feelings deep inside of him. The way he could never see himself in a positive light. How he blamed himself for everything bad in his life. He lived with too much pain inside. I tried to help him but there was only so much I could do. Being there for him didn't feel like enough. Especially not at times like this. When he sounded like he might break apart inside.

"I know we never talked about it, but I can come down and see you before Christmas."

"You'd do that?"

"Yeah… need to check on my sister too, you know."

He laughed a little.

"Your troublesome sister."

Meredith had been better over the summer now she wasn't seeing Cole all the time at school. She was happy to be at university. I'd helped her move into halls a couple of days ago. There was no way she wanted to stay with Mum and Grandma. I couldn't blame her, what with the way they treated my sister. I wasn't looking forward to moving back home when I'd finished up with university, but I could deal with them more than Meredith ever could. Probably since I didn't care what they thought of me any longer. Not when Mum had admitted she didn't want us. It made it easy to stop giving a shit. I'd grown a lot over the past couple of years whilst I'd been at university. Learnt how to survive on my own. I had a thicker skin. There were only two things in my life which made me vulnerable. My two weaknesses.

Firstly, my sister. And secondly, the boy I was talking to right now. The one who held my heart tight in his fist. He had the power to break me. I'd given that to him. When it came to love, you had to take the risk. Had to be willing to give up everything to be with the person you wanted more than life itself.

That was Raphi for me. I didn't doubt he would always be that person for me. Giving him up wasn't an option now he'd let me in. Now he'd shown me what true passion and a bond between two people felt like. How could I ever go back?

"She'll be fine without me. Besides, she has you."

"She's already been texting me, asking to meet up. Says I'm a dick for blowing her off most of the summer."

Meredith had no idea I was the reason he'd not seen much of her. We'd taken up most of each other's time knowing we had to be apart when university started. My sister didn't suspect a thing. She was happy I was getting out more and being sociable. I'd always been a loner on the whole considering crowds bothered me. Not to mention the multitude of emotions coming off all those people. That was the worst. I just about handled dealing with the emotional turmoil of those close to me.

"She just misses you is all."

"I've already arranged to meet up with her at the weekend. Don't worry, I'll keep an eye on her for you even if you don't really need me to."

He knew how much I worried about her. The whole thing between me, him, Cole and Meredith was water under the bridge. It happened. I couldn't take it back. Perhaps one day those two could work it out, but the last time I'd talked to

Meredith, she'd been pretty determined to forget Cole Carter ever existed.

"Thank you, it means a lot."

It hadn't surprised me she'd remained friends with Raphi after her breakup with his brother. Meredith had never been the type to take sides, only placing blame on the person who'd actually done wrong. I hadn't told her what Raphi had done to me three years ago. I hadn't wanted to ruin their friendship. Even when I'd been mad at him, I'd still appreciated the way he'd been there for my sister, especially after Celia turned on her. I couldn't say I was sorry they weren't friends any longer. That girl was cruel to people for the fun of it.

"You're welcome. I should go, this packing isn't going to do itself and my parents will be back from their meeting soon. I promised I'd help Dad with dinner, plus my parents are all like, you have to spend your last night with us. Going to be busy for the rest of the day."

"Okay. Text me before you go to sleep, yeah?"

"Will do, bye, J."

"Bye."

I love you.

It kept getting harder and harder to stop myself from saying those words to him. Raphi wasn't ready to hear them. Plus, I'd promised myself I wouldn't say them until he could be open about our relationship. The fact he'd even said yes to me telling Damien and Robin was a big step for him.

I stuffed my phone in my pocket and went downstairs again, dropping into the kitchen to make a cup of coffee. My two housemates were still watching TV when I sat down on the sofa again.

"Important phone call?" Robin asked.

I had a feeling he wouldn't drop it until I told him what I'd done over the summer.

"It was my boyfriend."

Both Damien and Robin stared at me. The entire time they'd known me, I'd never expressed interest in anyone. I hadn't even told Robin about Raphi when the whole topic of sex had come up that night. It didn't feel right.

"You got a boyfriend whilst you were back home?"

"Yeah."

"Well, fuck me."

"Congrats, J. Does he have a name?" Damien asked, giving Robin a scathing look.

I rubbed my chest before sipping my coffee.

"Raphi... I've known him for a long time. Guess we got closer over the summer."

It was the safest explanation. I didn't feel like getting into it with anyone about what had really gone down between me and Raphi.

"So it'll be long distance whilst you're up here?"

I nodded, hating the reminder.

"Well, I hope it all works out for you."

"He good in bed?" Robin asked.

Damien glared at him and I rolled my eyes.

"Yeah, I'm definitely not telling you that."

"Of course, that's all you care about," Damien muttered. "It's all sex, sex, sex with you."

"No point dating someone if they're shit in bed," Robin said, "A mundane sex life is the worst thing I could think of."

Robin let Damien's barbs roll off him all the time. The guy was way too laid back about everything in life. Probably why he was coasting through university, not really giving a shit about his grades and only caring about having fun.

"There's more to life than sex, Robin. Jonah knows that, but you don't seem to want to get it into your thick skull."

"Whatever, virgin boy. Sex is what gives us life."

"Fuck you, I'm not a virgin."

"No? How come in the two years I've known you, you've never brought a girl around?"

"As if I'd bring a girl anywhere near you. You'd be trying to get between her legs within two minutes of meeting her."

I sipped my coffee, ignoring their argument because it would no doubt escalate further. For once, I didn't feel like intervening. How they'd survived without me here as a buffer was beyond me, but they could fight it out all they wanted. It was all futile considering in less than a year, we'd all be finished with university and going our separate ways. No way in hell I was staying here any longer than I needed to. Not when I wanted to be back home with my sister. And not when I had Raphi.

I'd fight for what I had with him even if it broke me. I'd meant what I said to him weeks ago. He was worth all the pain. All of it. Every last second. I wouldn't let him go for anything.

CHAPTER THIRTY FOUR

Jonah

It took three weeks. Just three weeks for me to break. I had a lot of shit to get on with now I was back at university, but it didn't matter. I missed Raphi so much, it fucking hurt. Didn't help I'd had to listen about all the crazy shit he'd got up to during freshers. The parties. The drinking. All of it. I wasn't insecure and I didn't think he would do anything with another person, but I hated I wasn't having those experiences with him.

I stepped off the train at St Pancras into the late Friday afternoon rush hour. The sheer amount of people made my skin itch, but I followed the crowd on the platform towards the barriers. The journey down here had been long and boring. It would be worth it to see him for the weekend. I hadn't told my sister I was here, which was kind of shitty of me, but all I cared about was being with my boyfriend. Reminding myself we were okay. We had each other.

I swiped my card over the barriers and walked through into the station. What I was met with had me stopping in my tracks and someone almost bumped into the back of me. I heard some grumbling but I honestly didn't care. Standing several feet away by one of the big departure boards was my boyfriend. He had his hands in his coat pockets, his hair all windswept and the biggest smile on his face. I'd told Raphi what train I was getting, but I hadn't expected him to be here to meet me. I thought he had a lecture, so I was going to make my way to his halls and wait for him.

My feet carried me through the crowd to him. My hands itched to touch him. Every inch of me needed the man in front of me. When I reached him, I didn't know what to do. We were in public. It wasn't like I could grab him and kiss him.

Fuck, I've missed you so much.

"You're here," I said, all other words disappearing from my mind.

"You had the long journey down here, the least I could do was show up."

He shrugged and smiled wider. I could hardly breathe. Being close to him had me struggling not to melt into a puddle of goo. He looked good.

"You didn't skip your lecture, did you?"

He shook his head.

"No, I ran out the moment it was over so I could get the tube here. It's lucky your train was delayed by five minutes or I'd have been late and might have missed you."

The thought of him making the trip to meet me at the station had my heart racing in my chest. If I ever doubted his feelings for me, I had no reason to now.

"You should have texted me or something. I would have waited."

"And ruin the surprise?" Raphi reached out and took my hand, his green eyes twinkling. "Come on, let's go get dinner before we head to my halls."

I followed him through the crowd down to the tube. We were squished up together in the carriage after we got on, but it was okay. I was with Raphi. He kept me grounded. We didn't talk much during the journey, but he kept a tight hold of my hand. Raphi hadn't been particularly touchy-feely with me in public before. Made me wonder if he was finally coming around to the idea of being open about our relationship. It could be wishful thinking on my part. I wasn't going to get my hopes up.

When we got out of the underground up onto the street, I sucked in the cool air, finally able to breathe after being stuck in the stuffy atmosphere of the tube.

"You okay?" Raphi asked, squeezing my hand as he pulled me away from the entrance.

"Yeah. I don't miss rush hour."

He grinned and knocked my shoulder with his.

"Did you miss me?"

"Like you wouldn't know."

He bit his lip, making me wish I could kiss him. I'd not felt this man's hands and lips on me for three weeks. My skin craved his touch. I ached for him all over.

"I knew that already, considering you're here now. I distinctly remember you telling me two days ago you couldn't wait any longer."

"Shut up."

"You all shy today, J?"

I swear to god he loved to wind me up. And I did too because it was us. Raphi and me. That easiness between us when we weren't having emotionally charged conversations. When he didn't have the weight of the world on his shoulders and could just be with me.

"Maybe."

"I can tell, you're blushing."

I rolled my eyes, hating how hot my face felt.

"Totally your fault."

He leant closer, his breath dusting across my ear. I shivered. It didn't take much for me to get aroused when Raphi was near me. He knew exactly what he was doing as well.

"I'll take it. Your blushes are the most adorable thing in the world, especially when you're all hot and bothered from my words."

"You aren't playing fair."

"Have I ever?"

"Playing fair is boring."

He squeezed my hand, making me attempt to hide my smile, but I was completely unable to. Being with him again was the happiest I'd been since I'd left for Durham. Knowing I had almost two days of uninterrupted time with this man was like being brought back to life after my world went dark.

"How mad do you reckon Mer will be if she finds out you came down here and didn't see her?"

"I dread to even think about it. I reckon I'd be given the bollocking of the century."

Raphi snorted. My sister had one hell of a temper when she lost it. It was usually accompanied by tears of frustration, which she hated. It always made me feel shit when I made her cry. It broke my fucking heart to see her in pain, upset or angry.

Raphi pulled me into a little Vietnamese place. The wait staff seemed to recognise him as they seated us.

"You come here often?" I asked as I looked over the menu.

"Probably too much for only being here for three weeks. These girls on my floor suggested it and now you can't keep us away."

I'd promised myself I would not get jealousy issues over him hanging out with other people, especially not girls. Insecurity kept rearing its ugly fucking head because Raphi couldn't be honest about us being together with anyone else but Duke.

"What girls?"

I almost smacked my hand against my head.

You couldn't leave it alone, could you?

"Immi, Tara and Erica. They're cool, if a bit posh."

Do they like him? What if they ask if he's single? What's he going to say? That he is? He's not. He's mine.

I hated myself for those thoughts. He hadn't mentioned those three girls before. Maybe it's what set me off. Who fucking knew? I had to keep my shit together.

Raphi reached out and took one of my hands off the menu, entwining our fingers together on the table. I stared down at them, wondering if my insecurities were written all over my face. If he was capable of reading my moods.

"I told them about you."

My eyes flicked up to his, shock rushing through my system.

"What?"

"Well, I said I was seeing someone. They asked me all sorts of questions. I didn't answer, just said you were special, which you are, by the way. So special, *cuore mio*."

I swear my heart was going to burst out of my chest, it was so full. Raphi had admitted to people other than Duke he was taken. We were together. It might not be his parents, but it was another giant leap for him.

"I didn't want anyone getting the wrong idea, you know, because I'm yours."

"Raphi…"

"Don't make this into a big deal, J, please. It's not like I said you're a guy and I have a…" he faltered.

Raphi had a huge issue with saying the word boyfriend. I never called him it to his face. I'd not asked him why he couldn't say it. For some reason, I didn't think he had an explanation other than his inability to accept who he was.

"I'm not. I'm happy you could admit you have a partner is all. You have me."

He gave me a smile.

"You're all I need."

I swear my smile got way too wide. It was these moments which made the secrets worthwhile. Knowing I was the person he wanted. We didn't need anyone else. Just us together like this.

"Okay, since you've been here tons, you can tell me what's good."

He grinned wider and started talking up the menu to me. He didn't let go of my hand even after we'd ordered and been served drinks. This was his baby step towards being open. I appreciated it more than I could say. He didn't want me to make a fuss, so I wouldn't. I'd keep my joy inside.

"I'm glad you came," he said after a moment's silence. "I've missed you… a lot. Like uni has kept me busy and all, but when I'm alone, you're who I think about. When you said you were coming down, I couldn't wait to see you."

"Is that why you wanted to surprise me at the station?"

"Yeah… and I knew it'd make you happy."

I looked away, knowing I was only going to start blushing again.

"It did."

"You sure this is okay? I don't want you having a ton of work to do when you get back."

I shrugged. It didn't matter if I had to pull some late nights to get it done. My last year was kind of kicking my arse already, but I could deal. I had to do well then I could secure a postgraduate place. Besides, I'd studied on the way down here and planned to do more on the way home on Sunday evening.

"It's fine, I promise. I needed to see you."

He looked at me like he wanted to kiss me, but he didn't. A step too far for him right now. When we got back to his room, he'd be all over me. There was the undercurrent of need in the air between us. The desire to reaffirm our connection on a physical level.

"I take it Mer has forgiven you for her and Cole."

His change of subject took me by surprise.

"Um, yeah, to be honest, she wasn't that mad with me in the first place. More upset with him. I spent ages trying to make her feel better, which I don't think worked, but what else could I do? I don't think she's over him now even if she told me she wants to forget all about him."

"He never told me what happened, she did. He doesn't like talking about it. I've made my own assumptions about why he ended it despite how he feels about her."

I raised an eyebrow.

"And those would be?"

He fiddled his napkin, giving me a half shrug.

"He didn't want to make her choose between you and him. Cole is a lot of things, but he's not heartless. He values family. Pretty sure he knows how much you mean to her. Her superhero big brother."

"I didn't feel much like a superhero that day."

He rubbed his thumb over mine.

"You're allowed to make mistakes, J. She's your little sister. I know all about protective family members."

I smiled and turned the conversation to less charged topics, like how university was going for him. We spent the rest of our time at the restaurant laughing and joking with each other. I had a finite amount of time with him before I had to get back. I wasn't going to waste it with conversations about things best left in the past.

It wasn't a long walk to his student halls. This time, he didn't hold my hand but I didn't mind too much. We went straight up to his room, bypassing the communal areas and didn't encounter anyone on the way. Raphi said most people were probably getting ready to go out clubbing or down the student union bar. He unlocked his door and tugged me in. His room was a decent size for student accommodation. He took my bag from me and set it down on his desk before sliding out of his coat and hanging it up behind the door. I gave him mine and then we stood staring at each other for a long moment.

"Do you want to watch a film or do you want to…?" He indicated the bed with his head.

I couldn't fight my smile as I reached out and took his hand.

"I want you to come here and kiss me."

He stepped closer, bringing his other hand up to cup my face. His thumb ran along my cheek, those green eyes holding so many emotions.

"Mmm, have you missed my lips, J?"

"Yes."

"What else have you missed?"

I reached up and ran my hand down his chest.

"This… all of this. All of you."

His smile turned wicked, making me swallow hard.

"Can't have that now." Raphi leant closer, brushing his mouth over mine. "I better make sure I remind you exactly what you've been missing then, shouldn't I?"

"Please," I breathed, desperate for everything he had to offer.

"So. Fucking. Needy."

Then he kissed me and I was lost.

CHAPTER THIRTY FIVE

Raphael

He'd been waiting for it. For me to kiss him senseless. Ever since he'd spied me at the station, he'd had the look in his eyes. The desperate, needy one which scrambled my brain every single time I saw it. The one telling me he needed me to pin him down and take what I wanted.

I shoved my tongue in his mouth, gripping his face harder. My body pushed him back against the door, showing him who was in charge. Let's face it, Jonah always let me be in control. He thrived off it. He adored the way I kissed the shit out of him. Showing him how much I'd missed the taste of him on my tongue. Missed every inch of his hard body against mine. The way he moulded to me every time we came together like this, in a clash of desire and fucking need.

"Raphi," he whimpered as I traced a path down his jaw with my tongue.

"Tell me what you want," I murmured into his skin.

"You."

It was clear by the way his body arched into mine. I could feel his hard cock rubbing against me. His movements told me what he wanted, but I needed to hear it from his mouth. My hand slid from his face to his neck, loosely gripping it. My lips pressed to his ear.

"Not good enough, J. What exactly do you want?"

I sounded stern and unyielding even to my ears. It was all flooding out. I was untethered and unravelling because I'd been keeping my true self under lock and key. Only Jonah got to see this side of me. This man who liked to control everything in the bedroom. He trusted me not to go too far. I could be real with him. I could be me.

He swallowed at my words, the bobbing of his Adam's apple hitting my palm.

"I want you to fuck me hard. I need it."

"Need it, huh? Maybe I should make you ask me nicely. You only get what you want if you're good."

His harsh pant only turned me on further. I held myself back from showing him how much I wanted him. He didn't yet deserve my passion. My fire. My need to pound his tight little hole without a fucking care how rough I was.

"Please, I want your cock inside me, Raphi. Please give it to me. Give me what I need."

I shook my head, grazing my teeth over his earlobe. He whined in protest.

"You're going to sit on my cock like you were made to and show me you deserve to be fucked hard."

My hand around his neck tightened, demonstrating my seriousness. I could feel him trembling with all his pent up need. It was like a fucking heady cocktail, intoxicating me with his desire.

"I'll show you. I'll be good."

I smiled because fuck did he make me crazy. Jonah just did something to me. I let go of his neck and stepped back, taking in the wild look in his eyes, the flush of his cheeks and his hands fisted at his sides.

This was us. This was all us. Every part of our fucked up broken selves on show. We weren't normal. We weren't anything but two lost souls who kept drowning over and over. But we were each other's. When we were alone like this, all alone where we could be us, there were no barriers or walls. There was no judgement. There was nothing but this. Us. Me and him.

I started to strip out of my clothes, taking my glasses off and popping them on the desk. His eyes tracked my movements as I backed away towards my bed by the window. I could see his chest rising and falling rapidly with his ragged breath.

"Come show me," I told him as I sat up against the headboard of my bed.

He stayed against the door for two beats. When he moved, it was slow and cautious. I tugged the lube and condom I'd stashed off the windowsill and placed them on the covers. Jonah stripped with careful precision as if he was deliberately making me wait. I didn't care as it gave me a chance to admire him. To take in the way his muscles flexed with his movements. How his light green eyes were dark with arousal. The way he smiled at me with such wicked intent to drive me crazy. Fuck, he was so free right then. As if he'd embraced everything we were to each other and our serious problems, which would rear their ugly heads sooner or later, were dust in the wind. They floated away as the physical need took over.

Our bodies wanted to do the talking, not our mouths. No, our mouths wanted to kiss, fuck and love.

When he was bare, he crawled over me and straddled my hips. His smile grew lazy and languid. His fingers ran down my chest, making me stifle a groan. How did his touch have the power to render me incapable of doing anything else other than give in? Let him carry me off on the waves of pleasure. Watching him take both his cock and mine in his hand and stroke them together had me panting out his name like a fucking prayer.

"Give it to me," he murmured. "I know you want to."

The way he was staring at me had my heart pumping like wildfire in my chest. I grabbed the lube, not really giving a shit it was him telling me to do it. He was right. I did want to give it to him. I ached to be deep inside his body, showing him how much I desired the connection between us. Desired this man with every breath I took. Every beat of my heart. Every inch of my fucking soul cried out to keep him forever.

You don't deserve Jonah, and you know it.

I don't fucking care. He's mine. Mine. Fuck, he's all mine.

I popped the cap and coated my fingers. The moment I touched his hot skin, stroking over his tight entrance, he let out a whimper. Those fucking sounds he made were the music to my damn soul. More came as I circled him, making him grind against me as he continued to stroke both of our cocks in unison.

"Raphi," he moaned as I slid my finger in him.

He rocked against my hand as I worked him open, knowing exactly what he needed before I fucked him good and hard.

"Good," I grunted. "So fucking good for me."

"Please, please."

He was the one who grabbed the condom and ripped it open with his teeth, his green eyes glowing with desperation to have me. I bit my lip as he rolled it on before coating my cock with lube. My fingers slid from him as he shifted up on his knees. And then he sunk down on my cock like I'd told him to before we'd got on the bed. His hand curled around my shoulder to keep steady. His eyes were on mine, taking in my reactions. Taking in the way I'd clenched my jaw shut tight. He was fucking tight. I fought against every instinct to shove him down on me as I gripped his hips, my fingers digging into his skin.

"You're desperate to fuck me, aren't you?" his whispered breath came. "You want to pin me down on my stomach and take me with everything you have. I can see in your fucking eyes, Raphi. I can see how much you're holding back."

I grunted, the sound echoing around my skull as he bottomed out. My tells were obvious to him. We'd learnt so much about each other in the time we'd spent together over the summer. The intensity tonight had ratcheted up a notch since we'd been apart for weeks.

"You want me to show you I deserve it? I will. You can stop holding back. You can fuck me the way you and I need."

He rose and fell on my cock, proving he'd do what I asked of him. Giving me what I craved. Him. All of him. My grip on his hip was probably painful, but he didn't make a comment. No, he stared at me as he rode me. His eyes dared me. Taunted and teased me. They told me to stop being so fucking tense. To relax and give in to what we both wanted.

Jonah leant closer, his mouth brushing over mine, "Give in. Fuck me. Give it to me deep and hard. Don't hold back. Don't stop. Just give in."

Each word had my cock throbbing inside him. Had it aching with the need to do exactly as he said. I might be the one in charge of what happened, but Jonah had me wrapped around his little finger. He knew how to get what he wanted from me. So I did. I gave in. As he pulled up, I pushed him down, thrusting upwards to give him all of my cock. He yelped, his eyes going wide as I did it again.

"This is what you asked for," I told him, biting down on his bottom lip in the process. "What you need. You want me to have no mercy. That's why you fucking well taunted me."

Before he knew what was happening, I'd pulled him off me and slid out from underneath him. My hand went to his neck, shoving him down on my bed as I sat up on my knees behind him. I stared at my man waiting for me to do as I pleased. He didn't protest or try to dislodge my hand from the back of his neck.

"If you want my cock again, you better fucking show me."

There was no hesitation in his movements as he reached back and spread himself for me. I bit down on my bottom lip to stop from groaning at the sight of his compliance. The sight of him like this. I lost the fucking will to keep myself under control any longer as I leant over him. As I shoved my cock back inside him, making him moan. I gave it to him, fucking him into my mattress like my life depended on it.

"Raphi, fuck," he panted.

My hand was still wrapped around the back of his neck as my body pinned him to the bed. My lips were at his ear, kissing and sucking the lobe as I fucked him with punishing strokes.

"I missed you," I whispered, unable to stop the words any longer. "I've missed you every fucking second. I can't do this without you. I'm drowning, J. I'm fucking drowning."

I'd hidden all of my bullshit inside me for the past few weeks. Locked it down so I could concentrate on starting university. It festered there, making me crazy. Being without Jonah had left me vulnerable and lonely. Being away from my family should have been freeing, but it wasn't. It was fucking me up worse. I didn't have my brother right there to calm me. My parents to keep me from falling. I was alone. All a-fucking-lone.

"You're my anchor. My fucking lifeline. I didn't know how much I needed you until you were no longer there for me to touch, hold and care for. You are the best thing in my life. I hope you know that. I hope you realise how much you mean to me because I would break if you were gone. I would fucking disintegrate."

I didn't realise I was crying until my tears hit his cheek. The frustration with myself had bubbled over. Brought on by the intensity of this experience with him. Fuelled by my longing and loneliness.

I love you, Jonah. I fucking well love you. And I don't know how to be the man you deserve. I'm scared I'll never be able to find a way to accept myself enough to give you what you need.

If we parted, I'd be left with scars on my heart. Scars on my fucking soul. He'd marked me. He'd fucking branded himself on my skin. On my damn heart.

I didn't understand how I could love someone else so much and yet hate myself with the same intensity. With the same fucking breath.

"Raphi," he choked out.

"No, don't say anything. Don't... I can't take it." I kissed his damp skin where my tears had fallen. Where they were still falling. "I feel too much. Too fucking much and I can't do it any longer. I just can't. So don't say a word. Just be here. Be here for me... please."

He nodded against my lips before his hands came up and rested by his head. It was his way of showing his supplication. I wrapped my free hand around his, our fingers linking together. A physical manifestation of our bond with each other.

Jonah gave himself to me without a word. He let me use his body to drive away my fucking demons. To lose myself in the delirious pleasure and ecstasy. He moaned and whimpered with each one of my punishing thrusts, but he didn't speak. He didn't try to tell me it was going to be okay. I think deep down, he knew the truth. It wasn't going to be okay for me. I would continue to suffer when he went back to Durham and left me in London without his calming presence and soothing touch. I would suffer in silence.

I let out a guttural moan, my tears still soaking his skin when I came. All of my pent up fucking anger with myself seeped out of me. It drowned the both of us in this fucked up hell I'd consigned me and him to. He paid the price of my inability to be who I was. This beautiful, kind and caring man who deserved the entire world gave up pieces of his soul to be with me. And I couldn't forgive myself for it.

I pulled out of him, sitting up on my knees and dealing with the condom.

"Turn over," I murmured.

He did as I asked, his green eyes wide as he took me in. I dumped the condom on the wrapper. I would throw it away later, but right now, I wanted to take care of him.

Reaching out, I stroked my hand down his chest. I leant down and ran my tongue up his shaft, making him moan in response. My hand flattened on his stomach, keeping him pinned to the bed whilst my mouth closed over his cock. He whimpered and bucked under me. I only took him deeper in response, wanting to send him over the edge. Jonah was already worked up. I knew it wouldn't take much. I'd fucked him the way he needed. Now I was going to make him come.

His hand dug into my hair, grasping at the strands like he needed to hold on to something to keep him afloat. I wanted him drowning in me. Drowning in me like I fucking well drowned in him.

"Raphi," he whined. "Please."

I increased my pace, knowing it would be a matter of moments. And when he did explode, I tasted the saltiness on my tongue as his cock pumped inside my mouth. His fingers were wrapped up so tight in my hair, it hurt. I didn't give a shit. I deserved it. I deserved all the pain and agony I experienced for keeping someone who should be free from my fucked up messy bullshit. For making him mine when I had no fucking right to this man.

When he let me go, I pulled off him, swallowing. I picked up our discarded supplies, getting up to chuck some of it in the bin and set the rest on the desk. Then I lay down next to him and curled my body around his, resting my head on his chest. He wrapped his arms around me, stroking my hair with one hand.

"Do you want to talk about it?" he whispered.

He was referring to what I'd said when I was fucking him.

"No. Just be here with me, please."

"Okay." He kissed my hair. "I'm here. I'm right here. I'll always be here."

And that was the problem. The whole fucking problem. He should be saving himself from me, but he wasn't. I wondered if, eventually, I would have the strength. If I could let him go for his own good. So he could find someone who deserved him in all the ways I didn't.

Right now, I didn't have the strength… but would it be too late when I could?

Would the damage already be done?

You know deep down how he feels about you even if he's never said it. You know, Raphi. He loves you more than he loves anything in this world. Maybe more than Meredith. Don't fucking kid yourself otherwise.

The biggest problem I had with letting him go was I loved him too. It's why I wouldn't talk about it. Why I wouldn't admit it. If I did, it would force the conversation out into the open. It would force me to break his heart. And I couldn't do it. I couldn't shred him to pieces and leave him with scars like mine. It would destroy me. Ruin me entirely.

And fuck… I deserved it for everything I'd done to him.

I deserved it.

I deserved it all.

CHAPTER THIRTY SIX

Jonah

The weekend hadn't been entirely easy between me and Raphi. Not after the way he'd cried on Friday night and told me how much my absence was hurting him. He hadn't brought it up again. It was if he purged his soul to me during sex and now he was trying to forget it ever happened.

We went out yesterday, enjoying the autumn sunshine and did a spot of shopping. It had been nice to be with each other. And he held my hand all day. It showed me how much he was trying. How he wanted to make an effort to be open about us even if it was only in the smallest of ways.

Now he was napping as we'd had a lazy day in bed filled with sex, TV shows and snacks. Raphi looked troubled as he slept. His face was marred with frown lines. He wasn't looking forward to me leaving. And in all honesty, neither was I. Not when he needed me. I mean, really needed me. I kept thinking about his words, replaying them over and over in my head. Hearing the desperation in his shaky voice as he said them echoing in my ears.

"I would break if you were gone. I would fucking disintegrate."

Did he think I would leave him? Fuck, I couldn't. I loved him. He was the sun and stars to me. I wanted a future with him. Raphi was my person. My fucking one. I couldn't imagine anyone else taking his place. He belonged next to me.

I stroked his chestnut hair back from his forehead, hoping to soothe away the worry etched on his sleeping face.

"I'm not going anywhere," I whispered. "I'm here and I'm yours." I kissed his cheek. "I love you."

It was the first time I'd admitted it out loud. I couldn't say it when he was awake. My beautiful broken boy wasn't in a place to hear it. He wasn't ready.

"I want you forever, Raphi. If I told you that, I'd scare you, but it's true." I placed my hand over his heart. "There's so much I want to tell you but only when you're ready. Like how much I love you. How I want to marry you and have a family with you. We could work it out, adopt or something, but it's what I want… so much."

I felt stupid saying these things to him when he was sleeping. I had to admit to them. Give my feelings a voice because all of this was fucking killing me. I wanted to make him better. Slay his fucking demons to allow him to be at peace with himself. So he could look at the future and not be afraid. I wanted him to be happy. To be content.

It's why you don't treat the ones you love. You can't remain detached when your feelings are engaged. It didn't stop me wanting to try. I needed to help him. I wanted to save him from himself. It hurt to watch him go through all this shit. The pain was agonising. But I did it anyway. I stayed because I loved him with every breath I took. Every beat of my heart was his. He'd always held it in his fist. My heart belonged to him alone. And it always would.

I watched him sleeping and etched all of his features into my memory. I was terrified of losing the person I loved more than life itself. Afraid he would disappear on me and his ability to cope would run out.

Raphi needed help. Real help. But I knew in my heart he wouldn't ask for it. He wasn't there yet. Where he knew it was okay if he couldn't fix it himself. It wasn't a weakness.

I knew even without him having a proper diagnosis what was happening to him. I studied this shit. It's what I wanted to help people who suffered from it with. At the barest minimum, he had depression but I wasn't technically qualified to make that judgement. It's what I'd witnessed through knowing him the way I did. And only he could decide to go get a proper diagnosis.

I knew he'd spoken to his dad about his feelings of self-loathing. Eric had suggested he seek therapy. Raphi hadn't been receptive to it. It's why I didn't press the subject either. I didn't want him thinking I was trying to analyse him. I wasn't. I worried about him and his wellbeing.

I worried about him so much, sometimes it kept me awake at night. It kept me from focusing on what I should be doing, which was finishing my degree, getting some work experience, then I could do my postgraduate studies. He would hate it and blame himself. I kept my mouth shut and dealt with it for his sake. To keep him from imploding under his self-imposed guilt. It's why I didn't push him to tell everyone we were together. But I wanted him to. If only so I could stop lying to my sister about it. She was the one person I wanted to tell. Meredith would be happy for me. For us. She wanted me to find love.

Raphi stirred, opening his eyes and blinking. They focused on me a moment later.

"Were you watching me sleep?" he asked, his voice all groggy.

"Maybe."

He closed his eyes again.

"You're lucky you're so cute or I'd find it creepy."

He yawned and snuggled closer to me, burying his face in my chest and nuzzling his nose against it.

"Cute?"

"Mmm, as a button."

If anyone was cute right now, it was him cuddling up to me.

"I would prefer it if you thought I was sexy or something."

"Oh, I do think that as well, but mostly, you're just cute and adorable." He wrapped an arm around me and stroked my back. "How long have I been asleep?"

I looked at my watch.

"An hour or so."

"Did you sleep?"

"No, wasn't tired. Kept watch over you instead."

He pulled back and smiled up at me.

"My hero."

My heart hurt at his words even though he was being sarcastic. I wasn't his hero. I couldn't save him despite me trying so hard to. He couldn't know about the pain this was causing me.

I leant closer and kissed him. He responded, holding me closer as his tongue slid between my lips. I tried not to get aroused by it since we didn't have time for more sex.

When I moved back, I cupped his cheek, stroking my thumb across it.

I need you to be your own hero for me, Raphi. I need it so fucking badly. Save yourself before it's too late.

"I have to get up."

I didn't elaborate on the reason. We both knew I had a train to catch.

He let me pull away and climb out of bed. He watched me dress and pack my bag with sad eyes. I found the last vestiges of my inner strength and steeled myself against the waves of guilt and pain. I was leaving him here and it fucking killed me.

Raphi got dressed since he was insisting on coming along to see me off. I didn't stop him. The two of us were silent on the journey to St Pancras. He leant his head on my shoulder whilst we sat on the tube next to each other, his fingers tightly entwined with mine. When we trudged through the underground and up to the station, he seemed to get more and more agitated. The two of us stood near the barriers by the platform, staring at each other as if we couldn't yet say goodbye.

"Text me when you get home, yeah?" he said, his voice a little rough,

"I will."

I squeezed his hand to reassure him. His eyes searched my face for a long moment. I really had to go, but I was waiting for something from him. One last lingering look. Raphi let out a breath then he stepped closer. His hand slid from mine. Both of his were on my face, bringing me closer. And there, in a busy station, Raphi kissed me. He kissed me in front of hundreds of people. I almost died on the spot. Instead, my hands fisted in his coat. The kiss warmed me from the inside out. When he pulled back, he pressed his nose to mine for a moment.

"Safe trip, J."

I swallowed hard and smiled at him. My heart was ready to burst, but I wouldn't make it into a big deal.

"See you at Christmas."

He released me and I walked away to the barriers. I turned back after I went through. He was standing there, smiling at me and gave me a wave. I smiled before I walked up the platform and got on the train.

As it pulled away from the platform, I stared out of the window knowing I'd left a piece of myself on the platform with him. He already had my heart, but now, Raphael Nelson had something bigger. He had a part of my soul.

CHAPTER THIRTY SEVEN

Jonah

I sat at the kitchen table nursing a cup of coffee as I stared out the window at the dreary weather. It had been raining non-stop for two days. It echoed the misery inside me. It'd been two weeks since I'd been down to see Raphi and I was suffering. Lovesickness could do that to a person. Make them ache with longing for the one they cared about.

Raphi had become withdrawn and uncommunicative, which didn't help. We did talk a lot, but he refused to tell me how he was doing emotionally. Every time I attempted to ask, he shut down and said he'd speak to me later. I didn't want to stop trying to get him to open up to me. He needed someone to talk to about his feelings.

Damien walked into the kitchen in a dressing gown with his hair in disarray. He stuck the kettle on and rubbed his face. It was early, but I'd not been able to sleep much last night.

Too busy worrying about my boyfriend. I needed to see him in the flesh. Needed to hold him tight and tell him I was there. Show him he wasn't alone.

"Remind me again why we agreed to let the dickhead have a party later?"

"It's his birthday," I said, shrugging as Damien leant up against the counter.

Robin had twisted our arms over it. It was his twenty-first. He wanted a house party to celebrate rather than going out and hitting the clubs. Now the weather had turned shit, I couldn't really blame him. Damien and I weren't the clubbing types, anyway. Neither of us really drank much as it was.

"Still a pain. It'll be loud, people getting pissed to fuck and whatever else. If anyone is sick, he's cleaning it up."

"He knows that."

I'd been avoiding Robin a lot. He'd been acting weird ever since I'd told the two of them I had a boyfriend. It's not like I brought Raphi up often.

"Why do you look so miserable?"

I looked up at Damien who was grabbing a mug out of the cupboard.

"No reason."

"Hmm, yeah, okay. Do you want to talk about it?"

I shrugged.

"I'll take that as a no. Did you invite your boyfriend to the party?"

I looked down at my mug, tapping my fingers against my phone, which was resting on the kitchen table.

"I told Raphi about it, but it's a long trip to come to a party for someone he doesn't even know."

He wasn't too happy about it. He didn't like Robin even though he'd never met my housemate. After the way Robin had started acting, I didn't entirely blame Raphi. Robin kept making these snide little comments about me being in a relationship. Like how the single life was so much more fun than being tied down to one person. It was stupid considering I'd never indulged in the 'single life' anyway. The only reckless thing I'd done was sleep with Robin once. I knew better than to do stupid shit like that again.

"True, but it must be hard being away from each other."

I sipped my coffee and stared out the window again.

"It is. I miss him all the time."

Damien didn't say anything else for a long moment whilst he finished making himself a cup of tea. Then he came and sat at the table, running his fingers through his messy hair.

"What's he like?"

"Raphi? He's…" How did I even describe the love of my life? There didn't seem to be words which adequately explained who he was and how much I cared about him. "He's funny, smart and sweet. It's strange, but he's the person I can sit in silence with and feel… content… happy. It's as if we don't need to fill the void with words because we're together. Like, he's not perfect by any means, but he's the only person who just gets me without the need for explanation and I do the same for him." I shrugged and fiddled with my mug. "I just… love him."

Damien eyed me for a long moment.

"If you love him, why do you sound so sad about it?"

Raphi didn't make me sad in any way shape or form. It was the pain of being unable to help him.

"He's got problems and all I want to do is make it better for him."

"What kind of problems?"

I sipped my coffee again, trying to work out if I should tell Damien the truth. We'd always got on quite well even if we never discussed anything super personal. Maybe I'd feel better if I told someone about how hard it was for me to cope with Raphi's issues. Damien and Robin were the only people who knew about Raphi. Not like I could talk to my sister about it.

"Well, he's not had any official diagnosis, but I know he has depression. He has a hard time seeing himself positively and some days, he shuts down. The hardest part is knowing he won't ask for help. He thinks he has to fix himself, but we all need help. We all need someone. I want to be his someone even though he won't let me. At least not like that."

"I can see why that would be hard for you given what you're planning on doing in life. Not being able to help the person you care about the most even though it's what you're training for."

I nodded. Maybe when I was qualified, I'd be better at this shit. Right now, I could do nothing more than be there for him. Show him I'd never leave and he was worth everything. He would always be worth the heartache.

"He can't even accept he's bisexual. The only person who knows we're together is his older brother. It's hard for me, but he's trying to be more open about us. I mean, he kissed me in front of hundreds of strangers at the train station, but he won't tell his parents. Meredith doesn't even know and the two of them are friends. It's not like he's homophobic or anything. He has a bi dad and a pan dad, but it's his own self-image which is the problem. I don't put pressure on him to tell people because he's already hard on himself over it. Watching someone you love punish themselves for things they can't control is the worst thing imaginable."

Damien gave me a sad smile like he got where I was coming from.

"He has two dads?"

That made me smile.

"Technically he has four and a mum, along with two brothers and a sister. I know it sounds really messed up, but they work somehow. His family is probably the most loving I've ever met in the sense they all support each other no matter what."

I swear Damien's eyes were bugging out of their sockets.

"Hold on, are they're like all together? All five of them?"

"It's going to be hard for you to wrap your head around this, but all four of them are in a relationship with his mum. Two of them are straight and the other two, the bi and pan ones, are like together with each other as well."

Damien sat back and shook his head.

"Well, shit, that's enough to fuck any kid up for life."

"They're mostly well-adjusted actually, you'd be surprised at how normal their family is. Raphi got bullied the worst over the whole five parents thing, and I think that's where it all started... his issues I mean."

Honestly, after I'd spent some time with his parents, I understood what Raphi meant when he told me they weren't bad people. They really weren't. Just because they'd done bad shit in the past, didn't mean they were evil. They protected themselves and their family. Not that I agreed with their choices. I didn't have to. It was a long time ago and holding it against them felt wrong.

"That's rough. No one should give you shit for something you can't control."

"Yeah."

We heard a crash from outside the kitchen before Robin walked into the room without a care in the world.

"Morning."

"What was that noise?" Damien asked.

Robin shrugged and walked over to the fridge. Damien frowned. Had Robin been eavesdropping on our conversation? I didn't want to ask but I had my suspicions.

"Do you need us to help get supplies for later?" I asked.

"No, no. I told you, I've got it all covered," Robin replied, waving his hand.

I got up, snagging my mug and walking away towards the door.

"Okay, but if you need anything, let me know. I'll be in my room."

I made my way upstairs, trying to fight a niggling feeling in the back of my head I'd forgotten something. Instead, I thought about the fact Robin had probably heard what I'd said about Raphi. And it couldn't be a good thing.

Damien wouldn't be a dick over the fact Raphi wasn't open about my relationship with him. Robin would. He'd think I was stupid for being with someone like that. He wouldn't understand why my boyfriend struggled so much. Why I let him come to terms with it in his own time. You do crazy shit for the people you love, but that was the thing. I loved him without reservation. Without conditions. I'd do anything for him.

Hopefully, Robin wouldn't say a fucking word or he'd be admitting to eavesdropping on a conversation he had no business hearing in the first place. I didn't need his judgement. I didn't need anyone else butting into my relationship.

All I needed was Raphi. Nothing more. Nothing less. Just him and me together. I'd fight forever to stay by his side. I'd fight as long as he'd have me.

I loved him enough for both of us.

CHAPTER THIRTY EIGHT

Raphael

I 'd come home for the weekend knowing if I was alone right now, it wouldn't be a good thing. Not when Robin was having a party at their house. I knew Jonah wouldn't do anything stupid, but I didn't trust his housemate. The housemate he'd slept with. The whole thing still angered me, but I'd tried to get over it. Not very well, I might add.

Duke and I were in the games room. I was half-heartedly playing co-op with him, but I couldn't focus. Not when Jonah hadn't texted me since early this morning after he'd got up. We were usually in constant communication over the weekend. I was trying not to let it agitate me, but it was. I felt all sorts of crazy and slightly unhinged. I kept imagining horrifying scenarios as to why he'd not replied to my messages. Like what if he'd got into an accident? What if someone had hurt him? All stupid shit I shouldn't be worried about because it was completely irrational.

"For fuck's sake, Raphi," Duke grunted as he nudged my arm. "Are you even paying attention?"

I looked up at the screen, finding he'd died and my character was standing there doing fuck all.

"Sorry."

"What's wrong with you today?"

"Everything."

He gave me a look.

"I'm worried about J."

He continued looking at me.

"What?"

"What do you mean, what? You need to stop overthinking shit. He's fine. You're fine. What's not fine is you fucking up our play-through."

"I'm not fine, Duke." I rubbed my face. "I'm so not fine."

I didn't lie to him about my emotional state. He was the only one I opened up to. I'd been fobbing Jonah off because I didn't want to burden him with my shit. Not when he had to get through his third year of university and graduate. He needed to concentrate on that, not me. Not on my fucked up bullshit. I should be dealing with me.

"You want to talk about it?"

"What's the point? It doesn't change no matter what I say. I'm tired and I hate him being hundreds of miles away."

"You could have gone to the party, you know. I would've taken you."

I didn't want to go to Robin's birthday party. I had no interest in meeting him. Ever. Besides, I didn't trust myself not to do something stupid like punching him in the face. Not that I was even the violent type. I'd never hit anyone in my life, but the fucker rubbed me up the wrong way.

"I know, but it's better this way. I would've just brought J down."

"You really need to stop thinking like that. Just accept he wants to be with you without all this other shit. He doesn't care if you're having a bad day. He'll be there anyway because he cares about you. I mean, fuck, the guy blatantly loves the shit out of you."

I flinched. I knew Jonah loved me. It didn't make this any easier. It didn't stop the doubts. And it certainly didn't stop me from feeling like I didn't deserve someone like him.

My phone vibrated several times, making me frown. I tugged it out of my pocket and stared down at the screen. There were several picture messages from Jonah which was unusual since he normally didn't send me anything like that. I opened them up and my stomach dropped. Anger flooded my veins.

What the fuck?

There were pictures of Jonah talking to various people with a drink in his hand with a smile on his face.

Jonah: Your boyfriend is enjoying himself without you.

Jonah: Or should I really call him that since you can't even admit you're together.

Jonah: Maybe I should try again with him. Not like you're giving him what he needs.

Then another picture message came through and this time it was of someone I didn't recognise. I didn't need to because I knew exactly who the fuck it was.

Robin.

What the hell was this? How on earth did he know I couldn't tell people Jonah and I were in a relationship? I knew Jonah wouldn't have talked about it to him. How the fuck had he found out? And why the fuck did he have Jonah's phone?

This was clearly why Jonah hadn't texted me today. Robin had his phone. And the cunt was taunting me.

"I need you to take me to St Pancras."

"What?" Duke asked, frowning at me.

"I have to go see Jonah right now. Take me to the station because it would take too long to drive up there."

"Why? You said you didn't want to go to this party."

I shoved my phone at him.

"This is why! That fucker Robin has J's phone."

Duke took it from me and looked over the messages, his eyebrows shooting up. I'd told Duke about Robin and Jonah. He'd been on my side over it. If it was him, he wouldn't like his woman being around someone she'd slept with.

"What a prick. Who the fuck does he think he is?"

"Exactly. Who the fuck does he think he is giving me shit over something he doesn't even know a thing about."

Duke got up, giving my phone back to me.

"Right, let's go. This fucker isn't going to mess with you and him."

I jumped up and the two of us walked out of the games room, leaving the TV on and not even bothering to exit our game. We got coats and shoes on. Duke grabbed the car keys and then we were out on the street, getting in the car. I hadn't learnt how to drive, but Duke had.

"I'm coming with you to Durham," he told me as he pulled out on the main street.

"You don't have to do that."

"If you think I'm letting you go up there alone, you're fucking delusional. You need me."

My heart hurt at his words. He was right. I did need him. Duke and I would do anything for each other.

Duke parked the car in the nearby carpark at the station. The two of us got tickets, jumping on the next available train. The whole way to Durham I was a fucking wreck worrying about Jonah. I was also mad as hell. So mad I was liable to do something stupid, but I no longer cared. I cared about Jonah. He was mine. Robin needed to be put in his fucking place.

I swear I'd lost my mind or something because I wouldn't normally do something like this. Jump on a train and travel for three hours because some idiot had taunted me. It was the thought of someone messing with Jonah which brought out all of my instincts to keep him safe. I had to protect him. Protect what was mine.

When we reached Durham, Duke and I jumped in a taxi. Jonah had given me his address, so we had no problems getting there. It had been well over three hours since I'd got those text messages and it looked like the party was in full swing now. It made me angrier than ever.

I knocked at the front door, Duke hanging back behind me since he told me he was here for moral support. It was opened by someone I really didn't recognise.

"Hello, um, are you here for the party?"

"No, I'm here to see Jonah."

The guy's eyebrows rose.

"Are you… are you Raphi?"

I nodded, wondering who this was.

"Oh, he said you weren't coming. Hold on, come in… I'm Damien."

Jonah's other housemate who he'd told me was a really nice guy if a little quiet and reserved.

"Hi, Jonah's told me about you. This is my brother, Duke. Where's Jonah?"

Damien stepped back and let us both in.

"He's… somewhere. To be honest, I don't know. Hold on, I'll go find him for you."

Damien walked off down the hallway. Duke looked at me, but I was too busy staring at someone who'd walked out of what I assumed was the living room.

Robin.

"Well, hello, I haven't seen you two—"

He said no more because my fist connected with his jaw, causing to stumble backwards into the wall. I didn't stop there,

I hit him again. The only reason I wasn't able to do it a third time was because my brother grabbed my arm and pulled me back. Robin had his hand on his face, staring at me in shock.

"What the fuck, man?"

"That's for trying to fuck with me and Jonah. Where is his phone? You stole it, right?"

Robin's eyes widened. I tried to loosen Duke's hold on me, but he didn't let go.

"You're his boyfriend?"

"Yeah, I fucking am and I don't appreciate you butting into shit you don't know anything about."

Robin put his other hand up.

"Jesus, it was just a joke, man. There was no need to hit me."

I glared at him, wanting to punch him until his face was all messed up.

"Oh, trust me, there was every need. You stay away from Jonah, you hear me?"

"What's going on? Why are you shouting?" came Jonah's voice as him and Damien came out from the kitchen. His eyes went wide when he saw me. "Raphi? Duke? What… what are you doing here? Are you okay?"

I shook my fist out because it hurt from hitting Robin. Duke didn't let me go. It was probably a good thing because I really wasn't done with Robin.

"No, this prick stole your phone and decided to taunt me." I pointed at Robin who was rubbing his jaw still.

Jonah looked at Robin with a frown before patting himself down.

"Where's my phone?"

Robin tugged something out of his pocket and handed it to Jonah. I pulled at Duke's hold on me, not wanting Jonah anywhere near Robin.

Mine. He's mine. No one else can touch him. That man is mine.

Jonah looked through the messages Robin had sent me, his frown deepening. Then he raised his head and there was this horrified look on his face. He ignored everyone else and came towards me. Duke let me go. Jonah wrapped me up in his arms, holding me against him.

"I'm sorry, I'm so sorry, Raphi," he whispered. "I had no idea."

I hated the fact he was apologising. He had no reason to be sorry. No reason at all.

"It's not your fault."

No, it was Robin's. And mine. Having Jonah right there calmed my warring soul and made me realise what I'd just done. I'd punched a guy in the face with very little provocation because I'd lost my mind over the idea of him touching Jonah. The idea anyone would steal him from me.

Who does that? This wasn't me. I didn't hit people. Violence was never the answer. And yet I'd hit Robin. Twice.

Who are you right now?

"Should we go up to my room and talk?"

I nodded, still glaring at Robin over Jonah's shoulder. I noticed Damien was looking at his housemate with disgust too. At least I wasn't the only one who thought Robin was a cunt.

Jonah pulled away, reaching up and stroking my face. There was sadness in his eyes and it fucking broke me. The whole thing had broken me already. I was so messed up. I'd travelled over three hours to punch someone in the face. It was proof I'd lost it. Proof I'd gone off the rails. I'd never been violent in my whole entire life. I'd sworn to myself I would never hurt another person like that after going through it myself.

My hands shook at my sides. The weight of everything crashed down on me.

Keep it together. Don't fall apart now.

Jonah turned and looked at Robin.

"That was a shitty thing to do and you know it. I don't care what your excuse is. My relationship with Raphi is none of your business. So quite frankly, you can fuck off."

Jonah took my hand and pulled me upstairs. I looked back at Duke but he nodded at me. He'd be okay whilst I talked to Jonah. Whilst I dealt with what happened.

Jonah shut the door behind us when we got in his room. I didn't take in my surroundings because all I could see was him.

"Raphi…"

"I'm sorry."

"No, don't you apologise." He stepped towards me and cupped my face with both his hands. "What he did was really fucked up and not remotely okay."

"I shouldn't have hit him. I don't hurt people. That's not me. Why did I hit him? Oh my god. What is wrong with me?"

"Shh, it's okay."

My body trembled with the force of my emotions. It wasn't okay. It wasn't remotely okay. I couldn't do this any longer. I was broken. Utterly broken. Jonah deserved much more than this. More than me. He deserved the world.

I didn't recognise myself staring at the boy I loved with every inch of my being. This wasn't me. This person who got jealous and did stupid things like hit people.

I hate this. I hate me. I hate everything I've done. This isn't what he needs. He shouldn't have to deal with me. He should have someone who loves him and is open. Who can give him the world because I can't do that. I'm not capable of it.

"I'm… I'm sorry," I whispered even though he'd told me not to apologise.

I wasn't apologising for Robin.

I wasn't apologising for coming here.

I was apologising for what I was about to do.

For breaking his heart.

I had to for his sake. I had to save him from me. Set him free so he could be with someone who deserved him.

Because I didn't.

CHAPTER THIRTY NINE

Jonah

The way Raphi was looking at me physically pained me. It's like he had come to some horrifying realisation in his head. I didn't care if he'd hit Robin. Quite frankly, Robin deserved it after the shit he'd pulled. I felt bad for not realising I didn't have my phone on me. It's not that I hadn't thought about Raphi or wondered how he was. I was waiting for him to text me.

"I can't do this anymore, Jonah."

I frowned.

"Do what?"

"This. Everything. I can't... I'm broken. I'm so fucking broken."

I pulled him closer, resting my forehead against his.

"It's okay. I know you're hurting and I know it's hard, but it's okay. I'm here."

He shook his head but didn't step away.

"You can't fix me, J."

"I'm not trying to fix you." I wasn't. I just wanted to help him get better. Help him through this by standing by his side. "I want you to be happy, Raphi. I'm here for you. That's it."

I watched a tear leak out of his eye and it fucking killed me.

"I can't be happy. How can I be happy when I hate myself? I hate everything about me. Everything."

His words tore through me. They hurt because he couldn't see how wonderful he was. How amazing and precious he was to me.

"I know you do. It's okay to feel that way. You just need help to find yourself again."

He shook his head harder and more tears fell down his face. The sight of it destroyed something inside me.

"No." He wrenched himself away from me. "No. It's not okay. Nothing about this is okay. I fucking well came up here so I could hit your housemate for being a prick. It's not normal behaviour. I'm not normal and I'm not okay."

I watched him pace away, running his fingers through his hair and leaving it sticking up.

"You don't get it. I'm not right and all I'm doing is hurting you."

"What? That's not true, you're not hurting me, Raphi."

"Yes. I am. I'm hurting you because it hurts you to see me like this. It hurts you so fucking much but you stay silent. You suffer in silence like me because you and I are the fucking same. It's just you're okay with being who you are and I'm not. I'm fucking well not."

I couldn't lie to him. He was right. It did hurt me.

"I've told you why. You are worth it. You're worth everything. I'll go through all the pain because I want you. I need you."

His body shook as he paced the room. His hands kept fisting and un-fisting. I could see how worked up he was. How everything was crumbling around him and he could do nothing to stop it. Neither could I.

"You can't do that to yourself. It's not fair. You deserve more. So much more. I can't give you a happy, normal life, J. I can't. I'm not capable of it. I'm fucking selfish for keeping you when I don't deserve you."

My heart shattered at his words. How could he think he didn't deserve me?

What a stupid question! He thinks that because he hates himself. He doesn't think he deserves anything good.

"You're not selfish. I'm here with you because I want to be. You're not forcing me into staying in this relationship with you. I get to decide who I'm with. I want you. I've always wanted you no matter how hard it is."

It was the plain and simple truth of the matter. I didn't care what kind of pain I had to suffer. I didn't care about anything other than him.

"I can't let you do that. I can't… I'm not worth it."

"Yes, you are. You're worth it to me."

I felt like I was grasping at straws here. Trying to convince someone who'd already made up their mind. I could feel it. Feel him slipping away from me with every passing second.

"No. You think that now, but I'm just going to drag you down. I'm just going to ruin you and I can't do that to you. I just can't."

I shook my head. I couldn't take this. My feet carried me towards him, stopping his pacing when I stood in front of him. I took him by the arms and held him in place, forcing him to meet my eyes.

"You are worthy of me. You're fucking worthy of anyone you want. You think you're not, but that's because you don't see yourself like I do. Fuck, Raphi, I love you. I love everything about you. I don't care about your broken parts. I don't even care if you hate yourself because I love you. I love you enough for both of us."

He blinked. More tears ran down his cheeks and I realised they'd started falling down mine too. I just wanted him to let me hold him and make him feel better.

"I love you."

He let out this heart-wrenching sigh as if it was pulled from his chest by force.

"Love isn't enough. If it was, we wouldn't be here."

"What's that supposed to mean?"

"It means I love you too."

My heart squeezed hard in my chest. He was admitting it. He said it. He loved me.

"But if you think it changes anything, you're wrong. It doesn't fix what's wrong with me. It doesn't suddenly make this huge difference because you and I have loved each other since we were fifteen and seventeen. Love isn't enough to make everything okay."

His words left a bitter taste in my mouth. How could he think love wasn't enough?

"It is enough. If you've loved me that long, then it's enough. We belong together. You're it for me. You always have been."

The saddest of smiles graced his face. And I knew right then when he walked out of the door, he would break me.

"You think that now, J, but I can't give you everything you deserve. I'm too broken."

"You already give me everything I want because it's you. All I want is you. I love you."

He stepped back from me, forcing me to drop my hands from his arms.

"It's because I love you so much I have to do this." His words came out half whispered with agony lacing each one of them. "I have to set you free."

"I don't want to be free. I don't fucking well need that. I just need you."

He wasn't listening to me. It felt like nothing I said made any difference. Every part of me hurt with the knowledge Raphi was leaving me. He was fucking well saying goodbye because he thought it was for my own good. Nothing about it was for my own good. I wouldn't be okay without him.

"I'm sorry."

He reached up and cupped my cheek, making me choke on my own tears.

"Don't do this," I whispered.

He leant towards me. The moment our lips met, I fucking died. They were salty from our tears. My hands curled into his hair, tugging him closer as his tongue slid into my mouth. The desperate way we kissed each other was heart-breaking. It was fucking soul-destroying. It hurt way worse than anything else. Because this was the last time I'd kiss this boy. The very fucking last time I'd have him in my arms. Touching his skin.

I couldn't stop him from leaving me. I couldn't because Raphi wouldn't let it happen. He thought he was saving me by letting me go. I didn't want to be saved. I wanted him.

"Don't leave me," I whimpered against his mouth. "Please. You said you wouldn't run."

"I'm sorry."

"No, sorry isn't good enough. Don't do this."

"I love you, Jonah. I love you so much."

I didn't want to hear that either. I didn't want to hear it because it decimated me. Love wasn't enough. Love wasn't fucking well enough for him.

"Don't."

He pulled away and stared into my eyes.

"I'll always love you, but I want you to be with someone who deserves you even if it kills me to say that. You deserve someone who appreciates you and is proud to be yours. Who shows the world you're his everything. I'm not that man and I don't know if I ever will be. It won't stop me loving you or wishing everything was different, but I'm not going to be selfish any longer. I'm not going to keep you when I know it's wrong to have you."

His hands dropped and he turned, walking away from me towards the door.

"If… if you walk out that's it, Raphi. That's it. I won't forgive you for leaving me."

I was lying, but right then, I was desperate. I needed him to stay. He would utterly destroy me if he walked out.

"Then I guess I'll have to live with that too. I don't deserve your love or forgiveness." He sounded dejected and resigned.

"What do you mean, too?"

"I know what I'm doing, J. I'm breaking your heart and I hate myself for it, but you're better off without me. You'll see that in time."

"No. No, I'm not better off without you. I'm not!"

"Goodbye, Jonah."

I let him leave. I let him walk out on me because there was nothing left for me to say.

"I love you," I sobbed, but he couldn't hear me.

I stumbled backwards, my legs meeting the edge of my bed before I collapsed in a heap on it, burying my face in my hands. Agony ripped through my chest. I could hear my sobs echoing around my skull, but I didn't care any longer. I didn't care about anything other than my heart shattering over and over in my chest.

The boy I wanted so desperately to keep had left me. He'd left me because he couldn't believe he deserved me even though he loved me and I loved him. It's what hurt the most. The fact he loved me. We loved each other. And still… fucking still… he left.

Raphi was right about one thing. He was broken. Too fucking broken. But if he'd given me a chance… if he hadn't made decisions like this for me, he'd have seen how I'd have stood by him through thick and thin. How I'd have endured. How I'd have got him help so he could start the long, arduous journey of learning how to cope and manage with his mental health problems.

I would have done anything for Raphael Nelson if only he'd have let me. If only he'd have stayed. If only he hadn't walked out the door and destroyed everything we shared with each other. If only he hadn't taken everything from me when he left me.

You have my heart and my soul, Raphi. You have everything of mine. I'm nothing without you.

Nothing at all.

PART IV

save

verb, saved, sav·ing.

to keep safe, intact, or unhurt; safeguard; preserve.

CHAPTER FORTY

Raphael

Six and a half years later

I walked out of my counsellor's office with my head held high. Today was a milestone. A big one. I could finally say I was at peace with myself. And I didn't need to see Marvin any longer.

I'd gone through a thousand and one struggles over the years. Days when I wanted to give up. Days when I never thought I'd get better. Days when I wanted the world to disappear. But I was here now at the end of a road I couldn't believe I'd walked along. A journey to acceptance.

I smiled as my dad leant up against the car outside with his hands in his pockets.

"Hey, monkey."

He didn't have to be here to meet me. He wanted to get me after my last session and take me back to their house for Mum's fifty-first birthday.

My dad had been my rock. All my parents had, but my dad was the one who picked me up when I hit rock bottom almost five years ago. It was not long after Cole left the country. Seeing how it affected my whole family. How it affected Meredith. How I knew what it would have done to *him* because she was his sister. It sent me spiralling. I lost it. Not something I was proud of.

I'd hidden my illness for so many years, denying its very existence. When I finally had the courage to get a real diagnosis, it didn't come as a shock. Clinical depression. They tried several avenues to treat me, but nothing seemed to really help me. It was only after I finally asked Logan if his uncle, Jensen, could recommend a counsellor that we found something which worked for me. Seems ridiculous it was talking which helped the most, but it did. Talking. There was far more to it. After all, it had taken me years to find the right way to manage things with the help of medication and therapy.

My counsellor, Marvin, worked in Jensen's private practice. Jensen himself didn't practice any longer as he'd retired, but he still owned the place. My parents paid for my treatment. Not that initially I wanted them to, but they insisted. All they wanted was for me to be okay, so I allowed it. And it brought me to this moment.

I stepped up to my dad, who shoved off the car and gave me a hug.

"I'm proud of you," he whispered.

"I am too."

Proud for getting this far. For putting the work in. It seemed stupid this was my biggest life achievement, but it was.

He pulled back and smiled, ruffling my hair.

"So you should be."

"Are you making Mum's favourite?"

He walked around to the driver's side, shaking his head.

"You know I am."

I got in the passenger side after he opened his door and slid in.

"And did you make your cheesecake?"

"As if I would allow her birthday to pass without it, or yours for that matter."

I grinned. It was mine and Mum's absolute favourite. Dad always made it for our birthdays.

"Is Marvin sad to see you go?" he asked after we'd been driving in silence for a few minutes.

"Yes and no. He's happy I'm better and I don't need to see him any longer."

"We all are."

I knew I'd caused my parents a lot of stress over the years. They hated I hadn't come to them sooner. That's the thing about depression. It's hard to ask for help. Hard to admit you need it. I wanted to fix myself so badly, but I couldn't. Not without support and not without Marvin. I'd told him a thousand times over he'd saved my life. He kept telling me I'd saved myself. And I supposed I had.

I did what you wanted me to, J. I got help to be a better man. So I could perhaps deserve you. It's okay if you never forgive me. You're why I'm better.

I don't think I could ever forget Jonah. What I'd done had hurt him, but I couldn't drag him along through my hardships. He'd needed to live his life, not be shackled to a boy with undiagnosed clinical depression.

"Dad."

"Hmm?"

"Marvin gave me one last piece of homework before I left."

"Oh yeah?"

I smiled.

"Yeah. I know you already know this, but I never did the whole coming out thing properly, so here it goes."

I took a breath. He glanced at me, attempting not to smile.

"Dad, I'm bisexual."

"And I love you for that. I'd love you, regardless."

"I love you too."

He put a hand on my arm, giving it a squeeze before returning it to the gear stick.

Every day I felt grateful to have my parents in my life. After everything I'd been through, they'd stuck by me. They'd given me the strength to fight. No matter how many bad days I had, they were there, along with Duke. You don't know how much you need your family until they're the only people keeping you going.

"Dad."

"Yeah, monkey?"

"Do you think he'll forgive me?"

He glanced at me again.

"Jonah?"

"Yeah."

Dad knew the whole sorry story. It was one of the things I'd spoken to him about as part of my therapy. Admitting to all the shitty things I'd done to the person whose only real crime was loving me. And that was no real crime at all.

"Perhaps. It's been a long time. You can apologise and show him you're better. You worked hard on yourself. But don't expect things to go the way you hope they will, yeah? Maybe he's happy now and you should respect that."

I hadn't stopped loving Jonah Ethan Pope even through my darkest times. My love for him wasn't a part of my depression. It was a separate entity entirely. The man had etched himself on my soul. My first and only love.

"You're right. I won't expect anything. I hope he'll see me and allow me to apologise."

It's all I wanted, to make things right. I wouldn't ask him for anything else. I had no right to after the way I'd fucked everything up between us.

"You ready to ask Meredith then?"

I nodded. It had taken me a long time to be in a place where I felt strong enough to see him. Any sooner and I wouldn't have felt whole and complete in myself.

"I'll do it in person. She knows the whole story now, so if she doesn't think it's a good idea, I'll respect that."

Meredith must have heard the story from both mine and Jonah's perspectives. Whilst I was getting better, I sat her down and spilt the beans. She'd not judged me for it. She knew I was being treated for depression. It wasn't an excuse for my behaviour. I never hid behind my mental health problems.

Marvin told me it was important to make amends to the people you've hurt if you felt it was necessary. Jonah was the last person on my list.

"Maybe she'll surprise you."

I smiled and hoped she would understand. Meredith had been the only friend who'd never disappeared or left me. Everyone else drifted away. It was okay. I'd met other people and formed new bonds through work when I started to get better.

Dad and I walked up the steps to their house and he unlocked the door. We found everyone had gathered in the living room. The first person I went to was Mum.

"Happy birthday," I told her as I wrapped her up in my arms.

"Thank you, monkey," she whispered, holding onto me tight. "I'm proud of you. So, so proud."

My heart hurt in a good way and tears pricked behind my eyes.

"It's your day."

"No, it's our day. You've achieved so much." She pulled away and went up on her tiptoes to kiss my cheek. "Never forget how much I love you, baby boy."

I couldn't help smiling. Even though technically it was Cole who was the baby of the family, he wasn't home yet. Mum saw us all as her babies and that would never change. I found I no longer minded her overprotectiveness. She was only looking out for me. And she knew about Jonah too. All my family did now since I'd vowed not to keep secrets any longer.

"Love you too, Mum."

She took my hand and tugged me further into the room, handing me off onto Xav who wrapped me up in a bear hug.

"My cheeky little monkey. You're a superstar, you know that?"

I rolled my eyes.

"Yeah, you keep telling me."

He ruffled my hair, which made me shove him off. The biggest grin was on his face.

"I said it to Dad finally in the car on the way here."

"You did? Let me guess, E was happy and told you he loved you regardless, right?"

I nodded. Xav was the first person I'd officially come out to not long after I'd accepted who I was. It took a long time for me to be comfortable saying I was bisexual. And because Xav was too, he'd been the only person I wanted to share it with. He understood in a way the others didn't. Dad didn't like labels, but Xav got why I had to be able to say it and feel good about it being who I was.

"Yeah, just like you told me he would."

"Well, I do know your dad better than anyone."

Xav and Dad had been best friends for fifty-five years. They were lovers too, but they had a bond which went beyond that. Xav once told me my dad was his soulmate along with Mum, even though he didn't entirely believe in fate. He knew he couldn't live without Mum and Dad, nor Quinn and Rory for that matter, even though he and Quinn were constantly giving each other shit.

We both looked over at my dad, who was walking towards the dining room to go into the kitchen. He paused in the doorway as if he knew he was being watched and glanced at us. A smile formed on his lips.

"You know that man has stuck by me through thick and thin," Xav said, wrapping an arm around my shoulder. "I'm grateful in so many ways for his presence. And he gave me you. I love him even more for that."

Our parents saw us all as their children regardless of who had a hand in making us.

"You're making me emotional," I murmured.

Those tears were pricking again. I was so full of happiness, I didn't know what to do with myself. Some days I couldn't believe I actually felt happy and content. It was like a miracle after being in the dark for so long.

"I feel emotional today, monkey. Our family is almost whole again."

It would be when Cole came home, which he was due to very soon for Aurora's wedding. Mum had been ecstatic to find out her baby girl was getting married and her youngest son was returning to the UK.

I looked over the assembly of people in the living room. Quinn and Rory stood with my Grandpa and Lily. Grandma was with Aurora and Logan. Dad was still standing by the door to the dining room. Duke stood with Kira watching me and Xav with a smile on his face.

"Did Mum speak to Cole today?"

"He video-called us earlier to wish Ash a happy birthday. The boy got a tan since he's been sunning himself up whilst we're all freezing our arses off here."

I snorted. We were coming out of winter into spring, and it had been pretty cold for the past couple of months.

"Aren't you going away with the rest of them after Rora's wedding? You can attempt a tan then."

Xav rolled his eyes. The five of them were going to the Maldives for three weeks. I'd been surprised Rory agreed, but it was their thirtieth anniversary and Quinn's sixtieth birthday this year. Crazy to think my parents had been together that long, but it was a testament to their bond and love for each other.

"You know I just burn in the sun, right?"

"Poor you, I'm lucky I got Dad's complexion."

"Mmm, you grew up handsome like your dad, no wonder you've been fighting them off with a stick."

I prodded his chest.

"Shut up, I have not."

It's not that I hadn't dated or been with anyone since the fateful day I broke up with Jonah, but it wasn't a priority for me. Getting better had been. Xav was referring to the time a woman had asked me out at work. I'd respectfully declined. Then I'd had a guy hit on me whilst I'd been at a Christmas Market with Mum, Dad and Xav last year, which was extremely awkward. No one wants to get hit on when their parents are right next to them. I don't think he realised who they were, but I'd been left blushing. Xav had wound me up about it ever since.

"I know, I know. You're not a ladies' or gentleman's man like my idiotic son has been."

I laughed. Xav was well aware of Duke's faults, as was I.

"He's not so idiotic now." I waved at Duke and Kira. "He got his shit together."

"I've always told him she was the one, but he didn't want to listen to me."

"A father's intuition, was it?"

Xav shrugged and winked at me.

"More like you'd have to be stupid not to notice the way he's always looked at her. He never listened to anyone else but that girl. Duke needed time for his heart to catch up to his head."

"Like you with Dad then."

Xav gave me a dark look.

"And you wonder why I've always called you a cheeky monkey."

"Well, I am Dad's son, not sure why you're surprised."

He gave me a squeeze.

"You should go help said Dad finish up dinner for your mum."

"Are you trying to get rid of me?"

"Maybe."

I ducked out from under his arm and smiled.

"No wonder Mum calls you trouble."

"I'll have you know she calls me treasure, not trouble."

"Sometimes you are trouble, *tesoro*," Mum called from where she'd joined Quinn, Rory and my grandparents.

"Angel, don't be giving our son ammunition against me."

"As if you haven't given him enough already."

I shook my head as I followed Dad from the living room, who was chuckling at the exchange.

"That man will never stop being trouble," he said as we made into the kitchen.

"Duke's reformed, so why can't Xav?"

Dad snorted and checked the dishes in the oven.

"You try reforming a man whose goal in life is to wind everyone up all day. Besides, I wouldn't change him for the world. He makes me happy."

"Gross, Dad, I don't want to know about what he does to you."

He grinned.

"What? You don't want your old man to be happy?"

"Don't mention being old, Quinn might have a fit if he hears you."

Dad laughed and shook his head. Quinn did not like being reminded about his age, especially not from Mum. She'd started calling him an old man recently. The last time he'd carried her out of the room and told her just because she was in her fifties, didn't mean she didn't still require discipline. Me and Duke had found it amusing until we realised the implications of what he meant. Then we'd both felt a little sick. My parents were not shy about their relationship no matter how much it embarrassed us kids.

"You're right. No need to ruin Ash's birthday with all of that nonsense. I'm hoping your grandmother will be on her best behaviour so there's no drama there either."

"Grandma has literally got nothing to complain about."

Dad rolled his eyes.

"You know Bella always finds something to complain about regardless."

I got the plates out from the cupboard.

"You're right, but it's Mum's birthday and I want her to have a good day. She deserves it. The rock in our family, keeping us all from falling apart."

Dad walked over and gave me a squeeze.

"She is. Let's make sure she has the best day, hey? Even if we have to work hard to keep the peace."

I grinned.

"You can count on me, Dad."

The way he smiled made my chest hurt with happiness. This part of my life was wonderful, but one person was missing. One person who I couldn't stop loving even if I tried. And in all honesty, I hadn't made an effort to.

If Jonah couldn't forgive me or wouldn't see me, I'd accept it and try to move on. My heart had refused to let me do so all this time because we had unfinished businesses as far as it was concerned. Just as Jonah told me six and a half years ago, on the day I walked away from our relationship, I was it for him, he was it for me.

I'll make amends to you, Jonah Pope. I'll make sure you know it wasn't your fault. You weren't to blame.

I might have left him with scars. The same ones I owned. But I was determined to heal them. Only if he let me. I would never do anything to hurt him again. I wasn't broken any longer. And I'd learnt how to be a man who could deserve him. I'd be the man he could rely on when I'd made up for my wrongs… if he let me.

CHAPTER FORTY ONE

Raphael

Meredith and I had been sitting together in a bar for half an hour already. I didn't know how to broach the subject of her brother with her. Now I was going to see if she would be willing to ask Jonah to let me apologise to him, I found myself nervous. I didn't know how she felt about me when it came to him.

"You're really okay?" she asked, giving me a smile as she fiddled with her glass.

"Yeah, I am. It feels like I can breathe again."

She reached over and put her hand over mine.

"I'm glad... no, scratch that, I'm fucking happy. I know it's been hard, but you totally deserve to be happy, you know that, right?"

I nodded. It might have taken me a long time, but I'd got there. I realised the only person I was battling against was myself. I turned the tables and learnt how to love myself.

"I do. I really do."

She cocked her head to the side.

"I'm sensing there's a but here, Raphi."

I sighed and looked out over the bar. It's like Marvin always told me, you had to rip the bandage off. There was no point in stalling and waiting around for opportunities to drop into your lap. You had to go out and make them for yourself. I wondered what he'd think of me doing this. He knew all about Jonah, but I never told him how I planned to resolve my past with the boy whose heart I'd broken. It had nothing to do with my recovery. It was about me coming to terms with who I was inside.

"I didn't ask to meet up just to celebrate the whole end of counselling thing."

"Well, you know we don't need some jumped up excuse to hang out though, right?"

I smiled despite my nerves.

"Yeah. It's just… fuck, I don't know how to ask you this."

I hoped she didn't think this had anything to do with Cole. We didn't discuss him. My brother had been gone for a long time now. He'd asked us not to tell her he was coming back home. Cole didn't know how she would take it and honestly, neither did I. Meredith had seemingly moved on, but I think she still loved Cole. No, I knew she did. Cole loved her too. He'd been pestering me to tell him where she lived. I did know, but I'd never been there because she shared her flat with Jonah. If I didn't tell him, Cole would find out by himself. I might as well give in at this point.

"We don't have secrets anymore, so lay it out on the table."

I had one big secret. I still loved her brother. You'd think six and a half years would have dulled that. How could you love someone you hadn't seen in years? It was easy when the person was the one you couldn't forget. The one you wished you hadn't hurt so badly. I wasn't sure I'd forgiven myself for breaking his heart. It's why I had to make amends. I'd sought forgiveness for everything else I'd done in life, but when it came to Jonah Pope, I was still paying the price over and over again.

"But this is a big ask."

Meredith gave me a look as if to say give it to me straight or I'll force it out of you.

"Raphi, you're one of my oldest friends and this is clearly important, so tell me."

I stared down into my glass and took a deep breath.

"Do you think your brother will let me apologise to him?"

Meredith didn't say anything straight away. I looked up at her. Those green eyes which reminded me of Jonah's were full of understanding. I hadn't been expecting it.

"If I'm completely honest, I don't actually know. Jonah is…"

"He's what?"

I'd never asked after him. I had no idea what he was doing. It didn't seem right to dig for information from his sister when I was the one in the wrong.

"He's in a weird place right now."

"Oh… then maybe it's not a good idea for me to see him."

She squeezed my hand and smiled.

"I think he needs closure from what happened between you."

"He does? Has he said something about me?"

She shook her head.

"No, he's not said anything. I just know him. It's been a long time and he's happy in a lot of ways. He did it, you know, became a Chartered Psychologist like he's always wanted. He loves his career so much."

Knowing that warmed my heart. He hadn't fallen apart. Even though it was difficult for both of us, I had to set him free all those years ago to allow him to achieve his goals without me. He would never see it this way, but I was a burden to him back then. I was a fucking burden to myself. I wasn't capable of being in a relationship. Of giving another person my all because I couldn't even take care of myself.

"That's amazing… I'm happy he has. He worked so hard and I would have hated knowing he didn't get there in the end."

"It's funny because what he does now is exactly what you needed all those years ago… he's a counselling psychologist like Marvin."

Jonah must have known what was going on with me back then. He had to have. No wonder he wanted to help me so badly. I wasn't in a place to listen. I wasn't in a place to be good for anyone, especially not him.

"I think he knew I had depression even though I didn't."

"He's rather astute. To be honest, I can't get anything by him. He's like a hawk when it comes to my emotions."

It sounded exactly like Jonah. Always putting everyone else first.

"He loves you, Mer. You're the most important person in the world to him."

She waved me off and grinned.

"Oh, I know. That's never changed."

We sat in silence for a few minutes, sipping from our drinks.

"What's he got to be unhappy about? If it's okay to ask. You don't have to tell me."

Meredith appraised me for a long moment, her green eyes full of conflicting emotions.

"He's not really dated much since everything ended with you. I think he has a lot of confidence issues surrounding guys. Jonah doesn't trust people easily. Don't think of this as being your fault or that I'm blaming you, but honestly, I'm worried about him. It's why I think he needs closure. So, I'm glad you brought it up. I'm glad you're ready to say sorry because I think he needs to hear it even if he doesn't know it yet."

My heart hurt knowing he hadn't moved beyond us. I wanted him to find someone who deserved him.

"He's not with anyone right now, is he?"

"No. He doesn't have much of a social life. Work is his entire world and it takes its toll on him because, you know, he's sensitive to emotions."

I shouldn't feel relief at the fact he wasn't seeing anyone, but I did. It meant there was a tiny chance for me. I wasn't expecting anything but it gave me hope and hope meant everything to me.

"Why do you ask?"

I swallowed hard and took a sip of my drink.

"Because… because I still love your brother. Don't worry, I wouldn't tell him if he was to agree to see me. I don't want to hurt or upset him. This is purely me wanting to apologise for what I did to him."

I wasn't expecting her to sit back and smile at me.

"I knew it. I knew you still had feelings for him." She clapped her hands together. "You and J belong together in my opinion, and this confirms it."

"What?"

"We'll just have work at it, Raphi, get him to see he needs to open his heart back up to you."

I stared at her, wondering why, after everything I did to her brother, she would help me get him back. Because, ultimately, it's what I wanted. I wasn't going to hide or deny it.

"Have you lost your mind?"

"Nope. I'm going to ask him tonight when I get in if he'll see you. I won't tell him anything other than you want to apologise to him. I'll get him to say yes. Then you can see him and say your thing. Tell him how well you're doing now. We'll see what happens after that, but I'm determined to make sure you two get back together."

I couldn't speak for a long moment. Why on earth would she want us to be together?

"Can I ask what the hell has brought this on? You do remember what happened between me and Jonah, right?"

Meredith merely smiled wider.

"I'm feeling inspired after my best friend reconciled with the love of his life and they're getting married."

I knew all about Rhys and Aaron. Meredith wasn't particularly the romantic type, but she waxed poetic about how amazing the whole thing was. How it had changed her best friend for the better.

"So what, now you're going to matchmake for your brother?"

"I've been trying to get Jonah to meet a nice guy for years, but no, he's determined to be alone. And you know why I think that is?"

"No… why?"

She pointed at my chest.

"Me?"

"Yes, you. You're Jonah's one and we're going to remind him."

"I swear you've lost the plot."

She shrugged and sipped her cocktail.

"He's taken care of me our whole lives. I'm going to return the favour by giving him you."

I shook my head.

"You're making it sound like you're gifting me to him."

She threw back her head and laughed.

"Maybe I am. Hand you to him on a silver platter and all."

I frowned, wondering what I'd got myself into with her.

"What? Do you not want him back, Raphi?"

"I do, but I don't want to force him. If he doesn't want to be with me, I'm going to accept it."

"Well, I'm not."

I shook my head. As much as I appreciated her wanting to help me, I didn't want anyone interfering. Whatever Jonah wanted, I would be okay with it. All I wanted was his happiness. That's it. If it wasn't with me, I wouldn't push the subject.

"Meredith, promise me you won't meddle, please? All I want is for him to be happy."

She bit her lip, then sighed.

"Okay. I won't meddle. If he wants to get back with you, then I'm merely going to encourage it."

I could accept that. It's not like I could stop her from encouraging him. Maybe it's what he needed. Who knew. All I could feel was grateful she was even willing to ask him to see me. She wanted us to reconcile. Now I had to wait and see what he said, keeping my fingers crossed he would be open to it.

CHAPTER FORTY TWO

Jonah

*E*xhaustion plagued me. I'd literally worked myself to the bone this week. It was a small miracle the flat had been empty when I got in. Whilst I loved my job and my sister, my ability to be around people was shot to pieces. I needed to recharge and reset this weekend.

Meredith was consistently on my case about having a social life. I had friends. Mostly from work, but they were still friends. We went out for drinks and dinner to talk about our patients, keeping all details confidential, but it was good to have people who understood the job. It made it easier to cope with.

I suppose it wasn't the reason she kept hassling me. It'd been well over a year since I'd been out on a date. She said if I kept this up, I'd end up alone forever. I didn't want to be alone. I wanted a husband and a family, but it wasn't that simple. Not when my experience of dating was pretty fucking dire. Finding someone I was compatible with was hard enough without the fact none of the guys I'd been out with made me feel the way *he* did. I'd given up because what was the point? The only person I'd loved had up and left me for 'my own good'. The exact reason I had a habit of breaking up with someone before they could do the same to me.

It's not like I didn't realise I had issues with trusting people, opening up and giving them my heart. I wasn't one of these psychologists who wasn't self-aware. I didn't have the energy or the will to fix my own brokenness. Not when I didn't have any need or real reason to do so.

I'd crawled into bed after spending the evening in front of the TV when I heard the front door slam. Meredith was back. I hoped she wouldn't come to check on me. I wasn't in the mood.

It was my shitty luck when she came waltzing in two minutes later.

"Hey, J, you okay?"

I love you, Mer, but I don't want to deal with you right now.

"I'm tired and about to pass out. Did you have a nice evening?"

She hadn't told me what she was doing. Meredith had always been independent and did as she pleased.

"I did. Drinks with a friend."

"Glad to hear it."

I took her in properly then, noticing the twinkle in her eyes. It made me suspicious. She only ever had that look when she was about to either tell me something I didn't want to hear or ask me to do something I had no interest in doing. Not what I needed right now. I was liable to get snappy.

"Aren't you going to ask who it was?"

"No."

She pouted, giving me a sour look.

"You're a bit grumpy."

"I've had a really long week, Mer. All I want to do is sleep and be alone."

My sister always gave me space when I needed it. Usually, she'd apologise and leave but this time she didn't. She stood there, rocking back and forth on her heels. I wanted to tell her to go away but I couldn't. I wouldn't do that to her.

"J, I saw Raphi tonight."

My whole body went tense at the sound of his name on her lips. I thought I'd heard her incorrectly for the first few seconds, but no, Meredith had said his name in a very deliberate way.

Raphi.

I knew they were still friends. Not like I tried to stop her from doing what she wanted in life. Not after what happened with Cole. I wasn't my sister's keeper. I'd come to terms with it a long time ago. It was hearing his name which cut me. It made my chest burn. She made every effort not to bring him up in conversation. Why now? Why fucking well now?

"And?" I bit out, feeling like I was about to break in half.

"And I'd appreciate it if you listened to what I have to ask you without biting my head off."

I gritted my teeth against saying something I didn't mean. Instead, I nodded even though I didn't want to hear anything about him. It would only hurt. Anything to do with that name and what I had gone through with him hurt.

Raphael Nelson had left me with so many jagged scars on my heart and my soul, I no longer knew how to count them. When I said I didn't have the will to fix my problems with men, well, he was the reason. It always came back to him. The boy who'd broken me when he walked out the door. I shouldn't blame him for it. Not when I knew he'd been suffering. But I did. Fuck, did I. He crushed me.

"Love isn't enough."

It's not as if I'd ever thought love conquered all in life, but for him to tell me he loved me and then say it wasn't enough for him to stay? Well, it fucked with me. Royally.

It stayed with me. It changed the way I looked at relationships. It changed everything. It broke me.

For my sister to remind me of Raphi when she knew how I felt about him? It was fucking low.

I rubbed my face. No, I wasn't going to put that on her. None of this was Meredith's fault. She hadn't done anything wrong. She hadn't ripped my heart out of my chest and taken it with her when she left me for a second time. No, that was all Raphi. All of it.

I didn't think I was still so angry and upset about it. Fuck. Why did she have to go open my old wounds up?

"He wants to see you to apologise for what happened. I think you should seriously consider saying yes because he's gone through a lot to get to where he is now. And I really believe you need this because, Jonah, you have never closed that chapter of your life with him. You've never let go and I think it's time. It's time you find peace and closure with him."

It was as if she'd plucked my thoughts from right out of my head. Not the parts about finding peace, but the fact I'd never got closure. If I had, I wouldn't be feeling this way about him. Like I wanted to throw shit around the room to take out my frustration and anger on something.

"What?"

"I'm telling you this for your own good. See Raphi and let him say sorry."

"My own good? You think it's for my own good to see my ex-boyfriend? The person who fucked me over not once but twice? Who I gave everything I had to, but it still wasn't enough?"

Meredith raised an eyebrow.

"Yes, your ex-boyfriend who you clearly still have a lot of feelings towards or you wouldn't be getting worked up right now."

"I'm fucking tired. I told you that."

She shook her head and walked further into my room.

"Oh no, this isn't about your long week or your patients. This is about the fact I can't even say his name or mention his family without you flinching. You think I don't see how much you're affected by it even though it's been over six years? I'm not blind, Jonah. You might be the psychologist here, but I'm your sister and when it comes to matters of the heart, I know you."

I crossed my arms over my chest and looked away. I hated how right she was. I hated it so fucking much.

"Look, I could tell you why he wants to apologise, but I'm not going to because it's better coming from him. At least you can get closure with him. You get the chance to do that, J. Take it because fuck knows you need it."

My heart hurt at her words. She was talking about herself and her inability to get closure with Cole. How she'd gone five years without hearing a peep from him. How his family wouldn't tell her where he was. Meredith had basically been adopted by them. She felt like she had a real family now. I understood but at the same time, I couldn't help feeling as though she was punishing herself by being around them because all they did was remind her of Cole. Reminded her of how much she missed him. How she still loved him.

What a fucking pair we were. Completely messed up over boys in that family.

"I wouldn't tell you to do this if I didn't think it's what's best for you. All you've done since he ended it is punish yourself for not being enough. I'm not going to watch you do it any longer, not when you have the opportunity to shut the door on your past. Few people get that in life, Jonah, you, of all people, know this. I'm willing to bet many of your patients wish they could talk to the people they've loved and lost."

"I hate that you're using my patients against me right now," I muttered.

Why did she have to be right? By all accounts, I shouldn't see him. It would only hurt me, but sometimes you had to get hurt to heal properly.

"If it gets you to stop being an idiot."

418

"Excuse me if I have an issue with seeing the person who broke my fucking heart."

"I get this isn't going to be easy for you, but life isn't fucking easy. You've said that to me a million times."

I dropped my face into my hands. It wasn't the best time to be having this conversation since I was irritable. I didn't want her to be right about any of it, but she was. I couldn't deny it.

"So what, he wants to absolve his guilt over what happened? Is that what this is about?"

"No. You might not believe this but he wants you to be happy, J. And don't tell me you are, because we both know that's not true."

Why did the knowledge hurt so much? Maybe since it reminded me of what he'd said. Every word. Raphi had wanted me to be happy back then. He didn't want me to suffer. He never had. It's why he'd ended it. He felt like he wasn't good enough for me.

I knew Meredith wouldn't let this go. She'd keep pesetering me until I gave in. It was who she was. I couldn't hate her for it either.

I raised my head, dropping my hands. She stood there, giving me a sympathetic look, which I hated almost as much as this situation.

"If I say yes to seeing him, will you leave me alone? I need to sleep."

"I don't want you to say yes to get rid of me."

"Look, I get it. You're right. I need to move forward."

She stared at me for a long moment.

"Okay, I'll tell him to come over tomorrow afternoon. I'm out with Rhys, we have wedding stuff to do."

"What? Tomorrow? That's too soon."

"No, it's not, Jonah. I'm not letting you chicken out of it. I'll leave you a note on the fridge with the time. Sleep well."

And with that, she stalked out of the room, closing my door behind her. I didn't get a chance to tell her I didn't want to see anyone this weekend. I needed time to work out how I would approach this. How I would cope with him being in front of me.

I flopped back on my bed and rubbed my eyes.

Well, this is just fucking great. The weekend I need to myself and I have to see my ex-boyfriend.

I turned out the light and pulled the covers over my head, groaning. This was the very last thing I needed right now. I'd have to suck it up and deal. Whether or not I liked it, I was going to have to see Raphi and find out why the hell it was so important for him to apologise to me.

Damn my sister. Damn him. Damn everything.

CHAPTER FORTY THREE

Raphael

I hadn't expected Meredith to text me last night and tell me Jonah was willing to see me the very next day. I got the impression she'd strong-armed him into it. When she'd left the bar last night, the woman had been pretty determined to make sure I got my chance with Jonah.

Here I was, palms all sweaty and my heart racing, waiting outside their front door for him to open it. I hadn't given myself any wiggle room to chicken out or think too hard about seeing him again. There was no other choice but to go through with it now.

When the door opened, there was no one standing there, which confused me for a moment until I realised he was half-standing behind it. I took that as my cue to step in. The door shut behind me. I turned around, my breath catching in my throat at the sight of him.

Jonah had his hand dug in his pocket. It was the first thing I noticed as I'd always found his hands beautiful. The second was he looked exhausted and worn down. Lastly, I realised he'd only grown more handsome in the intervening years since I'd last laid eyes on him. His hair was longer and messy. His body was more toned and defined judging by the way his t-shirt clung to his chest.

I fiddled with my glasses, wondering how to stop myself from blurting out a whole series of compliments because they'd make him blush. I missed the way he blushed, his cheeks and ears going red.

Stop that. You are here for one reason and it's to say sorry. Do not ogle him.

The first thing which made me pause was seeing his light green eyes had lost some of that lustre they always seemed to possess whenever he was around me. It's like the lights had gone out. It made me very aware he wasn't doing as well as I hoped. And perhaps seeing me hurt him far more than it should.

"Hi," I said when he didn't make a sound.

"Hello, Raphael."

I didn't like the fact he'd used my full name and his tone was all formal as if I was one of his patients. I don't know why it felt that way, but it did. Probably because it was the way Marvin had talked to me for a long time. It gradually changed when I started to open up to him. Even though I knew I'd needed counselling, I'd resisted talking about my feelings towards myself for a long time.

"How are you?"

"I'm fine."

His tone was clipped, indicating he was anything but fine. I didn't try to push the subject. Instead, I looked around at the open plan living area.

"Can I get you something to drink?" he asked a moment later.

"Sure, um, tea is fine. Thank you."

He nodded and then waved at the sofa as if to say sit down. I watched him walk away from me into the kitchen area and fill up the kettle. The stiffness of his back and his general demeanour only confirmed what I suspected. Meredith had forced this on him. It didn't make me feel good about coming here. I was in half a mind to text her and give her hell for not giving Jonah a real choice in the matter.

I shrugged out of my coat, hanging it up by the door where his and Meredith's sat before walking over to the sofa and taking a seat.

"You and Mer have a nice place."

He flinched as if the sound of my voice cut him.

Fuck, I shouldn't be here. He doesn't want me here.

"Thank you."

Right now, he and I felt like strangers making stupid small talk. We weren't strangers. Jonah and I knew each other intimately. This didn't feel right. It just plain hurt. I knew I wasn't entitled to feel that way considering I was the one who'd hurt him. Marvin had told me to own my feelings. I wasn't going to push them away.

It's okay if it hurts you. It should. He meant a lot to you. He still means everything to you.

I didn't speak whilst he made tea and brought it over, setting it on the coffee table. He took a seat in the armchair diagonally across from the sofa. When he levelled his gaze on me, I felt exposed. Jonah had always seen through me.

Would he know I still cared about him?

Could he see how much I wished to make things right?

"So, you have something to say to me."

I swallowed and fiddled with the end of my jumper.

"Yes, I do."

"Well…" He splayed out his hands. "I'm listening."

I'd gone over in my head what I would tell him. It seemed best to start at the beginning. Start back when I'd fucked up my life. Before I'd found a way to get better.

"Did you know?"

He frowned.

"Know what?"

"That I had depression."

He stiffened in his seat, his hand curling around the arm.

"Yes. I suspected it, anyway. I take it you got an official diagnosis, then."

I nodded.

"Not straight away, but yes. I… I came here today not to drag up things from the past or to upset you, but to tell you I'm sorry for what I put you through. I don't want to make excuses or justifications for what I did. I don't blame my mental health for the way I acted. My actions are my responsibility and I know that."

His eyes softened a fraction. They'd been hard since the moment he'd opened the door to me, but my words had pushed past that.

"Back then… back when we were together, I wasn't in a good place. Every day I'd wake up wishing I could be different. Wishing I didn't hurt people the way I did. I wasn't going to give up, but I felt like it. All the time. I wasn't coping well. I didn't want to be a burden to anyone else. Especially not you."

I paused to take a sip of my tea as my mouth had gone dry.

"You were never a burden to anyone, but I understand why you felt that way at the time."

I set the mug back down. His words gave me the courage to continue.

"I didn't get any better after we broke up. To be honest, I was incredibly self-destructive and did a lot of things I'm not proud of. I pushed away everyone who cared about me. It wasn't until… until Cole left, I hit my lowest point. Him leaving left a gaping hole in my family. It hurt Meredith and honestly, I knew it would have affected you because of that."

I didn't look at him when I said those words. Admitting I'd still thought about him wasn't what I intended, but I found I couldn't lie to him. Lies and secrets had all but destroyed me before. I wouldn't let them do it to me again.

"I lost it and almost had to drop out of university. That's when I went to the doctor and got my diagnosis for clinical depression. They tried to treat me in various ways, but nothing seemed to make me feel okay. Logan's uncle is retired, but he still owns a private practice. He found the right person for me and worked out the right combination of meds. I started seeing Marvin every week and did so until a week ago when I had my last session. It's taken me a long time to be in a place where I can finally say I'm okay and at peace with myself."

It's not like I thought I would never suffer another bout of depression, but I was in a place where I could handle it if it happened. I was stronger now. So much stronger than I'd ever been before. Plus, I had my meds to help keep me on a more even keel.

I looked up at Jonah then. His expression was neutral, but his eyes betrayed everything. They told me on some level, he was proud of me for getting help. For sorting my life out. The part of Jonah who helped people like me knew how difficult it was for me to even come here today and tell him this. To have made this journey to acceptance. It didn't change the fact all the other parts of him probably hated me for what I'd done to him. Hated me for breaking his heart.

"I know this is all probably irrelevant to you, but one of my goals when I decided I needed to get better, was to get to a place where I could see you and apologise. So, I want to thank you for seeing me today, for hearing me out and again to say I'm sorry. I realise it isn't easy. I'm not expecting anything here. I'm not asking for forgiveness. All I want… all I've ever wanted, Jonah, is for you to be happy. I hope you are."

He didn't say a word. It gave me the impression he wasn't happy just like Meredith had said. I hated it. Knowing even though I'd let him go because I wasn't capable of being the person he needed at the time, he still wasn't happy.

I want to make you happy, Jonah, so fucking badly. Fuck, seeing you is like being able to breathe after being underwater for too long. Those choking gasps you take as your lungs struggle to regain their equilibrium.

I'd once wondered how it was possible to love someone as much as I'd always loved him. Now I knew. There was no explanation. Love wasn't this quantifiable force. It was wild and unpredictable. But when you found it, when you truly found it, you had to hold on to it. You had to be willing to walk through fire for it.

I hadn't been capable of doing that back then, but I was now. I'd thought love wasn't enough. Love hadn't fixed me. I was stupid to think I didn't deserve love. I didn't deserve to be loved the way he'd loved me. Stupid and naïve. He wasn't the man I'd become. I knew better. I knew love was enough. Love would mend my heart and his, if he let it. Love wouldn't erase our scars, but it would soothe them.

I didn't push Jonah for a response to anything I'd said. I picked up my mug and sipped at my tea as we sat in silence. He was clearly digesting everything I'd told him. Being with him only made me want to reach out and hold his hand. To remind myself of what his skin felt like.

When we'd been together, we only had eyes for each other. It was the same for me right now. The same feeling. Like his image was the only one I wanted to fall asleep to and wake up with. I couldn't help it. I still loved him. I just fucking well loved him.

"I accept your apology, Raphael, and I'm truly glad you're doing better…" He looked away, his eyes growing sad. "But I don't think we should see each other again after this."

My fingers tightened around the mug, but I didn't allow myself to react any further. No matter how much it hurt, I understood and would respect his wishes. I set the mug down and stood up. If he didn't think we should see each other again, then I needed to leave and respect what he wanted.

"Okay. I understand. I'm sorry to have taken up your time like this."

He stood too. Those green eyes of his were so full of wildly conflicting emotions. One second it looked like anger, the next, sadness and heartache. I steeled myself against it and walked towards the door, taking my coat and sliding it on. I found he'd followed me to the door looking like he wanted to say more but was unable to. It would be better for me to go now before I made this any worse for either of us.

He opened the door for me and I stepped out, turning back to him one last time.

"I meant what I said, I hope… I hope you find happiness one day."

Then I walked away. When I reached the stairs, the sound of his voice stopped me.

"Raphi!"

I glanced over my shoulder. He'd stepped out from his flat, holding the door open with his foot. Fuck, he was stunning. Absolutely stunning and everything I'd ever wanted. But I couldn't have him. He wasn't mine. He never really had been in the first place.

"I hope you find happiness too."

I smiled, giving him a nod and a wave before I started down the stairs. I stayed strong whilst I made my way home.

It was only when I walked through the door of my house and sat down on my sofa, my heart started to burn.

I'd done it. I'd seen him and told him I was okay now. It hadn't made me feel better. If anything, it had only confirmed something I already knew to be true. I loved that man with every inch of my fucking being. And he didn't want to see me again.

I deserved what he'd said. I hadn't expected anything else. But it didn't change how my body flooded with pain at the knowledge I had to let go of the person I'd loved for almost ten years.

It's time you move on. It's time to give up on the hope he could ever forgive you and give you another chance.

"I can do this," I whispered to myself. "I'm strong enough. I can."

I would be strong enough, but right then, I let myself feel the weight of his loss all over again. I let myself cry those tears of loss knowing I couldn't hide from them. It was the only way. I had to purge them from my system, then I could do what was best for both of us.

I'm going to let you go, J, even if a part of you will remain in my heart forever.

CHAPTER FORTY FOUR

Jonah

It only took me shutting the door and walking two steps before my knees gave out. Pain. All I felt was pain. I curled up on the floor, unable to go anywhere. Tears came, blurring my vision as I stared at my hands.

Raphi. Fuck.

I knew I wasn't ready for this. No part of me was ready to let go and move on. Especially not now I'd seen him.

It hurts. God, it hurts. Why does it hurt so much?

Why did he have to look so good? And happy. He seemed so fucking happy. Here I was lying on the floor crying like a fool over him. I sent him away. I'd done this to myself by allowing my sister to interfere. By not saying no when she told me he wanted to see me.

Why are you such an idiot?

When I'd opened the door to him it was as if no time at all had passed. Probably why I'd all but hidden myself behind it to stop myself from grabbing hold of him. He'd grown into himself more. He still had those wide framed glasses which suited him, but he had a scruff of beard too. His green eyes were bright and full of life. And his clothes fit him like they were made for him. Moulding to his body which I had, admittedly, checked out whilst he'd been talking to me. I couldn't help it. Raphi was beautiful. He always had been. The years had not changed that one bit.

Why did you send him away when you want him?

Maybe it was my self-preservation kicking in. Or maybe I was scared. Who the hell knew.

I was genuinely happy he'd got help. He needed it. It only hurt because I wasn't there to help him through all of it. All the hardships he must have faced trying to find himself. It's all I'd ever wanted to do. Be there for him. For the boy I loved more than life itself.

I wasn't there. He needed me and he wouldn't let me be there.

It was ridiculous to be so upset by that fact. And yet, it was how I felt. I hated him and myself for it. Hated how I'd punished myself all these years. For not being enough for him. For not being strong enough to stop him from leaving me. For not keeping him from imploding on himself. I'd failed him. And yet… he'd saved himself like I wanted him to.

Why did it still hurt? Why did I still feel shit about it? How could I feel proud of him and hate everything about it at the same time?

I don't know how much time went by as I lay there, my tears falling unheeded as I continued to stare at my hands. The key in the front door alerted me to the fact my sister was home. It was the door knocking against my back which made me flinch.

"What the—"

Two feet came into my field of vision as the door slammed shut.

"Jonah? Oh my god."

Meredith dropped to her knees and pulled my hands away, checking me over. Her face came into view as she lay next to me and stroked my face.

"What happened?"

I shook my head. Talking about it would only hurt more.

"Is it him?"

Another tear leaked out. I wasn't angry at her. Just at myself.

"I told him we shouldn't see each other again."

"Okay, and that's upset you?"

I nodded.

"Why's that, J?"

It seemed so ridiculous. So stupid. I was the absolute worst.

"I love him."

Meredith didn't say a word. She merely gave me a sad smile and moved closer, wrapping an arm around me and pressing her forehead to mine. It only made me cry harder.

"Why did I send him away? He told me... he told me he was better. He got better and... and I wasn't there for him."

Her face crumpled.

"Oh, Jonah. You know he had to do it on his own. How many times have you told me you can't help someone who doesn't want to help themselves? He wasn't ready."

"No, Meredith, I wasn't enough for him. He said love wasn't enough."

My sister stroked my cheek again. I felt like I was breaking. I was back there on the day he left me. It hurt more than anything had ever hurt before. All I could think about was how much it hurt.

"You are more than enough. It wasn't why he left and you know it. He wasn't well. You can't take what he said to heart."

Rationally, I knew that. My heart wasn't being particularly rational right now. Meredith was right. I was losing it over Raphi and all the reminders of that day. I should pull myself together. Start actually listening to reason. Raphi hadn't been well. He hadn't been ready to get help. He had been self-destructive and it wasn't good for him or me. Loving someone didn't necessarily mean they were good for you.

"Since when did you become the psychologist and me the patient?"

Meredith grinned.

"All your advice and lectures have worn off on me."

"I don't lecture you."

Her eyebrow shot up and she pulled away slightly.

"Only sometimes when I'm being stupid. Now, let's get you up off the floor and I'll make you some coffee and food, okay?"

I let her help me up and bring me over to the sofa, making me sit down. She tucked a blanket around me and wiped my face with some tissues. I couldn't help but give her a grateful smile because it was the exact same thing I would have done with her. She left me there to walk over to the kitchen and start preparing something for us.

"Why did you make me see him?" I asked as she pulled stuff out of the fridge.

"Many reasons, J. I've seen how much he's been through over the years. How hard he's worked. He's doing so well. I would have never allowed it if I thought he wasn't in a good place. You might not see it now, but you need this. You can't spend the rest of your life punishing yourself over him."

I looked down at the blanket. Meredith had seen right through me. She knew I'd consigned myself to purgatory over Raphi. I couldn't hate her for it. Not when she wanted what was best for me. I'd spent my whole life fighting for her. She wanted to do the same for me.

The truth was I should know better. I'd built my career on helping people like Raphi and others who suffered from mental health problems. Guess when it came to my personal life, I was bad at taking my own advice and helping myself.

"I hate how you know I do that."

"Well, big brother, you can't hide from me. Firstly, I love you, and secondly, I want to help you. Now, tell me honestly, do you really think it's best for you two not to see each other again?"

I didn't have an answer for her. Was I even in the right frame of mine to make that judgement?

"I don't know."

"Okay, let me put this another way. Regardless of whether or not it's a good idea, do you want to see him?"

I looked inside myself. Raphi was the only person I'd cared about without reservation outside of Meredith. He'd always been the one. I'd accepted it long ago. I hadn't wanted to change it because deep down, I hadn't stopped wanting him. Hadn't stopped hoping one day he would come back to me. Now he had, I didn't know what the fuck to do with myself.

"Yes."

"And why's that?"

I almost smiled when the answer came to mind.

"I love him."

"See? That wasn't so hard, was it?"

I looked over at her.

"It doesn't matter what I want. I don't know if being around him is good for me. It hurt so much having him here and not being able to tell him how he made me feel."

Meredith glanced over her shoulder from where she was standing by the stove and frowned.

"What exactly did you say to him?"

"Not very much. He did the talking, not me."

"Jonah, you know I wanted you to see him so you could have an honest discussion as opposed to it being one-sided."

I wanted to hang my head. It wasn't particularly adult of me to have sent him away when we clearly needed a conversation. Why had I been so stupid? Probably because I was way too messed up over him, I couldn't think straight.

Self-preservation. Definitely self-preservation.

But what the fuck was I even preserving myself from? He wasn't the same boy he'd been when he was eighteen. He wasn't fucked up and hating himself. I'd heard what he said and then dismissed it like it meant nothing even though it meant he was better. He'd changed.

"I know and I fucked that up."

"Well, we all make mistakes. You can fix this."

"How? I told him I didn't want to see him."

She snorted and shook her head.

"You think that's a hindrance? God, you really are useless at relationships. You are allowed to change your mind. I doubt he's going to tell you to get lost if you tell him you want to talk."

"Oh yeah, and what makes you so sure about that, huh?"

I was acting childish, but my emotions were all over the place. The thought of seeing him again made my heart race. Plus, this was my sister. We ribbed each other all the time.

"He didn't just get better for himself, J. He did it for you too."

"What?"

"Do you really think he stopped caring about you? Wow, you're stupider than I thought."

"Hey! That is not fair."

"It is when my idiot brother can't see what's right in front of his face."

I crossed my arms over my chest and glared at her.

"Why are you so annoying?"

"I'm your little sister and it's my job. Did you ever stop to think why Raphi made it a personal goal to be well enough to face you again, hmm? No, because you're too busy being stupid and acting like he broke your heart all over again when it's your doing. You didn't have to send him off without talking to him. Don't you sit there and get all high and mighty with me."

My sister was too damn smart for her own good. Calling me out on my own shit. I didn't even want to dispute what she'd said.

"What should I do?"

"About what?"

"Raphi, what should I do about him?"

"Talk to him."

"As if it's that simple."

Talking to him felt impossible when all my feelings were whirling around inside me. I didn't know what I wanted when it came to him. I hadn't thought past getting him out of the flat so I could fall apart without an audience. I'd had one anyway in my sister. Instead of letting me drown, she'd picked me up and shook some sense into me. Stopped me from losing it. Maybe she was right. Maybe I did need to talk to him.

"It is. I'll give you his phone number and address. Then you have no excuse."

I didn't answer. Meredith left me to my own thoughts whilst she finished making me coffee and food. When she brought it over, she sat down next to me and rubbed my knee.

"I know it's hard, J, but you have to deal with this. Either find closure or find a way to forgive him. That's it. It's not rocket science. I mean, shit, look at Rhys and Aaron. Trust me when I tell you I'm pretty sure what happened between them is way worse than you and Raphi, and they still found a way back to each other. You're both human. You've both made mistakes. Now it's time to put the past to bed and move on with your lives."

"I'm not ready to make a decision about him yet."

She smiled at me.

"You don't have to be. He's not going anywhere."

I didn't know about that. He did look pretty resigned when I said we shouldn't see each other. If I didn't see and talk to him soon, would it be too late?

I couldn't bear the thought of it. I had to get my act together and see him again. Just to have a conversation. To talk things out. I didn't have to decide right then what I wanted to do about the two of us. Getting it all out in the open would be better than keeping my feelings bottled up. Meredith was right. I needed to deal with it once and for all. I couldn't let myself remain like this. Just as Raphi had saved himself, I had to do the same for me. Save myself from purgatory and find peace again. Whether it was with Raphi or without him, it didn't matter.

I had to do this for myself then I could be free, like he'd wanted for me all those years ago when he left me with nothing.

CHAPTER FORTY FIVE

Raphael

The doorbell went, making me frown as I got up. I hadn't been expecting anyone, so I had zero clue who it was. I walked out of my living room into the hallway and pulled the door open. My heart just about stopped when I saw who it was. My hand shook as my world tilted on its axis. The one person I was trying to move on from was standing in front of me after telling me we shouldn't see each other again.

"Jonah? What are you—"

I didn't get a chance to finish my sentence. He stepped in, grabbed me by the face and kissed me. I froze, unable to comprehend what was happening. He walked us backwards despite the fact I hadn't responded to his kiss. I let go of the door to make sure my arm didn't get ripped out of its socket. For a long moment, I thought I might be dreaming as the door slammed shut and he shoved me up against a wall, pressing his body into mine.

What do I do? What the fuck is he doing here? Why is he kissing me?

My whirling thoughts didn't stop my body reacting to his. The years hadn't dulled my attraction to Jonah. I hardened under his touch as I responded to his kiss. My lips moved against his as all our pent up longing and need took over. My hands went to his hair, tugging at the blonde strands and pulling him even closer.

"Fuck," he muttered against my lips.

Fuck indeed. Fuck have I missed you.

In response to his curse, I flipped us around, pushing him up against the wall instead. He ground against me, making it very clear he liked this. He wanted it. I released his mouth for a moment so I could look at him. His green eyes were wild and I imagined mine were too.

"Jonah, what—"

"Don't speak."

"What?"

"I said don't speak. I don't want to talk."

"Then what—"

He kissed me again to stop me from asking. I groaned as he dug a hand between us and stroked my cock. Jonah didn't want to talk, but he certainly wanted something else. He wanted me. I didn't know if this was a good idea or not but my body was on board with his desire.

"Remind me of how we were," he whispered against my mouth. "I need it, Raphi. Please."

442

"You need me to do what?"

He knew this game. How we worked. I didn't give him things unless he asked for them. This time it was imperative I had his words. So we both knew who'd initiated this. Who'd asked for it.

"Take me to your bed, strip me down, kiss me, touch me and… and… fuck me like you used to. I need it. I need you to remind me of what we were to each other."

Whilst I had no real fucking clue why he needed this, I couldn't deny him. Instead of talking like we really should, I took his hand and led him upstairs. His breathing was heavy as if this scared and excited him at the same time. Hell, I was scared and excited too. Scared of what this meant. What if this was his way of being able to let go? I didn't want him to let go of me. I wanted him to stay forever and for us to work things out.

When we reached my bedroom, I took my glasses off and set them on the bedside table. Jonah curled himself around my back and kissed my neck, running his hands down my stomach. I turned in his arms, wrapping my hand around the back of his neck and kissing him again. His fingers explored the contours of my body as mine did so to his. It'd been such a long time. Whilst I'd memorised every inch of him, this felt different. It felt better.

He went willingly when I pressed him down on my bed. I shoved his coat off his shoulders and threw it away. My hands went to his jumper next, pushing it up his chest along with his t-shirt. He'd got more toned. It only made my mouth water.

"Still hot as fuck," I murmured.

Seeing him blush made it completely worth it. I leant down and ran my tongue along his collarbone. He panted, his hands coming up to fist in my hair. I moved lower, circling his nipple which made him moan and buck underneath me.

"Raphi," he whimpered. "Please."

"A little impatient, are we?"

His light green eyes were on me, begging me to keep going.

"I've been too scared to ask anyone else to give me what you do."

I didn't want to think of Jonah with anyone else when we were about to have sex but knowing I was the only one who'd ever given him what he truly needed made my chest swell.

"I see." My hands went to his belt, tugging it open and unbuttoning his fly. "So, you're saying you need to be pinned down and made to take it without mercy, hmm? Have you missed it? The way I take and you give?"

He moaned as my hand ran down his hard cock. There was no doubt he'd missed it. He craved it.

"Yes, I have. I need it."

I tugged off the rest of his clothes, stopping to untie his trainers on the way. Reaching over, I ripped my bedside drawer open and pulled out the lube. I sat up on my knees, proceeding to coat my fingers. He watched me, his hands fisted at his sides as if his patience had worn thin. I leant over Jonah, reaching between us as he shifted, bending his legs at the knees to give me better access. My lips brushed against his, taking in every one of his tiny reactions to my touch.

"Do you want me to take you here, J?" I brushed my fingers over him. "Do you want me to pound your tight little hole with my cock, huh? Make you cry out and beg me not to stop?"

I slid my first finger inside him, trying not to groan at how hot he was.

"Please, fuck me."

"Tell me how you want it."

"Rough, I want it fucking rough, Raphi. I don't care if it hurts. Just give it to me."

It's not like I was going to tell him no. Every part of me had missed Jonah. Missed the way we were together. It's not like I'd been this way with anyone else either. It hadn't occurred to me. This was me and him. I'd wanted to keep it that way. I felt like I'd be tarnishing our memory otherwise.

"You're going to get it rough and without mercy. Even if you want me to stop, I won't."

He moaned as I worked my finger inside him before inserting another.

"I don't want you to stop."

"I wouldn't be so sure of that. You have no idea what I'm about to do to you."

He shivered and I kissed him. I wasn't going to be all talk and no action. He had told me to remind him of how we were. I was going to go one step further. Give him an experience he'd likely never forget. I wanted to brand myself on him the way he had me.

I took my time working him up, getting him ready for me. He whined and begged me to give it to him, but I had more patience than he did. When I was sure he could take it, I pulled my fingers from him.

445

"I want you to bend over the bed and put your hands behind your back."

I shifted off him so he could obey my command, standing up and wiping my fingers down with a tissue. Jonah did as I asked whilst I tugged my t-shirt off. He looked back at me, his eyes roaming across my bare chest. I smiled as I pulled the rest of my clothes off. Jonah could barely keep his eyes off me and it made me feel good. Like he needed to see me to feel alive.

I might not have let my true self out with anyone else, but I'd learnt a few things, regardless. Things I liked in the bedroom. I pulled a length of silk rope from the bedside and wrapped it around his wrists, tying them together. He didn't object or tell me no. I took the next thing out. Jonah let out a little pant as I wrapped a length of silk around his eyes and tied it behind his head, depriving him of his sight.

"Now you won't see me coming," I whispered in his ear before pressing a kiss to his cheek.

"Raphi…"

I stroked my hand down his back.

"Shh, it's okay. I've got you. You don't need to be scared."

"I'm not. I need this… I need you."

My heart hurt at his words. The desperation in his voice. I didn't know how he could place so much trust in me after all this time. I wouldn't question it when he was being honest with me.

I shifted lower, pressing soft kisses down the column of his spine, my fingers stroking along his skin. He whimpered, the most beautiful sound imaginable. I hadn't heard it in what felt like forever.

"More," he panted. "Please, fuck, please."

"Needy and begging," I whispered. "Could you be more perfect right now?"

He struggled against his bound wrists.

"Please, I want you to fuck me."

I dug my fingers into his hair and pulled his head back. The way his neck stretched made my cock throb.

"No patience. That's not being good, J. Don't you want to be good for me?"

"I do, please, Raphi. I'll do anything."

I placed a kiss between his shoulder blades.

"Spread your legs wider."

He widened his stance without objection or hesitation.

"All you need to do is make all those beautiful sounds whilst I fuck this tight hole of yours." To make my point, I pressed a finger inside him again. "Do you hear me? Moan, pant, mewl and beg. Fucking beg me."

He tried to press himself back on my finger, making me smile.

"Please fuck me."

"Are you hard for me? Are you fucking throbbing for my touch? If I wrap my hand around your dick, will it be leaking for me?"

I pressed my finger deeper, making him arch his back.

"Yes, fuck. I'm so hard for you."

"Good."

I released him then, allowing his head to flop back on the bed. His breathing was erratic, his chest heaving. He trembled all over with want and need. Fuck. I made him like this. Only me.

I straightened and reached for a condom. I might love teasing him, but I was fucking hard and aching to be inside him. Rolling it on after I ripped the foil open, I coated myself to make sure I didn't hurt him. No matter how hard I wanted to fuck Jonah, I wanted him to enjoy it too.

Placing my hand on his hip, I lined myself up, rubbing my cock against him. He shifted, letting out these harsh breaths as if he was too desperate to even moan. I didn't deny him. My hips shunted forward, my cock sliding inside him with little resistance.

"Oh fuck," he cried out.

I stopped, wanting to give him time since I had no idea when he'd last done this. His hands moved on his back, his wrists rubbing together under the bonds.

"Raphi."

"Yes, J?"

"Can… can you go slow for me, please? Just at first."

My hand tightened around his hip.

"As you wish."

That told me one thing. He hadn't slept with anyone in a long time. It had been a good long while for me too. I hadn't been ready for a relationship whilst I was being treated. Not to say I didn't date, but it never got serious. The only person I'd ever wanted to be this way with was Jonah. I wanted the whole fucking shebang with him, including marriage, but I especially wanted forever. If he'd let me. I wanted it to be on his terms this time. I would do whatever it took to get him back.

I did exactly as Jonah asked. I went slow, giving him a little more at a time until I was pressed right up against him. He groaned and I let out a harsh breath. He was so fucking hot and I struggled to hold back.

"Thank you," he whispered.

"For what?"

"Giving me what I need."

I leant over and kissed his cheek.

"Anything for you, J. Anything at all."

I meant those words in every way he could think of.

"Kiss me?"

I smiled, moving my head lower and capturing his lips. Whilst I kissed him, I gave him deep and gentle thrusts, opening him up further to me. He moaned in my mouth, his hands shifting on his back again. Jonah clearly wanted to touch me but he wasn't allowed. Not yet.

"Are you ready for me? Ready for the way I'm going to fuck you," I hissed against his mouth.

"Yes, fuck, please."

I pushed off the bed and straightened. Gripping both his hips, I pulled out almost all the way before thrusting back in. He yelped but there were no other sounds of complaint. I gave it to him again and again, getting harder and deeper each time. And he gave me those noises. Those moans of pleasure which had always intoxicated me.

"That's it," I ground out through gritted teeth as sweat beaded on the back of my neck. "Take it. Fucking take it."

"Fuck. Raphi. Fuck. Me." The way he panted out his words as if forcing them from his lungs turned me on further.

No matter how many times I'd given it to Jonah before, I don't think I'd ever fucked him as hard as I did now. My hips slammed against him over and over. He just took it. Every thrust. Every inch.

"Don't stop, please, fuck."

No, Jonah was begging for more. Begging me to never let up. To show him how good we'd been together. How right we were.

I was so lost in giving it to him, my orgasm crept up on me. It came without warning, slamming into me as I grunted and moaned his name. My body shuddered, my cock pulsing inside him as pleasure washed over me.

"Fuck!"

"Raphi!"

I felt him clench hard around me with his own release. The two of us had been so worked up, it wasn't surprising it had come on fast.

When we'd both stopped shaking, I pulled out of him, tying off the condom and throwing it away. Then I collapsed next to him, knowing now we'd fucked, we needed to talk. I was too wrung out to move right then. And by the looks of it, Jonah was too. He lay there panting, looking like he'd been thoroughly ravaged.

God, J, you're fucking beautiful. I adore you. I love you so much. I don't want to let you go.

CHAPTER FORTY SIX

Jonah

When I came over to see Raphi, it had not been my intention to kiss him and tell him to take me to bed. I swore to myself I only wanted to talk to him. It had taken me almost a week to find the courage to visit him. When he'd opened his front door, all I could think was how perfect he looked. And how much I wanted him. My need had overridden my common sense. The need to be reminded of what we were to each other.

The way he'd taken care of me had my heart in knots. He'd done everything I asked. Went slow when I needed it then fucked me so hard I thought I was going to pass out from the pleasure. I'd even come without him touching my dick, not something that happened often but he kept hitting just the right spot. It had been a long time since I'd been with anyone intimately. He reminded me of exactly what I'd been missing with everyone else.

Passion. Fire. Desire.

Raphi untied my hands first before removing the blindfold he'd put on me. He had a tired but happy smile on his face. His perfect face I'd longed to see again.

Fuck, I'm still so in love with you.

It seemed strange to me I could have such intense feelings for someone I'd not seen in six and a half years. Perhaps what they say about first loves is true. You never forget them. Considering Raphi was my first and only love, it shouldn't come as a surprise to me. I'd never tried to get over him or let go.

"Hey," he murmured, stroking my cheek.

I flexed my fingers, resting my arms by my sides.

"I'm not sure I can move."

He smiled wider.

"Mmm, then I need to take care of you."

He kissed my cheek before getting up. I heard his footsteps retreating from the room and wondered where he was going. I somehow got on the bed properly, laying there feeling as though my world just got rocked.

"J, do you drink wine?" I heard his voice calling from somewhere.

"Um, on occasion," I called back.

"Red or white?"

"Red, please."

Then there was silence apart from the sound of running water. I should get up and go find him, but my legs felt like jelly. Raphi had learnt some new tricks in the bedroom. Being tied up wasn't something I'd considered. Him doing it had been hot. The whole thing had been incredible. I knew sex between us could be like that, but this was on a whole other level.

When Raphi returned, he grinned at me before helping me up off the bed. He frowned down at the covers, realising we'd made a bit of a mess. It was lucky it was only on the blanket covering his bed.

"One sec."

He tugged it off the bed and took it out of the room. I heard his footsteps going downstairs. I waited a few minutes until he came back. Raphi grabbed my hand and gave me a smile.

"Where are we going?" I asked as he pulled me out of the room.

"You'll see."

He took me into a bathroom. I stood on the threshold, staring at the huge claw-footed bathtub which looked like the one at his parents' house. It was filled with hot water and the room smelt of citrus. The lighting was turned down low and two filled wine glasses sat on a low small side table next to the bath.

"What's this?"

"I told you, I'm taking care of you," Raphi replied as if it was obvious.

He tugged on my hand, leading me over to the bath and encouraging me to step in. What I wasn't counting on was for him to get in with me. He sat back against one end and made me sit between his legs. I felt weird about it considering I'd never done this before. He wrapped his arms around me and kissed my shoulder.

"Isn't this something straight couples do in romance books and films?"

He snorted and rubbed my chest.

"And?"

"I forgot, you date girls too."

"Would you have preferred it if we'd showered together? Is that the more manly thing to do?"

"Shut up, that's not what I meant."

"You have a problem with me being bi, J?"

I laid my hand against his where it was resting on my chest.

"No. I never have. So, you've accepted it now then."

"Yeah, it is what it is. I don't run away from who I am any longer. I told you, I'm better."

I had believed him when he said it but hearing it and seeing it in evidence were two very different things.

"I know."

This wasn't how I meant for any of this to go. For us to be intimate with each other again, like no time at all had passed.

Raphi reached over to the table and handed me a glass of wine. I took it and sipped at it, trying to work out what I should say to him now.

"Why did you come here?" he asked me, his fingers dancing over my shoulder.

"To talk to you."

"So the fucking part was just spontaneous, was it?"

"You could say that."

He leant his head against mine.

"Then talk, J, because you told me we shouldn't see each other."

I sighed and stared down at our legs. Mine sat between his. It was a huge bath. We fit in it together without any issues.

"Why do you have such a big bath?"

I hadn't meant to ask the question but my thoughts were scattered after the sex we'd had. I didn't know where to begin.

"When my parents bought me this place as a graduation gift, they had the whole thing gutted and redone. I wanted a similar bath to the one at home. It was my favourite place to be. I could forget the world for a while whilst I was in there."

"They bought you a house for finishing university?"

Raphi rubbed his head against mine.

"You do remember they're loaded, right? They were proud of me for getting my act together. I was going to counselling every week and improving. Dad knew I didn't want to live at home so they did this for me. It gave me the independence I'd always craved. I still go back to theirs like at least once a week for dinner. It makes Mum happy and, well, I need my family."

I hadn't forgotten how rich his parents were. They were worth billions. I knew as well as Raphi not all of their wealth had been obtained by legal means. I supposed it didn't really matter now. They'd left their criminal lives behind.

"What do you even do now?"

"I work for the local council in recycling and waste management. And yes, I do enjoy my job even if it isn't glamorous like working at the casino would be. It's rewarding in its own way. Do you have any other questions or are you going to tell me why you really came to see me?"

I was stalling and he knew it. It was time to bite the bullet and admit the truth to him.

"I lied when I told you I didn't think we should see each other. Seeing you again… I wasn't ready for it. Meredith kind of made me agree to it, saying it was for my own good. She's not wrong but I wasn't ready."

I took a huge gulp of wine then set it back on the table.

"It reminded me of how much it hurt when you left me. I know you weren't well and thought you were protecting me. It didn't feel like that at the time. I was heartbroken and hated you for it. I realise now it wasn't good for either of us to be together at the time, but it still hurt. You kind of destroyed my view of love if I'm honest."

Raphi didn't say a word. He waited, probably knowing I wasn't done. One of the things I'd always adored about him was his ability to listen. It was always me who people told their problems to. Having someone who did that for me, who listened, it was something I never knew I needed until it got taken away from me. Until he left me.

"I've spent so long helping other people and wishing I could have helped you, I forgot about myself along the way. About how what happened broke me. I need to fix me. I can't move forward without dealing with the source of the problem. That's why I'm here. It all starts with you."

Raphi leant back against the bath. I turned my head to look at his face. There was contemplation there as if he was processing my words. I let him digest. Hell, I was still trying to work out why I needed it to be him. A part of me held out hope when Meredith said Raphi still cared about me, it meant more than only caring. Perhaps it meant he'd continued to love me just as I loved him.

"I want you to know you were enough for me. Your love was enough. I couldn't see it because I was too wrapped up in myself and my problems. I'm sorry I said those things and made you think you weren't enough. It was wrong of me."

My heart ached at his words. I'd needed to hear them for such a long time. I hadn't failed him. He wasn't ready for us.

"I want to help you if I can."

I hadn't expected him to make the offer. To want to help me like I'd wanted to help him all those years ago.

"You do?"

"Mmm, I still care about you. I never stopped. But I don't think this is the right way for me to help you."

"What do you mean?"

He stroked my shoulder again.

"Us sleeping together. It's not going to help you trust in love again. It doesn't mean I'm going anywhere. If you'll let me, I want to see you and do things with you."

"What... like dating?"

He chuckled.

"I wasn't going to presume that's what you wanted."

I felt my face growing hot, knowing now he'd meant spending time together as friends.

"Is it not what you want?"

"This isn't about me. I'm here for what you need. So you tell me. Do you want me to date you, J?"

"I don't know."

He leant his chin on my shoulder.

"That's okay. We'll just be friends for now. You tell me if you want more at any point. This is on your terms. I don't want to hurt you again so I'm not going to ask you for anything."

I nodded, not trusting myself to speak. It felt strange us agreeing to be friends whilst we were naked together in the bath. It wasn't particularly friend-like.

"Is that a yes to being friends, J?" he murmured.

"Yes," I whispered.

"Good."

Then he grabbed a couple of things from a shelf above us. I watched him as he squirted soap onto a loofa and washed me with a gentle touch. He started with my shoulders, making me lean forward. Again, this wasn't something friends did but I didn't object. No, I relaxed into his gentle touch. I'd missed the way he always took care of me. It felt good to let someone else be in control. To let him look after me. When he was done cleaning my whole body, he kissed my shoulder again.

"Do you want to stay the night?"

"Where, in your spare room?"

He chuckled again.

"No, J, with me. I promise no funny business."

I swallowed, unsure of how I would deal with being close to him and knowing he wasn't going to touch me.

"Okay."

What the hell? Why did you just agree to that?

I must've lost my mind, but I didn't take it back. Raphi simply asked me if I wanted to get out and after we did, he dried and dressed me. Then he tucked me up in his bed with the wine and we talked into the small hours about everything and nothing. I fell asleep feeling content and at home for the first time in a long time. Raphi was so familiar to me. His scent. His smile. The way we could sit there in silence without feeling weird or awkward.

Even though I was scared of what the future held for me and him, I didn't allow it to stop me from being happy in his company. From feeling like I could see a light at the end of the dark tunnel I'd been trapped in. Maybe Raphi was right. Maybe this would help me.

It had been forever since I felt any sort of hope for myself, but being here with him, I felt that spark again. It might only be small, but it was there.

You can do this. If Raphi can save himself, so can you. You've just got to try.

CHAPTER FORTY SEVEN

Raphael

*L*ast night I'd taken Jonah out for the second time this week. We might have agreed we were only friends, but I was treating it as if I was dating him. I'd picked him up from his flat and dropped him off afterwards, kissing his cheek both times. I didn't want him thinking I wasn't interested in more than being friends but kissing him on the lips would negate the friendship part. I'd settled for subtly indicating this was more. I wasn't sure if it was working, but I was trying.

The first 'date' had been at a bar where we'd had drinks and talked the night away. And this time, we'd gone to the cinema and had dinner afterwards. It felt like we'd not spent any time apart. Jonah and I had always had an easy friendship. We'd never run out of things to talk about and when we did, we were content to be in each other's company. It was all the other stuff surrounding our bond which had made things complicated. Like my depression. Like the fact I couldn't be open about our relationship. Too many fucking things. It was different now though. I was better. And had no issues with being honest.

"So, you haven't yet told us what's happening with Jonah," Mum said, nudging me with her shoulder. "I hope it's good news."

Duke and I were at our parents' house having dinner with them. Quinn and Rory were busy talking to each other about something to do with the casino at the other end of the table, but Mum, Xav, Dad and Duke were all staring at me with expectant looks on their faces.

I'd told them I was going to see Jonah to apologise, but not what happened afterwards. Well, Duke knew since I told him absolutely everything, but my parents didn't.

"Um, well…"

"You're embarrassing our monkey here, angel," Xav said, giving me a wink.

I hadn't realised I'd gone red until he said it. My hand went to my burning cheeks and I almost sighed in frustration. Whilst I no longer kept things from my parents, Jonah was the first and only man I'd ever been with. I'd only ever introduced my parents to girlfriends, and those were very few and far between. I found other guys attractive but they didn't match up to Jonah. I don't think anyone could regardless of whether they were male or female.

"Am I not allowed to be invested in my son's happiness?"

"I'll tell you if he keeps tripping up on his words," Duke said, waving a hand at me.

I glared at him.

"No need, I'm perfectly capable of telling them myself."

"I was only offering out of the kindness of my heart."

"Your heart isn't kind or nice so pipe the fuck down."

Duke stuck his finger up at me. Our parents didn't stop us from giving each other shit as they were used to it by now. It was how Duke and I were together.

"You going to answer our darling mother's question then?"

I looked at Mum, giving her a half-smile.

"Well, I did see him and do the whole apology thing, which he accepted but then told me he didn't think we should see each other again."

Mum's face fell. I put a hand on her arm.

"I'm not done yet. A week later he turns up on my doorstep, presumably Meredith told him where I live. We had a talk and—"

"More than just a talk," Duke interrupted, waggling his eyebrows. "There was nakedness involved."

"Oh shut up, they don't need to know about that part."

I saw Xav grinning from ear to ear and Dad shaking head from across the table.

"Don't even think about making a comment," I said to Xav before he could open his mouth.

He put his hands up.

"Oh no, I'm not going there with your mother giving me daggers."

I glanced at Mum, finding her glaring at Xav and making it very clear he needed to behave. I sent a silent thank you her way because I really didn't need any of them giving me a hard time over Jonah or what I'd got up to with him. It's not like I initiated the whole sex part. It had all been him. He'd asked me for it and how the fuck could I refuse the man I loved? I mean, I could have denied him, but I didn't want to. My goal here was to give Jonah everything he needed and wanted. To make him happy.

"As I was saying, we had a talk and agreed to spend time together… as friends. So, I've been taking him out. I saw him last night, actually."

"What did you do together?" Mum asked.

"I took him to see that new thriller and then we had dinner."

"What Raphi isn't saying is they're dating but not actually calling it that," Duke said.

"Would you stop interrupting?"

"I'm interrupting because I think it's stupid and you should just tell him how you feel."

I rubbed my face, wishing Duke would drop it. He didn't understand how scared Jonah was about me hurting him all over again. He needed time to adjust. He'd told me he needed to fix himself and it started with me. I was merely allowing Jonah to heal.

"And scare him away? I don't think so. He needs time and I'm giving him that. I've told you, it's not about what I want, it's about him. I'll do anything to get him back, including being friends whilst he deals with his own insecurities. Please stop with this shit already."

Mum rubbed my arm. I looked over at her.

"I think that's a good plan, monkey. If he needs time, then don't rush him. Just like we couldn't rush you to get help, it's the same situation here."

"Thank you, Mum."

Unlike Duke, she understood what I was trying to do. It was about restoring Jonah's confidence in me and showing him I could be someone he could rely on.

"I still think it's better in the long run if you're honest with him," Duke muttered. "I should know."

We all stared at Duke, well aware of the turmoil he'd gone through over him and Kira not being honest with each other.

"Your situation was entirely different to monkey's," Dad said. "I don't recall your brother running off and doing something incredibly reckless and stupid all because of a dare."

I put a hand over my mouth to stifle my urge to laugh. Even after all this time, my parents weren't exactly happy with Duke for the way he handled everything between him and Kira. Sometimes I thought I might be the black sheep of the family, but honestly, all four of us had done things our parents weren't best pleased about.

"Oh great, thanks for the reminder, E."

"You're welcome."

"I never said I wasn't going to be honest with Jonah," I put in. "He's not ready to hear it yet. Can you really blame me for wanting to be careful? I broke his heart. Me." I pointed at my chest. "I carry that. You know what it feels like, to be the cause of his pain, so stop giving me a hard time. I'm trying to atone for the things I've done to the person I want forever with. If Jonah needs time, I'll give it to him. I'll give him everything he needs because I wasn't there for him in the way I should have been when we were together. And yes, I'm well aware I was unwell and unable to be the person he needed, but I'm that person now."

Mum put an arm around my shoulder and gave me a squeeze before she kissed my forehead.

"I'm so proud of you," she whispered. "You've grown into such a strong and self-assured man who takes responsibility for everything he's done. I didn't think I could love you anymore but I do."

My mum's words made me emotional. I bit my lip to fight back the tears threatening behind my eyes. After all the difficulties I'd been through with my mother, having her say those things was almost too much for me to take.

"I love you too, Mum," I whispered back.

She merely stroked my hair in response, the simple gesture telling me everything she couldn't say. How she knew she had to let me be my own person and make my own mistakes. How her stepping back and allowing everything to run its course had brought us all to the here and now. Where I was better and my family was almost whole again.

The rest of the dinner was a quieter affair. No one else asked me any further questions about Jonah. To be honest, I was kind of glad of it. Talking about him made my heart ache. Even though I'd seen him last night, I missed his face. The way he smiled. The light in his green eyes when he was amused by something I'd said. It was safe to say Jonah was everything to me.

As I helped Rory load the dishwasher, my phone went off. I dug it out of my pocket and couldn't help the smile on my face when I read the message.

Jonah: Thank you for yesterday. I had a really nice time.

Raphi: You're welcome. I had a nice time too. Can I take you out on Saturday?

Jonah: What did you have in mind?

I bit my lip and noticed Rory was eyeing me with a raised eyebrow. Quinn wandered in with more dishes.

Raphi: Why don't we see where the afternoon takes us? Pick you up at 12?

Jonah: No elaborate plan? I like the sound of that. 12 it is.

"What?" I asked Rory now he'd leant up against the counter.

"Nothing."

"I don't believe you."

"He wants to know if you're texting your almost-boyfriend," Quinn said, giving Rory a look.

"He's not my almost-boyfriend."

Quinn snorted and shook his head.

"Okay, do you want me to call him your almost-husband then?"

I stared at him in disbelief.

"Quinn! He's not… how did you even know… oh my god, why is this my life?"

I buried my face in one hand, squishing my glasses up against my nose in the process.

"I saw the way you looked at him when we met him, monkey, that's how I know."

I dropped my hand.

"What is that supposed to mean?"

He leant his elbows on the kitchen island and levelled his gaze on me with a sly smile.

"It means you look at him the same way E has looked at Xav since the two of them were kids and later on, he looked at Ash that way too. Now, we've all told you why the five of us never considered marriage an option, but I know that's what you would like to happen in the future, is it not?"

I had no idea Quinn had noticed. My parents were far more astute than I gave them credit for.

"It is. Has Rory been rubbing off on you or something? I thought he was the only one who had eyes like a hawk."

Rory grinned, which made Quinn give him another look.

"Rory isn't the only one who pays attention. You're my son, of course, I'm going to notice these things. That's what parents do, isn't it?"

I raised an eyebrow.

"Huh. You approve of my choice then? Or are you just being nice because you don't have to like Jonah? You don't like Logan."

Quinn scowled, but it was the same way every time Aurora's fiancé's name got brought up.

"I never said I didn't like Logan. I gave him my blessing to marry Aurora, didn't I?"

"You forgot to add eventually," Rory said, waving his hand at Quinn. "You *eventually* gave Logan your blessing."

"Shut up, Rory."

I looked down at my phone again.

Raphi: My parents are actually the worst sometimes.

Jonah: That's nothing new.

Raphi: They're being all astute about me and shit.

Jonah: You're with them now?

Raphi: Yes, came over for dinner with Duke. We're being dutiful sons.

Jonah: Do you want a gold star for being son of the year?

Raphi: Funny. Real funny.

"And for your information, monkey, I do approve of Jonah. From what I knew of him six years ago, he seemed very nice and good for you. I doubt that's changed, has it?" Quinn said, bringing my attention back to him and Rory.

I shook my head. Jonah was nice and he was definitely good for me. He was sweet, kind, funny and everything I'd ever wanted in another person.

Jonah: You sure? I can buy you some on Saturday.

Raphi: You going to arrange some kind of presentation ceremony for me as well?

Jonah: That's actually a really good idea.

Raphi: And you're officially ridiculous, but I kind of love it anyway.

Jonah: My ideas are amazing, not ridiculous.

Raphi: You keep telling yourself that.

Jonah: I think you love my idea really. You'd look cute with a gold star on your coat.

I just about died. He still thought I was cute.
Why are you the most adorable person in the world, J? I love that about you.

Raphi: Well, if you *really* want to get me a gold star, I won't complain.

Jonah: You'll just have to wait and see!

"I'd prefer it if you waited a while before any engagements or weddings, monkey. As much as I love Rora, this wedding has caused us all a fucking headache. Why she had to choose a man whose family is in the public eye is beyond me sometimes."

Rory and I shared a look. Quinn might say he was okay with Aurora and Logan's relationship, but I didn't think he'd ever really approve of it.

"Don't worry, I have no plans to spring an engagement on the man I'm not even in a relationship with yet, Quinn," I said to reassure him there were no more weddings on the horizon quite yet.

"Good, because your mother is exhausting all of us with this wedding and Cole coming home, so you on top of that would be the last straw."

And with that, he walked out of the kitchen leaving me staring after him.

"I swear to god he loves to have the last word at all times," I muttered.

"He doesn't get it very often with Ash. He likes to take advantage of it with everyone else," Rory said with a grin.

"Don't I know it!" I adjusted my glasses. "Did Dad make dessert?"

"Maybe he did."

I hastily made my way over to the fridge and peered inside. There sat the dessert to end all desserts. Dad's cheesecake. He had made it for Mum's birthday a few weeks ago, but the fact he'd produced one now made me smile wider.

"No offence to the rest of you, but he's my favourite for this."

Rory chuckled as I took it out of the fridge and started getting plates out of the cupboard. He knew I was only joking. I didn't play favourites with our parents.

As Rory and I took it into the dining room, I couldn't help feeling like I'd won a huge battle here. Even if Jonah didn't know it yet, I'd conquered my fear of telling my parents the truth about him. I couldn't wait to show him how far I'd come if and when he was ready to give us a shot.

CHAPTER FORTY EIGHT

Jonah

After Raphi took me out on our afternoon adventure which involved sightseeing I'd not done in forever, and me buying him a gold star as a joke, the next three weeks went by in the blink of the eye. We'd been out a total of eight times since he'd come back into my life. We'd laugh, have fun with each other, talk about what we'd done over the years and enjoy each other's company. At the end of each night, the same thing would happen. He walked me up to my door. We'd stand staring at each other for a time. Then he'd kiss me on the cheek and wish me goodnight. Whilst I appreciated him being so gentlemanly and we'd agreed to be friends, it was driving me absolutely insane.

I didn't want him to kiss me on the cheek. I didn't want him to wish me goodnight. No, I wanted Raphi to kiss me like he meant it, push me inside my flat and give it to me the way I craved. He'd told me if I wanted more, I had to say it. I had to ask for it. Every time I tried, I got all tongue-tied instead. It was ridiculous, but I was scared.

Was it too soon?

Did we still need to spend more time getting to know each other again?

Did he even want to have a relationship with me?

I had no idea. When I'd asked him if he wanted to date me the day I'd gone over to his house, he'd told me it wasn't about him. I needed him to tell me what he wanted. How else could I know if we were on the same page or not?

You're being a coward, you know that right?

Apparently, my fears were getting the better of me. I didn't know how to fix it. Raphi and I had always attempted to be honest with each other and here I was holding back.

"Why do you look so fucking miserable, J? Are things not going well with lover boy?"

I looked up from where I was sat at the kitchen table going over some patient notes. Meredith was watching TV with her feet up on the coffee table. Something she knew I hated her doing but had given up on complaining about.

"He's not my lover boy. We're not… we're just friends."

"Friends." She did double air quotes with her fingers. "Yeah okay, friends who clearly are in love with each other and won't say it to each other's faces."

"He doesn't love me, does he?"

She shook her head and rolled her eyes.

"Oh my god, Jonah. Would you open your fucking eyes? The man has taken you out several times and made every effort to make sure you have a good time together. You two are dating in case you hadn't noticed whether he kisses you at the end of the night or not. And here I thought I was shit at reading men, but you are the absolute worst."

My sister did not mince words with me. I kind of deserved it since I kept questioning everything to do with me and Raphi. She was the one on the receiving end of my endless fucking indecisiveness about what I was going to do.

"You don't have to be so mean about it."

"And you need to tell him how you feel. How many more times do we have to have this conversation? Talk to him. It's not hard to have an adult discussion about the state of your relationship, you know. For a psychologist, you really are shit at dealing with your own love life."

I ignored her comment and looked at my laptop again. She was right. I needed to get my act together.

"What if he doesn't want to get back together? What if he's doing this because he just wants to make up for everything he did to me?"

"Then he doesn't and you move on. And you know as well as I do, that's not what he's doing so stop asking stupid questions."

"Move on like you've moved on from his brother?"

She gave me a death stare.

"Shut. Up."

"Hey, I'm not judging. Just like I never got closure, neither have you."

She went back to staring at the TV. I'd hit a nerve and it wasn't fair, but she was giving me way too much shit over Raphi. I couldn't help it. He was the only person I'd loved.

Who I wanted forever with. I didn't want closure with him. No, my heart was set on marriage and a family with Raphi. Maybe it was stupid for me to wish for those things when he'd given me no real indication he wanted that with me.

When I told Meredith what happened the night I'd gone over to Raphi's, she'd smiled and told me it was a good thing. I could start to heal from the wounds Raphi had inflicted on me. The more time that went by, the more I became sure of what I wanted. Him. I'd told her my heart wanted what it wanted. It wanted Raphi and it wanted him for the rest of our lives. I had to stop being a big fucking coward and be honest with him.

"Is Raphi going to Rhys and Aaron's wedding?"

It was tomorrow and I realised I'd never asked Raphi about it.

"No, he's got some public consultation event for work he can't get out of."

Meredith had asked me to be her plus one. I was more than happy to go with her since I liked her best friend and his husband-to-be. Their love story had inspired my sister.

"Okay."

I'd kind of hoped he'd be there, but it didn't matter. He'd let me know when he wanted to take me out again.

"Look, J, I'm pretty sure Raphi wants you too."

"Did he say something to you?"

"If he had, I wouldn't tell you. You warned me not to meddle. This is me, not meddling and telling you to talk to him."

She clearly knew how he felt about me, but I didn't blame her for not divulging. I had told her not to meddle because I was going to do this in my own time. Meredith had tried to continually matchmake for me over the years and I was fed up with it.

"You do still love him, right?"

"Yes."

"Then your answer is right there. Trust in love."

I didn't know if I did yet or not. It was hard to trust in something which had burnt you so badly before. Trust the person who hurt you and hope they wouldn't do it again.

Making a decision, I pulled out my phone and fired off a message to Raphi.

Jonah: Would it be okay if I came over after Rhys' wedding tomorrow night?

I wanted to see him, and maybe I could actually have the conversation about what we were. I wasn't going to make myself any promises, but the thought of seeing him made me feel warm inside.

Raphi: Yes, I won't be home until like eight so would have to be after then. Meredith mentioned you were her plus one.

He hadn't even questioned it. He was always the one initiating us seeing each other and never leaving me guessing. I hoped he was happy I'd asked to see him.

Would you quit overthinking this? You're going to give yourself a headache.

Jonah: She would never forgive me if I didn't go.

Raphi: As if you would ever say no to your sister.

Jonah: Do you say no to yours?

Raphi: All the time. Aurora is the worst. Especially right now with the wedding coming up.

Meredith had mentioned Raphi's sister was getting married a while back.

Jonah: Everyone is getting married it seems.

Raphi: Don't remind me. Wedding mania has taken over my family and it's exhausting. I don't blame Logan for taking so long to ask Aurora. It seems like a lot of effort for just one day.

What he said didn't make it seem like Raphi was keen on the wedding thing. Why did it make my heart sink?

Jonah: Oh? How long were they together before he popped the question?

Raphi: Over five years. Personally, I think Logan was too scared to ask Quinn for Aurora's hand.

Raphi had mentioned Quinn didn't approve of Aurora's choice in partner when we were together. Having spent a little time with his parents, I could readily understand why. Quinn seemed incredibly protective of his family. Raphi said no one would be good enough for Aurora in her father's eyes.

Jonah: Wow, I wouldn't want anyone to wait that long to ask me. It's kind of outdated to be asking someone's dad for his daughter's hand as well.

Raphi: I'll keep that in mind.

What the fuck does that mean?

Jonah: You planning on asking someone to marry you?

Raphi: Not currently, but you never know.

Did he have any idea what he was doing right now? Confusing the fuck out of me and making me wonder what he wanted to happen between the two of us.

That's unfair. He has no idea how you feel. You haven't told him.

Raphi: You say it's outdated, but if Logan hadn't asked Quinn, there'd have been hell to pay. Though, it was bad enough when he did. The word trainwreck comes to mind.

I was sort of glad he'd moved on from what he'd said since I had no idea how to respond to it.

Jonah: Doesn't surprise me, knowing your crazy overprotective family.

Raphi: Not quite as bad as Duke's scandalous exploits but I'll tell you about those another time. My parents have dealt with a lot from the four of us over the years.

Jonah: Isn't it our job to drive our parents crazy?

Raphi: True. I suppose that no longer applies to you.

It didn't. I hadn't seen or spoken to my mother in years. Not since Meredith graduated university and the two of us moved out. I wasn't like my sister who'd found a surrogate family. I only had her and it was okay with me to an extent. Maybe it was why I wanted to create a family of my own.

I'd always known I couldn't have one in the most traditional of ways. It's why I never cared if I had biological children. There were too many kids out there who needed loving families. For me, adoption would be my first choice. I had no idea if I was to get back together with Raphi whether or not he'd want that too. It was a conversation for the future. When I'd stopped being too scared to admit I wanted us to be together again.

Jonah: No, but it's like I said to you, I'm better off without her in my life. Sometimes you have to know when something is a lost cause.

I hoped he didn't think I meant me and him. I almost sent him another message but decided against it. Raphi wouldn't read into it.

Raphi: You're right. Duke is here so I have to go. I'll see you tomorrow.

It shouldn't feel like a dismissal but kind of did. Like maybe I was wrong about him reading into what I'd said.

Cut it out. You are your own worst enemy, you know that?

He'd told me he was seeing his brother tonight. He'd invited me to come along. I'd declined as I had paperwork to catch up on. He'd also asked me if I wanted to go to dinner at his parents' house at some point. Raphi said they'd love to see me. I was beginning to think maybe I was being a bit stupid. And maybe Raphi did want to be with me. And maybe he was just waiting for me to say something.

Your terms and at your pace, remember? He set the pace last time. He's waiting for you to ask him for more.

I clearly had to stop being so scared. The only question which remained was did I believe in love enough to push past that fear? Did I believe in me and him enough to ask for what I wanted?

I guess I had to find out.

CHAPTER FORTY NINE

Raphael

Ever since the night when Jonah had turned up on my doorstep, I'd been taking him out and trying to show him I wanted us to be together. The whole situation was frustrating me and my patience had begun to wear thin. It'd become clear to me, Jonah wanted more but he hadn't said it yet. He hadn't voiced his feelings out loud. I needed him to. The more time I spent around him, taking him out, giving him all my attention and learning about him all over again, the surer I became about wanting to make him mine for good this time.

I didn't want to only be his boyfriend, I wanted to be his everything. The future I had mapped out in my head for the two of us was so clear. Us together. Him moving into my place. The two of us getting married and maybe having a family. Fuck knows my mother would love grandchildren.

She'd worry over them, of course, but she'd love them to death. All of my parents would, but especially Mum.

It was crazy to think I was dead set on these things with Jonah when we weren't even back together yet. I'd been in love with him for almost ten years. I couldn't think of anyone else I wanted to spend the rest of my life with.

I'd given him my word I would be okay with what he wanted. I had to have patience and let him go at his own pace. I imagined this was how he felt when I was all over the place about our relationship before. It made me all the more aware of what I'd put him through. And how I never wanted to cause him pain again. Now I would nurture and care for him. Show him how precious he was to me. How I'd fought so hard to be a man who could deserve someone like Jonah. No, not someone like him, just him. I wanted to deserve him. And now I felt as though I'd reached a point in my life where I did. I deserved to be happy with him. If he let me.

Fuck, I hope he'll let me.

Duke had given me a whole load more shit over it yesterday. Like asking yet again why I didn't just tell Jonah I wanted him and make my intentions clear. I didn't want Jonah to think he was under any obligation. If he wanted to be with me after everything that had happened between us, then it had to be his choice. I didn't want my feelings coming into it.

Maybe I was more like my younger brother than I realised. He'd always told me he wanted Meredith to make her own choices without his influence. Probably why I'd given him her address a week ago right before he'd flown home. He wanted to be with her so badly, he was willing to do anything to make it happen. I just hoped he and our parents sorted out the mess he'd gotten into with the Russian mafia. The less I thought about that fucked up situation, the better.

I'd made peace with my parents' past a long time ago. And wasn't surprised when it came back to bite them either. Out of the four of us, the fact it had fallen on Cole was kind of par for the course given how impulsive and cocky he'd always been. Sometimes I wondered where he'd got all that confidence from considering Rory was the quietest of our dads. Probably from Mum. Dad said she had an impulsive streak which is what led to the formation of her relationship with my dads in the first place.

The doorbell rang, making my nerves prickle. Last night was the first time Jonah had asked to see me. I'd been nervous about what he might have to say when he got here. I was also shattered from a long day at work. The consultation this evening had gone on way longer than I expected. It was lucky Jonah had stayed at the wedding later since we never specified a time.

When I opened the door to find him in a suit as he'd come straight from the wedding, my mouth went very dry. I felt completely underdressed since I'd changed into comfortable clothes when I'd got in. Jonah looked fucking hot. I had to clench my fist to prevent my impulse to tell him exactly that. His suit was navy, complete with a waistcoat and he had a grey tie on. Sure, I'd found other guys attractive before, but no one measured up to Jonah for me. No one had ever looked so damn good in my eyes.

"Hey, come in."

I stepped back and allowed him into my house. The last time he'd been on my doorstep, he'd grabbed me and kissed me. This time he just looked plain scared. I didn't know how to feel about it.

What did he have to be scared about?

"You want a drink or something?" I asked, shutting the door behind us.

"Just water. Had enough to drink at the wedding."

It sucked I hadn't been able to go since I knew Rhys reasonably well, what with him being Meredith's best friend. We'd spent a lot of time together over the years and since his new husband had arrived on the scene, we'd only gotten closer as a group.

Jonah followed me down the hall into the kitchen.

"Was it nice?"

"Yeah, I swear I've never seen two people more in love. It's like that all-consuming kind between them."

"They are kind of sickening at times. Mer is always complaining about it in one breath and going on about how sweet it is in the next."

I opened the fridge door and pulled out the Brita filter, grabbing a glass from the cupboard and pouring water in it. I put the jug back in the fridge and handed the glass to Jonah. Our fingers brushed, sending a wave of need up my arm. Judging by his reaction, he felt it too. His eyes widened and his breath hitched. I was so aware of him, I noticed every little thing he did.

Jonah, please be here to tell me you want this. That it's not just me, because I don't know how much more I can take.

"I guess they are," he murmured.

I snatched my hand back but the damage was already done. The urge to crush him to me sunk into my bones. I was about to step back when he reached out and brushed his fingers along mine as he took a sip of his water. My throat worked as I swallowed, heat rushing up my skin from our simple touch. He set the glass on the counter and stepped into my personal space.

"I need to say something to you."

"And what's that?"

His brows furrowed, leaving little lines between them which I wanted to smooth away.

"I don't know how to do this. I'm… scared."

He dropped his hand from mine and fidgeted instead.

"Scared of what?"

"You and me."

What is that supposed to mean?

"What about you and me?"

His expression grew troubled. I reached out and brushed a thumb across his cheek. His breathing accelerated, making me aware I was affecting him. Well fuck, he affected me too. Far too much.

"I don't know what you want, Raphi, and it fucking terrifies me." His words came out rushed and in one long breath. "Because… because I feel so much and I don't want… I don't want…"

I cupped his cheek and forced him to look at me.

"You don't want what?"

"I don't want my heart broken again." It came out as a whisper, his voice shaking on each and every word.

My own heart squeezed in my chest. I could only take what he was saying one way. Perhaps Duke was right last night. Maybe what Jonah needed was for me to give him my truth. The one thing I'd held back on.

"Do you think I'm going to do that?"

"I don't know."

I dropped my hand from his face. He watched me unbutton his suit jacket followed by his waistcoat before I slid my hand underneath the fabric, brushing along his waist. I could feel the heat of him through his shirt. He let out a harsh breath which fanned across my face because we were standing so close to each other.

"You're allowed to be afraid. I've never asked you to forgive me or trust me again. There are no expectations here. Perhaps it's my mistake not to have told you how I feel. Maybe you need to hear it before you'll tell me what's inside here."

I lifted my other hand and placed it on his heart. It was pounding so hard, I could feel it on the pads of my fingers. He didn't say a word, just watched me with caution. I couldn't blame him. He needed me to own up to my feelings.

"I told you I got help for me so I could get better, but that's not the whole truth. I once told you I didn't feel like I deserved you. Ever since then, I've tried to find a way to be the person who could deserve you. To be someone who could offer you the world. I would never have asked to see you again if I didn't think I could be that man for you."

I could see all of his emotions clear as day on his face. He had no idea it's what I'd spent six and a half years trying to achieve. Yes, I'd got better for me, but I'd done it for him too. I'd walked through fucking fire to be exactly where we were today. At a crossroads where a few words from him had the power to make me the happiest man alive or rip my heart to shreds. I couldn't say I would blame him if it turned out to be the latter. I'd put him through too much.

"I'm offering you everything I have. Everything I am now. And that's the man who fucking well adores the shit out of you. Who looks at you like you're his everything because that's exactly what you are to me. I want to give you my love so badly, it kills me inside to hold back. Fuck… Jonah, I love you so much and I will continue to love you until the end. Please, tell me what it is you want here. Tell me why you wanted to see me tonight."

His green eyes were wide. He opened and closed his mouth like he didn't know what to say. I dropped my hand from his heart and picked up one of his instead. I placed it over my heart so he could feel it. Then he could fucking well know he was the one.

"This is yours. I'm yours, only if you'll have me. If you can look past all of the shit we've been through and find a way to—"

He cut my words off by putting his free hand over my mouth. I stared at him, wondering why he needed to shut me up. Had I said too much? Admitted too many things?

"I love you, Raphi. I love you. I can't stop loving you. I can't… every part of me loves you. You're the one. You're always going to be the one. I don't care about the past. The past doesn't fucking matter when you're standing here in front of me telling me you love me. Telling me you'll give me the world. I'm done living in the past. I'm fucking done with punishing myself over not being enough for you. I know I'm enough. Love is enough. It has to be. Please tell me it is."

Those words about him punishing himself over not being enough for me almost had me breaking down in tears. Jonah had always been enough. He was more. He was the only person for me in this fucked up world we lived in. I couldn't imagine life without him in it. It was my fault this had happened. My depression had ruined everything. I wasn't going to let it do that again. Not now I'd learnt how to manage it and how to love myself. That had been the hardest part. I was determined to get better for me and him. I'd had no other choice. I had to find myself and accept the man I saw in the mirror.

Jonah dropped his hand from my mouth. His breathing was heavy like it took him too much effort to get those words out. But he'd said it. He'd finally told me the truth. I was going to give him what he asked for.

"You're more than enough," I whispered. "You're the whole universe to me. Love is enough. It's always been enough."

"Then ask me… ask me to be yours."

I couldn't help smiling. My hand around his waist tightened as I pulled him that much closer.

"Jonah, will you be my boyfriend?"

I knew I couldn't ask him to be my husband yet. It was far too soon. But I would eventually because there was no doubt in my mind I needed Jonah as much as he needed me.

He let out this choked sound like he couldn't believe I'd actually used the word boyfriend. Given my aversion to it, I understood why. I leant closer and brushed my lips over his.

"Is that a yes to the boyfriend thing?"

He nodded profusely, his lips rubbing against mine. I could take that. I kissed him. And Jonah kissed me back. His hands went to my hair, digging into the strands and keeping me right there with him. As if I was ever going anywhere. I never wanted to be apart from him again.

CHAPTER FIFTY

Jonah

The word boyfriend echoed in my ears as Raphi kissed me. He kissed like he was drowning in me. And well, I was pretty fucking unstable too right then. But only because he'd told me he loved me. Love was enough. I was enough.

I believed him. The sincere and honest look in his eyes when he'd said he got better for me made my heart hurt. This man made me ache all over for so many things.

His touch. His affection. His love. His forever.

I pressed him back until he hit the counter. I gripped the edge of it as my body came in full contact with his. My other hand fisted his hair and all I wanted was more. Raphi tugged his glasses off his face and fumbled with placing them on the counter. His hands curled around me underneath my suit jacket and waistcoat. His fingers dug beneath my trousers, tugging at my shirt until he met bare skin. Then he groaned in my mouth as our tongues tangled in a rough dance of affection and desire.

"I want to make love to you, *cuore mio*," he whispered when he pulled back slightly.

Fuck, I can't believe he still wants to call me his heart.

I swallowed since we'd only ever called sex between us, fucking. But I supposed this time it would be more. The look in his eyes told me so. It was gentle and full of adoration. Like I was the universe to him. Just like he said.

"What, you don't want to order me into your bed?"

He smirked which only set my blood on fire.

"No, but if you go willingly, I'd be much obliged."

"I've never been anything but willing with you."

His hand tightened around me.

"I know and it's a problem, J. You make it hard for me to be gentle and sweet since you're always begging for it to be anything but."

I smiled. Raphi and I didn't do loving and caring in the bedroom. It was raw and unbridled.

"Maybe I won't beg."

His smirk didn't disappear, if anything, it grew more deviant.

"We both know that's never going to happen."

And then his face did fall, his demeanour turning serious. It was as if a switch flipped and talk of sex was over.

"I need you to tell me what you were going to say before I told you how I feel."

I wanted to ask why but the way he said it made it seem like this mattered a great deal to him.

"Well, before I came here, my sister told me I needed to give you an ultimatum."

His brow arched.

"Did she now?"

"Yeah, I was supposed to tell you either we get back together or I'm done for good."

His fingers brushed across my bare back and lower. I shuddered, trying not to get too distracted by his wandering hand.

"And is that really what you were going to say to me?"

"No. I wanted to tell you I love you and I want you back. That the way you've treated me over these past weeks you've been back in my life has meant everything. And I've hated all the cheek kissing since it was not where I wanted your lips. So no. No ultimatums. They're not really me."

He smiled again, the warmth of it lighting up his eyes. I don't think I'd ever issued one to Raphi. The only time I had was about Cole and Meredith. It went horribly wrong. I'd decided ultimatums were terrible from then on.

"Your sister is quite something, you know, considering she already knew I was waiting for you to tell me you wanted more."

I had a suspicion that was the case and the reason she kept calling me an idiot. She was right since I should have known Raphi wanted to be with me again. Now I thought about it, he'd made it very clear the first time I'd come over here. He asked if I wanted him to date me, implying it's what he'd do if I said yes. I guess I should have listened properly.

"She did, huh?"

"Mmm, she told me when I said to her I still loved you, she was determined to make sure we got back together. I think she's been playing matchmaker even if she promised both of us not to meddle."

Meredith was going to get an earful from me over this. Her meddling wasn't exactly helpful though it had forced me to admit I needed to say something to Raphi.

"But don't be too hard on her, J."

I frowned.

"Why not? You have no idea of the abuse I've had off her over you. I mean, okay, maybe I kind of deserved it since I was fretting over telling you how I felt, but still, she took it too far."

Raphi gave me a sad smile and pulled his hands from under my shirt. Instead, he brought them up and rested them on my chest.

"Cole came home two days ago."

I froze. Cole was back. Well, that complicated matters a great deal since my sister had got emotional over him at Rhys' wedding. I didn't know how she would react to seeing him. No doubt he intended to get her back since this was Cole. I don't think I'd ever met a more determined boy in my life. It was my sister or no one.

"And you are not supposed to know about that so when you do see him, please be surprised. I'll be in trouble otherwise."

I didn't want Raphi to get in any shit. I would do my level best to make sure I didn't let on I already knew.

"He wants her back."

"Yes… but it's more than that." Raphi looked off into the distance over my shoulder. "He asked our parents to get him a ring for her."

"Wait… he wants to marry Mer?"

Raphi nodded. I thought about all of the reasons why it was completely insane. Then I remembered my sister was still in love with Cole. She always would be. Their story was all kinds of fucked up but they still shared one thing together. Love.

"Well, fuck. I thought your brother was reckless and impulsive before but this… I mean, fuck."

Raphi merely shrugged, dropping his hands from my chest. I guessed he was used to his brother's antics by now.

"It's Cole. He might have been gone for five years but he's still Cole. Not that I've seen him yet since he's been staying with Rora and Logan. I'm avoiding them because of the wedding shit. Honestly, the only reason it's so complicated is because Logan's family are kind of famous. Add my parents into the mix and you have a recipe for madness. I swear if I ever do the wedding thing it's family only and none of this huge reception with a fucking six-tiered cake business."

Raphi and the word wedding made my heart feel like it'd skipped a hundred beats.

"If?"

"Do you want to come to their wedding with me?"

My heart sunk a little at him ignoring my question since it didn't exactly make it clear if Raphi wanted to get married or not in the future. But I had to get my head on straight as he'd just asked me to go to Aurora and Logan's wedding with him.

"Isn't that really soon?"

"Mmm, like two weeks, and if I ask my sister nicely, she'll make room for a plus one."

"Are you sure about that?"

He gave me a look.

"Do you want to come with me or not?"

"I mean, of course I want to come, but it depends on work."

"It's on a Saturday." Raphi was still eyeing me as if to say I wouldn't have asked you if I didn't think you'd be available. "And you're my boyfriend. Attendance is non-negotiable."

I snorted and shook my head. He was joking about the last part, but it still made me feel all warm inside. He wanted me there as his boyfriend. The word had the ability to melt my brain when he said it.

"Okay, just tell me the place and time, I'll be there."

"I was hoping you'd stay here the night before and we could go together. You don't like crowds. It's a big wedding. I figured you'd want to be close to me at all times."

I swallowed as his lip curved up into a smile. He was right. I still hated crowds and Raphi had always kept me grounded.

"You said you didn't do sweet."

"I do when you're not getting all needy and shit, J."

He could be incredibly sweet. In fact, he had been since he'd come back into my life. Always attentive. Always making sure I was happy. It's how he'd been on each and every one of our dates. I was going to call them that now because, in reality, we had been dating for the past few weeks even though we'd said we were just friends. Raphi and I couldn't be *just* friends. We'd always been so much more to each other. Even back when we were getting to know each other as teenagers. He'd known that when he was fifteen. It was about time I caught up.

"What if I'm needy now?"

I was still pressed right up against him, pinning him to the counter with my body. I couldn't help feeling aroused by his presence. Raphi did all kinds of shit to me.

"Then I'd remind you of what I said about getting into my bed willingly."

I reached up and ran a hand through his chestnut hair.

"If I go right now, will you follow… and make love to me?"

His eyebrow slowly rose and the smirk reappeared.

"I guess you'll have to find out."

"Tease."

He shook his head.

"Oh, Jonah, you have no idea of the teasing I'm capable of. This is nothing compared to what I might do to you, so… you going to get that sexy suited arse upstairs or not?"

Raphi had done a heck of a lot of teasing in bed. This made me nervous. What on earth else could he do to me?

"Sexy, eh?"

His eyes darkened, making me shiver.

"Very. Every part of you is sexy to me, especially those eyes of yours. They tell me a lot of things. Like how you're having a hard time moving away right now because even though you want me to make love to you, a part of you wants to stay right here against me."

He leant his hands back against the counter as if waiting for me to dispute his statement.

"You're almost as annoying as Meredith when it comes to reading me."

"Me? Annoying?"

"Mmm, being right about how I feel and all."

He cocked his head to the side and searched my face for a long moment.

"I'm going to make this easy for you. Go upstairs and sit on my bed, but don't get undressed. I plan to take my time in stripping you out of this." He lifted a hand from the counter and waved at me. "Fuck, J… you look so damn hot in a suit, it's short-circuiting my brain and I don't know how I've managed to have a conversation with you for however long it's been without ripping your clothes off and having you on my kitchen counter."

The thought of him stripping me down made my cock jerk in response. I wanted him too. So damn much.

"Is that an order?"

"You're damn fucking right it's an order."

I backed away from him, giving him a grin.

"Well, I better obey or no doubt you'll find a way to punish me."

I heard his laughter as I turned and quick-walked out of the kitchen towards the stairs. The faster I got up to his room, the faster he'd be on me and I'd be experiencing the exquisite pleasure he'd reminded me of the last time I was here at his place.

CHAPTER FIFTY ONE

Raphael

I listened to Jonah's footsteps as he climbed the stairs and was pretty sure he was taking them two by two. It didn't surprise me he was eager. I'd waited weeks for this moment and I was going to take my time with him. Show him why we belonged together.

I made my way upstairs slowly, my thoughts running rampant with what I wanted to do. The first and most important thing was I wanted to see his face. I needed his expressions and to watch those beautiful sounds he made fall out of his mouth. The image of it in my mind made me smile wide. The fact we'd agreed to be together again made my heart fucking swell. I could touch him, taste him, feel him and love him without needing to restrain myself. I'd offered Jonah all of me and that's what he was going to get.

When I reached my bedroom, Jonah was sat on the edge of my bed, his hands resting on the covers next to him. His blonde hair was a little messy and his green eyes were dark with need. My eyes roamed over him as I walked into the room with measured steps.

"I see I won't have to punish you."

"I want to be good for you, Raphi."

Why did he have to say stuff like that? He knew what he was doing to me. The man knew how to push my buttons. And I loved it.

"You do, huh? Maybe I should reward you."

He bit his lip, opening his legs and I came to rest between them. I tucked my finger under his chin and forced his head up so he'd meet my eyes.

"Do you want a reward, *cuore mio?*"

"Yes… please."

I leant down towards him, my fingers dancing down his throat before sliding underneath his suit jacket. I pushed it off his shoulders, leaving it pooled at his wrists.

"Fuck. Just look at you," I murmured. "The star of all my dirty fantasies."

His lips parted but no sound came out. I wanted him to know exactly how much I desired him. Tell him how he made me feel. Jonah was it for me. I think he'd been it for me since I'd been a teenager.

I slid his waistcoat down his arms next. Then I took his tie between my fingers and loosened it. His eyes were on what I was doing as if he didn't want to miss a single thing.

"I love you, J. Every part of you. When you're around me, all I can see is you. You take up all the space in my vision and nothing else matters but you."

I tugged his tie off and threw it away, not caring where it landed. I carefully extracted his wrists from his suit jacket and waistcoat but didn't throw those. No, I took them and hung them up behind my door on some hooks I had there. The only other thing hanging up was my dressing gown.

"Raphi…"

I turned and met his eyes. He reached out a hand to me and I went to him, taking it. He brought it up to his face and kissed my palm.

"I forgive you."

I swallowed hard at his words. They made my heart squeeze tightly in my chest.

"I know you've not asked me for it, but I do. There's no blame here between us. I want to let go of the past. You know me, I don't hold grudges or hate in my heart. The only thing I want in there is love. Your love and mine. I love you. I never stopped. I held out hope that one day you'd find your way back to me when you were whole again and here you are. Here we are. It's all that matters."

I leant down until we were eye-level and cupped his face.

"Thank you for forgiving me. Thank you for loving me even after everything we've been through. I appreciate you more than words can say and I will show you every day for the rest of our lives because, J, that's what I want. You and me… forever."

I pressed a kiss to the side of his mouth.

"I want that too," he whispered.

I let go of him and unbuttoned his shirt. He raised his hands, allowing me to undo the little buttons at his wrists and

503

tug it off him. For a second I just looked at him bare-chested. All I could think about was how lucky I was. How I owed so much to Jonah.

He reached out and tucked his fingers under my t-shirt, brushing them along the waistband of my jogging bottoms. I didn't stop him from exploring. His touch electrified me.

"Did you want something?"

He nodded, staring up at me with a little twinkle in his green eyes.

"You… without anything on."

"Is that because you like looking at me?"

"More than anything."

I grabbed the bottom of my t-shirt and tugged it off, dropping it on the floor. His hands splayed out over my stomach, making me suck in a breath.

"You are perfect."

I didn't dispute his words since they made me feel good. Jonah looked at me with no small amount of admiration and desire. I couldn't help but want to hear all his inner thoughts about how he saw me.

"You want more, J?"

He nodded, his fingers still exploring the groves of my abs.

"You can have everything if you want it."

The smile spreading across his face had me trying to stifle mine.

"I want it."

I placed a hand on his shoulder and pushed him back on the bed, crawling over his body. He stared up at me as I unbuckled his belt. I took my time unzipping his trousers, wanting to prolong the anticipation he was surely feeling. Jonah's breathing became heavier as his hands curled around my thighs. Thankfully he'd kicked off his shoes before coming upstairs, meaning I could easily tug the rest of his clothes off his body.

I stared down at my beautiful man waiting for my next move. I leant down and kissed his chest before trailing my tongue lower. His breathing hitched and a moan left his lips. I watched him as I dropped off the end of the bed and kissed his stomach, my fingers trailing along his hips. His eyes were intent on me and what I was doing to him.

"You ready for your reward?"

He nodded, biting down on his bottom lip.

I circled the crown of his cock with my tongue, making him buck and let out a harsh pant. His fingers fisted in the covers when I licked down his shaft. Fuck, he was stunning like this. His chest rising and falling rapidly as he fought not to lose control. Those green eyes unfocused.

"Ah, fuck, Raphi," he cried when I took his cock in my mouth, my fingers fisting around the bottom and giving him a languid stroke.

I wouldn't let him come yet, but he deserved his pleasure. He deserved everything I was going to give him. I sucked him deeper, revelling in the way he felt and tasted on my tongue. He released the covers and dragged a hand up his face. His fingers twisted in his hair as I continued to work his cock in my mouth. The little noises of ecstasy erupting from his mouth spurred me on. They always had. His pants and moans were toxins to me. Infecting my blood and making me crazy for him.

And the whine he made when I pulled away, made me smile.

"Don't worry, *cuore mio*, I intend to take care of you. We're only just getting started."

I grabbed his calf and shoved his leg up on the bed. He obliged me by lifting the other. Rising to my feet, I walked over to the bedside table and pulled out the necessary supplies. His eyes followed me as I made my way to the end of the bed again. This time when I dropped to my knees and took his cock in my mouth, I had my fingers lubed up and stroked them across his tight little hole. His gasp when I slid one inside him only had me eager to open him up to me.

"Raphi," he groaned whilst I worked him with my mouth and my fingers. "Fuck, don't stop."

It didn't take long before he was begging and all but demanding I give him my cock. I was rock hard and throbbing at the thought of being in him.

"You are always so impatient, J," I told him as I tugged off my jogging bottoms and boxers.

I knelt on the bed, encouraging him to move up it.

"I can't help it. You feel so good inside me."

"You're lucky I adore the way you're needy for me, and I'm just as desperate to be in you."

He smiled wide. My hand landed on his thigh, pushing his leg up higher to give me a better angle. After rolling on a condom and liberally applying lube, I shifted closer, pressing my cock to him. He let out a groan when it slid up inside him.

I bit back my own need to moan. A few shallow thrusts had him opening up more. This wasn't going to be a fast, hard fuck like we sometimes had in the past. I wanted slow and sensual. I wanted him to feel every inch of me as I thrust inside him.

When I was fully seated in his heat, I leant forward, forcing his legs higher and kissed him. I buried my fist in his hair as I devoured his mouth, giving him slow rolls of my hips at just the right angle. He moaned in my mouth as his hands curled around my back, holding me to him.

"You feel so good," I told him when I shifted back slightly. "I've missed this. I've missed you so much."

He brought his hand around from my back to cup my face, dragging his thumb across my bottom lip.

"I've missed you too." Then he smiled. "Is this you making love to me then?"

I nuzzled my nose against his.

"Mmm, why? Is it not rough enough for you?"

I thrust harder to prove a point. He whimpered in response.

"I think you want it harder. You don't like me holding back."

His hand left my face, curling around my shoulder. I kept my rhythm slow but drove into him with more force. I could tell it pleased him by the flush of his cheeks and the way he let out a series of short, harsh pants.

Leaning down, I brushed my mouth along his earlobe, "I love you, J. And I love how much you want me. How much you need this. You're intoxicating, you know that? You're like

507

my own personal drug… or should I say medicine since you saved me even when you weren't here."

His fingers on my shoulder tightened.

"You saved me too," he whispered. "You've reminded me of how precious love is and how I should fight for it. No matter what happens in the future, I'll keep fighting for us because I love you."

I kissed his ear and along his jaw.

"I'll protect you and keep you safe."

I captured his mouth and the two of us drowned in our kiss whilst I continued to make love to him. To show him with my body how much I needed him. He was my medicine. My happiness. My home.

I reached between us, wrapping my hand around his cock and stroking it. Jonah moaned in my mouth. I was getting close and I wanted to bring him off too. Being with him like this had me almost at the brink. This closeness and connection I felt. The intimacy between us. It was unlike anything else I'd ever experienced. I never wanted to be without this man again.

I adjusted the angle of my thrusts. Jonah turned his face from mine and whimpered. I was hitting right where I wanted. I knew exactly what he needed.

"Raphi!"

His cock pulsed in my hand, hot, sticky streams coating it and our stomachs. I could only smile and grunt as I followed him over the edge, letting go of everything in those few moments where my body trembled and my cock spurted inside him over and over.

I buried my face in his neck to catch my breath. Jonah held me and kissed my hair. Contentment washed over me. I had my man back and nothing in this world felt better. This time I'd keep him by my side.

I rolled off him a moment later and stared up at the ceiling. Jonah propped himself up on his elbow and stroked a hand down my chest.

"We made a mess."

I looked down at what was talking about.

"Just a little."

He kissed my cheek and grabbed the tissues off the bed whilst I disposed of the condom. We cleaned each other up and got under the covers together. Jonah curled up against my chest, running his fingers down my side.

"You staying the night?" I asked, hoping he would say yes.

"If that's okay. I don't want to leave you."

I kissed his forehead.

"I don't want you to go."

He snuggled closer to me. We lay in silence for a long time, happy to be together again.

"I'm going to dinner at my parents on Wednesday night."

Jonah turned his head and looked up at me.

"Okay."

"If you're not busy, I'd like you to come with me."

He blinked. I'd already told Jonah my parents would love to see him again, but I hadn't yet said they were aware of my intention to get him back.

"I'm not busy. I'd love to go."

"Then I'll let them know."

He smiled at me.

"Your siblings going to be there?"

"No, it'll just be the parents and us, so you won't see them until Rora's wedding."

"I like your siblings."

"What? Even Duke?"

Jonah dug his fingers into my side.

"Duke's your favourite brother."

"He's also a pain in the butt who is way too much like Xav for his own good."

"I bet all of you are like your respective fathers."

I grinned.

"Yeah, you're totally right, we are. Though Cole is way more like Mum than he is Rory. But enough about my family. You need to tell me all about Rhys' wedding since I didn't get to go."

Jonah reached up and stroked my face.

"Well okay… if you insist."

And the two of us spent the rest of the night trading stories. He told me about Rhys' wedding and I discussed Aurora's upcoming one. It struck me how normal this felt to be with him like this. How right we were together. Jonah and I weren't just lovers, we were friends and companions. He got me and I got him. That's why our bond ran so deep. We were it for each other.

I couldn't wait to properly introduce him to my family as my boyfriend. When he was ready, I would make sure Jonah and I were tied together forever because I loved this man more than life itself. And I would never let him go again.

CHAPTER FIFTY TWO

Jonah

R aphi unlocked the door to his parents' house and stepped in, leaving me to trail in behind him. My palms had got all sweaty with nerves. This whole officially meeting the parents of my boyfriend thing had me feeling all kinds of crazy. Stupid really since I'd already met his parents years ago. This was different. We were openly together this time. And we'd only just re-established our relationship.

Raphi took my coat after sliding out of his and hung them both up. He linked his fingers with mine and pulled me towards the living room, a smile lighting up his face. I kept my expression neutral so as not to show how scared I was.

"Hello everyone," Raphi said as he walked into the room, pulling me along behind him.

All five of Raphi's parents were sat down on the sofas and armchairs in the room. His mother, Ash, jumped up immediately when she spied us. She came around and enveloped her son in a hug.

"My cheeky monkey."

"Hi, Mum."

When she pulled back, she smiled and turned to me. I don't know what I was expecting, but it wasn't to have his mother embrace me.

"Hello, Jonah, it's so nice to see you."

"Hi, um, it's nice to see you too, Ash," I replied, trying not to allow my voice to get all high pitched.

"I hope you don't mind me saying I'm overjoyed you and Raphi are together. You make my son come alive when he talks about you. I've never seen him this happy. He's smiling all the time because of you."

Raphi must have heard her as he squeezed my fingers. Ash drew away and patted my arm.

"I do hope he does the same for you."

I had no idea how to respond to any of what she'd said. Raphi hadn't told me he'd informed his parents of our relationship yet.

"Mum, you're embarrassing him," Raphi murmured.

"Oh, shush you, I'm just welcoming your boyfriend into our family."

She gave me another smile.

"I… um… yes, your son makes me very happy," I managed to say.

I could feel my cheeks burning. Why didn't he tell me? I had prepared myself for the whole 'this is my boyfriend' talk. I looked over at him, finding a twinkle in his green eyes.

"I told you I'd accepted myself, J. I'm not hiding who you are to me."

"I can see that," I all but hissed back.

This had caught me off guard. I wasn't annoyed by any means. Merely shocked.

Raphi searched my face for a long moment as Ash stepped away, clearly noticing the tension between us. Then my boyfriend tugged me from the room with a tight smile and a nod to his mother. We ended up in the dining room and he closed the door behind us.

"Are you okay?"

I looked down at the floor.

"Yes… no… I don't know."

I felt fingers under my chin.

"Hey, J, look at me."

I raised my eyes and took in the concern on his face. Fuck, I loved his face. I loved everything about him and here I was being stupid.

"Are you upset I already told them about us?"

"No, of course not. I'm happy… you just didn't tell me and I wasn't expecting… Raphi, I've never met anyone's parents before as a boyfriend. I know I've already met them but this is different. I… I've been nervous and your mum is so nice and caring, your whole family is. I just don't know how to react to it. I'm not used to it."

He framed my face with both his hands. I sucked in a breath. His touch soothed me. What was it about him which kept me grounded? Honestly, I didn't care. Raphi liked taking care of me. It made him happy and I couldn't deny I needed him to.

"It's okay. I'm sorry I didn't tell you. You seemed to be fine with seeing them tonight so I didn't think."

"It's not your fault—"

"No, don't do that. I should know better. You don't have this in your life and my family can be intense, which I'm sure Meredith has told you. But you don't need to be scared. I'm right here and they're happy for us. Hell, even Quinn said he approves of you and we both know he doesn't entirely approve of Logan so that's saying something."

He smiled at me in that heart-stopping way of his. It made me melt immediately and relax into his touch.

"All they want to do is get to know the man I'm intending to spend the rest of my life with and make you a part of our family."

He stroked my cheek with such reverence, I couldn't take it any longer.

"Raphi?"

"Yes, *cuore mio*?"

"Will you hold me?"

He dropped his hands from my face and pulled me into his arms, kissing my hair and stroking my back. I curled my arms around him, burying my face in his shoulder and breathing him in.

"I don't know what I'd do without you," I whispered into his jumper.

"We already know what it's like to be without each other and I can tell you now, that's not happening again, okay? I love you."

I could hear the words 'I love you' from his lips forever. They wrapped around my heart and kept me from drowning.

"I love you too."

He pulled away and smiled at me.

"You always see me at my most vulnerable," I said with a shrug.

It only made him smile wider.

"I love that about you. Knowing you feel safe with me."

"I do. You keep me grounded when I'm anxious."

"I want to make sure you're comfortable and happy. It's all I ever want."

I took his hand and brought it to my lips, placing a kiss on his knuckles.

"I'm your heart."

Those green eyes behind his glasses softened.

"You are so ridiculously adorable and if you don't stop it, I might say fuck my parents and kiss you for hours instead."

"I'd like that."

He chuckled and shook his head, making me smile wide.

"I know you would, but they wouldn't be happy with me, so come on, they don't bite."

Raphi pulled me towards the door, opening it and walking through into the living room again. None of them said anything about what happened. His dads merely came up one by one and shook my hand, telling me they were happy to have me here. Eric, Raphi's biological father, was last, and in all honesty, I was most nervous about his opinion of me. Only because Raphi was closest to his dad. Well, technically Duke was the person Raphi was closest to, but I already had his approval. Raphi said Duke's reaction to us getting back together was "thank fuck for that," something which did not surprise me in the slightest.

"Raphi said you got all your qualifications and are now working as a psychologist," Eric said after he shook my hand.

"Yes, I do love my work. As Raphi knows, helping people is something I've always wanted to do."

Eric reached out and squeezed Raphi's shoulder.

"Then I know my son is in good hands. He speaks very highly of you as it is."

"Dad!" Raphi groaned.

"Don't mind this one, we're apparently always embarrassing him, especially now he's an adult."

"Dad, please stop talking, you're almost as bad as Xav, but at least he didn't make a crude joke."

Eric grinned.

"Not yet, monkey, but the night is still young."

Raphi shook his head, his hand tightening around mine.

"Oh great. You sure Mum didn't tell you all to be on your best behaviour tonight? I distinctly remember every other time one of us brought a partner around, she threatened you into being good."

Eric bit his lip in the way Raphi did.

"She did, but you know Xav likes to bend the rules somewhat."

Raphi rubbed his face.

516

"Welcome to my version of hell," he muttered to me.

I kept from commenting but it didn't stop me smiling. Seeing him all worked up over his parents not behaving in front of me somehow made this less awkward and uncomfortable for me. They were a normal family and they'd accepted me. They approved of me being his boyfriend. It's all I wanted.

Ash disappeared to get dinner out of the oven, and told the rest of us to sit at the table. I was thankful Raphi sat next to me and laced our fingers together on his knee under the table.

"You okay?" he whispered as his dads all sat down.

"Yeah, I'm good."

He glanced at me, his green eyes shining.

"Did I tell you how handsome you look this evening?"

I shook my head. Raphi had picked me up from my flat before we made our way over here. It turned out my boyfriend was a perfect gentleman outside of the bedroom and a dominant one inside. I loved that about him. Those two sides of my man excited me in the best way possible.

"Does that mean I scrubbed up well for your parents?"

"Fuck yes, possibly too good. I can't wait to get my hands on you later."

My cheeks heated. I didn't think I'd made a huge effort even though it'd taken me half an hour and pestering Meredith to help me choose an outfit. I'd settled on smart casual. Dark jeans and a navy short-sleeved shirt.

"Your parents are right there," I hissed, feeling embarrassed about how openly he was admitting to wanting to fuck me later.

He grinned and winked at me. No wonder his parents called him a cheeky monkey.

"Don't worry, they're not listening."

"You are something else."

"You love that about me."

I smiled and squeezed his hand. I loved everything about him. Nothing could make me want to leave this man ever again.

Dinner was a rather lively affair amongst the seven of us. His parents asked me all sorts of questions and made every effort to engage me in conversation. The whole time Raphi kept looking at me as if I was everything to him. As if it made him happy I was getting along with his family. It helped me relax and allayed my anxiety.

When dinner was over and we'd had dessert, Raphi leant over to Rory and asked him something I didn't hear. I gathered by the smiles they shared, it was something good. Raphi then tugged me up out of my chair whilst his parents started to clear the table.

"Come with me."

I was unceremoniously dragged out of the room, which didn't seem to faze his parents. We were their guests tonight after all.

"Where are we going?"

"I have something to show you."

I kept quiet as he took me down a hallway. He stopped outside some patio doors and opened them. The two of us stepped into what looked like a conservatory, but it was nothing like any normal conservatory I'd ever seen in my life. Raphi closed the door behind us and swept his hand out.

"Welcome to what my parents like to call Rory's sanctuary."

I looked around. There were a variety of plants everywhere, some of them as tall as the glass ceiling. It was like we'd stepped into a mini version of Kew Gardens.

"This is… amazing."

He smiled and pulled me further in. There was a seating area amongst the plants. The lighting in here was low and made it almost seem magical.

"Are we allowed to be in here?"

"Yeah, I asked Rory if I could show you. He doesn't like too many people being in here, but you're special to me."

"Well, I'll have to thank him."

Raphi pulled me closer and cupped my face with his free hand.

"I have to admit, I also have an ulterior motive for bringing you in here."

I raised an eyebrow.

"And what would that be?"

He placed a gentle kiss to my mouth, making my heart go haywire in my chest.

"I want to ask you some things. I want to be on the same page about the future or at least, I would like to know what you want."

I swallowed. It had crossed my mind many times what our future would look like. I knew what I wanted with him. And here I'd told Meredith not to mention anything to Raphi, but he'd been thinking about it himself.

"Okay… you sure it's not too soon to discuss this?"

"No, J, it's not. I don't want to waste time second-guessing your feelings about it."

I gave him a nod. If he wanted to do this now, then we could. Raphi dropped his hand from my face.

"It didn't escape my notice when I told you about Aurora's wedding, or more like I complained about it, you questioned if I wanted to get married."

I bit my lip. He'd deliberately avoided the question at the time. Was he waiting until now to talk to me about it?

"I want to get married in the future… to you, obviously."

I tried not to smile. My heart was doing all sorts of crazy shit in my chest at the knowledge that's what he planned for us.

"Obviously."

"And I want to know if it's what you want."

"That's easy. Yes, in the future."

He let out a breath.

"And a family… is that something you'd want too?"

I had to make a conscious effort not to let my mouth drop open.

"I've thought about it."

"And?"

Honesty. You and Raphi have to have honesty between you even if it's scary.

520

"I've always envisioned I'd adopt with whoever I ended up with."

It took a second before he smiled at me. Then his hand came up and cupped the back of my neck, drawing me closer to him.

"We can talk about specifics when the time comes, but know I want that with you."

I didn't get a chance to respond. He kissed me again and my body reacted to his like it belonged to him. I curled my arm around his back and held him close. Many times in this life I'd wondered if I could ever be truly happy. Right there at that moment, knowing Raphi was mine and we wanted the same things in the future made my heart swell.

When he pulled away, he raised our joined hands and started to sway slightly. I raised an eyebrow.

"What are you doing?"

He started to hum in answer to my question. I let him rock us from side to side, shaking my head and smiling at him.

"Really, Raphi, what are you doing?"

"I'm celebrating the moment."

He made me twirl around like we were dancing whilst continuing to hum a tune. I started laughing at the ridiculousness of this man. He never ceased to amaze me.

"You say I'm adorable, but I think you are."

"I'll take that."

I allowed Raphi to spin me around and dance with me in Rory's conservatory because apparently, this is how he wanted to mark the moment. It felt like we'd taken a giant leap of faith with each other tonight. I leant my head on his shoulder, feeling content, happy and in love.

"You're not going to run away from me again?" I whispered.

"Never, *cuore mio*, you're stuck with me for life so you better get used to it."

"I'll try."

He laughed. We both knew there was no trying involved. Raphi was the one I wanted to be beside forever.

"Haven't I shown you how much I love you yet?"

I raised my head from his shoulder and smiled at him.

"You have, but later, I think I'm going to need you to show me all over again."

The way his eyes darkened made me shiver.

"Make no mistake, I fully intend to show you as many times as you ask for it."

"I can't wait."

He squeezed my hand and I knew we were going to be okay. Raphi wasn't going anywhere. And I'd been welcomed into a family I knew would treat me like one of their own just as they did with my sister. Who could ask for more from this life?

All I really needed was Raphi and me together. The rest... well, that was a bonus.

CHAPTER FIFTY THREE

Jonah

I looked up at the man I'd married as he stood, smoothing out the paper in his hand. Raphi had kept a lot of his speech a secret from me because he wanted me to hear it on our wedding day. I had no clue why it was this important to him, but I didn't question it.

Our love affair had been tumultuous at times, but when we came back together as adults who'd gone through hell and back just over a year ago, it was for good. We both knew what it felt like to be apart and it had only made us appreciate what we had in each other.

I remembered the day Raphi asked me to marry him six months ago. It'd been two days after I'd moved into his place. A normal day in our lives, yet it took a turn when I went upstairs to get ready for bed and found a note sitting on our bed which said turn around. Somehow the damn man had managed to sneak up behind me and get down on one knee.

What followed was me crying buckets and just about managing to say yes to his proposal. Raphi had spent the rest of the night calming me the fuck down and telling me how he couldn't wait to be my husband. Then he'd made love to me, which stopped me crying because how the hell could I cry when he'd been giving me so much pleasure.

Neither of us had wanted a big affair. It was just family and a few close friends. I'd loved every moment of saying I do to him. Raphi had spent the entire ceremony staring at me as if I was the only person in the room. I don't think I could have asked for more.

Raphi knocked a knife against his wine glass, bringing the attention of the room to us. He cleared his throat and looked around.

"Okay, so I'm not very good at talking in public, but here it goes."

I smiled and reached out, linking his fingers with mine. He looked down at me and gave me a subtle nod.

"Jonah and I would firstly like to thank everyone for being here on our special day. And it has been truly special. I got to marry this one, so nothing really beats that." He indicated me with his head which garnered some chuckles from our guests. "Some of you will know we've not had the easiest time together, but the journey has been worth every moment. There is no one else in this world I would want to spend my life with but Jonah."

My heart started to race and my fingers tightened in his. I had a feeling Raphi might end up making me cry, but I was going to try hold back on those tears.

"Now, we didn't want to do traditional speeches hence why I'm not letting this guy over here talk even though he's my best man." Raphi waved a hand at Duke who winked at him. "Mostly because his stories about me would be inappropriate and quite frankly, I don't trust him not to embarrass me."

"Aw, Raphi, I would never," Duke said, putting a hand to his chest.

"You say that, but no one in this room believes you."

That brought more laughter from our guests, especially their parents.

"Anyway," Raphi continued when everyone had settled down a bit. "I did want to say a few things to mark the occasion because, for me, there was a point when I didn't know if I would have a day like this. For Jonah to agree to marry me after everything we've been through, well, that's pretty big for me. Words cannot express how much I appreciate having him in my life."

I bit the inside of my cheek as tears threatened.

No. No crying!

"I thought I'd tell you about the first time Jonah and I actually had a real conversation." He smiled down at me. "You remember that, right?"

I nodded, relatively sure of the day he was referring to.

"I was fifteen at the time… crazy to think it was over ten years ago now, but anyway… I didn't always have the best time at school, though what kid would when they have a family like ours."

He glanced at his parents, giving them a smile to let them know he wasn't giving them any shit for it.

"I'd just had a bunch of kids giving me a hard time and I ended up in the toilets, bawling my eyes out. If that wasn't bad enough, I heard someone come in and tried to be as quiet as possible, but it clearly didn't work because here they were asking me if I was okay. I'm there like, shit, why did someone have to come in here, but there was also something very familiar about the person's voice which made me not want them to leave."

I remembered that day vividly as Raphi clearly did. It was the very first time I noticed how attractive he was. I hadn't looked before because he was Meredith's friend.

"So imagine my surprise when I walk out of the cubicle and find my friend's older brother standing there. Now, Jonah doesn't know this because I've never actually told him, but I'd always felt a little awkward around him. We'd only ever shared hellos and small talk before, but every time he was around me, I'd get this weird feeling in my chest."

Raphi rubbed his chest as if he was still feeling it now.

"I did eventually work out why later on, but at the time, I had no clue why Meredith's older brother made me feel so odd."

"You going to tell me what it was?" I asked, interrupting him.

He smiled and let go of my hand, only to ruffle my hair.

"Yeah, silly, I had a crush on you."

"What?"

"Well, you know when you're a kid and you look up to and admire someone, that's a crush, J."

I gave him a look.

"You're so not funny."

"I like to think you find me hilarious, but are you going to let me get on with the story?"

I rolled my eyes then felt a little sheepish since we had an audience. It was hard sometimes to remember other people were around us when he was next to me. Just as I took up all of Raphi's vision when I was with him, he took up mine.

"Go ahead."

"Thank you." He turned his attention back to the room. "Anyway, Jonah offered to lend me an ear, I think out of the kindness of his heart, but he can tell you why. I agreed because I mean, I trusted him to an extent, like he was my friend's brother. Jonah takes me off to this café and buys me tea and a slice of Victoria sponge. Here's me thinking, doesn't he know my parents are loaded and he really doesn't need to do this. But… we ended up having this deep conversation. I remember feeling like I'd found a connection with someone who actually understood me, but I felt incredibly guilty about it too."

I stared up at him. I had no idea he'd felt that way the first day we'd talked. It was such a long time ago and we'd been through so many things since then.

"This was my friend's brother and I shouldn't be taking up his time, but in a lot of ways, I'm glad we did talk that day. I'm glad he gave me his number and told me I could talk to him if

I needed to. It was the first time I had someone offering me something without asking for anything in return."

He looked down at me.

"It's one of the things I love the most about you, J. All you want to do in life is to help other people. You helped me that day. You were just what I needed only I didn't realise it until much later on. I wanted to say thank you for talking to me because if you hadn't, we might not be here today."

I took his hand again and brought it to my lips, kissing his knuckles. Raphi smiled at me in that beautiful way of his, letting me know how much he adored me.

"It wasn't out of the kindness of my heart," I said, giving him a shake of the head.

"No?"

"Well, maybe a little, but there was just something about you. I wanted to help you. And I guess I kind of liked you too."

His eyebrow curved upwards.

"Kind of?"

"Yeah, just a little."

His smile told me he was messing with me. I batted his arm.

"All right, lovebirds, get on with it," Duke said.

Raphi smacked his brother around the back of the head which earned him a scowl.

"Okay, okay… I'll try and wrap this up." Raphi shook his paper out. "I'd like you all to raise your glasses to my wonderful, kind, caring and incredibly handsome husband here who is my entire world and I couldn't do without him."

He picked up his champagne glass and raised it.

"To Jonah."

Our guests echoed his sentiments as Raphi peered over his glass at me whilst he took a sip. Those green eyes were full of affection. Then he sat down and rested his head on my shoulder. I placed a kiss on top of his head.

"I love you," I whispered.

"Love you too, *cuore mio*."

Duke stood up and Raphi tensed.

"Since my brother is refusing to let me do a speech... I'd like you to all raise your glasses again to the happy couple. To Raphi and Jonah."

There were cheers and whoops as everyone raised their glasses and toasted us. My heart was full. This had to be the happiest day of my life. How could any other day match this? I'd married the man I'd loved and wanted forever with. It meant everything to me.

"I loved your speech," I told him a while later when we were dancing together.

"You did?"

"Yes, especially the part where you admitted to having a crush on me."

He smiled and I rested my head on his shoulder.

"How could I not? You're hot as hell."

"So are you."

"I'm counting down the minutes until we can leave. I swear you in a suit does things to me."

I laughed. I didn't wear them all that often but every time I did, it drove my husband crazy. He looked just as good in my eyes. I couldn't wait until we could be alone too. And tomorrow, we'd have three whole weeks to ourselves in the sun when we jetted off to the Caribbean. Raphi's parents had insisted on paying for our honeymoon. I'd learnt not to object to their generosity in the time Raphi and I had been back together. It never ended well when anyone did.

"And here I thought I was the one with no patience."

"You telling me you're not already thinking about what I have planned for you?"

"You know very well I am since you refuse to tell me."

"Anticipation always makes it sweeter, J. Haven't you learnt that yet?"

Raphi made me wait for a lot of things in the bedroom, which had done little to prevent my impatience when it came to him. He kept saying I was still just as needy as ever. Lucky for me, it made him want me all the more.

"No, I'm never going to like your insistence on taking everything at a snail's pace when all I want you to do is fuck me."

He laughed and I adored the rich sound of it.

"I always reward you when you're good for me."

I stroked his nape with my fingers.

"I'm going to be very good for you later."

"I'm counting on it."

The thought of it excited me no end, but I kept a lid on it.

"Thank you for giving me the perfect wedding," I whispered into his neck. "And thank you for loving me. You're the best person in my life."

"I thought that was Meredith."

"Don't be smart right now when I'm trying to tell you how much I appreciate you."

He held me closer and kissed my hair.

"I'm sorry."

"Mmm, you will be."

He chuckled.

"Is it time for us to leave yet?"

I lifted my head from his shoulder. We were staying at the hotel we were having the reception in so we could sneak away if we wanted.

"You think anyone will notice?"

"They will, but I no longer care since it's our day."

I grinned and took his hand. Raphi eyed me for a moment. Then the two of us snuck off the dancefloor together and hot-footed it towards the doors to the room. We glanced back before we left. All of Raphi's parents were huddled in a corner talking. His siblings were on the dancefloor with their partners. Meredith spied me and Raphi from over Cole's shoulder, her eyes widening.

"We've been spotted," I hissed at Raphi.

He gave Meredith a wave and a wink. She shooed away us with a flick of her wrist, essentially giving us the go-ahead to get out of here for the night. We'd see everyone in the morning when we came down for breakfast. Then it'd be home to get our suitcases and off to the airport. I really couldn't wait.

I smiled at my sister and tugged my husband from the room. The two of us were laughing all the way up to our suite.

And when we got in the room, we only had eyes for each other.

My beautiful man and I were going to make it this time. We had forever ahead of us and nothing would come between us again.

EPILOGUE

Raphael

Lots of people say your wedding is the best day of your life. I would have agreed a few days ago. That was before I got to see the beautiful sight in front of me. The most picture-perfect moment of my life. I wondered if anything could ever top this feeling I had right then.

I leant my head against the doorframe, watching my husband with our baby girl resting on his shoulder whilst he hummed a little lullaby and rocked her. We'd brought Elodie home two days ago. My parents were coming over later to meet her but she needed a nap. Jonah volunteered to put her down for a couple of hours.

It had taken us a year and a half to through the adoption process and be matched with a child. Jonah had become frustrated at times but when they'd placed Elodie in his arms, all the stress of the process melted away. She was only two months old and had lived with a foster family before she came to us. We were told her birth parents had died in a tragic accident. Elodie needed a family. Jonah and I were it.

"Your dad and I are going to give you the whole world," Jonah murmured as he continued to rock her to sleep.

I swear my heart hurt at his words.

"We are?" I asked, keeping my voice low.

Jonah looked over at me, his light green eyes full of happiness.

"You hear that, Lo-Lo? Daddy doesn't think we can give you the world."

I shook my head. For all the shit I gave Jonah, he gave it right back.

"Don't be making our daughter think I'm the bad dad here already."

He kissed the small tuft of light brown hair on her head.

"Your dad has clearly forgotten how much I love him and he could never be bad in my eyes."

I approached them with a smile.

"Is that so?"

I wrapped an arm around Jonah's waist and stroked Elodie's head.

"Mmm, yes it is."

"Good thing I love your daddy too, isn't it, baby girl?"

Elodie closed her eyes, her little fist gripping Jonah's t-shirt. Fuck, she was beautiful and perfect in every single way. I fell in love with her the moment I saw her. It was the same for my husband.

I leant closer to Jonah and kissed his cheek. He turned his face into mine to catch my lips. When I pulled back, he was smiling softly.

"Mum is going to lose her mind over her," I murmured, staring down at our sleeping daughter.

"Oh, I'm sure. Our girl is going to get so spoilt by your parents."

I was in absolutely no doubt of that. When I told Dad about the adoption, he got teary-eyed and told me how much he was looking forward to meeting his granddaughter. The way my parents had not only accepted Jonah into our family but hadn't batted an eyelid about us adopting made my heart ache. They were the most supportive and loving parents anyone could ever have. Whilst some people would never understand their relationship, I wouldn't change having Dad, Mum, Xav, Quinn and Rory as my parents for anything.

"I bet Mum has filled the car with gifts and my dads are totally complaining about it."

Jonah laughed quietly so as not to wake our daughter. I let him go and he placed her down in her bassinet. He tucked a blanket around her and wrapped his arm around me this time. I leant my head on his shoulder as the two of us stared down at Elodie.

"I can't get over how perfect she is," he whispered.

"Neither can I."

"Can we just stay here and watch her for a while?"

"If you want."

He kissed the top of my head, making me sigh with contentment.

There was nowhere else on earth I would rather be but right here with my husband and my baby girl. Life had thrown a lot my way. I'd had a lot of ups and downs. Been through so many hardships. And coming out the other side of all of it had been a blessing. I couldn't ask for more now I was with the love of my life.

"Jonah."

"Mmm?"

"We're parents. How fucking crazy is that?"

"Batshit."

It might be crazy but I had this guy to keep me steady. There were days I still struggled and Jonah was there to pick me up. He never made me feel as though I was any less because of my battles with mental health. He was the one person I could rely on every day to help see me through. And I'd be forever grateful I'd found my way back to the man who had always been there for me even when we'd been apart.

"We'll be okay though because I'm doing it with you, *cuore mio*. You make everything easier."

"Don't make me cry," he muttered.

I lifted my head from his shoulder and turned to him, framing his face with both my hands.

"Will you cry if I tell you I'm going to love you forever?"

He shook his head even as tears welled in his eyes.

"No… because I'll love you forever too."

I rested my forehead against his knowing this was all I ever needed to get me through the rest of my life.

Just him.

Just Jonah Ethan Nelson-Pope.

My beautiful, perfectly handsome husband.

I needed him.

Always.

ACKNOWLEDGEMENTS

Thank you so much for taking the time to read this book. I really appreciate all of my readers and hope this book gave you as much joy reading it as I did writing it.

The only thanks I have to give for this book is to Raphi and Jonah.

Thank you for letting me tell this story. For giving me the opportunity to dig deep into my soul and drag this out into the open. To let me speak of something I've personally kept hidden for a long time.

I'm not ashamed of my history of mental illness. It's been a long and arduous journey to find myself in a position today where I'm good. Where I don't wake up every morning hating my existence. Suffering from depression is no walk in the park. There's no quick fix or way out for most. But I can say I'm okay. I manage. I cope. Every day is a new one and in a lot of ways, creating helps keep me sane.

Writing a story from the perspective of a person suffering with depression forced me to relive experiences probably best left in the past. I was able to give Raphi's struggle that much more because of it. And as for Jonah, well, he was just as hard on me. He's an introvert and shares the part of me which suffers in silence so I can help those I love. For me, this book was a double whammy in terms of emotional taxation. Yet, it was worth every moment. Every tear I shed in process. Their journey wouldn't be what it is without the pain I went through to give them a voice.

I want to thank them for who they are as characters. They taught me a lot of lessons during the process of bringing their story to fruition. Ones I will carry with me along my path as a person and as a writer. And for that, I am eternally grateful.

ABOUT THE AUTHOR

Sarah writes dark, contemporary, erotic and paranormal romances. She adores all forms of steamy romance and can always be found with a book or ten on her Kindle. She loves anti-heroes, alpha males and flawed characters with a little bit of darkness lurking within. Her writing buddies nicknamed her 'The Queen of Steam' for her pulse racing sex scenes which will leave you a little hot under the collar.

Born and raised in Sussex, UK near the Ashdown Forest where she grew up climbing trees and building Lego towns with her younger brother. Sarah fell in love with novels when she was a teenager reading her aunt's historical regency romances. She has always loved the supernatural and exploring the darker side of romance and fantasy novels.

Sarah currently resides in the Scottish Highlands with her husband. Music is one of her biggest inspirations and she always has something on in the background whilst writing. She is an avid gamer and is often found hogging her husband's Xbox.

Printed in Great Britain
by Amazon

78577455R00312